street money

BILL KENT
street money

Thomas Dunne Books / St. Martin's Minotaur ⚏ New York

THOMAS DUNNE BOOKS
An imprint of St. Martin's Press

www.minotaurbooks.com

Book design by Michael Collica

ISBN 0-312-28585-X

First Edition: October 2002

10 9 8 7 6 5 4 3 2 1

author's note

This novel is fiction. Although the story is set in Philadelphia, a city with newspapers, none of the characters described here is a depiction of any existing personalities currently or previously employed by the Philadelphia news media. The story was inspired, in part, by the superb obituaries written by Jim Nicholson of the *Philadelphia Daily News*. I have never met Mr. Nicholson. I respect his work because it says so much about what really holds a city, and its people, together.

acknowledgments

I want to thank my wife, Elaine, my son, Stephen, as well as family and friends who provided support in a time of extraordinary trial and effort.

Philadelphia is a great city, a marvelous city; I am not saying it is a cesspool.

—Larry Sabato, University of Virginia professor of political science and author of *Dirty Little Secrets: The Persistence of Corruption in American Politics*, quoted in the *Philadelphia Inquirer*.

street money

1get yourself dead

In some parts of Philadelphia, you don't die, you don't get murdered, you don't commit suicide or fall off a roof or come home and light a cigarette when the oven's pilot light has gone out, blowing half the block to Kingdom Come.

You get yourself dead.

And like a lot of things that happen in a neighborhood when you're not watching your back, this isn't particularly good. Because, maybe you really did make a mistake that you could've avoided, but it is also possible that there were real reasons, people, money, or other things involved that had something to do with the neighborhood, and that can bother people.

It bothered Andrea—call her Andy—Cosicki that her father, "Benny Lunch" Cosicki, got himself dead, but, if you listen to some people, Benny shouldn't've gotten her that job with the *Philadelphia Press* because the media always gets it wrong, even when they get it right, and you don't want no one in the media looking over your shoulder, asking you questions about who you've been breaking the bread with. Especially if you come up from a neighborhood like Redmonton, make enough money cutting deals—you know, making some things happen sweet and easy for some people in the city, and not so easy for others—then move out to the suburbs—the Main Line, no less. He figured he could drop back in on the place where he got his start, that he could drive into Redmonton in his gray suit and his yellow Buick and that wouldn't bother people.

It bothered people and then he got himself dead.

And that bothered N. S. Ladderback, the guy that writes the obituaries at the *Press*. They say he made some calls, just the way he does when somebody gets dead in the city, somebody who isn't big or rich or famous, but important enough to get a mention.

So why was it nobody in town, not the *Press* or the *Standard* or the little newspapers, the freebies that you see blowing around all over the streets, did an obituary about Benny Lunch? It could've had something to do with Benny Lunch working a deal that settled the newspaper-delivery truck drivers' strike in such a way that the drivers made out okay but the newspaper owners got a little bit screwed.

Or maybe it was because Benny Lunch never liked seeing his name in the papers and that, even when he was dead, he could call in favors.

You'd think he get an obit because Benny Lunch had this faith in people, places, and things: That no matter how bad things got, no matter how much people hated each other and tried to kill each other, you could get them to sit down at a meal and work out their differences.

The cops found his body in the basement of the Straight Up Club, a place at North Seventeenth and Sackawinick where he used to tend bar before it caught fire and was never rebuilt. They figured he fell through a hole that the fire had made in the second floor of the club, in what had been an apartment where the sarge—retired Philadelphia Police Sergeant Francis McMann—lived with his daughter Charlotte (her mother, a Polish woman named Natalie, had died of some kind of cancer a few years before that).

Everybody knows that the sarge died in that fire while helping to rescue the club's patrons. N. S. Ladderback wrote a great obituary of him in the *Press*—it hung in a frame on the wall of Bep 'n' Betty's Luncheonette at Eighteenth and Sackawinick until the place closed. Ben Cosicki, who was really, really short, married Charlotte McMann, who was really, really tall, not long after what was left of the sarge was buried. The baby came a little too quick—but that didn't stop Ben from strolling Andrea around the neighborhood. He let everybody admire her and wonder if she was going to grow up tall, like her mother, or short, like her father, while Ben handed out the street money from Councilman Szathmary's office, right upstairs of Bep 'n' Betty's Luncheonette.

Now Cosicki had a real job that the councilman got him, riding a trash truck, but everybody knows when you get your job through politics, your job is just what you do when you're not working for the person who got you the job.

Oh, you should have seen Ben working the street money on election day, walking fast and wearing the big smile of somebody who knows he's on the bottom but thinks if he plays the game right, and performs an occasional miracle, he'll go right to the top.

There was one election day coming on and the weatherman was calling for rain, which meant that it would cost more to get out the vote, because there are people in the city who will walk from Redmonton all the way down to Broad and Market to watch the Mummers on a freezing New Years Day if the sun is shining. But these very same people will not go two blocks to the polling booths at the Gerrold Street VFW Hall if there's a drop of rain on the sidewalk, unless they can expect something for their effort.

Up in Councilman Szathmary's office, Bep Adamo had wrung every penny he could out of the businessmen, shopkeepers, laborers, tradesmen, bookies, drug dealers, pimps, and any other fine, upstanding citizen who wanted the very best government money could buy. But there just wasn't enough.

That was when Ben Cosicki saved the day. He was strolling his baby daughter around with him when he heard that the councilman had come up short. He parked his daughter in the stroller in front of Bep 'n' Betty's Luncheonette, and got Betty to go up on a stepladder and hand him down one of the cookie jars she kept on shelves above the tables. Then then he took the cookie jar into the Hampton Bank branch, this big, old, domed, marble-sheathed monster of a building that stood just across Sackawinick Street from Bep 'n' Betty's, but could be miles away.

The Hampton Bank, like a lot of Philadelphia institutions that survive, persist, and endure, in spite of the offspring that inherit them, was not the biggest, richest, or most powerful financial institution in the country, but it was the oldest. The bank's chairman, Kellum Brickle, a New England blue blood who married into the Wadcalader family that had owned the bank since before the Revolutionary War, sometimes used that branch as his office because he liked to wander down to the sarge's nightclub and drink himself blind listening to the jazz music there before the limo came to take him back to his estate in the suburbs. They say Brickle, no spring chicken, had had himself a stroke the night that the Straight Up Club caught on fire, and that Ben Cosicki had helped get him out of the fire and into an ambulance.

Brickle wasn't in his office that day—he hadn't been seen around Redmonton since he had that stroke. But Ben made one phone call and came out with a cookie jar considerably heavier than when he went in.

Everybody stood around and cheered when Ben put that cookie jar in his daughter's tiny arms and carried her, and the jar, up the stairs to the councilman's office, as shining with pride as one of those lights they used to put on the front of the locomotives that came roaring out of the factory just down from the bank.

No doubt about it, at that moment, everybody thought Ben Cosicki was going places. "You'll see, as soon as the results are counted the next day, Ben will be off that trash truck and behind a desk."

On election day some of this street money came back to Betty, because she got paid at a discount rate to make coffee and donuts (no cookies, though) to give to the people when they showed up at the VFW Hall to vote, as well as the buffet for the victory party later that night. Some of the street money went to people you never saw or heard of, who had gone around the neighborhood at night and put up signs for the state representatives, judges, and functionaries major and minor, sharp and flat, that Councilman Szathmary wanted to boost into office. Some of the street money went to cab and limousine drivers working out of Hank Norwood's garage to pick up the people that needed picking up and bring them to the VFW Hall, and, later, to the victory party, those that were invited and should be there to show their consideration. And because a few of the more progressively minded of the neighborhood's clergy made sermons about how it was important to remember who takes care of you, in this world as well as the next, some of the street money went their way, too.

But because Councilman Szathmary wasn't running for reelection that day, and Redmonton was considered a knee that jerked when Councilman Szathmary tapped it, most of that street money went to other districts where the election results might not be so predictable.

In some of those districts, due to many reasons that people are still guessing about, the election turned into what the *Press* called "a bloodbath that money couldn't buy."

But, as an old hand like Bep Adamo would tell you, that's the way it goes in politics: You only win when you win big. Win small, or lose big, and people look for someone to blame.

Ben Cosicki got blamed. He was picking up trash when some creeps threw him into the hopper, turned on the hydraulics, and crushed him half to death. Not long after that, Hampton Bank announced that, due to low customer demand, it was closing its Redmonton branch, for good.

By the time Ben Cosicki got himself dead in his old neighborhood, the bank building, Bep 'n' Betty's Luncheonette, the locomotive factory, and the sarge's ruin of a nightclub had all been bought by the Reverend Hooks, a crazy preacher who, because he could tell his parishoners who to vote for *without* passing out street money (at least, that's what people said), was the new force to be reckoned with in neighborhood politics.

What Ben Cosicki was doing getting himself dead in the sarge's club, nobody could figure. The club had been boarded up more than twenty years since the fire, but you could get into it if you wanted. Some people say the second floor was used as a place to stash drugs that the dealers were selling on street corners. The same streets had once been filled with Cadillacs and limousines belonging to suburbanites who'd come to listen to jazz at the sarge's club.

Other people say Ben had set up a meeting on the second floor with people who maybe didn't want to be in the same room with each other, and that things got out of hand. This, in itself, was a little hard to believe because getting people who couldn't stand each other to sit down for lunch was Benny Lunch's thing. Supposedly, there was not a soul in the entire city—good, bad, or whatever—that Ben couldn't invite to sit down for a bite. They'd meet and eat, and, somehow, arrangements were made, deals were greased, details would get ironed out, and if you were to ask Ben how it came down, he'd just shrug his shoulders and say in that side-of-the-mouth way he had of talking, that all he did was pick up a check.

So, it makes you wonder, what kind of check is it that somebody like Benny Lunch would not want to pick up, especially in a place like Redmonton, a neighborhood that has been going downhill ever since they closed the locomotive factory. (Tell people that they used to make big huge monster locomotives in Philadelphia and they won't believe you until you show them the wider-than-usual streets where the tracks used to run up to those big doors that no longer open in the walls of that big monster of a brick building that's now the First Church of God Harmonious). All the Irish, Polish, Ukranian, Italian, German, Spanish, and Jewish people that lived in Redmonton who were content to hate each other in peace as long as they all had jobs found themselves having to go farther and farther out of the neighborhood for work. Used to be, there were half a dozen nightclubs like the Straight Up in Redmonton, and, from six in the morning until three o'clock in the afternoon, you'd see everybody coming in and out of Bep 'n' Betty's Luncheonette, the place that had all the cookie jars on the shelves.

That the restaurant was lined with cookie jars had nothing to do with Betty's saving habits. There was a time her marriage to Bep hit one of those potholes that you read about in the *Press*'s "Tell Tracy" advice column and Betty exhibited what everybody thought was cruel and unusual fascination for the custom-order porcelain restaurant crockery items proffered by a salesman who blew in from a redware china factory up in Phoenixville because—he said—he'd heard she served the best scrapple this side east of Mantua, and would she like to come out and see the factory one day?

So one day after Betty was gone for a long weekend that Bep said was to visit family but everybody knew was a factory tour (you *know* what kind of free samples were being passed out). Betty comes back like a cat that had been left out all night and nobody says anything until a truck pulls up and there's all these boxes of all these pink porcelain cookie jars with Bep 'n' Betty's Luncheonette written on them in blue letters.

Bep starts to smash them on the street in front of the driver but Betty comes out and asks if there was a bill with the shipment, and the driver said there was no bill—as far as he knew, the shipment had been paid for in advance. Bep turns to his wife and realizes that, whatever happened on that tour, he is suddenly richer by twenty-four—actually twenty-two because he smashed two—porcelain cookie jars.

Such a look of love you have never seen between two people, at least, not on that day. They should start baking cookies, Bep said. When I'm ready, Betty said. So he built shelves all around the restaurant just high enough to be out of anybody's reach, put the cookie jars on them, and one day some idiot reporter from the *Philadelphia Press* named Howard Lange (who's now running the newspaper—can you believe that?) did one of those don't-you-love-those-mom-and-pop-restaurants and wrote the place up as "The Cookie Jar." Nine months later, Betty gives birth to a girl, Maria, who would grow up waiting tables at the luncheonette, try to become a nightclub singer at the sarge's place, drop out of sight for a while after the indictments came down, and then come back to work in a soup kitchen run by the Reverend Jeffrey Hooks's First Church of God Harmonious.

If you asked anybody from Redmonton, they'd tell you Maria didn't look as much like Bep as she looked like a gingerbread girl, and that that was enough to make Ben Cosicki fall in love with her, but marry somebody else. Councilman Szathmary married Ben and Charlotte McMann in his office. Then they went downstairs to have the party at Bep 'n' Betty's.

Councilman Szathmary got the city to pay to convert Bep 'n' Betty's upstairs apartment into his office so he could set up a kind of one-stop service in Redmonton. You'd just follow the aroma of scrapple, kielbasa, and Italian sausage and eggs in the morning, and marinara sauce and steak sandwiches cooking in onions and olive oil in the afternoon, and if you had a problem, like a pothole in the street, or if you were waiting on your driver's license from Harrisburg, or you couldn't pay your gas bill that month, you went upstairs to Councilman Szathmary's office and you'd see Bep Adamo, who always sat by the front window so he could see who was coming and going (but it might've been really because he had the worst breath and it was better if he was talking to you near an open window), and if Bep liked the way you looked, he'd say, "We got a visitor," and show you into the backroom that was the councilman's office, which they called the "Doug Out" because his first name was Douglas and that's supposed to be funny.

The councilman was a Redmonton legend, a bachelor who always seemed too old for the young girls and not old enough for the widows and divorcees. He never forgot a name or a face, and if he couldn't remember if you voted the full Democratic ticket on election day, Bep Adamo did. The lone Hungarian in Redmonton, Douglas Szathmary would have had one of the longest ethically conflicted political careers in Philadelphia history if an FBI agent posing as a parking-lot developer didn't make a tape recording of him spelling out that to get "things built right in town you have to take care of people, you have to show consideration, you have to put out street money."

Some people say that it was Ben Cosicki who told Bep Adamo that some well-off developer from the suburbs, who used to hang around at the Straight Up Club and knew Ben when he was tending bar there, was willing to "show consideration" in order to get city approval to build a multistory parking garage next to the sports stadiums down in South Philly. They also say that the meeting was going to be local, for lunch, at a place convenient to the councilman and that the councilman picked Bep 'n' Betty's.

The developer, who was actually an FBI agent, supposedly told Bep Adamo when they set up the lunch that he'd heard the scrapple there was the best west of Mantua.

Now Redmonton is *east* of Mantua. Always has been. Always will be. When the developer got out of his limo, Bep sent Whitey Goohan, this creepy orphan kid who was always hanging out in the councilman's office paring his fingernails with a switchblade, down to the street corner to check the man out. The agent later said Goohan asked him if he was wearing a wire. The agent said, "No," and he was telling the truth. The councilman came down, with Bep Adamo behind him.

They picked the table that was always the councilman's table, and they sat down, and it all went on tape because Bep was wearing the wire.

Now there were those who say that "Double-Dip" Szathmary (as he was nicknamed by Howard Lange, then a general-assignment reporter) went to jail because Anthony "Bep" Adamo became a government witness. On the witness stand, and later, in a series of interviews with Howard Lange, Adamo spelled out that there were daytime rackets and nighttime rackets running out of Redmonton and that the councilman had a piece of the daytime rackets. Adamo said he was going to help the Feds get the guy running the nighttime rackets after he was done with the councilman.

People who were close to Szathmary when the indictment came down said that it was like Szathmary had been laid low with a case of the stupids. Given the adversarial nature of Philadelphia ward politics, he could have kicked up a fuss, hired the best criminal lawyers in the galaxy, and pulled all kinds of favors to get himself off. People in the wards and neighborhoods may not admire a man who is willing to lie, cheat, and extort money to benefit himself, but if they can see him walking the streets, if they can walk up to him and ask him to get a pothole fixed, if he can get some lousy city building inspector off the backs of the widow running the apartment house down the block, if he'll show up at the banquet and give a gold-plated watch to the janitor who was a drunk but is finally retiring after thirty years of hard labor, and if they have proof, in the form of street money given out on election day, not as a bribe, but as a reminder that their support is dearly and truly appreciated by the powers that be, why, they'll vote for him for the rest of their lives.

Councilman Szathmary did the wrong thing. He got a local lawyer nobody had ever heard of (who moved out of the neighborhood to the suburbs after Szathmary was found guilty), who happened to be a Vietnam vet, as Szathmary was. Szathmary refused to say or do anything, on the witness stand or off, that he thought was in the slightest way dishonest, compromising, or underhanded. By the time the federal prosecutor was done with him, Szathmary looked like the worst kind of loser: a guy who plays by the rules even though he knows the rules are out to get him. And they got him, bad, finding ways to stick him with enough stuff to keep him in jail for his entire life. Why didn't Szathmary fight it, just a little bit?

People didn't need a reason to stay away from Bep 'n' Betty's after the indictments came down. Bep Adamo closed the place, got himself and Betty put in the Witness Protection Program, and was all set to embark on a career of ratting out more politicians, mobsters, and petty scumbags, but, what should happen, but he got himself dead.

It happened after the FBI grabbed Jeffrey Hooks, the bass player in the sarge's old club. According to the FBI, Hooks had stepped into Bep Adamo's shoes after Adamo turned straight. Bep Adamo said as much at Hook's trial, though he wasn't as convincing as the Feds had hoped.

At the climax of a boring trial in the big, boring federal office building off Independence Square, Bep sat and sweated and told the jury it was his mission in life to put creeps like Hooks away. Hooks, who was half asleep during the trial up until now, jumped out of his chair and screamed that he was innocent, that he'd found God and that if he got off he would dedicate his life to making things better in the neighborhood.

The judge asked Hook's celebrity lawyer from New York to restrain his client. Naturally, the celebrity did no such thing and Hooks pointed a finger at Bep and said, "You are a devil and a liar and you will die for your sins." When the judge adjourned for the day, Bep went back to where he and Betty were living on the Witness Protection Program's tab, had himself a heart attack, and died.

The judge instructed the jury not to pay attention to "coincidental events" in determining the defendant's guilt, but they sure did and Hooks founded that church of his the very next day.

Encased in plaster from head to toe, Ben Cosicki kept track of the fates of Councilman Szathmary, Bep Adamo, and the Reverend Hooks of the First Church of God Harmonious by watching the televions bolted to the ceiling over his hospital bed. When the somebody from the U.S. Attorney's office showed him mug shots and asked him who among these distinguished gentlemen had tossed him into the back of the trash truck, Cosicki said the incident had "messed up" his brain.

Cosicki couldn't do much on a trash truck when he got out of the hospital, so he got a position in the Sanitation Workers Union office, and sometimes he'd fetch a take-out order from the kind of places that catered to the people who catered to the people who like very much to be catered to. He started to wear suits, nothing fancy, always gray, but nice, real nice. Then, wouldn't you know it, Ben started having his lunches at Jimmy D's. It wasn't long before Benny Take-Out became Benny Lunch. The Lunchman figured out he could do more, and do it more lucratively, if he became a consultant. He left his job at the union office so quietly that it was a week before anybody knew he was gone.

Leaving quietly was Ben Cosicki's style. He never talked about himself, never talked about much of anything, really. But he kept in touch, even when he moved out of the neighborhood, to the Main Line, where his wife, the sarge's daughter, got a job selling art to rich people, and his daughter Andy, who used to be so small, grew up real tall and went to the University of Pennsylvania.

Ben kept in touch, even when he had to bring bad news.

For Betty Adamo, who had renamed herself Beatrice Adams and was living in sin with the executive chef of a Main Line banquet hall she had bought into, the bad news was that Szathmary was finally getting out of jail.

Ben brought his daughter along to visit Betty—very strange for a guy who always worked alone, or always seemed to. Was it just an accident, her being with him, or was there something she was supposed to see, and remember, and do something about?

From Andy's point of view, it was just one more of those boring things her father did when he should be doing just for her. She had taken a history of psychology course in college and when the professor was talking about Freud's definition of a narcissist, a lightbulb had gone off in Andy's head and she thought of both her parents and opened her mouth and said "Bingo" just a little bit too loud, the way they say bingo in the church basements that her father took her to when he was doing more of those boring things he did when he had *promised* he was going to do something for her. The man couldn't leave the house to go to a supermarket for a dozen eggs without driving off into the city to drop in on this one or that one, to stop by a bar in this neighborhood or blow into a party or a get-together or diner where short, thick, fat guys who looked like they never did anything but eat would look up and say they were happy to see him in such a way that Andy wondered if they really meant it.

Her parents were both narcissists, Andy decided. Everything that happened to them, they related to themselves, even if there was no relation to themselves. The only difference was, her mother would talk about herself and whatever was going on at the gallery, while her father wouldn't say a thing, but gave off little hints with his body language, or the speed in which he'd get into his screaming-yellow Buick and start doing things.

That very morning, she had asked him to do one thing for her, and, as he always did, he'd promised that he would do it "the next thing." This thing she wanted was for him to drive her to an interview she'd set up. After sending out five different packages containing articles she'd written for the University of Pennsylvania student newspaper and getting no response at all, she was going to meet with the *Morning Standard*'s Montgomery County bureau chief.

She'd set up the interview days after she graduated from the university by telling that lie you're supposed to to tell if you're going to get a job in any ruthless, highly competitive organization that pays well: You call up and press all kinds of numbers to blow past the phone tree until a human being answers, and then you ask to get transferred to the top man or woman and try not to go crazy when you're cut off or somebody snide gets on and asks, "What's this in reference to?" Sooner or later, if you can tolerate the fact that you are contributing to the amount of suffering in the world by annoying people you have never met, you are transferred to the top man or top woman's secretary and then you start saying how much you've always admired this top man (even if you really hate this creep because you sent him all this stuff about you that either never got to him, or he threw out) and that you'd love to meet him and just ask him all sorts of questions about what it's like to be the top man and how you break into such an exciting field.

This hallowed and time-honored act of craven brown-nosing is known in student job-placement offices as an "informational interview" and, like the pickup lines that buzz like flies around the pickup bars on Delaware Avenue, it works more often than not because those who are truly weak but acquire power cannot resist the attentions of attractive youngsters who are willing to listen to them talk about themselves.

Of course, Andy had done her homework in advance. She had grown up reading the *Evening Standard*, the broadsheet newspaper published out of Philadelphia that, even when it found good things to say about the city, was primarily interested in assuring people who lived in the suburbs and had their kids educated in the suburbs and bought everything they needed in the suburbs and dreamed of the day they might get jobs in the suburbs so they wouldn't have to pay that stupid Philadelphia city wage tax and put up with a horrible commute where it takes an hour in a car or a train or god forbid a bus, to go a few miles and you could probably travel faster if you walked but who walks when you live in the suburbs?—that the city was an incompetent cesspool of corruption, ineptitude at all levels, and enigmatic ethnic intrigue, and that they were better off where they were.

Now, the editors who decided what went into the Philadelphia *Morning Standard* didn't sit at a table every morning at ten A.M. and say, "What are we going to do next to stick it to the city?" They didn't put themselves in the shoes of the typical suburban reader and contemplate what would make this reader grateful that he put a few miles of lawns and malls and school systems between so much poverty, crime, and vicious urban rage.

No, what these editors did every morning was get into their cars and leave their suburban houses and put up with that horrible commute where they can see the landscape change from green-this and green-that and everything works and boy-oh-boy-wasn't-that-a-great-barbecue, to smog-stained concrete, potholed asphalt, broken-down storefronts on streets where weird people stood on the corner and shouted obscenities at the traffic, and they'd wonder why the City of Love had sunk so low and swear that they were going to get to the bottom of it and find out.

And they would think about bottoms, pits, dark pockets of shame and degradation that were just so different from happy shopping and never-ending errands and trips to specialty shops, specialty restaurants, specialty health care, specialty warehouse clubs where, for a small annual membership fee, they could load up the sport utility vehicle with a year's supply of toilet paper, frozen pizza, and bottled mayonnaise and congratulate themselves on how much they'd saved.

These editors would summon their very best reporters—dynamic, hard-charging kids who had been hired after they won awards writing for tiny newspapers in towns these editors had never heard of—who would fill their front pages with horrifying multi-part series in which the city became a gruesome setting for the specialty wretched of the earth.

These series would provoke outrage, investigations, protests, lawsuits, firings, and hirings within the city, and then the editors would have these series reprinted in lavishly illustrated packages that they would send to the Pulitzer committee in New York, gratified that, even if the New York papers grabbed half the awards the way they always did, the editors of the *Philadelphia Morning Standard* had gotten to the bottom of something.

That these bottoms never quite disappeared was not necessarily the editor's primary concern. If the city was a place of dark valleys, it would also be a place of lofty peaks, though scaling those peaks required money to spend on restaurant food, performances, sports, exotic medical treatments, books, recordings, art, antiques, education, history, experiences, *things you couldn't find in the suburbs*. Thus, the *Standard*'s editors perpetuated a vision that had nothing to do with the day-to-day life experienced by the majority of the city's inhabitants, who might spend long fruitful years of their existence without encountering any of the bipolar dysfunctions that delighted and horrified the paper's readers.

The possibility of filling the *Standard* with even more Philadelphia bottoms and tops was not why Andy Cosicki had spent several days after she graduated annoying anyone who answered the telephone at the *Standard*'s Montgomery County bureau, trying to land a precious informational interview with the bureau chief. Ever since her parents had moved to a succession of larger houses culminating in the huge stone knock-off, an Italian villa on Albemarle Way, she had pored over the Local News section of the *Standard*, hunting for articles about similar bottoms in Montgomery County, a rolling spread of lumpy hills, rippling streams, spectacular golf courses, superb school systems, magnificent malls, great colleges, stupendous hospitals, a few good restaurants, and, thanks to a solid population of old-money families, still one of the largest concentrations of wealth on the East Coast.

She hadn't found any. She had been thrilled at the *Standard*'s revelations of inner city scandals, crimes, and shameful goings-on detailed elsewhere in the newspaper, but, beyond an occasional murder or swindle that was always reported as having "shocked the neighbors in this quiet, affluent suburban community," she found nothing in the *Standard*'s Local News that was as unbearably, relentlessly, impossibly bad as the *Standard*'s Metro section.

Andy was certain there was something rotten hiding behind so much green-this and green-that because her mother could never stop talking about them. When she wasn't in New York at the gallery's office and showroom, Charlotte Cosicki flitted and fluttered to the luncheons, banquets, teas, and galas of the Main Line social scene which, if her gossip was even *slightly* accurate, was more spectacularly shameless, sinful, vicious, and venal than anything that gray, grimy, sunk-so-low Philadelphia could produce.

When Andy was in middle school she figured out that some of the people her mother was dishing about on late-night phone conversations with Abigail and Belisaria and Georgiana were parents of kids who seemed no worse for wear, in spite of the affairs, embezzling, frauds, and other polymorphously perverse misadventures their parents were allegedly enjoying.

Andy, at six feet and maybe half an inch extra, was just about as tall as her mother, had always been shy, and so never really asked any of these kids if their parents were carrying on, until that magic day in her English class when the teacher decided to make some of the students reporters and some editors, and Andy got a note pad and a pencil and was told that, as a reporter, she had to "find out the truth about something."

During a social-whirl-type visit to the Brickle estate in St. Anne's with her mother, she found Logan Marius "Logo" Brickle, the prodigal son of the Hampton Bank chairman Kellum Brickle and his insufferable wife Belisaria Wadcalader Brickle, trying unsuccessfully to ride his motorcycle into the estate's swimming pool (he couldn't quite get the motorcycle to start) as part of his lifelong ambition to disgrace himself. Andy asked him why it was that her parents saw so much of his parents, or rather, parent, since Kellum had died from a series of strokes shortly after Logo was born.

Logo was Andy's pathetic excuse for a best friend. They were both only children, and, though Logo had numerous disreputable acquaintances in Bermuda, Bar Harbor, and other places the Brickles had residences, they had known each other longer and closer than anyone else.

Logo might be a best friend, but he was never friendly. Obnoxious, sarcastic, and whiney, he would be utterly loathsome if he weren't harmless, ineffectual, and more than a little bit pathetic.

So his answer to Andy's question was predictably mean. "We use each other," Logo said. He was being predictably obnoxious in a dinner jacket and denim shorts, both perfectly pressed. "We keep each other's secrets. And your father thinks of me as a son."

He went back to trying to kick start the motorcycle and Andy wanted to tell him that her mother didn't keep anything secret, at least, not on the phone.

"Like what kind of secrets?" she asked him.

He shook his head until she said, "I have an assignment for my school newspaper. We're supposed to find out something."

"Like, how it is rich people never seem to get into trouble?"

"Everybody gets into trouble," Andy said.

"But some people never pay for it," Logo replied. "Even if they can afford it. Is that what you want to find out?"

Andy became aware that Logo wanted to tell her something and he was just waiting for her to listen. So she said, "Sure."

And he told her of times he was busted for drugs, and her father helped pay off the cops. He told her of moments that his mother, who was legally blind, bought art that was fake or merely bad, and how Andy's mother sold it off through the New York gallery. And he told her about his father, the late Kellum Brickle, who liked to stay in the city and listen to jazz music, get drunk, have a fling with a whore, and drive home and forget about it.

"Your father was a bartender at one of those clubs," Logo said. "He used to pour my father back into his limo after the place closed down. One night it burned down and your father pulled my father out. Am I telling you anything you didn't know?"

Andy tried to pretend that she had heard this before, but she hadn't. Her parents never talked about her grandfather's nightclub, other than to say it was where they met.

"And what about my mother?" Andy said.

"At least you have one," Logo snarled. He got his motorcycle started and drove it into the pool, which brought Mrs. Peters, the Brickle family's personal secretary, out into the open with a train of servants while Andy looked across the pool at her mother, in a black-and-white vertical striped couture dress that made her look like a cell phone antenna tower, standing next to her father in one of his anonymous off-the-rack gray suits.

Andy got an A for her school newspaper project when she wrote about the effect of swimming-pool water on a motorcycle engine and, from then on, Andy understood that you get a weird kind of courage from having a pad and pen in your hand that you don't get from merely being curious. She never had a reason, or the guts, to ask questions around her parents because her parents discouraged such questions by either talking too much about what she didn't want to know (her mother) or glaring at her and saying nothing (her father).

Andy became a regular member of various student publications and discovered the corollary to the courage-from-the-pad rule, which was that if certain people saw you with a pad and pen in your hands, if they knew you were "the media," they'd tell you things about themselves they wouldn't tell their best friends.

For a teenager who was too tall, too shy, but smart enough to find compensations, Andy was hooked. Her curiosity became almost insatiable. She wanted to work for the *Morning Standard* so she could ask questions and find out the truth about things for the newspaper she'd read for so many years. But not in Philadelphia. She didn't want to learn about a place invented just so the *Standard* could fill itself with risible tales of vice and venality. She wanted to find out about her own neighborhood, if not her own backyard.

After long years of education and a degree in journalism from one of the best Ivy League schools in the country, she was ready to grab a shovel and start digging. She had no doubt that the Montgomery County bureau chief would put her to work after she listened to him blather on about himself. That she had zoomed through Penn with straight A's and done the kind of work that made her professors volunteer to write recommendations was certainly a plus. That she'd sent those recommendations, with samples of her work, to the bureau chief five times previously without reply did not daunt her enthusiasm. That her parents had both tried to talk her out of working for the *Standard* only made her want the job more.

But her dented, rusting Ford Escort wouldn't start on the morning of the interview and her mother had gone before the sun came up to attend a breakfast meeting at the gallery in New York.

Her father was in his underwear, muttering into the phone in his little office in the bedroom on the second floor. He seemed nervous. "She ain't going to like it with Doug getting out. She never forgot about the street money."

Andy knew better than to ask to borrow his car. She waited until he finished the conversation. She asked him to take her to the bureau's office and, of course, he agreed.

"I'll take my girl anywhere she wants," he said, dialing another number. "It'll be the very next thing."

When she heard that, she walked right out the door.

Maybe it was the slam of the door, the *front* door, which nobody uses much in the suburbs (like the four-wheel drive in a sport utility vehicle, it's there if you need it but you're better off not needing it) when you have a kitchen door or door through the garage, that made Ben Cosicki sit up and remember what his daughter was wearing when she walked out of the house.

It was all legs, with a jacket that just came down over a skirt that was so short and tight that when you saw it, you wondered if it came with instructions on how to sit down. Charlotte must have picked it out. Ben paused in mid conversation and had a vision of his wife blowing into his daughter's room and flinging down half a dozen outfits that she bought for herself in New York boutiques and then decided that maybe they might not necessarily work for the vice president of an art gallery, but, what the heck, Andy was just about her height, and she was young enough, and what's wrong with wearing something that would cause a car wreck?

Charlotte was like that: Getting these ideas into her head about how a person should behave, forgetting that this was the suburbs, the Main Line, and you just don't push things, not in that way. Even if the only people up and about at 9:30 were the landscape services mowing lawns or the maids cleaning up inside the houses set so far back into the trees you could only imagine what kind of cars the owners of those houses drove. People had a way of finding out that Benny Lunch's daughter was dressed up like she had to sleep her way to a job and, with three-quarters of the politicians in Philadelphia owing him deep, most of them ready, willing, and able to put Andy on any patronage job he could ask for (and enough that he couldn't), it didn't look good for the Lunchman's daughter to dress up like she was answering a want-ad for a management position at an exotic dance club on Delaware Avenue.

So he got dressed the way he always got dressed: fast, wincing when he had to pull a shirt or trouser leg over joints in his body that never quite worked right after he got crunched in back of the trash truck. Or maybe he was just getting old: *finally*. All his life, Ben

Cosicki had wanted to be old because, growing up in the Catholic home without a mother and father, all the old people either had all the cards or could act like they didn't need to play the game.

So here he was, racing down the stairs while pulling up his tie, fishing the car keys out of his pocket as he went through the kitchen door with that stupid alarm system keypad that he had insisted Charlotte never should have put in, but she did because she wanted people who came through the back door to know that the junk she had hanging on the walls was worth stealing. Into the car, the Buick, yellow because when he finally started driving his own car, he figured he'd be able to find a yellow car faster than one that was black, white, or red, so it was always a yellow, American-made car so as not to piss off the union people. He bought them used, at first taking them back to Redmonton for Hank Norwood to work on and then later to places closer to home where parents or relatives worked in the unions in the city. That's the way you do whatever it is you have to do: through people who know you from someplace or someone. You walk into an establishment where they don't know you, and you're expecting to get treated good, you're just going to get screwed.

So he started his Buick, his yellow Buick sitting in the big, separate three-car garage next to Andy's beat-up Escort. He expected to see Charlotte's silver Mercedes in the last bay but then he remembered she had gone to New York, having driven it into Thirtieth Street Station and left it in the lot down there. He briefly imagined his wife in New York, lighting that town up like she used to when she waited tables at the sarge's nightclub. The woman was born to get attention and keep it. You have to admire people who know where they belong, from birth. He had to find out the hard way.

The Buick's engine groaned and heaved and it didn't want to start. Ben had that momentary fear you get when you remember the face of the mechanic who knows you and talks to you and you talk to him like you're both equals and you pretend that this mechanic, with grease under his fingernails that he'll never wash out, wants nothing more than to make you, the guy in the gray suit and the shiny brogans, the owner of a flawlessly performing vehicle. And you know that's a crock of shit because the guy with the grease under his fingernails can do the job right or he can screw up and sometimes he'll do one instead of the other just for variety's sake, and the guy in the suit will never know.

As the engine coughed and wheezed, Ben wanted to call up his mechanic and tell him that before he started seeing people that expected him to wear a suit, he used to stink so bad from a day of hauling trash that it would never wash out, and that there's something to be said for hauling trash, for the feeling you get when you see the stuff that people throw away and you think about the places in the world where people would be so grateful to have half of what we leave at the curb, and that this knowledge, as simple and uncomplicated as it is, can give you a feeling of power, a strange certainty, that the people who are the real masters of their fate are those who use everything they have because everything that comes to them is a gift. Even before Councilman Szathmary got him that job on the trash truck, Ben Cosicki wanted to be the kind of guy who used what he got, everything he got, and see where it took him.

And then, as if such humble thoughts pleased the Lord above, the engine woke up, grumbled, and roared as he tapped the gas pedal. Ben backed out and tried to remember where his daughter said she was going when up ahead he saw her, a vision in black and gray and white piping that didn't look at all like him and, if his prayers were answered and he could work the right kind of deals with the right kind of people, she would get a job where she could make things better and help people and be able to sleep at night.

How much had he slept last night, knowing that Szathmary had finally used up every favor he had, and that, as much as Szathmary loved the prison and everything about it, he was going to be a free man, whether he liked it or not. He was most certainly not going to like it because Doug Szathmary was one of those rare people who, once they are in prison, not only adapt to it, but maybe even do good things for the inmates, and for the people on the outside who still came to him and asked for things.

But on this bright, slightly chilly, spectacularly green June morning, Ben Cosicki put such potentially nauseating thoughts from his mind as he snuck his car up on the street behind this fantastic female with that dumb shoulder bag she always dragged around with her, her hair bouncing and swaying as those legs that had been sharpened to sculptural magnificence by long hours spent doing layups with a basketball at the single wire hoop mounted over the garage—those incredible legs that she got from her mother moved with a long, strong, this-world-belongs-to-*me* stride (that she also got from her mother)—that would have been such a knockout combination if each step wasn't wobbling from wearing shoes she obviously hated but wore because they went with the outfit. Taking all in, Ben Cosicki felt that warm numbness of parental pride rise in his chest like the sun shining over creation.

Until he remembered where it was she was going, and he had that parental thought that is the exact opposite of pride, when you wonder if everything and anything your kid has accomplished up to this very moment was done because your kid knew that it was precisely what pissed you off.

And Andy, who heard the engine of his yellow Buick ker-chunking behind her, was thinking the kid-version of the same thought: Was he coming up behind her in the car because he had finally decided to do what he was supposed to, or was he just going to make things worse?

"How's my girl?" her father called behind her.

She stopped and let him drive up, as if he just happened to be out for a morning drive.

"I'm telling you, you don't want to work for those creeps," he called out to her over the weird, rhythmic ker-*chunk* of the engine, which was always sounding slightly off because the guy who worked on her father's car was such a terrible mechanic but her father was loyal to anyone who was loyal to him, so the car ker-*chunked* and ker-*chunked* until it threw a rod or broke down in some spectacular fashion on a road to the mall or in one of the cruddy neighborhoods where he went to visit the geezers and wheezers, and the girlfriend that her mother swore he was seeing.

She resumed walking, and whatever had been cool and pleasant in the morning changed into the hint of heat and humidity that would turn this dumb gray-and-black pinstriped suit her mother had gotten her in Manhattan with the little label inside the jacket that was supposed to make all the difference into a soggy sack. She heard him follow her in the car but she looked straight ahead, knowing that it was two miles to the offices of the Montgomery County bureau of the *Philadelphia Morning Standard* and she would be a liquid mess of sweat by the time she got there but that maybe this was the story they would tell, years later, after she was a brand-name journalist, a veritable truth-squad shock-jock always flying off to the places on the planet where the world was coming apart, or coming back together; where it was interesting all the time and your father and mother didn't try to tell you what you should be doing with your life.

"I tell you, Andy, they won't put you on unless they have a reason," her father said. "And if there's one thing most of those media creeps are, it's being unreasonable. They don't even play by their own rules."

She closed her eyes, continued walking. She hoped nobody was hearing this. She told herself that everybody's got the air-conditioning on and the windows closed, except if they're a gardener mowing the lawns or cutting the hedges and then they're working machines so loud they don't hear anything. Maybe she was thinking too much about this because then she didn't feel the changing texture of the ground beneath the overpriced half-heeled square-toed pumps that were pinching her heels. The texture changed rapidly, from the bleak and wretched flatness of the sidewalk to the foamy mush of an over-protected lawn, and then it was too late, and the steel truss that the stop sign was mounted on smacked her hard in the shoulder, sending her backward until the balance that she'd developed from doing layups clicked in. She planted her feet in the grass, and took the battered shoulder bag that had gotten her through four years at the University of Pennsylvania and hauled back and let the stop sign *have* it, right there.

She smacked the sign two more times before he said, "Okay. I give."

Not give up. Not give in. Just give. Sometimes her father was such a miser with words, as if he truly believed that what went out of his mouth diminished him in some way and that, whatever he did, he could never put back what sneaked out. Other times, it was like all junk and he couldn't get rid of the words fast enough.

She heard him open the Buick's passenger-side door.

"You don't want to stand here all day," he said. "You'll waste the air-conditioning."

This was a man who would drive with the air-conditioning off in summer, the heat as high as it would go in winter, and always have his window down wherever he was going, unless it was on a highway, and then he would have it down at least a quarter of the way, the wind making a rip-roaring sound so you just couldn't talk, even if you wanted to.

She looked at him, this short, frail, puny guy with glasses and a crew cut, in a gray suit with a blue button-down shirt and a tie that didn't quite match, his eyes on her, knowing exactly that she was going to get into the car.

She had to say, "You're taking me."

"The very next thing."

"I don't want you parking the car and leaving me in it. I want you to take me directly there."

"Direct." He agreed, or seemed to.

She came around and got in, feeling the freezing blast of air from the dash hitting her in the chest. She pulled the door shut and the car was moving when he said, "After."

"Nothing after," Andy said. "You're taking me now."

"I'm taking," her father said. "You got time."

"Now."

"You don't got an appointment," her father said.

"He said I should feel free to come in."

"You know what it is, when they say feel free? That means they don't give a shit."

"I'll make him give a shit."

"Only one way you're going to do that, and you're not going to do that."

"There's more than one way."

"You got that right. Let me handle it."

"You're not handling it," she said. "But I'll let you do this: You tell me something I can tell him to show him I know what's going on."

He said nothing as he steered the car out onto Montgomery Avenue.

She said, "I'm not asking to get anybody in trouble—"

"Yet."

"Only if they deserve it."

"Everybody deserves it. It's what they don't deserve that they worry about."

"You tell me something I can tell the bureau chief, so after he finishes telling me his life story, I can impress him."

"This something," he said. "Does it have to be true?"

She sighed.

"I'm serious," her father continued. "You're going up to this guy, who don't know what's going on or he wouldn't be in the business he's in, and you think you have to give him something that shows you know what's going on, and you think if you tell him, it'll be like going down to Atlantic City and hitting the jackpot, and he'll be so grateful, he'll put you on, which is the number one thing he won't do, because if it's really something that's going on, he figures out that you're right, he'll get pissed at you for telling him something that he's supposed to know, and he'll never want to see you again."

She shook her head. "This is an editor with one of the top ten newspapers in the country. He gets a hundred resumes a week from college journalism majors. I have to make him see I'm different."

"You just stand there in what you got on and he'll see enough. He might even fall in love."

She folded her arms and glared at the storefronts. "You don't like the media, do you, Dad?"

"As long as I'm not in it, I like it just fine."

He stopped the car at a traffic light, then turned right into the driveway of an apartment house and before she could say anything, he stopped the car in front and said, "You wait. I gotta stop in here for a minute."

"You're not stopping here. You're taking me to the bureau office."

"I'm stopping here and I'm taking you to the bureau office the very next thing."

"I'm not staying in the car."

He got out and she followed him. He stopped, thought about it for a second, then turned and went through the glass doors into a lobby so small they must have cut the single chair into three sections and then glued the ends back together with the middle section left out so it would fit into the space between the second door and the wall with the mailboxes.

"What do you have to do here that's so important?" She knew better than to ask, but she asked anyway.

"Let's hope it isn't important," he said quickly, pressing a buzzer over a mailbox that said B. ADAMS.

An old woman's voice came out of the speaker by the door and said, "Who is it?"

Her father said, "Hey."

The door buzzed open and Andy followed her father into a narrow hall that was painted what she would call cooking-odor brown. He went into the elevator, which was cooking-odor beige, and into another hall that was cleaning-odor blue.

Halfway down the hall, a door was open. Her father went in and stopped in front of a dining room table set for four in a small living room. Two women sat at the table, one of them in a wheelchair. A man was shuffling cards. He looked up and said, "The Lunchman."

Her father said, as if it was all a big accident that he happened to show up, "I was in the neighborhood."

A tiny, dried-up bump of a woman came out of the kitchen. "You coming here, this better be good."

"It ain't," her father said.

The guy shuffling dropped one of his cards.

The tension in the room made Andy want to turn around and leave. She moved away from the table, feeling herself being appraised, and pretended to be studying the shelf of pink-and-blue cookie jars along the far wall of the living room, the same cookie jars as the one back in the kitchen of Andy's house. They'd come from a restaurant her father used to take her to, the place they would end up at when he'd say, "Let's get ussa ice cream," and an hour or so later after he'd gone up and down so many streets, knocking on doors, taking payments from some people and giving out money to others, he'd park her in the restaurant and go upstairs to the councilman's office and stay there while she watched her ice cream melt and the old woman who ran the restaurant always sat down next to her and said, "What's a matter? You're not hungry?"

The woman was a dried-up bun now, shorter than she used to be, more wrinkled than she used to be, in a silver pantsuit with white hair and eyes just as mean as they used to be. She looked at the cards that had been dealt to her on the table, examined them, and said, "What is this?" Then she put her cards down and went back into the kitchen and came out with a tray with a pot of coffee, six cups, six spoons, a sugar bowl, a small pitcher of milk, and a dish of little packets of artificial sweeteners.

She put down the tray and looked Andy right in the eye and Andy felt herself being swept by friend-or-foe radar as the woman said, "Decaf okay?"

"Uh, sure," Andy said, suddenly nervous because these were people she'd never seen before who weren't necessarily happy to see her or her father.

The woman poured the coffee, sat down, took up her cards again, and said, "Big girl."

"You remember my daughter, Andrea," her father said.

"She used to be a baby," the woman said.

"They all used to be a baby," the guy at the table said.

"She's with me, is all," her father said. He picked up a mug of coffee and a minute went by as the people playing cards began to bid. Andy had the feeling that something should have been said by now, whatever her father was going to hear from these people. Andy moved out of the small dining area and saw in the living room over the TV, a color picture that had faded mostly to red of a bright-eyed little girl in a Catholic school uniform.

The woman said, "We fed your girl good, Benny, when you brought her around. How come she don't look like you?"

"It's her mother she looks like," her father said.

"How come a guy like you gets a daughter like her?"

"Things happen," her father said.

"Only once?" the woman asked.

"You take what you get," Andy's father replied.

"It's the other way around, Benny," the woman said firmly.

Andy watched her father fold his arms. "You know, the councilman is going to come out soon, and I think it's time to make peace."

Andy heard cards move across the table and then the woman said, "How much are they asking to keep him in there?"

Andy's father said, "He's done his time."

The woman smacked her cards on the table and said, "He stays in."

"Hey," the man cut in. "No need to get excited. You don't live in the city no more. You could forget about it."

The woman said again, "How much to keep him in?"

Andy's father said, "From what I hear, he don't exactly want to come out. He's made friends in there. He's gotten comfortable."

"He would," the woman said.

"But he's got to come out because there's no more reasons left to keep him in," Andy's father said. "And what we have to think about is, maybe, sometime after he's out, we sit down, we have something to eat—"

The woman said, "What he did to Maria, there's no excuse."

Her father folded his arms even tighter. "I still see her, you know."

"You should stay away. She should see me. Why is it she sees you but she doesn't see me?"

Andy's father said, "It's been long enough. We should sit down and make peace."

The woman said, "With Szathmary? I would spit at myself in the mirror if I was in the same room with him."

"He's coming out no matter what," Andy's father said. "I can see us all sitting down and putting it behind us."

"What good would it do?"

"Maybe show our kids that things aren't completely hopeless."

The woman slammed down her cards. "They can get him in the jail. They put a pillow on his head and smother him. There are people I can pay to do that. He can come down with a disease and they can take him to the hospital and he can have a heart attack. If he comes out, it might not be so easy for him to have accidents. You said you could arrange it to keep him in."

"What I said," her father replied, "was that there are no more ways to keep him in. Now, I can have a meal with some people who might give me an indication of a date. Or they might give me no indication. What you could do is . . ." Andy heard her father deliberately let a second pass before he said, "you should visit."

A cup dropped. Chairs moved. The man said, "Let me have that. There's a spot you missed."

After the movement subsided, the woman said, "You have some nerve bringing me that kind of news, Ben."

"Nerve is what I don't have, okay? If there's anybody who never took a chance in his life, it's me."

"You took plenty of chances. For her and for him."

The man said, "Betty, he's done his time. We should let bygones be bygones."

"Get me close enough to him," the woman said, "and I'll cut his heart out and eat it."

The man said, "Hey." Her father said something about great coffee and in a few minutes Andy was out and in the elevator with him, saying nothing until she checked the name on the mailbox that her father had buzzed going in.

When they were in the sunlight, Andy said, "I get an explanation?"

Her father didn't say anything as he got into the car, but it took him a few tries getting the key into the ignition.

"Why is she so mad at him?" she asked with just enough of a hint in her voice that he'd better answer her this time or she'd keep asking even more questions.

Benjamin Cosicki, of Cosicki & Associates, also known as Benny

Lunch, steered the car back onto Lancaster Avenue. "What it is, is, she's still mad."

"So you going to set up a lunch?"

"It's my business to set things up, but with Betty and the councilman, and some of the other people I know, getting them to settle up and make peace after twenty years of wanting to stab each other in the back—I would only set that up to show somebody I could do it. And who would I show?"

"Me," Andy said.

"And what would I be showing you?"

"Something I could write up in the newspaper."

"I don't want you writing nothing about me. What you see and hear, you keep to yourself."

She said, "Can I at least tell the bureau chief what I heard? That Szathmary's coming out and there's some unfinished business with him and an old lady that used to run a restaurant whose husband used to be his right-hand man?"

He almost laughed. "No. Just go in there and say nothing and watch him fall asleep."

"I'll make him talk about himself and then I'll show him my stuff. He won't fall asleep."

He stopped for a red light. "You're going to go in there and even if he does talk to you, you're going to figure out real fast that he doesn't care how good you are, because hiring somebody who's good isn't going to do anything for him. Hiring somebody who's famous, or connected, or who can sweep his dirt under a rug, or who can get him free tickets to a show down in Atlantic City—that's the person he's going to hire."

He pulled into the parking lot of a profoundly boring office building with a sign by the road that read: PHILADELPHIA MORNING STANDARD.

"And you're going to sit there," he continued, "and it's going to become obvious to you that what I'm telling you is the truth, and you're going to want to tell him that Benny Lunch is your father, because while Benny Lunch might not be the most famous expediter around City Hall, Benny Lunch is connected. Can he sweep dirt under the rug? You don't even have to show him the rug. Can he get tickets? Just tell me where you want to sit. And can he get two people, any two people, especially if they hate each other enough to want to kill each other, can he get these two people to sit down for a sandwich and have these same two people, at the end of the meal, push themselves back from the table like they were long-lost buddies? Can he do that? Can anybody do that? Benny Lunch can do that and nobody has to know how. Nobody has to know that it's me doing a thing. You might want to tell him that, but you won't, because the one thing you don't want him to say is the one thing he's probably going to say, and you know what that is?"

She looked him in the eye. "Who's Benny Lunch?"

He grinned, gave her a hug, and said, "That's my girl."

2 mr. action

An hour later, he was waiting for her, right on time, the car parked in the fire lane. How could he do that, she wanted to know. Most people, if they park out front of a building, even if it's just one of a number of office buildings in an office park off the King of Prussia Road butting up against the Blue Route, somebody tells them they have to move the car. Or they get a ticket.

Her father just did it and he never got in trouble. For her entire life, Andy could never remember her father ever getting in trouble for anything, though her mother hinted that he learned a lesson back in the days when Andy was too young to go to school and they were living in Redmonton. Her father injured his back while working on a trash truck for the Philadelphia Sanitation Department. Hauling trash was his second job, after the bartending job he had before her grandfather's nightclub burned down, if you don't count the errands he ran for the councilman. The injury put him in the hospital and, after three months of rehab, he went to work in the office of the Sanitation Workers' Union. The union would send him out on errands, to get lunch sometimes and to pass on messages that you couldn't say over the telephone because you never knew who was listening in. Her father had a memory that was nothing short of incredible: Say something to him once, and he got it. He couldn't remember stuff he read, though. Show him something written on a piece of paper and he'd have to look at it for a long time. He never liked reading anything, especially newspapers. Later, her father found out that he was dyslexic but he never seemed to care. "Some people read books," he told her once. "I read people."

What he read, he remembered. He could be unnoticeable as he hung around the courtrooms inside City Hall, waiting for the lawyers to come out so he could do a "once around" with them. He'd walk them around the building's rectangular corridor once, or maybe twice, and, by the time they got back to the courtroom, perhaps, he'd have gotten the lawyers to reach some kind of agreement over whatever it was that they couldn't resolve in the courtroom. By the time he went into business for himself as Cosicki & Associates, he was known in City Hall as the Lunchman, one of the people you should see if you wanted things to happen, or maybe not to happen, with some of the city's unions, and with departments and divisions within the city government.

He made enough money to move into a succession of houses in Philadelphia, and finally to a nineteenth-century house in Merion that her mother, who had gotten herself an art history degree at Bryn Mawr while Andy was at Penn, had picked out. They needed a really big house, her mother had said, so she could hang some "seriously huge goods" that she would rave about to the women who bought from her, goods that she would absolutely *refuse* to sell unless they begged her and even then, she might hesitate until the check cleared.

Growing up, for Andy, was mostly watching her parents grow apart from each other. It got to the point, around the time Andy was in her sophomore year at Penn, that the only thing these two people could agree about was that, when it came to what they saw and did, "nobody knows anything." Her mother, Charlotte "Cos" Cosicki (the partners at her gallery were aping some kind of Manhattan trend by calling themselves by abbreviated versions of their last names) despised art critics because you could buy them so cheap: lend them art, provide access to the artist, hire them to write catalog copy and throw in invitations to the right parties, fly them out to openings in London and the West Coast. Do that often enough and it doesn't matter who your artists are and what they make: The critics will talk about it, and talk, as Cos told her daughter, sells anything.

Her father would say the opposite: "If you tell 'em nothing, they got nothing." When clients worried about the media, he'd tell them the media was a follower, never a leader. "They don't even know what they don't know," he liked to say.

What happened was that either the bureau chief refused to see her, or nobody bothered to tell him that the woman in the drop-dead New York boutique suit who was sitting patiently in the bland mauve, beige, and boysenberry reception area with its TV set playing a loop about how "The *Standard* in news is the *Standard* for reaching your customers," was the same woman who had called in and was told she could show up anytime today and he would tell her how great he was. Sure, Andy told the receptionist her name, told the receptionist who she was supposed to see, signed in, and clipped on the big red plastic guest badge that hung off her jacket lapel like a price tag. Andy watched the receptionist call in. She heard the receptionist mention her name. The receptionist told Andy that the bureau chief was in a meeting but if she would wait, someone would be right with her.

So she waited and she began to think about what she'd heard in Betty Adamo's apartment, and she went over things she had heard her mother talking about. She thought about things she'd heard at the Brickle estate, which was looking shabbier and more run-down than it ever had before. She remembered Logo complaining about how the bank was being run, how his mother had to sell the cottage in Bermuda, how they missed "the hunt" that year, how they had to fire some of the servants because they were "too greedy," how some of what Andy's mother had called "the most vital objects" in the Brickle art collection had found their way to Andy's house in the prime display sections, and how Andy's mother was careful when showing them to potential customers to mention that "objects of this significance appear when the seller is distressed."

So even if her mother was telling another lie for the sake of art, the Brickles seemed to be cutting corners lately. The Hampton Bank had printed scrip during the Revolutionary War (and smuggled it out under the noses of the British who had occupied Philadelphia) so that George Washington could feed the Continental Army at Valley Forge, and had managed to survive President Andrew Jackson's attempt to take away its charter, a shift off the gold standard, changes in federal banking laws, plus numerous depressions, recessions, and financial panics. If the bank was in trouble, then she should forget about her informational interview and just tell the bureau chief, because this was information that would affect the city, perhaps even the country.

But she never met the bureau chief. The receptionist had enough explanations: the bureau chief was in a meeting, the line going into the bureau chief's office was busy, could she talk to someone else or leave a detailed message? Andy said she would wait a little longer and when it had been an hour she took herself out of the waiting room and saw her father parked in the fire lane.

She tried not to look too dejected when she came out, but he picked up on her mood as soon as she slid into the car. "He didn't see you," he said.

"They told me he was in a meeting."

He said, "They lied to you. He wasn't even there."

She shook her head. It couldn't be that bad. Newspapers were about the truth. They were custodians of the public trust. They don't like to lie to smart, straight-A Penn grads looking for work.

She told him, "If he hadn't been there, they would have said he was out of the building."

"But they didn't, did they? Maybe, wherever he is, it's not the kind of place he should be on the morning of a working day. Look over there."

He pointed to a row of reserved parking spaces. "See the space that's closest to the door? The one that says BUREAU CHIEF? It was empty when I dropped you off and it's still empty now."

Andy wasn't convinced. "What if he didn't drive his own car and someone dropped him off?"

"It don't change the fact that you got treated like shit for no reason you know about," he said.

She wouldn't cry and he didn't take her directly home, but went down Lancaster Avenue, going past City Line Avenue into west Philadelphia and into Center City, where he put the car in an illegal space on a street crossing Chestnut.

She watched him as he looked at the front door of a corner bar. He could have dropped her off at the house, where she would have peeled off the outfit she was in. She'd have put on shorts and a shirt and basketball shoes and shot layups for three hours until she was so tired she couldn't feel mad or depressed or mad *and* depressed, which was how she was feeling at the moment.

"So what are we supposed to be doing?" she said finally.

He put a music cassette into the tape player. "Billie Holiday did this song called 'Don't Explain.' Mara Rimes did it better."

"So I'm not supposed to ask?"

"You can watch and listen and not be so curious."

So she sat and listened.

Then this bulky geezer in a milky blue suit came out the front door of the Chestnut Street bar with his hands in his pockets and her father sat up and said, "See that? See that?"

"See what?"

"Doesn't matter. He's got his hands in his pockets, like he's so casual, like he don't have a care in the world."

Her father started the car and drove off in the opposite direction.

"Aren't you going to follow him?"

"No need."

She turned back to her father. "So we just sat here to see if some guy would come out of a bar with his hands in his pockets?"

"He wasn't supposed to be in that bar," her father said, squinting as he negotiated a turn.

"So what were we just doing?"

"It all depends. The bar he came out of is not just a bar. There's no such thing as just a bar in the city. What that is, is the Penny Saved, a dark, brass-and-carpet joint for the banking and finance people that is supposed to go all the way back to Ben Franklin, but you never know about that. We don't ask ourselves what an ex-FBI guy is doing mixing it up with the bank people, walking around in Center City in broad daylight like we should all be grateful. What we think about is, sure, there are things that a bank gets scared about, that a bank needs to cover up, that a bank needs to get done what won't get done if somebody like Fenestra doesn't come in and break some fingers and bust some heads. I spent my whole life trying to keep people from using scum like him."

"So what's it to us?"

"A challenge, is all. Do we do nothing or do we do something?"

"Is there money in it?" Andy said, amazed at how much her father was telling her.

"Could be. It all depends.'

"On what?"

"On how much we want people to stay stupid and mad at each other. You gotta read people like you read those newspapers. No, you gotta read them better than that. It don't matter why you got lied to at the *Standard*. What matters is that you didn't see it coming."

He was silent on the way home and after he put the car in the three-bay garage with the basketball hoop on the side where she did layups for hours on end, he turned to her as if she'd just appeared beside him. "Look at this college graduate I have here. So, what you going to do for a living, now that you have this diploma that says you know something?"

She hesitated.

He folded his arms. "Back when I was busting my rump with the Sanitation Department, I never thought I'd live to see the day my baby got her college diploma."

Where was this dreamy-eyed nostalgia coming from? He hadn't attended her graduation at Penn. He hadn't seen a damned thing.

"Mom saw me at the ceremony. I didn't see you."

"Something came up. Things always come up but, you ever need something, you just ask. That's what it is with me and people. Things come up, people want a miracle every day of their lives and . . ." he hesitated, "it's always me that ends up being the one getting asked to pull the rabbit out of a hat."

He was setting her up. She could feel it. There was one thing he wanted her to do more than anything, and it was the one thing she had forbidden herself to do, and there's nothing like telling yourself you can't do something to make you want to do it.

So she folded her arms and she asked.

"And this is our guy on the Dead Beat."

For the second time, Howard Lange, the editor of the *Philadelphia Press*, put his hand on Andy's waist, nudging her toward the back of the newsroom where a pair of desks were shoved up against a windowless part of the wall. There a soft, pale, rounded lump sat, wearing a black suit so old it was flaking, fraying, and fading, even as she looked.

Lange patted her waist again. "Shep Ladderback, meet the new Mr. Action."

Andy was used to men waiting a second before they checked her out. Ladderback took so long she began to get mad. His head was turned toward his word processor screen, his short, thick fingers were poking and pecking the keyboard. He moved his head, covered by a thick, matted mess of yellow-gray hair, which moved from side to side as his fingers worked.

His head stopped moving with his fingers. He turned, with slow, careful effort and his eyes swam behind his glasses, as if they couldn't quite find her.

"Shep's been around here the longest of anybody on the staff," Lange said. "He could retire, move someplace sunny tomorrow, but the man is *dedicated*, you know? Obits are his thing. Somebody you never heard of dies—Shep writes 'em up. He's been doing it longer than he can remember."

Andy saw that Ladderback's eyes had settled on her hands. *Why is he looking at my hands?*

"Now Shep," Lange said, "when Andy here has a free moment, I want you to show her how it's done. I want you to let her help you out. Let her learn from the master."

Ladderback didn't move. His voice was almost a whisper: "I don't need an assistant."

Lange patted Andy's waist. "Well, you got one now. Show her the ropes."

Andy looked down on Lange and found her eyes resting on the bald spot on the back of his head. In the last fifteen minutes he had put his hands on her waist, and both arms had brushed up against her legs and behind—all of it very casual, nonspecifically sexual but very much I-am-doing-this-because-I-can. He had nudged and towed her about the newsroom, introducing her first to the reporters—mostly women of every ethnic group—who wrote things, and editors—mostly older white men with guts bulging out of their pressed shirts—who cut, chopped, spliced, diced, and titled what these reporters wrote.

"What you have to do," Lange told her, "is find something that makes you famous. I got famous as a street reporter. Wrote some kick-ass stuff. It's the ass-kickers we promote around here. Everybody else rots in their boots, unless you go to sports, or you become a columnist."

The *Press*'s sports coverage was considered the finest in the city, as good as any city's in the country, with a cadre of mostly male writers in a section of the newsroom set off by a bank of wide-screen TVs that always showed some game in progress. The prose ground out by these writers could hush a noisy barroom, make drunks cry, start fights, and precipitate hundreds of calls to the paper's "Answer Line," where questions of who hit what, when, where, and to what extent the hit was a record, were answered with lightning rapidity by the famous Janine "Bar Bet" Schroeder, the daughter of a northeast Philadelphia tavern owner whose ability to recall sports trivia got her a half-time TV show, a weekend call-in talk radio program, and a contract that was supposed to be higher in pay and benefits than any other journalist in town.

"Without her," Lange pointed to an empty chair, "we're nothing. The focus groups, marketing, and demographic surveys say she's the reason that eighty-six percent of the people who can read in this city open our paper."

He steered her toward the music columnist, a guy who almost yelled at her as he said hello, because, Lange explained, he had gone deaf from attending too many arena concerts; the movie columnist who had autographed pictures of herself with movie stars attached to the wall over her desk; the cadaverously thin restaurant reviewer nervously gobbling vitamin pills as she hunched over her keyboard; and the androgynous elf of a book columnist, whose waist-length gray hair covered her like Spanish moss behind a crenelated wall of stacked books.

"We would have fired her because the last demographic survey we did indicated our readers don't have time to read books anymore,"

Lange told Andy as he steered her away from her desk. "But they still buy them, and they all wish they could write them, so we kept her on to do the buy-my-book interviews with the big-name authors, like our City Hall columnist here."

The columnist was older, fatter, flakier, and more fragile than he looked in his picture. He had copies of his latest book in a cardboard box under his desk and he had just been about to autograph a copy for her when Lange said that she wasn't visiting, that she had an actual job at the *Press*, and then the columnist had stuttered, "Wel-wel-welcome aboard," and put the book back.

It had taken less than twenty-four hours. She had asked and her father had gone into the house, up to his office in the smallest bedroom on the second floor. He put one of his tapes into his stereo—another woman warbling about how she got the blues—and made three phone calls, speaking low enough into the phone so Andy couldn't hear. Then he went behind his shelf of cassette tapes to a shelf of orange Monopoly playing cards. He picked out one that said "Free Parking," put it in a small envelope, and wrote on the envelope with the tortured, forced script of a man who can't even stand printing block letters, MR. LANGE.

He handed it to her. "What you're going to do, tomorrow morning, is you're going to put on clothes," he had said, "and take the train into the city, to the *Press* Building—what is it—Eleventh and Market. Go up to the eleventh floor and tell them this is for Lange personally, and that he's expecting it. Make sure you say it's personal. That means you're not supposed to give it to anybody but him. Lange'll look you over, but, whatever he does, you don't do it back. Don't let him take you out to lunch. Don't get into any room with him that doesn't have a lot of glass where people can see in. He'll give you something to do and don't let him, or anybody else, help you figure it out. Don't try to be nice. Get mad if you want. Don't make friends. Don't tell anybody who you're related to. Don't tell no one the story of your life. Don't try to figure nothing out. Just watch and listen and try to fit in and call me if my name comes up about anything I could be working on."

She had to let him know she was curious. "What are you working on that would come up?"

And he had to let her know that he was in control, even if he was still fidgeting and nervous. "You don't need to worry about that. I get tied to all kinds of stuff that maybe I don't have anything to do with. Something comes up you think I shouldn't be surprised about, you call me. And make sure they don't have any pictures of me in their files."

She wanted to thank him but she knew he wasn't doing this quite for her, that, by agreeing to ask him to get her a job at the *Philadelphia Press*, a scrappy little tabloid that was one major economic disaster away from going under, she owed him.

And Andy didn't like owing anybody anything.

Then he said something strange. "You're going to hate working at that place. You think that newspapers are supposed to help people and solve problems and all you're going to find is a bunch of people tormenting each other and covering their asses and working out their frustrations on the people they write about."

"So, what I'm going to do is, your first day on the job, I'm going to set something up. A lunch."

"Who with?" she asked warily.

"You and me. And I'm going to show you how people are really helped and problems are really solved."

"How are you going to do that?"

"Hey, let me set it up, okay? I know what I'm doing. I've always known what I'm doing."

Her mother had come home later from the gallery in St. David's, a satellite of the New York gallery, and had sensed a shift in loyalties: that Andy no longer despised her parents equally. Charlotte Cosicki retired to her sixties retro office in what had been a butler's pantry behind the kitchen, and made arrangements for an overnight in New York.

The next day, in the newsroom of the *Philadelphia Press* with Lange nudging up against her, Andy wondered why it was that you have to get something you've always wanted, to find out that maybe you shouldn't have wanted it. She reminded herself that a job at the *Philadelphia Press* was not what she wanted, but that it might work out okay, if she could get used to the rest of the people in the newsroom staring at her, not because she was tall or good looking or young or female, but because she was *new*. Every person Lange introduced her to *except* Ladderback had a hunger for newness, and it made Andy's eyes go, not to the person she was being introduced to, but to the person's desk, to the knickknacks, tchotchkes, pictures of family, friends, lovers, odd vacation souvenirs, plastic frogs, stuffed toy animals, Star Wars spaceships, and other clutter that turned the forlornly drab off-white walls, off-white dropped ceiling, off-white fluorescent lights, and gray industrial carpeting into something similar to a pavilion in a zoo, in which each cage had objects designed to keep the imprisoned animal occupied and, perhaps, remind an outside viewer of the far-off realms from whence the animal came.

Ladderback's desk was utterly blank, empty of everything but a notepad and printout of the day's death notice advertisements. Its lack of adornment was, at first, a relief. Then it began to unnerve her. Who is this guy who thinks he's so different he can't keep some cheap junk on his desk that makes it personal?

Andy looked down at Lange and waited for his hand to come and take her toward the newsroom's next denizen. But Lange didn't take her anywhere. She felt both hands on her waist, pushing her toward the empty chair.

Andy did NOT want Lange's hands on her body and she suppressed an urge to elbow Lange in his chest, or, rather, in his neck, because he was so short her elbow would probably catch him there if she hauled back and slammed him one, the way the really hard pro basketball stars did when they were trying to justify their seven-figure signing bonuses. Something about Lange clued her in that he sensed that he was bugging her and that he liked making her uncomfortable, so, for her to indicate to him that she was ready to stomp him into the carpet would only make him happier.

What should she do with a jerk like this? Her mother would have given him one of her glowering looks and watched him shrivel. Her father, on the other hand, would keep cool, focused on what was supposed to happen, and on what wasn't supposed to happen.

So she kept cool, looked him in the eye and figured that, so far, what was supposed to happen had happened, and now something else was supposed to happen. She clamped her right hand around Lange's fingers, crushed them until he flinched, and let go of his hand as if it wasn't worth the effort to fling it away. She said to him, "*Don't* touch me."

The newsroom's background noises, the clattering of keyboards, the mumbled conversations on telephones, suddenly ceased.

"Something bothering you?" Lange asked innocently.

She turned to Ladderback and extended her right hand toward him and said, "How you doing?"

Ladderback stared at her hand. Then he moved one of his hands away from the keyboard and touched hers. His grip was dry, warm, and strangely comforting, as if he absorbed some of her nervous jangling tension. "You're an athlete," he said quietly.

She pulled her hand back.

"You can't keep secrets from Shep," Lange said. He cupped his hands over his mouth and said in a stage whisper, "His folks are retired medical examiners. They taught him how to read bodies, you know, the dead kind."

Ladderback looked away, embarrassed.

Andy said, "I'm not really an athlete. I'm not into sports."

Lange pretended to be horrified. "Not into sports? In this town, that's like going down to South Philly and dissing the Pope."

"I do like sports, actually," Andy said, flustered. "I just don't . . ."

"Compete," Ladderback said quietly. "You don't compete." There was the smallest grin at the edge of Ladderback's mouth when he said, "You're not a team player."

"Whatever she does and doesn't do," Lange began, "Andy is going to help you out when she isn't being Mr. Action. People with problems that aren't rich, aren't famous, aren't anybody we ever heard of and won't want to hear from again, probably—Mr. Action here is going to solve their problems."

Ladderback said to Lange, "You canceled the Mr. Action feature two months ago."

"Because our previous Mr. Action was lazy and careless and sucked at the job," Lange said. "Andy here," he patted her thigh, "is an expert."

She had imagined it millions of times while she was doing layups at the backboard mounted on the garage behind her house—a guy trying to take the ball away from her moves in, moves too close, does something to annoy her, so she raises the foot that's closest to the guy, raises it up just a few inches and then brings it down, heel first, *hard*, on the guy's toe.

It was not a legal defensive move. If a referee saw it he'd call for a foul. Andy crushed Lange's toe and she heard a gust of air blow out of Lange's mouth. She looked down and saw that bald spot on Lange's head wobble slightly. She ground her heel in just a little bit more, then she took her foot away.

Lange swallowed and planted his butt on the desk next to Ladderback's, which was piled high with envelopes, papers, note cards, and other printed effluvia.

He narrowed his eyes at her. He took a breath. "I hope you really and truly hate this job, because, if you don't, I can't think of any worse thing for you to do here, with the possible exception of writing obits. Obits will make you depressed. This, this will make you choke."

Andy looked closely at one of the envelopes. It had been addressed in red felt-tip marker to Mr. Action. It was one of thousands.

Lange patted the pile, pointed a finger at her mouth, and said, "Open wide."

Mr. Action's job wasn't to solve problems, Lange told Andy, but to make it appear that by giving equal time to both sides, the problem would somehow go away.

"Say there's a dog barking, or cops who were slow to respond to an emergency call, or a reader bought a used car that died and the dealer won't pay for the tow, or there's a leak that the plumber was supposed to fix and it's still leaking, a magazine subscription paid for that hasn't arrived, a pothole in the street that's already large enough to swallow an entire SUV; what you do is, you call up the dog owner, the police community relations officer, the car dealer, the plumber, the magazine subscription service, the Philadelphia Department of Streets and Public Conveyances. You get both sides. If it's funny, if it's stupid, if there's passion in it, or if it's insanely trivial and you think they're both nuts, you write it up, supercondensed. If there's any result coming up, like, say, the plumber says he'll visit again or the car owner didn't buy an optional protection plan or Department of Streets and Conveyances says they've had the pothole on a list of potholes and they'll be repairing it soon, try to get a date, and put that in. Magazine subscription problems go to this magazine subscription company that gives them an introductory subscription to the same magazine and sends 'em a new bill—either way, they start getting issues. Don't write up anything involving lawyers or that might be covered in other sections. Don't write up anything involving mid- to high-end city government. Don't write up anything involving the state or the Feds. Don't write up anything that happens outside our circulation area. Don't

49

write up anything involving *Press* staffers, newspaper employees, or their relatives, or their friends. Anything political has to be checked with the City Desk. This is supposed to be lively, upbeat, entertaining fluff that makes the *Press* look like we're concerned and we're on the side of the readers, who only really care about seeing their names in print. Got me?"

He glanced at the dent she'd made in his shoe. "You had your word processor orientation this morning and you have your temporary sign-on. So go for it. You got any problems, you ask Shep. He asks you to do anything, you do it. You need a shoulder to cry on, quit." He got up and she watched him try to walk without favoring his toe as he moved back across the tangle of newsroom desks toward his glassed-in office.

After a while, she heard Ladderback's tapping on his keyboard. The tapping stopped. She turned and saw his eyes on her again. She waited for him to say something.

"Look, I'm just here, okay? I don't want to be your assistant."

Ladderback said, "The obituary desk is the traditional training station for new reporters. They either develop skills and move on to other desks, or they quit."

She didn't ask him, if the obituary desk was such a great training ground for young bloods, why he was a little past due for moving on. She said, "I'm just doing this until I can move on to what I really want to do."

He stopped typing and said, "I told myself the same thing, some years ago."

That's not my problem, Andy thought as she opened her first letter. She found it mildly annoying, a stilted, whining rant about the city snow plows blocking cars parked on city streets. It had been written in February. It was now June.

She opened the next letter. It was typed on stationery with a swastika in the letterhead. The writer was complaining about minorities who were polluting the white races with their inferior mutant seed.

Another letter asked if the newspaper would buy an expensive medical machine that the author's insurance plan wouldn't pay for. It was a matter of life and death. Andy checked the postmark. The letter had been written a *year* ago and had sat on this desk, unopened. Of course, the newspaper wasn't going to buy a machine for this person but there must be some way the insurance company dealt with matters this important. She called the insurance company six times. Each time she got lost in the phone tree.

Here was a letter from a purchaser of a computer that wouldn't work correctly. The letter didn't have a phone number but Andy identified the sender from directory assistance. She called and got an old man on the phone who said he was blind and didn't know what a computer looked like and why was she bothering him?

Three other letters about HMOs not paying. Ten failed attempts to get through the phone tree to a customer account service representative.

She tried the voicemail, starting with today's. An old man was complaining about a cat yowling at all hours of the night, and the owners, who used to work for the CIA and are now drug dealers who use computers to tap the phones. These no-good owners leave the windows open so the cat can keep everybody awake. Where is there any consideration?

She sighed and went to the next message. A woman, complaining about noise in the burned-out building across the alley. "They boarded it up but the kids, the kids took the boards down and they're in it all the time, and not just kids. I swear, somebody's going to get killed in that thing, one of these days."

The third message was a tape recording telling her about a great time-share opportunity in West Virginia.

One hour and fifteen letters later, Andy wanted to scream. She hadn't found one problem that she could deal with, and, when she couldn't get to the right people, the people she could get through to were filling her ear with so much hate-filled whining and complaining that she would eventually tap a button on her phone to make it sound as if she had a call on the other line. She'd tell the people to hold and put them on hold and glare at the blinking HOLD light until it stopped blinking.

"I hate them," Andy said, her head in her hands. "I hate them all."

"Try listening next time," Ladderback muttered.

She didn't want to give him the satisfaction of knowing that he had annoyed her, so she just lifted her head and leaned back in the swivel chair, which chose that moment to throw a screw so that the backrest slipped down and dug into her butt.

She did not scream, largely because she heard the City Hall columnist slam his phone down and say, "Yowza, yowza, yowza. Double-Dip's getting out today! Can you believe it?"

She didn't even make that tiny I-am-not-screaming noise as the newsroom revved up and Lange strutted out, making noise about "pulling the cover" and "getting art on the Big Dipper." She didn't turn around as she felt the temperature in the newsroom rise. The low level of chatter increased. Papers dropped. People picked up phones and stabbed the numbers with new energy.

Should she call her father? She saw from the clock over the newsroom reception desk that it was close enough to the lunch hour, so maybe she should wait until she saw him then.

She put her shoes back on, slid back on her swivel chair, hoisted up her shoulder bag, and took off. On her way out of the newsroom she passed the glass wall that divided Howard Lange's office from the rest of the newsroom. Lange bounded out as if he had been waiting for her, his dark, navy-blue suit jacket blowing open to display the monogram over his salmon-colored shirt pocket and the cascade of his emerald, azure, and rust zigzag-patterned tie, as if to say, isn't it great that I can wear this, and get away with it?

He looked up at her, gave her a tiny half smile, and asked her, as if he wanted to know the time of day, what she was doing for lunch.

"I'm meeting my father," she said quickly.

"You could do better," Lange said. He raised his hand to touch her, but withdrew it when he saw her tense. "You keep in mind that I have a hundred and fifty letters and resumes from people all over the country, some of them reporters with master's degrees in journalism and ten, fifteen years of experience; prize winners that would perform unnatural acts to be doing what you're doing, and all I have to do is pick up the phone and they're in and you're out. Make sure you understand that, okay?"

Andy fought back an urge to step on his foot again. "I think I do," she said.

"Your father and I had some run-ins over a strike we had here," Lange went on, bringing his arm back. "But I put it behind me. You want to go places, I can take you there. You cross me, and I'll run over you with a truck."

Andy felt that sudden clammy feeling she got when she was doing layups and she knew instantly that whatever she did, not only was the ball going to miss the hoop, it was going to miss the backboard and end up someplace out of the court where it would bounce out and away into the darkness and into the hands of the idiot males who hooted and snarled at her: A tall, strong white female who was so good at putting a ball into a hoop that they would not play with her because she would beat them so badly.

Whenever she felt this way, she knew that, no matter what happened, she would lose: the ball, her pride, the flowing sense of grace and harmony that made doing layups (which is *not* the same thing as playing basketball on a team) so necessary, or, in this case, the choice of quitting a job she hated because she didn't like it, didn't want it, and could do much better at something—anything—else, and not because this asshole who owed her father a favor was being an even bigger asshole than she had thought possible.

God created rich assholes, her mother had told her, so that art dealers could sell them art at prices high enough for the these assholes to compensate for every repulsive, irritating, or merely inept thing that assholes ever did.

But she didn't think that rich assholes could ever compensate for Howard Lange. Pawing an employee is so stupid, why would anyone in a position of authority do it? Did the guy *like* being hated?

Andy told herself she was going to quit this job anyway, but she wanted to do it on her terms, and not give this asshole a reason to get rid of her.

But, before she could yell that at Lange loud enough for the rest of the newsroom to hear, a voice behind her asked, "What kind of truck, Howard?"

Lange stared past her. She turned and saw Ladderback, close enough to be in her shadow.

"The kind you'll never afford," Lange muttered. He spun around and went back into his office, and Andy became so angry that she lost her chance to put the asshole in his place. Even if Ladderback appeared to want to say something to her, she wouldn't give him the chance. She pretended she was checking the sports digital watch on her wrist and said, "I'm going."

She wasn't followed to the elevator, didn't look at anyone until she was out, on the street, heading up Market Street. She walked quickly, purposefully, ignoring simmering heat and the brackish odors of diesel exhaust, the honks from passing cars, and the drivers who hooted "Yo, legs!" at her. She crossed Market, went south on a traffic-snarled Twelfth Street to Sansom Street and the Italian place where her father said he'd meet her.

She took a seat at a tiny, walnut-and-brass bar in front of the dining room, asked for a real iced tea, and waited.

Andy found herself at the bar two stools down from a scrawny pigeon of a woman with a lip that curled whenever she caught her eye.

She switched to a Ukrainian pepper vodka, then another, and maybe one more, as she tried to ignore the clumps of casuals and toots (what the guys in their $250 cotton summer sweaters called the perkier females that accompanied them, when they thought females couldn't hear them) saying, "Yo Jimmy, howya doon?" to the bald buzzard (who wasn't named Jimmy because he answered the phone "Jimmy D's, whaddya want? Yeah, this is Angie. I got called in because the other guy had to be someplace.") in reading glasses, black bow tie, ruffled shirt, and cummerbund, who ran a chewed pencil down the list of names with reservations while his other hand hung low enough to take whatever rolled dollar bills were passed his way, and then lead them to a table whose location in the dining room was supposed to be a profound indication of the suit's style, substance, and need to be observed.

After the third pepper vodka, Andy, who had always been too tall not to be observed, tried to figure out why her father would take her to a noisy Center City steak-and-fish joint where paralegals, wet-eared MBAs and commuter worker bees pretended they were on the fast track. Paneled in dark woods, with a black-and-white tiled floor and dingy, painted tin ceiling, Jimmy D's was probably as old as it looked, and it appealed to people who wanted to believe that the narrow tables with oyster crackers and horseradish on them, and the dusty paintings on the walls of weirdly motionless leaping stags, running dogs, and men sitting in hunting uniforms looking bored on horses, were indications of a Philadelphia that was more real than the one they inhabited.

Was this going to be business, or something else? She tried to remember what he had said earlier that morning before he dropped her off at the SEPTA train station. (He had insisted she take the train, even though she had a car and he had a car and he always drove into the city so why couldn't he give her a lift?) He had had a faraway look in his eyes as the train pulled in and he said, "I'm going to set something up." He told her a time and the address of Jimmy D's.

So, what was going to be set up? Was he going to have her meet with someone? Or would he do what he always did when she was angry— sit and listen and tell her that sooner or later she'd feel different?

She told herself that she'd feel different if she wasn't really working for him. Though her father worked without a secretary or an assistant, he always had these associates calling him, knocking at the door of the house at all hours, some of them walking in because her father never locked anything. Andy was told to never ask who these men or women were, they were "just people," he would say, "who are paying me to do what they think they can't do themselfs," and Andy would blush, wanting to tell her father she should say *themselves* so he wouldn't sound so . . . so dumb all the time.

But she wouldn't correct him. "I may not know when I'm right," he had once yelled at her mother when her parents used to fight, "but I don't need nobody telling me when I'm wrong."

So, she wouldn't tell him he was wrong in letting her sit at a bar with the casuals muttering behind her back about how they liked big girls and then one of them coming on, real friendly, tapping the expense-account credit card on the bar and asking, as if he had just noticed her, if she didn't mind him buying her a drink.

And then there was the asshole who looked her right in the eye and said, "You hear that song on the radio? Every time I hear that song I want to fall in love."

She could have told him she didn't listen to music, didn't like it much, that she may have been born with this neurological disorder called amusa that Sigmund Freud may have had that makes everything that people like about music sound like noise. Her mother never danced and preferred silence or talk radio stations. Her father hoarded cassette tapes of too-drunk-to-sing-straight blues and jazz singers.

So why did this asshole at the bar come on to her about music to let her know what kind of asshole he was? This was turning into a day for not talking to assholes. After the eighth guy went down in flames she decided that she didn't care if her father showed up or not. She went out, began to sweat, and began to hunt for windows of shops that sold things she didn't want to buy.

If she was in need of further disappointment, she could call her mother on her mother's portable phone, and listen to her mother tell her about how things were going at the gallery in New York. She could call Logo, who had an apartment in the city and might just be obnoxious enough to lift her wilting spirit.

But she didn't want to call Logo because, if he bothered to answer the phone, he would either promise to pick her up in his banged-up Porsche and then never show up, and then tell her when she ran into him again that she was not allowed to get mad at him because his mother was her mother's first and best art collector and the customer is always right, right? He would make her so angry that she would want to hit him, but she wouldn't hit him because making her angry was Logo's twisted way of showing affection. Ever since they were kids he found ways to get under her skin and she let him because it was something he had to do, and, as angry as she would get, her anger blew off quickly enough, and then the two of them would be able to put up with each other, to "run along and play together" as Logo's mother Belisaria would advise. While Logo was seeing expensive psychiatrists and getting thrown out of private schools, Andy went to public schools and brought home straight A's. Belisaria would always tell Charlotte that Andy was the daughter Belisaria had always wanted, which would embarrass the hell out of Andy and make Logo go out and wreck his Porsche.

Logo was currently enrolled in summer classes at Penn in an attempt to make up enough credits to graduate. His apartment was in Center City and the Porsche was in a garage and all she had to do was call.

But she didn't. She had had enough disappointments. She decided to take the train home.

And what should happen on the train but she saw a guy who could have been her age, maybe a little older, in the seat that faced toward the other seats. He was in a nice, casual suit of one of those strange colors that is somewhere between gray and brown but wasn't quite either. It was dressy but neat, no tie, deep dark blue shirt buttoned up, with dark black hair pulled back over his head in a style that was, let's face it, slightly out of date, but on him it looked like he was allowing himself a small indulgence. He could have been Italian or Spanish, there was something dark about him but not so dark that he couldn't fit in, if he wanted to, at the kind of dressy Main Line weddings her mother was always getting her invited to—"not" her mother would tell her "to find a guy or get involved with anyone specific, but to learn the rituals, to understand these people, to know the kind of buttons you're going to want to push one day, even if you think you'll never want to push them now."

Andy found herself staring at him and he probably sensed it in the same way that she sensed when people were looking at her. He fidgeted a little as he turned the pages of the *Press*—he was actually reading the *Press*, which, because of its tabloid shape, could be opened like a big book—and Andy wondered how she would feel it if he read something she wrote but then she remembered she hadn't written anything. She tried to spot the page and—yes, there it was, the obituary page, *not* the sports, *not* the comics, *not* the columnists with their fake friend-of-the-people grins.

Wouldn't he like to know that the guy who did those was so old, like he'd been there forever. Old and strange . . . but nice enough to blow off Lange before she had gotten mad enough to do something stupid to him.

She studied his nose and decided it might have been broken once, so the face, with its dark five o'clock shadow, wasn't as perfect as it could be. But even if she didn't see those eyes, she knew that if he bothered to look up out of the paper and see her, they would melt her where she sat.

She shuddered then, pulled her shoulder bag over her. She told herself it was the air-conditioning on the train. She told herself that even if she wanted the guy to look up and catch her eye and do something stupid so he could come over and start talking with her, that it simply wouldn't happen because things like that just don't happen, not when you want them to, or exactly the way you want them to.

She waited for him to pick his nose, chew his lip, stick his finger in his ear or do something else that she wouldn't like, so she could turn away and think about her father not showing up or how he would react when she told him the job wasn't working out.

The train lurched to the side and she pulled her shoulder bag in closer when she saw him look at her. Just as she made sure that his eyes really could liquefy her, he looked away like he was a little kid and he had been doing something wrong. She didn't figure it out until she remembered that those eyes hadn't really been moving when he had the *Press* open, that they had, in fact, been looking a little bit past the paper at a window and that if she looked at the window she could see him, reflected, looking right at her!

She was dizzy when she got up but her stop was coming and when she got off she didn't look back to see if he was also getting off.

The train hadn't begun to leave when she heard him say, "'Scuse me, but . . ."

She started walking away from him as fast as she could. Well, maybe not that fast, because it just wouldn't be right, with the old train station with its platform just about empty at this time of the afternoon, to break into a run—

"'Scuse me, but, would you please wait up?"

She wanted to say, NO! But she moved a little faster, or was it slower, she wasn't sure. She came to the stairs she'd have to descend and the leaky, stinking tunnel under the tracks that she'd have to go through to get to the other side to walk home. No way was she going to let this guy catch up with her in that tunnel.

So she stopped, turned around, and he wasn't looking right at her so he almost collided with her, came close enough for her to smell after-shave and wonder if there was something about his voice that was a little familiar, some twangy flattening of the vowels that said the guy was from the city, but what came between him and her was her shoulder bag.

Just as she remembered that she wasn't feeling the convenient weight of the bag's strap on her shoulder, her eyes locked into his— big, gray with flecks of gold—and he said, "Uh."

Was it just a second that she felt herself stop breathing?

Then he looked down and she saw the beginnings of a blush flood into his face, and he said, "You left this on the train."

"Yes," she agreed, immediately feeling stupid for agreeing because the last thing she wanted this guy to think was that she left her shoulder bag on the train so he could grab it and give it to her and then she would have no alternative but—

She looked past him at the train receding up the tracks and said, "The train—you have to get back on."

He shook his head just enough for her to see the muscles move on his neck. The guy worked out. Or maybe he had one of those bodies that guys wish they had, so they work out and they never quite get it. So if he had one of those bodies and he didn't work out, it was only a matter of time before that thin skin would grow thick and he would turn into another male food-bag watching football games and packing in the beer and pierogies.

"Actually this is my stop," he said, too quickly. "I know how that sounds, but it's true."

Now *that* was dumb. He should never have told her that he, too, was aware that it was just *so* coincidental that she would leave her shoulder bag on the train and he would just pick it up and hand it to her because he happened to be getting off at that stop.

Then she became a tiny bit miffed: why *shouldn't* he miss his stop to give her her shoulder bag? What's wrong with a guy who had been staring at her and had been ashamed when she caught him in the act, what's wrong with him missing his train so he could give her something she would have regretted losing? Next he was going to ask her if she wanted a lift. She did a quick scan of the narrow station parking lot and didn't see anything that she could see this guy driving.

"Well, thanks," she said, taking the bag and pushing the strap onto her shoulder, wondering if that's all she should say.

He smiled bashfully. "These things happen to me all the time."

She was about to say, *what's that supposed to mean?*, when she saw him squint and look around the station. "You're from around here, right? You know where the streets are? I mean, there's this place I'm supposed to go, to just check it out. The property, I mean. It's a house on this street called Albemarle Way. You know where Albemarle Way is?"

Of *course* she knew where Albemarle was, but she wasn't going to be obvious about it. There were a few ways to get to Albemarle from the station, one that was fast but you had to make a lot of turns down streets that didn't always have the intersections well marked, and another, the idiot-proof way, that was longer but . . .

She gave him directions for the idiot-proof way. He nodded, repeated them, looked across the parking lot at that first left he was supposed to make. "You have to go through this tunnel to get to the other side," she added.

He peered down the stairs. "Right," he said, and began to move past her.

He was halfway down the stairs leading to the tunnel when Andy said, "You came out here without knowing where you were supposed to go?"

He turned slowly around and looked up with a half smile on his face. "I could've driven but, you want to know the truth, I found this great parking space, the kind of space you always want that's, like, close to everything, but not directly out front. It was so perfect, my car just sitting there, against the curb, just like it belonged there. I couldn't bear to move, knowing that I come back an hour later, I have to drive around, a half an hour, sometimes, just to find the right space."

The guy was broke, she decided. Anyone in the city with any money and a decent car would put the car in a lot. Well, maybe not anyone. You meet people on the Main Line who are wealthy beyond their dreams, and they still scrimp and save and pinch pennies and dress like they can't afford decent dry cleaning because . . . because they don't have to. Being cheap for these people is a choice, rather than a necessity, a little game they play with themselves. This guy was wearing a suit that wasn't cheap. And it wasn't the kind of suit that the suits in that restaurant were wearing: dark things that say finance, law, I-have-to-wear-this-because-I-have-to-impress-some-asshole.

"Besides," he added, "when I have the time, I like to find my own way."

"You must get lost a lot."

He shook his head. "I don't look at it that way. A day like this, with everything nice and peaceful, it's okay to let a few things happen as they will. In my line of work, sooner or later things get . . ." he crunched up the left side of his face, "different."

"What do you mean different?"

He regarded her for a moment, as if he was asking himself if she really wanted to know, and if he really wanted to tell her and spoil it all. Instead, he said, "You want to go for coffee or something?"

Oh, God did she ever. But she had to say no.

He seemed genuinely disappointed. "Let's leave it like this: Next time, you'll say yes."

"What makes you think there's going to be a next time?"

"What makes you think there isn't?" Then he turned and went into the tunnel. Andy didn't move until she saw him emerge, go through the parking lot, and disappear at the end of the first street along the idiot-proof way.

He didn't turn around to look back at her. Not once. She waited a few minutes after he'd gone. Then started down the stairs into the tunnel and took the shortcut automatically, without even thinking about where she was going. She didn't see him again on the way to her house.

Was it the walk along shady streets that hummed with the sounds of landscaping machinery, or the pepper vodka, or the late afternoon haze that made her want to fall into a pool filled with ice cubes and just a little bit of water? No such pool existed behind her house because the rolling acreage that had once come with the house had been subdivided long before her parents bought it.

But the house was still impressive. Even before her American Vernacular Architecture course, she could appreciate the feeling of grandeur invoked by the three story, late-nineteenth-century Bryn Mawr stone plantation house, with its white Doric portico over the front entrance (that nobody used), an end-wall porch on the west side, and a porte cochere that opened into the salon on the east (another entrance that nobody used). The driveway passed around and through the porte cochere and continued back to the garage, the asphalt parking deck, and the basketball hoop that had been the center of her adolescent universe and still was.

Andy checked the mailbox, found it empty, twisted the front doorknob, and found that locked. Her father wasn't home. If her father were here, the door would be unlocked because he had a thing about locks, refusing even to lock his car. "If you want to let the whole world know you got something worth stealing, you lock it up," he'd say.

Though her father had never had a car stolen from him, he would return from wood-paneled union halls and noisy roofer bars to discover the glove compartment open and paper scattered on the floor, or a big hole in the dashboard where the tape player had been. When Andy had asked him if it would be less expensive to put up the windows, he said, "If it ain't sticking with me, it deserves to go." The hardness in his eyes told Andy he was so serious that she never said anything about it again.

She had a key to the front door but if she opened it she would have exactly ten seconds to find the alarm keypad and turn the alarm off, and the keypad was in the coat closet at knee level because her mother felt alarm system keypads were tacky when they were mounted right next to the formal entryway. Andy didn't feel like squatting down in flat heels and a soggy dress to turn the thing off, so she went back to the driveway toward the kitchen door, where the keypad looked like one more in a row of high-tech kitchen controls.

On the way she passed the viciously beautiful pink-and-white cluster of rosebushes her mother had ordered planted around the side of the house, then the heat bump that whirred ceaselessly on its low pedestal. A wall of hedges and trees ran behind the garage and blocked most of the view of the houses that had sprouted from the land an earlier owner had sold off in odd lots so that the streets surrounding the house looped and whirled back on each other without seeming to go anywhere.

In one corner, beyond the rosebushes, just inside the hedge, was an overgrown, tumbled-down brick outdoor barbecue that a previous owner had left unfinished. It remained unfinished and occasionally her father would mumble about getting it cleared out. "Can't have no barbecues around here," he'd tell Andy, "because if your mother could put up with the kind of crooks, deadbeats, and degenerate scum that I'd have to invite, I'd have to put up with them too."

Her crumpled red Ford Escort slumbered silently in the garage where her father's mechanic had dropped it off. The bays for her father's yellow Buick and her mother's silver Mercedes were empty.

She unlocked the house's back door, turned off the security system, and heard a phone ringing in the house. It wasn't her mother's line, which chimed like a bell in a cathedral. It wasn't either of her father's two lines. Her father's business line had a ring that sounded like a chirping, energetic, happy-to-see-you bird, and the second, his private line, had a low, muttering rattle.

It was her *own* line ringing and the house's heavy wood paneling created an echoing effect, transforming the cheap digital whistle into a hysterical shriek.

She let her answering machine take it. She stood in the vestibule at the back, the familiar aromas of the house welcoming her. She stepped into the spaceship-modern kitchen with the blue-and-pink porcelain Bep 'n' Betty's Luncheonette cookie jar on top of the refrigerator. A pile of unwashed breakfast dishes were piled high in the sink. Andy saw a fry pan with some of her father's gray scrambled eggs adhering to it. They were gray because of the things he put in them: mushrooms, garlic, sardines, and leftovers chopped and diced and included into the curdling mix that was different every time he made it, but still came out colored gray.

The chopping block didn't have the paper and plastic packaging of a no-need-to-refrigerate microwave meal on it. Her mother had not come back for lunch.

The kitchen opened onto a formal dining room with a long table that could seat twenty. Track lights hung from the ceiling like theater spots. Her mother had hooked the lights up to a motion detector. Enter the dining room and the dark landscape paintings of cows and sheep floating over grass hills winked on. Andy used to try to fool the motion detector by moving as slowly as possible into the room. Sometimes she'd blast into the room and then stand as still as a mannequin, until she became invisible to the motion detector and the lights shut off and she saw the paintings in pearl-gray natural light.

The lights blinked out as she went into a heavily wood-paneled hall, passing what her mother called the salon, with its tremendous fireplace, tall windows shrouded in complicated drapery cascades, sprawling Oriental rugs, clusters of reupholstered antique furniture, portraits of stiff, bearded, bewigged and bespectacled people that weren't from her family but appeared as if they were, a spangled Venetian glass chandelier, and, located conspicuously over the mantel, the latest painting she was trying to unload. No matter how the painting appeared, her father always called it "the Art."

Andy went up the wide, formal staircase in the hall, taking the stairs two and three at a time, not because she was hurrying, but out of habit.

Her room was on the second floor, facing the back, between one bedroom that her mother had turned into a clothes closet and a storage area for art and antiques, and another that was her father's home office, which was never locked but always closed.

With her father's car missing from the garage, the office would be empty. She opened the door. Her eyes fell on the cheap, dented, black metal-and-walnut veneer desk, an old Tensor table-lamp, a few filing cabinets, the two telephones, and his luxuriously plush coffee-brown leather chair, which was supposed to be good for the pains her father got in his back, souvenirs from a beating he had before she was born.

She went past the office to her bedroom. It was a mess, but it had always been. The phone rang again and, before she could stop herself, she picked it up.

"This is N. S. Ladderback from the *Philadelphia Press*. May I speak to Mrs. Cosicki?"

"It's Ms.," she told him. "I'm quitting. I'm not coming back. Tell Lange to find another Mr. Action."

She heard him take a breath. "You're Ben Cosicki's daughter."

"So?"

He paused, "I'm sorry. Is your mother available?"

"Talking to her isn't going to help."

"I was hoping that your mother or, perhaps you might have access to a photograph of Mr. Cosicki. A recent, black-and-white head shot? We don't have anything usable here."

"What do you need a picture of him for?"

She heard the breath again. "Oh, no. I am very, *very* sorry."

She became surly. "Sorry for what?"

"No one told you?"

"I just got home. If you wait long enough," she said, "my father will be back and I can find out if there's a picture that you could use, but I don't think there is one, because he never liked getting his picture taken."

She remembered she was supposed to call her father if she heard his name mentioned. So she would call him on his portable phone, right after she got off with the old man.

"What do you need his picture for?"

"I'm . . . sorry."

"About what?"

"He died, Ms. Cosicki."

She didn't move. She couldn't speak.

"It came in over the police wire a little more than an hour after you left. He was found inside an abandoned building in Redmonton. Do you have any idea why he would be there? The police feel it was accidental, that he fell through a weak area on the second floor and died of his injuries."

She didn't hear what he had said. She heard him talking, though. Something about a picture.

"Ms. Cosicki, if you're alone, please, you must find someone who can be with you at this time."

"Wait," she said. She put the phone down, went out into the hall, and pushed open the door of her father's office. She looked at his empty chair. There was no way her father would have a picture of himself. She felt her knees giving out and she sat on the floor. She felt her back growing weak so she put her head on his chair. She felt her throat tightening and her vision blur so she closed her eyes.

She couldn't feel herself crying. She couldn't feel anything for quite a while.

what you pay for

When the police report came in, Lange burst out of his office, plopped down at the copy desk where everyone in the newsroom could see him, ordered out for a latte, and, as he signed on to the terminal, demanded that "Somebody get me some art on this Lunchman."

Art was newsroom slang for a photo. The photo editor was on vacation and his assistant, a wide, crew-cutted woman named Snag, replied with an unflappably calm voice that suggested a regimen of antidepressants that she'd already checked the archives and that they had no art.

"What do you mean, you already checked," Lange snapped, his fingers flying over the keyboard.

"What I mean is somebody already asked and I checked and we don't have any."

"Not even a group shot?"

"Not even."

Photos were crucial in a newspaper like the *Press*, where, many times, the picture grabbed readers' attention faster than a headline. To not have a picture in time for deadline might mean that the news item would not run, and, for Lange, to have one precious word beneath his byline fail to see print, was unthinkable.

Lange's eyebrows slouched together. "You said somebody checked. Who was it that checked?"

"Mr. Action. First thing when she came in."

Lange glanced around the newsroom. "Anybody not on deadline, get me some art on Ben-jam-in Co-sick-ee, with a C. Now."

Lange was caught up in the flamboyance of the creative act, when any frustration demanded a dramatic response. Newsroom etiquette required that reporters, a handful of whom had been writing furiously for more than an hour to meet the deadline for tomorrow's morning edition, had to pause and notice Lange's passion, and then become busier. Even reporters who were in limbo—waiting for a source to call them back, reviewing their notes, or slacking off into a late afternoon brown-out when there was nothing to do but call up friends, lovers, or relatives and gossip until it was late enough to leave—became animated, moving papers here and there, tapping their keyboards with renewed energy, hunching forward so it would appear that the doodles they had been making in their notepads were indications of serious activity.

The idea was not to appear idle when Lange, who normally spent most of his time in his office where he could observe the newsroom that he was supposed to be running, wanted to show everyone that he knew how to bang out a story to meet a deadline.

"I'm going to roast this roadkill," Lange mused, like a coach trying to rally a losing team. He called over to Ladderback. "Shep, don't leave this place until you've got me every damn thing you can find about this Lunchman. Somebody must have wanted him dead."

Ladderback wanted to tell him that there wasn't much to be found, but he said nothing. The idea that Cosicki had been murdered was hopelessly lurid. Cosicki wasn't the kind of man that people wanted to kill. Cosicki didn't make speeches. He didn't take credit or blame for mysterious occurrences between City Hall and the numerous unions that could, and frequently did, paralyze the city and its institutions. He didn't make threats. He never got into the kind of trouble that would put him in the media spotlight and he certainly hadn't gone to jail. So why was Lange so worked up about him?

Ladderback pulled up a copy of the police report on his terminal. Benjamin Cosicki, Caucasian male, five feet four inches tall, approximately 135 pounds, age middle fifties, was pronounced dead at the scene after police responded to a 911 call from a location on Sackawinick Street reporting a loud crashing noise inside an abandoned, boarded-up, fire-damaged nightclub at 1662 East Nephro Street in the Redmonton section.

The medical examiner determined that Cosicki had been on the second floor of the rowhouse and fallen through. An area of flooring that had been weakened by fire and rot had apparently collapsed. Cosicki's body was found on the earthen floor of the basement—the first floor had been destroyed by fire though several wood beams remained. One ankle was broken when his body hit, and his skull had been smashed in the back, presumably from having struck a wooden beam on the way down.

At the bottom of the report was "RT: 8:23." The new police commissioner had insisted that a response time be added to all police reports in an effort to encourage faster service, and this was one more annotation that was supposed to mean one thing but actually indicated something else. Since when, Ladderback asked himself, do the Philadelphia police, who have been known to take as many as two hours to respond to a burglary-in-process call from an affluent neighborhood like Rittenhouse Square or Chestnut Hill, show up within eight minutes to investigate a noise in a burnt-out block of Redmonton?

Ladderback gazed across the newsroom at one of several large street maps of Philadelphia. Shielding his eyes from the open windows near the sports desk, he wandered toward the maps and looked for a tangled snarl of streets where Polish, Russian, Ukrainian, Hungarian, Irish, and African Americans lived in narrow, nineteenth-century row-houses and worked in the factory of the old Redmonton Locomotive Works. On the map an X had been drawn, right across from the old Hampton Bank building, at what had been the former office of At-Large Councilman Douglas Szathmary. On top of the old locomotive factory someone had written in pencil *church?*

Sackawinick Street, where the caller had summoned the police, was just off the old factory. He remembered an obituary he wrote, could it have been twenty years ago?

More than twenty. He went back to his desk, pausing before the wall of dark, mildew-green steel file cabinets that extended from the side of his desk back along the wall to the photocopying machine. They were stuffed thick with files containing copies of every obituary he had ever written, with his notes, telephone numbers of sources, photos that the families did not want returned, and every letter ever written to him about an obituary—hundreds of thousands of mostly grateful letters, some carefully splotched and wilted with the letter writers' tears. A few were composed in jagged script, angry that the obituary had lacked essential information about the decedent. Ladderback responded to those letters with copies of his original obituary, and an explanation of how the details about the decedent winning the Employee-of-the-Year Award twice in a row, the vice chairmanship of the Shackamaxon Bowling League, the citation as honorary Clean Up Stamenko Park Day grand marshal had been excised in the composing room due to lack of space, always ending with, "Sincere regret, N. S. Ladderback."

He ended his letters that way because he did regret how the newspaper's rush to deadline, if not judgment, trampled on the feelings of people who were already suffering too much.

It took him a few minutes to find a yellowed cutting with a small cut-out of the police officer. One of his first obituaries, it had been rewritten at the last minute and bumped up to the News section.

Beside the head, FIRE KILLS POLICE HERO, was the Philadelphia Police Department mug-shot photo of Sergeant Frank McMann who died when burning portions of the Straight Up Club lounge at 1662 East Nephro Street collapsed on him. McMann, who was assisting firefighters at the scene, went into the building to rescue patrons who were believed to have been trapped in the blaze. Among the people McMann was supposed to have rescued was his daughter, who shortly became Charlotte McMann Cosicki.

Ladderback then read the obituary he had written, the tiny words on the brittle paper arousing memories of how surprised he had been by the emotional response the dead policeman brought from the racially and ethnically mixed Redmonton community. Ladderback had quoted, among others, Jeffrey Hooks, a jazz musician who had been performing in the club that night, praising the Irish officer, a widower, as an "honorable man, a decent human being, a big fan of the music, and a loving father."

He dug deeper into the file and removed his notes. Many of the jottings, done in the cheap ballpoint pens that the newsroom still stocked by the thousands, remained oblique. There was one, though, that he recognized, next to the quote: He had written a capital L and circled it.

That mark meant that Ladderback had believed while he was taking down Hooks's statement that Hooks had been lying.

Still, Ladderback had quoted Hooks because Hooks was African American and McMann had been Irish and it looked nice in print when an African American said nice things about an Irish cop, who, Ladderback saw in his notes, had been cited dozens of times in brutality cases involving neighborhood drug pushers and petty criminals, many of whom were African American. Newspapers could, and frequently did, print outright lies—quotes from a politician's speech, for example, or a defense lawyer's claim that his mobster client was innocent—because the quotes represented a response, a point of view, a statement freely given that only needed to be reported fairly and accurately, and not questioned or probed.

Sergeant McMann was not as admirable as Ladderback had portrayed him, but the man had died a hero's death and the fewer questions asked of dead heroes, the better.

A third clipping was in the file, not quite as fragile as the last two. The headline read PREACHER: A LIFE IN HARMONY. The article, by a general-assignment features reporter who now worked at the *Morning Standard,* was a profile of the Reverend Jeffrey Hooks, whose First Church of God Harmonious had taken over a portion of the Redmonton Locomotive Factory and led late-evening and early-morning services "because that's when grown-ups play, or pray, and I like to do both."

Ladderback skimmed it, noting that Hooks had grown up in Redmonton and played in some of the neighborhood's jazz clubs and even recorded on a few albums. "I backed up Mara Rimes in a live set we recorded at the old Straight Up Club," he was quoted as saying. "Man, that place was so hot. We used to get all kinds of people in there from all over. Rich, poor, good, bad, and everybody in the middle. We get some of the same people now. We've just changed from the Devil's music to God's, that's all."

It was when Hooks was acquitted for drug possession that he experienced his religious conversion. "I'd been paying and praying to the wrong people to help me out. Then God spoke to me and said, 'Help me in.'"

He removed one last file from his cabinet. It contained the notes and clippings of one of the first articles he had ever written for the *Press*: a neighborhood success story about a jazz club called the Straight Up, and its street-wise owner, Sergeant Frank McMann.

Clipped to the article was a scrap of paper, his notes and quotes from a phone conversation with a Ben Cosicki, the "B-Man," the bartender at the Straight Up. He had said the story Ladderback had written about the Straight Up Club was great, but there were "things going on" in the neighborhood that he might be interested in that "aren't quite legit." "You got one side going up against the other. If they'd make peace it would be okay, but nobody wants to make peace." Cosicki had given him three names and three telephone numbers to call for "proof." Ladderback had told Abe Donitz, the former editor, that he had it from a confidential source that illegal activities had been taking place at the Straight Up Club.

Donitz told Ladderback that he was too inexperienced to pursue such a story. Donitz said he would give it to another reporter, who "seemed to have a feel for these kinds of stories."

That reporter was Lange, who had done a series of stories on the downfall of Councilman "Double-Dip" Szathmary that might, or might not, have led to his promotion to editor after Abe Donitz retired.

Lange now sat, not in his office, but at the copy desk, the U-shaped table that was the newspaper's nerve center where stories were edited and processed. By pressing a few keys on his terminal, Ladderback could access Lange's terminal and watch the words of Lange's column appear as Lange wrote them. What Ladderback saw bothered him enough to make him stand and move slowly across the newsroom until he hovered at Lange's side.

"Shep, you're not making phone calls," Lange began. He ripped a scrap of paper, rolled it into a ball between his fingers, popped it in his mouth, and began to chew.

Ladderback did a telephone number search for Cosicki. There was no answer at the Philadelphia number of Cosicki & Associates. There was no answer at the Merion number of Cosicki & Associates. There was an A. Cosicki in Merion. He dialed it and, when the girl answered and he found out that she had been sitting beside him all that morning, that she had been answering the phone as "Mr. Action," that she had not once used her last name and he had been stupid enough to tell her to listen to her callers when he didn't even have the courtesy to call her by her full name, he wished, for the umpteenth time, he had gotten into some other kind of business.

He heard her put down the phone. He heard her begin to sob.

Lange shouted, "Where's my art on that Cosicki bastard?" Then he peered closer to the terminal. "Oh fuck. Ads coming in. Move Cosicki back to the obit desk. Shep? Are you going to do one of your sob stories or are you going to nail that bastard?"

Andrea shouldn't have to hear this, Ladderback decided as he hung up the phone. No one should.

Lange pushed himself out of the copy desk slot and started heading toward Ladderback. "Shep, I want to know what I'm going to get from you."

Ladderback looked straight at him and said, "Contempt."

In her bedroom Andy found a photo of her father in a drawer where she kept her high school yearbook, her high school diploma, awards and certificates for being smart, pictures of Logo Brickle, and other things she'd rather not have sitting on a shelf, hanging from a wall, or propped up in a frame on her desk where she could see them.

The photo had been taken four years ago during a summer when her father, in opposition to her mother (who wanted to go to Bermuda with Mrs. Brickle) had taken a client's offer and driven his yellow Buick (keeping his window down and the doors unlocked even when it rained in the car one afternoon and somebody stole his tape player the day before they left) to inhabit a house down the shore in Sea Isle City, as always, rent-free. The picture brought back memories of fried calamari so hot it burned the roof of her mouth, of the afternoon aroma of garlic simmering in olive oil. The house had been near the southern bulge of the island, close to the Italian enclave. A short drive over the bridge in Avalon, the next island down, was a really great basketball court, where these preppie snots in surfer shorts, college T-shirts, and pricey sneakers hooted at her through the chain-link fence, and then walked onto the court and tried to take the ball away from her.

She wouldn't let them take the ball away and they got mad and disgusted and drove off in their fire-engine-red sports cars. When they left, she felt an enormous, overwhelming sense of pride.

Her father had spent most of the two weeks at the shore in the house, on the phone, while her mother, who was going through an antiques craze, was gone for most of the day and sometimes well into the night, hitting every antiques shop on Route 9. She returned one night with a fabulous, heavily padded, coffee-brown leather bomber jacket she'd bought in a Cape May boutique. She draped it over her daughter's bony shoulders and Andy couldn't wait for the air to turn cold. The jacket became such a part of Andy's personality that she had worn it on nearly every cold day since.

Mom *could* score occasionally, Andy admitted. When it came to buying things, her father was the strike-out. He almost never spent money on himself—everything was for his business, which meant it had to be like his clothes: bland, inoffensive, fade-into-the-background-gray suits, pale blue shirts, and a tie that was merely dark. Every once in a while, deliverymen would arrive mysteriously and deliver big boxes of stuff: TV sets, rolls of vinyl floor covering, an entire sink in some awful color that made her mother choke. Andy could tell from the way her father reacted when her mother gave the stuff to her maid, pitched it out with the trash, or dragged the box at night to the front of a house whose occupants were on vacation, where, the next morning, a truck from the Salvation Army carried it away ("God forbid they should know this came from us!" she wailed), that these things had special value for him, even if, when she asked where they had come from, he would say "It's here, ain't it? Wherever it was, it ain't there no more."

In the picture she held he was in one of his silent moods. His mouth was closed, lips pressed together, with a slight curl at either end. His eyes were characteristically blank and unsmiling.

She should cry more now, she told herself. She was supposed to feel bad, but there was nothing inside her that could feel. She and her father had never been *close*, but he loved her, right?

She tried to think of the times she felt loved by her father. He paid for things, but he never seemed to take any pleasure from them, and he was never there when she needed him, not even when she just wanted him around. He rarely ate his meals at home. Sometimes, coming home late, he would watch television. Once she wanted to tell him that she was taking a course at Penn in which she was required to watch television. It was called "Running on Empty: The Emerging Global Visual Culture" and it was taught by this bald guy with tiny eyes and a single, two-inch-wide braided column of hair hanging down from his chin. The course was part of his big post-doctoral research and there were no books, no assigned readings, no exams, no studying, only watching a stack of videos that contained pieces of foreign movies, blurry newscasts read by ugly people in bad clothes, and American TV shows that had been dubbed in another language. The professor was always canceling classes to fly to Los Angeles to meet with "studio people." Halfway through the semester, he let the school know he wasn't coming back and they put a grad student in who led discussions in "visual idioms" and showed slides of her trip to Disney World.

But she never told him because he wasn't watching the set as much as he was losing himself in it. He was always drifting off, especially when he played his music in his office.

She sat on the floor of her room with the picture in her hand, and noticed that her phone was off the hook. She was about to hang it up when she thought of the framed picture her mother had downstairs in her office that looked so out of place with all the 1960s furnishings and memorabilia.

Andy went downstairs into the wood-paneled "rec room" tucked behind the kitchen that her mother used as a private sanctum. There, beneath the Coca-Cola-branded Tiffany swag lamp, tangerine-colored shag carpeting, the lava lamp that was only lit for special occasions, the faded reproduction of a poster for the movie *Blow Up* on one wall, a pole lamp in a corner, a bulky "early American" sideboard that held exhibition catalogs and art-world magazines, her computer and telephones, crowned by a molded plastic table lamp whose globe light said BAR, was a single, yellowed, black-and-white newspaper photograph of Andy's grandfather, his Philadelphia police uniform with the sergeant's stripes glowing at his shoulders, his former boxer's mug thick and puffy but cracked into a definite smile, with one long arm up, over, and around his wife—an uncomfortable, fretful woman in an apron and lumpy blouse holding a dish towel and beer glass in her hand (who had probably been behind the bar, drying the glass while the tumor in her brain was growing, making her hear and see things that weren't there, forcing Pops McMann to yell repeatedly for her to come out into the street and be in the picture). Pops had his other arm up and around Charlotte McMann. The girl who would become Andy's mother did not resemble either of her parents. She was as tall as her father, but seemed shorter (Pops had his police cap on), narrow-shouldered, wide-hipped, potato-nosed, and thoroughly awkward beneath a sign that said STRAIGHT UP CLUB.

And in the back, just in the shadow of the open door leading in, was a face, with thick eyebrows, crew-cut hair, and haunted eyes that peered, carefully, wary and with a touch of fear that Andy had seen in some of the animals at the zoo who were (she could only guess) worried about what would happen if the bars on the cages came down and the people who stared and threw junk at them came closer and closer until it was impossible to get away from them.

Her grandfather and grandmother used to take in foster children, her mother had said. Ben Cosicki was one of them. He never talked about where he came from, but there was always a problem with immigrants, with families breaking up, kids running off, whatever. After the cancer killed Ma McMann, Pops took Ben out of the stockroom and put him to work behind the bar. He didn't say much but he worked well with the customers, who came from all over to hear the music at night.

The kid that owned that wary face became a little brother to Charlotte McMann. She never imagined that she would marry him. Her father would never have allowed it while he was alive. But Pops died in the fire and Charlotte was pregnant so it just seemed the right thing to do.

Andy focused on the photograph, and brought her eye so close that she could see that the faces, smiling, awkward, were composed of dots. She was not surprised that the picture had been cut from a newspaper, but had never been quite aware of that until now. She saw the type on the opposite page faintly visible in the lighter places. Was that "McMann" in backward type?

She took the photograph off the wall, turned it over, and slid a fingernail that needed trimming under the cardboard backing. Inside she found an entire yellowed newspaper page folded carefully so that only the photograph showed through the glass. Though she unfolded it slowly, pieces of the paper crumbled in her hands.

The photo illustrated an article, surrounded by anachronistic advertisements for restaurants specializing in thick steaks, cigarette brands she'd never heard of, and Orlon sweaters worn by perky models in hair styles that were ludicrously out-of-date. The headline read, COP STILL SERVES with a one-column split about Sergeant Frank McMann's "night spot" doing better than ever in its tenth year of operation.

The page was from the *Philadelphia Press* and the story was written by N. S. Ladderback.

Andy ran upstairs to call Ladderback and tell him she had found something, but the line had gone dead.

She went back down, put the article back in its frame, and returned the frame to its spot on the wall. She sat down again on the shag carpet and thought that if she was going to cry, now would be another good time. She waited and couldn't stand how terribly quiet the house was. She dialed her mother's wireless phone and got the gallery's voice-mail.

She hung up without leaving a message. She sensed the house wasn't so quiet anymore. She got up, moved into the hall, and stopped when she heard, through the open window in her father's office, a pair of cars pull into the driveway, the thunk of doors opening, and a voice announce that "We'll have the place surrounded in thirty seconds."

Andy could identify the self-absorbed hum of her mother's Mercedes, the throaty shudder of her father's Buick, and the malignant buzz of Logo's Porsche.

The two cars she heard coming up her driveway were not among them.

She rushed downstairs and ducked behind the living room couch.

She heard the engines go off. A minute later, a car door opened and shut, making a faint groan. She heard the back doorknob twist, the door open.

Instead of moving, getting up, going to the hallway where there was a panic button that would trip the alarm whether it had been deactivated or not, she stayed down in the salon, on her knees, her heart beating madly, her blood racing, her brain thinking was this another of her father's repairmen or was somebody going to break into the house?

She'd seen a TV cop show once explaining that most burglars aren't just *anybody*. Some of them live in the neighborhood, or they know the owner, or they were inside the house on a plumbing or meter-reading job so *they knew what they were after*.

She heard the door shut. A heavy step on the kitchen floor. The kitchen was set up so that if you walked a straight line, you went directly into the dining room. If the intruder knew the layout of the house, he would turn to the right and through the doors into the hall, and bypass the dining room, avoiding the motion detectors her mother had put there.

The dining room lights came on in a sudden blaze. She heard a clink of crockery. Whoever was in the dining room must have bumped into the sideboard.

The dining room opened directly into the living room through two broad, heavy, swinging, wood-paneled doors that were weighted and counterbalanced so that a gentle touch would send them moving. If the touch was more than gentle, the doors would rush over the threshold but would slow as the counterweights took over. Andy's mother liked to leave the doors open in the living room, restrained by a pair of decorative sashes, so as to better display the long dining room table.

Andy stationed herself beside a door and silently slipped off the sash. She'd seen movies about a lone woman or cute kid in a house having to fend off an invader by turning common household items into instruments of torture and violence. She learned, in her Film Criticism course (which she took because it was fun to go to a class that required you to watch movies) that the transformation of familiar household icons into instruments of pain and destruction relieved the audience's anxiety about the dehumanizing power of materialistic goods.

As she heard the whispering slip of a shoe on the dining room rug, and an answering creak of a floorboard beneath it, she imagined herself in a movie, eager to trash sideboard, china plates, chairs, tables, and awful art of her mother's life; tear it all down, mess it up, break it, step on it, and hurl it at this unknown enemy. Her escape route was suddenly clear: She had to find that all-important catharsis.

She gripped the door handle.

She saw a shadow grow in the light spilling from the dining room, heard a foot clunk into the large legs of one of the dining room chairs, caught the intake of breath, counted *one two, three*, and shoved the dining room door with all her strength.

The door was followed by the thud of a body wrapped in oversized thrift-shop clothing hitting the dining room rug. The door stopped, caught on the body. Andy saw one of the feet. She recognized the black, chunky leather shoe. She stepped behind the door and saw the dirty black trousers, rumpled thrift-shop corduroy jacket, magenta T-shirt, mildewed mountain boots, unshaven face, tangled hair, open mouth, and tiny, blinking eyes of Logan Marius Brickle.

"You're not supposed to be here," he said, rubbing his nose. He pulled himself up on his elbows.

"Neither are you," she said. "This is my house."

Logo touched his nose again. "I'm not hurt, by the way."

"Too bad."

"Listen, there's a guy with me named Fenestra. My mother hired him to do security for the bank. He's got some people with him. We're looking for some things your father had, old papers, records, stuff that's got to do with the bank—and he'd never been to your house so . . ."

She remembered the man she had seen from her father's car, coming out of the Center City bar "mixing it up with bank people."

"You helped him break in."

He couldn't quite look at her.

"And he thinks *you're* going to find this now?"

"Hey," Logo said, "I might be incompetent and a more-or-less total fuck-up, but that bank is going to be mine one day, whether my mother wants to give it to me or not, and your father is supposed to have some documents in his possession that I was supposed to get when I inherited, but now that he's gone, I sort of want them now."

"Mr. Brickle, permit me to handle this." The voice came from a bulky geezer in a tan suit, pink tie, and azure shirt that broke over his paunch. His perfectly white teeth gleamed but he had apparently eaten something rotten because his breath made Andy almost gag. Flanking him on both sides were two taller, wider, younger versions of himself, in darker gray suits.

"James Fenestra." He examined Andy intensely but didn't offer his hand. "I've met your father. We've shared a meal or two. I don't expect he would have mentioned me to you."

"Mr. Fenestra, here, is a kind of corporate samurai," Logo said proudly. "Used to be in the FBI."

"Mr. Brickle is correct, I did work for the Bureau," Fenestra said firmly. "My associates and I have been retained by Mrs. Belisaria Brickle to reacquire materials belonging to the bank that were in your father's possession. Pardon my bluntness, Ms. Cosicki, but the law requires that a person's possessions be sealed immediately after death. A safe deposit box, for example, cannot be opened upon a person's expiration until after several formalities are taken care of. If the items we are seeking were in a safe deposit box, we would not be here. As far as we can ascertain, your father did not maintain a safe deposit box in a banking institution—"

"He always said he never wanted to have anything that was worth stealing," Andy said. "There's no safe here, if that's what you're looking for."

"Because your father's death was unexpected and unanticipated," Fenestra continued, "we are under time constraints. You can save us some time if you can tell me where he might have put these things. If you save us time, I can be very grateful. If you resist us in any way, if you interfere or frustrate us, you will regret it, extremely."

Andy heard a crashing sound in the dining room. "My father *does not* steal!"

"I am in complete agreement," Fenestra said. "Ben Cosicki was incapable of providing a full range of services in a negotiating capacity."

"Mr. Fenestra can make accidents happen to people," Logo said proudly.

Fenestra scrutinized her again. "Have you been grieving, Ms. Cosicki?"

Andy felt herself weaken.

Fenestra became solemn. "It's been my experience that bad news travels quickest. In my estimation," he continued, his eyes scanning the room, "your father was an honorable, forthright, thoroughly respectable gentleman, of which there are few and far between. He was a credit to his profession. My associates and myself wish to extend our sympathies."

Andy glared at Logo. How could he bring these people here? She said, "Okay. Thanks for your sympathies. Now leave me alone."

"We intend to do that," Mr. Fenestra said, "after we have searched the premises."

"I TOLD YOU MY FATHER DIDN'T STEAL ANYTHING!"

Fenestra let out a slow breath. "There is no question of your father's integrity, Ms. Cosicki. He had access to these items. We want them."

He turned to Logo, "Console the lady," and then stepped past her.

Logo put himself between Fenestra and Andy. "Fenestra does a lot of the same stuff your dad did, not so much lunches. Remember when your father would get me off for the drug busts? Fenestra does that kind of stuff too, but on a grander scale. Much more expensive. Nasty, if it has to be. He's supposedly had people killed. He has a line into every police department. He can get I.D.'s changed, wipe out criminal records—not that I have any to wipe out. When he found out what happened to your dad, well, he wanted me here to help him search because he figured you'd need someone to talk to."

Andy felt the room beginning to spin. "Logo, I really can't deal with this. If these guys are working for you, then you can tell them to get out and come back . . . later."

"Excuse the interruption, Ms. Cosicki," Fenestra said, "but could you show me where your father kept his records?"

"He is dyslexic. He almost never reads or writes anything down," Andy said. She watched Fenestra's goons move about the living room, prying paintings away from walls, turning back the edges of rugs.

"There are two business telephone lines coming into this house registered in your father's name," Fenestra said, eyeing the stairs. "They must go into an office somewhere. Did he listen to music in his office? Did he have tape recordings of music?"

"Please, GET OUT!" Andy yelled.

"I don't want to cause a problem, Mr. Brickle," Fenestra looked at Logo. "But if you don't console the lady, you could have yourself one."

Andy pulled a big, pretentious, wooden pepper mill off the dining room wall. "Like what kind?" Andy asked, hefting the pepper mill.

"Andy can be feisty," Logo said.

Fenestra said, "Mr. Piper," and a bulky man whose cheeks were pocked with adolescent acne rushed in and clamped a hand on her right wrist so that she felt a shocking, stabbing pain shooting up her arm. Then he took the pepper mill away.

"Never liked pepper," Piper grinned. "Makes me sneeze."

Andy tried to smack Piper but he held her wrist and cranked it up so that the pain shot again into her forearm. Then he gently released her.

"We'll be happy to leave you all in perfect comfort when we've found what we're looking for," Fenestra continued. "This will all be over in a few minutes."

"You hope," Logo said.

Andy moved back to get into kicking range and was about to let Fenestra have it in the shins when Fenestra said kindly, "Mr. Piper is right behind you, Ms. Cosicki. And he still has the pepper mill."

He turned his back on her and began to explore the living room. He touched the walls and followed the cords of lamps until he appeared satisfied. He straightened his jacket and approached the staircase.

Logo said, "Andy, just let him do whatever his thing is. If your mother were here, she'd ignore him."

If her mother were here, she'd get them out, Andy told herself. Or she'd try to sell him a painting. "He has no right to be here!" Andy said. "Get him out or I'll get him out."

"Let's chat," Logo said, leading her to a couch whose cushions Fenestra's associates had just finished poking, prodding, and squeezing. "I bet you didn't know your father thought of me as the son he never had."

"I don't care," she said, even if she did, just a little bit.

He drew close enough for her to smell scotch on his breath, which, she reflected, was probably close enough for him to smell the vodka on her breath.

"He was aware that the bank hasn't been in the best shape lately. There were talks of selling out—I mean, merging—with another bank, Confidential Financial—they're a vicious, predatory, black-hat merchant bank that's based in Cleveland, don't ask me why. They want to buy our name and our history, and I think that might be cool, you know? More money for everybody, and a management position for me, if it goes through. Before we announce, Confidential Financial is doing a routine check on operations and, given the way things were, with my father, well, we, that is, Mr. Fenestra and I, think it would be much better if they didn't find what we don't want them to find. Not that Confidential Financial is squeaky clean—they got into a lot of trouble with their last merger—they basically paid themselves a few billion that they sucked out of what was a healthy institution and put it in the financial equivalent of intensive care. So they want to suck up some integrity by buying the Hampton."

She closed her eyes. "Logo, I can't listen to this now."

Logo put his arm around her and she found herself liking his arm around her. She didn't want to be comforted but if he was going to do it, she wouldn't stop him.

"Your father thought the merger wasn't going to go over well with the unions that represent some of our clerical and engineering employees because Confidential Financial fired all the union employees of the last bank they absorbed, claiming that they did not have to abide by the old bank's labor policies. Your father felt that Philadelphia, being such a strong union town, would react negatively to the deal, especially considering that a quarter of Hampton's shares are in Philadelphia union pension funds. He also felt that there was something in the bank's background, something that may go way back, that shouldn't come out. He suggested that, given the way my mother is about the bank, I shouldn't be afraid to walk away from it all. Can you imagine that? Me walking away from the bank? He was going to set something up today."

Andy grabbed him. "What was he going to set up?"

"A lunch meeting. Me and some people and—"

"At Jimmy D's, right?" Andy said. "It was supposed to be for me!"

"I hate to break it to you, but it was supposed to be for a lot of people. Well, I don't know if it was actually a lot of people, but I was going to be there, and some people from your folks' old neighborhood."

"Did he say why?"

Logo pulled out a pack of cigarette rolling papers and a silver cigarette case filled with marijuana. "All I know is he died and it didn't happen."

"Oh God, Logo," Andy put her head in her hands. "Just stop it, okay?"

"I can't stop," Logo said. "I want to take charge and I want to deal with all of my nervous tension, okay? I have my own ways of dealing with loss, especially when I might have had something to do with it."

Andy grabbed him again. "What could you possibly have to do with it?"

"Whatever this bad thing about the bank is, well, if he knew about it, there might be people who didn't want him to know and—"

She was about to smack him when she felt her arm gripped from behind. Piper said, "Easy, Miss. Leave the fighting to us."

Logo rolled rolled a joint, licked the paper, and asked Piper for a match.

"You know we're not supposed to smoke that shit," Piper said. Piper looked up the stairs and tossed him a lighter.

Logo snatched the lighter out of the air, torched the end of the joint, puffed on it, and passed it to Andy, who told him to take that thing away from her.

He shrugged and handed it to Piper, who grabbed it and almost smoked it up in a single drag.

"I admit," Logo continued, taking what was left of the joint from Piper, "there was a lot of the lizard in your dad, like he was, you know, just sitting there on a rock, not moving, not doing anything, but his eyes were always on you, all the time. I would think, sometimes, what would happen if things were switched, like I had grown up with your folks and you had grown up with mine."

"Shut up, Logo," Andy said.

Logo passed the joint to Piper. "Hey, everybody gets nightmares once in a while."

Piper was smoking so Andy punched Logo as hard as she could on his shoulder and he fell off the couch, coughing smoke.

Andy stood back and away from Piper. "Logo, you're going to get these people out of my house now, or I'm going to call the cops, you hear me?"

Logo giggled. "Andy, that would be too stupid. The cops would come here, smell these pony feathers I'm cooking, and arrest you, too."

Andy asked herself, as she had asked herself for so many, many years, what it was she saw in Logo that made her tolerate him, for even one second.

"Try to *endure* it, dahling," Logo murmured, as if he read her mind. "Pretend I'm fun to be around."

Then she heard Fenestra call down, "I've found his office." Andy raced up the stairs and saw Fenestra, who had put on a pair of surgical gloves, opening and shutting her father's desk drawers.

"Stop it, *now.*"

Fenestra stopped. He gazed at the wall of cassette tapes, boxed, dated, and meticulously arranged. "I like jazz myself, but my tastes run to the hillbilly variety."

He called down to Piper and told him to bring up a box.

Andy approached him. "I've already called the police."

"It's a sin to lie, Ms. Cosicki," Fenestra said.

"Then just leave, right now."

"I'm about to. Go downstairs and tell your boyfriend to stop playing with fire."

"He is not my boyfriend!"

He turned to her and she backed away before he could touch her. She tripped against the door and fell down so hard on the hall floor that she saw stars.

He looked down at her as if she were an insect and he wasn't sure if he should step on her or ignore her.

Then he returned to the office.

Andy ran down the stairs, passed Logo, grabbed her purse, and went out the kitchen door. She didn't think as her hand pulled out her keys, locked the back door, and activated the security system.

Then she ducked past Piper, who had a large file box in his arms. She saw that the two gray Lincolns were parked in such a way that she could still squeeze her Escort out. She slipped past Piper again and activated the burglar alarm.

Piper moved toward her.

At this point Andy experienced what she had learned in her Ethics of Ecstasy seminar to call a "ludic moment." That is, she reacted to a set of familiar stimuli that caused a significant new alignment of synapses within her brain that created the illusion that she was entering a level of heightened sensitivity that was nevertheless determined by cultural antecedents. So, instead of responding to Piper with fear, she viewed the business-suited oaf—with his sun-blotched skin, disturbingly blow-dried chestnut hair that leaked a milky goo down his forehead, and the sweat-soaked ecru shirt pulled so tight over his chest that she could see the rough outline of the metal cross he wore over his chest—as an awkward, bumbling cartoon villain, a stuttering, effeminized Elmer Fudd without a rifle, and herself as a cartoon version of the trickster hero, a lanky, street-wise Bugs Bunny who responded effortlessly to the threats of danger or civilized compromise with violent, potentially antisocial acts that, because of their narrative context, were perceived as stylish demonstrations of social aplomb.

It was important to remember, her professor had emphasized, that ludic moments were not epiphanies or Jamesian religious experiences. They were, in fact, psychological releases of stress that created new contexts for discordant cultural appropriations. Thus, middle-class Americans, familiar with suburban cultural antecedents, feel a slight uplift when passing from the passively threatening structure of the parking lot to the presumptuously safe, simultaneously comforting but architecturally enervating entrance of a shopping mall or theme park.

Having entered a cartoon world, she sought a cartoon remedy for distress: She picked up one of the bricks from the ruined, weed-and-vine choked barbecue and, instead of throwing it at Piper, hurled it high, in the manner of a center-court foul-shot, so that the brick tumbled overhead and landed with a loud, violating smack on the hood of the Lincoln.

She expected Piper to charge toward her and so she threw another brick overhand, straight at him. He ducked away from it, moving dangerously close to the rosebushes, and, just as the third brick she threw slammed into the Lincoln's windshield, she threw a fourth. Instead of charging her, Piper jumped up with his arms raised and tried to block the brick from hitting the car. He failed, of course, but Andy adjusted the arc of the fifth brick so that Piper jumped to the right, reaching just slightly off center to come down like a stuffed bag of soiled laundry onto the rosebushes.

He screamed in pain something about HATING THESE GUD-DAMMED SONS-A-BITCHIN RAT BASTADS as she dived for her car and got it going and backed it out before the other goon arrived.

The ludic moment faded as she wondered why she didn't hear the burglar alarm. Once activated, it could only be shut off by Andy's family or the police. She remembered that her mother had wanted it, not merely to protect the house, but to inform the neighborhood, if it should ever go off, that there were things in the Cosicki residence worth stealing. What she couldn't recall was if this was a silent alarm that would, at first, lull intruders with a feeling of confidence, followed by a loud, obnoxious claxon that screamed out in pain and violation.

She was turning out of the driveway onto the street and hoping the system hadn't sprung a wire when she heard a siren go off that was so obnoxiously, repulsively, painfully loud that she had to disagree with her mother's favorite expression.

Every once in a while, it seems, you *do* get what you pay for.

4 an acceptable use of clichés

Andy threw her shoulder bag down next to Mr. Action's swivel chair. "You hung up on me!"

Ladderback stopped writing. His eyes moved first behind his glasses, and then he turned his entire round, rumpled self toward her.

"I'm sorry," he said.

Andy looked him right in the eye. "No you're not."

He looked away.

"I was going to tell you that there are no pictures and there won't be anything about my father in the paper. Nothing. Not one word."

Ladderback folded his hands in his lap. "It would have been easier for you if you called me back."

Andy paused. He was right. She could have called him. So she made a mistake. So what? "I don't do the easiest thing all the time," she told him. "Besides, I didn't want you blowing me off."

Ladderback's face grew dark. "I don't blow people off."

"You don't hit that button on your phone and say you have a call on the other line and put whoever's calling on hold and wait for them to hang up?"

"As you were doing this morning?" Ladderback said. "I listen to people. Even when it's difficult. Especially when it's difficult."

She sat down in Mr. Action's swivel chair and faced him. "So listen to me now. So I'm telling you, right now: I don't want anything about my father going into the paper."

He turned his attention to the terminal and sat quietly for awhile. She folded her arms and stared at him and when she got tired of listening to him breathe, she said, "I don't hear an answer."

He glanced at his notes. "You should be with loved ones."

"My mother's in New York. She goes to New York twice a week to the gallery that she works out of."

"Have you spoken with her?"

"She's not answering her cell phone, which is typical when she's with a client or at a meal. She makes a big deal of turning it off, so whoever she's with knows how important she thinks they are. I left a message at the gallery."

He seemed uncomfortable. "Is there anyone you can go to?"

"Why should I go to anyone?"

Ladderback stopped typing. "It's important for you to be with someone who can provide emotional support. The loss of a parent is devastating."

Andy felt herself tremble slightly. "I'll worry about being devastated after you kill the obituary about my father."

"That," Ladderback said crisply, "is not your decision."

"So whose is it?" Andy demanded. "Lange's?"

"The subject meets the criteria," Ladderback began. "Your father is—was—a significant individual in the city."

"You go down to City Hall and ask twenty people if they ever heard of him and they'll say no," Andy said. "I know, I had to do that, once, for a high school project—we had to ask twenty people who worked in the same place or business as one of our parents what they thought about our parent. My mother begged me to do her, but I did him. I mean, there was no question who I was going to do. And would you know it, I went down to City Hall. I went up to the big hallways they have that go around the whole building, and, the first doors I came to, if they were open, I went right in. If they were closed, I knocked until somebody opened them. You know what happened? I almost got thrown out of there until somebody said, 'Oh, you mean Benny Lunch.' And they *still* couldn't tell me. It would be, like, 'Oh, he's just somebody you see around.' Or, 'When he says something, you can believe it.' My favorite was, 'He always picks up the check. Never says a thing about it.' "

"Did you identify yourself as his daughter?"

"I did, for a while. But so many people hadn't heard of him, and those that did, they looked at me, being six foot one, and they said, 'No way a shrimpy guy like Benny Lunch could have you for a daughter.' So I said, 'I get my height from my mom,' and then they started asking questions about her and, I mean, I wasn't there to talk about my mom. It got to the point, I'd just bang on the door and say, 'Anybody know anything about Benny Lunch?' Then one of the aides in the Mayor's office comes up to me and says, 'Benny likes it, if you have questions about him, you ask him direct.' And he gives me one of my father's business cards."

Ladderback waited, and then said, "What did this indicate to you?"

"That I should've done my high school project on my mother."

"Your mother . . ." Ladderback examined his notes, "is the vice president of the Kaplan Gallery."

"She's *a* vice president. One of six. What she really is, is a saleswoman. She's goes to openings and museum shows with her customers. She's out almost all the time."

Ladderback turned his monitor toward her. Andy saw the screen divided into several sections. "Here are the names of those whose obituaries have appeared in the last seven days. The newspaper must not appear to be favoring, or denying coverage of, any specific ethnic, racial, economic, religious, or regional group. Your father is a white, middle-class male of no known religious affiliation."

"You have a shortage of dead white males?"

Ladderback's expression hardened. "The newspaper must not appear biased in its coverage. In a given day, an average of one hundred and fifty people die within our circulation area. Of that number, twenty may meet the criteria for an obituary. Of that number, five will be researched, three will be written. They may not appear if larger stories or paid death announcements take up space."

"What are you telling me? I should be happy my father beat the competition?" Andy said. "Let's talk about the real reason you're writing him up. You're afraid the competition will do something on him and, if you don't, everybody will wonder why."

Ladderback turned his monitor away from her. "I am not concerned with what the *Standard* prints."

"If there's an obituary about my father in the *Standard* tomorrow, and there's nothing in the *Press*, Lange will use that as one more reason to make you retire."

Ladderback's lip curled slightly. "My job does not depend on what the *Standard* does. My job depends on what I've done for others."

"Do you really believe that?" Andy said.

He retrieved a file from the huge wall of cabinets, glanced at the contents, returned to his seat, and picked up the phone. "Listen," he said.

Andy picked up her phone, punched the conference line, and heard him dial. "*Standard*, computer maintenance, Benedetto."

"This is N. S. Ladderback, Mr. Benedetto. I wonder if I may ask something of the dairyman."

"Mr. Ladderback! I don't think I called to thank you, but, that was a great write-up you did about Aunt Anna. The way you put it, about our family name being the good word, and how she always had a good word, that was a really decent thing."

"I studied Latin a long time ago," Ladderback said.

"You know the *Standard* didn't run anything about her? I mean, what could it have cost them? So what if she lived in South Philly all her life and never bothered no one? They had to run these ads and there was no space. Even I after I told them you called me for background, they wouldn't write her up. Maybe an old lady who raised her family right wasn't famous enough, I don't know. I tell you, there's a reason we read the *Press* in computer maintenance, and it isn't just because the Sports page is so good."

"I'm glad to hear that," Ladderback said.

"So how you want me to show my appreciation?"

"I was wondering if you could do a database search for me, including the active files."

"Keyword, date, what is it?"

"Keyword. Cosicki." He spelled it.

Andy heard typing on the phone. "Wasn't he the one that got the newspaper-delivery truck drivers to go back to work when they struck?"

Ladderback glanced at Andy. She shrugged.

"Cosicki is hated around here by management. He was supposed to prevent the strike altogether and then the drivers struck the *Press*, too."

"I believe that occurred when the editor tried to fire a driver who had backed a truck into his car," Ladderback said. "The editor's car was illegally parked."

"So Cosicki got the drivers of both papers a better deal. They hire back that driver?"

Ladderback opened one the files in his cabinet, checked a clipping. "He was forced to take early retirement," Ladderback said.

"And that editor?"

"Nothing from management—though, the day after the driver

retired, his car was booted by the Parking Authority." Ladderback studied a note he had appended to the file. "He had to pay $896 in fines and penalties."

"And he paid it, and meanwhile the driver who hit him with his truck is screwed. See what kind of business this is? The paper dumps on the government and the other businesses all the time for not being on the up-and-up, but, when it comes to their own people, they're just as petty and disgusting, only they don't like to talk about it and God help anybody who does. I thank God we have a union here or they'd be putting this paper together in Mexico."

He paused. "Now let's see what we have with Cosicki in it. There's a lot about a Charlotte Cosicki in the Art and the Society columns. Her and this Brickle woman just donated a pile of paintings to the art museum."

On a pad, Andy wrote, *My mother. Donated works appraised by museum so Brickle can sell similar stuff through Kaplan at highest $$.*

She showed it to Ladderback who asked if there was anything in the search about a Benjamin Cosicki.

"Something in April about negotiations involving the Sanitation Workers' contract, but that's it."

"Nothing current?"

"Zip, zero, zilch. I figure, if you're calling me about him, something must have happened to him, right?"

"He died today," Ladderback said.

"No need to worry about the *Standard* beating you to anything, Mr. Ladderback. Ever since they didn't run anything about my Aunt Anna, the obit guy's computer's been screwing up. Nobody can figure out what the problem is, but we're working on it, you know?"

Ladderback thanked him and hung up.

"So, you know somebody at the *Standard*. I'm supposed to be impressed?" Andy said.

"You were supposed to listen," Ladderback said. "We know the contents of a search of the *Standard*'s active editorial files. Obituaries can run several days after the death. It's possible that an assignment has been made that hasn't appeared yet in text on the *Standard*'s word processing system."

He pressed some keys. "You can help." He pointed to his monitor. "This is the formula. Three to five paragraphs, ending with the time, date, and address of the funeral, and an address for memorial donations, if any.

"The first paragraph is the lead paragraph, a modified version of the who-what-when-where-why opener: '*Benjamin Cosicki, a City Hall expediter, political consultant, and negotiator specializing in labor issues, was found by police on Friday inside an abandoned Redmonton nightclub. He had died from injuries due to a fall.*' "

She held her breath. She didn't know if she could endure this.

"The paragraph that follows is an amplification," Ladderback continued. "We note here that your father was forty-two years of age, and that police determined his death was accidental. The third paragraph begins with the subject's birth. I have no information about your father's birth. He is believed to have been an orphan."

Her eyes opened. "Who told you?"

"I was informed by a source that your father was at the Saint John Cantius Boys and Girls Home." Ladderback opened a slender folder and showed her a yellowed newspaper clipping. "This is from my files, actually. It mentions a reunion of members of the Saint John's home."

She fingered the scrap and saw a picture of conservatively dressed men and women her parent's age gathered around an older man, a tailor, who worked there. "You kept this?"

"These," he nodded at the wall of dark green filing cabinets behind him, "are mine." He turned to the screen. "Did your father ever tell you who his parents might have been?"

She shook her head. "He never said he had another name. He said his parents died when they got here."

"He was born elsewhere?"

"He said he was Ukrainian."

Ladderback wrote *Born in the Ukraine, Cosicki came to the United States as a child and was a resident of the former Saint John Cantius Home for Boys and Girls.*

"Did he say what city or region in the Ukraine he may have come from?"

"He said he was too young to remember."

Ladderback opened a third file. "Did he ever say anything in Ukrainian?"

"I'd ask him sometimes, but he'd say he forgot it all, almost like he didn't want to remember it."

"Did you meet any of his friends?"

"Nobody," Andy said. "He had people he called associates that he'd show up with, but he never called them friends. He always worked alone. He was proud of that."

Ladderback moved the cursor down to another paragraph and wrote *In the intensely social field of political consultation, Cosicki proudly worked alone.* "This is the character paragraph. Here we say things about the decedent that evoke personality. Is there anything we can add to this? Traits, hobbies, eccentricities?"

"He listened to music. Women singing, usually. He had tapes from when he worked in that nightclub and he'd listen to them."

Ladderback wrote *an aficionado of jazz ballads and blues singers.*

"And he hated the media."

"That is not eccentric."

"But he also admired it, I think. He was dyslexic, so it was really hard for him to read and write, but he read every word I wrote. He got me in here."

Ladderback wrote *Ever sensitive to the nuances of public opinion,*

Cosicki, who suffered from dyslexia, admired the power of the written word.

"He would say all the time that you just have to say the right things with people, which, for him, wasn't like being tactful as much as it was . . . like finding the key to someone and opening them up so they," she felt tears welling up, "so they let you into their world."

Ladderback changed the sentence to read *Cosicki, who suffered from dyslexia, enjoyed conversing with many people, from all walks of life.*

" 'Walks of life' is a cliche," Andy said. "You're not supposed to use cliches."

"Cliches are appropriate in obituaries," Ladderback said. "In an obituary, a cliche brings to an unfamiliar subject connotations of familiarity that do not necessarily breed contempt."

Ladderback scrolled up to the third paragraph. "The Cantius Home was closed shortly after your father arrived there and what records were kept have been lost. Your father was put in a foster home with . . ." he held another clipping, "a Francis R. McMann."

"My grandfather," Andy said, blinking back the tears. "He died before I was born. You wrote his place up."

"I also wrote his obituary," Ladderback said. "Your father was found in that nightclub, in the cellar area. The police believe he fell, most probably through a burned-out section of the second floor. Do you know why he was there?"

She could see the blackened, boarded-up facade of the nightclub in her mind's eye. Before they moved out of the city, when he was still working for the Department of Sanitation, her father took her there when she'd walk with him to the pharmacy on Brown Street, which still had a soda fountain. On hot nights he'd buy her an ice cream cone at the pharmacy's fountain and he'd tell her they were taking the long way back, which meant he would stop by her grandfather's old place and tell her that he had met her mother there, and that "this used to be some place. People used to come from all over to hear the music. And now, look at it."

Andy glanced at the police report and shuddered. Why had he gone back to the old neighborhood? Why had he gone into her grandfather's old nightclub? She had never seen him go in there. It was all burned out and boarded up. What was there to see? She tried to imagine him in there and the tears came. She was aware of Ladderback giving her a handkerchief and the sounds of other people in the newsroom coming over to her, asking if there was something wrong and if there was anything they could get her.

Something wrong? Andy wanted to shout out that her father was dead, but she couldn't say that. She couldn't say anything for a while. By then, anyone who was going to ask her if they could get something had gone back to their desks. She heard Ladderback's fingers tapping on the keyboard. She moved her chair around to read her father's obituary.

"The five paragraphs you see may be cut," Ladderback said. "And I can't run this until I find out if there is to be a funeral and where it will be. I presume I can obtain that information from your mother."

He folded his hands. "If space permits, I might have room for some topical detail. What activities had your father planned today?"

"He was going to have lunch," Andy said slowly. "With me. He said he was setting something up at a place called Jimmy D's."

"Jimmy D's," Ladderback repeated. "The maitre d' there is a reliable source. He might provide additional insights into your father's character." He reread the obituary and turned to Andy. "This is incomplete, but it can give you an idea of what is possible, with the information available. It is likely that your father would not have wanted anything like this published about him, but obituaries, like funerals, are for the living. They are a way of coping with the ending of lives, certainly not the only way, but a reliable one. Look at this. Do you feel this might help some of those who knew him?"

She read it and she wasn't sure who it was about. The man who died seemed be a nice, quiet kind of guy, a "former city sanitation worker who rose through the ranks to become a skilled union negotiator and expediter. He was known affectionately as Benny Lunch because at the noon hour he was typically found dining with powerful and influential figures."

There was a quote from an aide to the mayor, "Ben Cosicki came out of Redmonton with Juliet Masco, but he was different because he never said much, never held a grudge and always picked up the check. He was the kind of guy, he would put things in cookie jars, you know? And whatever he took from the cookie jar, he shared. Everybody owed him."

Cosicki was *survived by his wife, Charlotte, a New York art dealer, and a daughter, Andrea, a journalist.*

"It's wrong," Andy said.

"As long as you sit in that chair, you are a journalist."

"It's not that," Andy said.

Ladderback stiffened. "You've found mistakes?"

"He couldn't have just fallen. He was too careful. After he got hurt working for the Sanitation Department, he was always checking his back. He had a way of walking like he thought the ground would cut out from under him at any moment." She picked up the printout of the police report, read it more closely this time. "There's something else. Here, where it says they found his car on the street."

Ladderback appeared peeved. "He drove, presumably."

"They say they found his car locked. My father never locked his car. He never locked anything. He'd let people steal from him before he'd lock anything. So there was no way he would've locked his car. Whoever he was with must have locked that car."

"The police report says that they were summoned by a nine-one-one call mentioning a loud noise in the building. That someone may have been with him does not change anything."

"It changes everything if somebody killed him!"

Ladderback put his hands back on the keyboard. "Those who are confronted with a sudden loss tend to embrace complicated explanations. Explanations cannot change the facts. They don't bring anyone back. You need to be with someone who can help you come to terms with this. Would you please call your mother, just one more time?"

"What I need to do," Andy said, "is find out who was with him and why and what he was doing that would get him killed." She shoved a stack of Mr. Action letters on the floor and put one hand on the police report and another on Mr. Action's telephone.

She heard Ladderback's phone ring. She was dialing the number of the officer who had written the report when she heard Ladderback answer his phone. She saw, from the corner of her eye, Ladderback point to his phone and mouth the words, *pick up.*

She looked at the number of his extension, tapped it into her telephone, and listened in as Howard Lange said, "So we're just going to let it go."

Ladderback caught Andy's eye and said, "It is possible that the *Standard* might run something on him."

"They're not. As for us, I changed my mind. I don't want Benny Lunch's name in my newspaper, okay? He fucked us over with the newspaper-drivers strike. I put in anything by him in the paper, the publisher's going to ask what I'm doing, mentioning someone who fucked us over. Bad enough I had to give his kid a job. If his kid comes back, you tell her she's fired."

"I need an assistant," Ladderback said.

"All of a sudden? You're not into Cosicki for anything?" Lange said.

Ladderback paused. "We only spoke on the telephone. He was a competent source."

"About me?"

Ladderback said nothing.

"I'm not so sure you need an assistant," Lange said. "I'm not sure she's right for the paper. The only thing I'm sure about is that the Cosicki obit gets killed because he's a scum and I don't want him in my newspaper. You got that?" He cut the connection.

Ladderback slowly hung up the phone. He printed out the obit, then typed KILL across the control bar.

With the phone still in her hand, Andy hung up and watched the words wink out. Andy tried to tell Ladderback that she wanted to cry, but the best she could do was pull her knees tightly into her chest, causing the swivel chair to bend backward and almost tip over. Then she let go of her legs and put her head down on her desk. She wasn't sure how much time had passed when she opened her eyes and Ladderback said, "While you were resting an arson attempt was reported at a church office in the Redmonton neighborhood. It was adjacent to the building in which your father died."

Ladderback didn't ask for an explanation and Andy had none. She had no memory of any church office near her grandfather's club. "There was a bank there, once."

"Yes. One of the earliest branches of the Hampton Bank," Ladderback said. "The branch was opened before the Revolutionary War and was rebuilt several times before it was closed and sold to this church."

"I remember going into it with my father when I was really little. The bank was this big domed thing, like the Pantheon in Rome. And . . ."

"What?"

"Kellum Brickle and my father were friendly. Brickle was always holding me up to mirrors and giving me lollipops."

"Did your father have money in the bank?"

"Everybody used it to cash paychecks. He could have. He met Kellum at my grandfather's place. Kellum liked the music, at least, that's what my mother told me."

Ladderback nodded. "I called the Kaplan Gallery in New York.

They gave me your mother's portable phone number. I called her and she said her train will be coming in soon. She said the problem at your house has been resolved. She wants to know if she should drive here to get you, or if she should meet you back at your house."

"I can drive," Andy said, blinking. "I drove my car here. I'll drive back. You can tell her that."

"You should tell her that yourself."

Andy looked around at the drab, stuffy, nearly lifeless newsroom. There was activity down by the sports desk and a few of the reporters were talking on their phones. She recalled the ugliness of Lange's conversation with Ladderback and she wanted to get the hell out.

She stood and hoisted her shoulder bag.

"You should have someone walk you to your car," Ladderback said, not looking at her.

"No thanks," she said. "I don't think anybody here meets the criteria."

5 lies that people agree with

When she parked in the garage she saw her mother's silver Mercedes in the bay beside her. The third bay would have had her father's yellow Buick.

She had had nights when she shot layups under the floodlight and made a bet with herself: Would his car come back from wherever he was, and would he come out reeking of roasted garlic, cilantro, and stewed tomatoes, with that pep in his step that meant he had been with his girlfriend, or would he drive up and stay in his car for a while, as she was staying in hers, and think about how you can start a day one way, and something will happen, big or small, and you'll slide into another world and end the day feeling so strange and different that you wonder who was that person you thought you were fifteen, sixteen hours before.

She liked to imagine, on those nights when he lingered in his car while she beat out a rhythm on the asphalt and tossed the basketball into the air, that they shared a moment in common, for, whatever kept him brooding might be the same kind of pressures, complications, and screw-ups that made her hunger for those hours when she didn't have to worry how she looked, or who was looking at her, or what was supposed to happen, or why things didn't fall into place; when she could get one of those basketballs, put on shorts and an old T-shirt and one of the twenty-two pairs of cross-training athletic shoes, all in her size, that one of her father's "associates" had left in a big cardboard box at the front door—explaining, after he rung the doorbell that "these here fell off a truck" and that she should let her father know that "what it was, was okay. You got that?"—and just be with the ball, or, more accurately, disappear into the arc and swing and bounce-bounce-bounce rhythm that was the ball doing whatever it had to do to go through the hoop, or refuse to go through the hoop, as the case may be.

Some nights he would get out of the car and stop and watch her quietly, and though what she was doing with the ball was so very private and personal, his interest gave her a lift, the same lift she felt when some of the kids in high school and at Penn who knew her would come up to her and tell her they'd read something she wrote in the student newspaper and they liked it, they understood what she was writing about, they agreed with her that somebody had gotten a raw deal, or that things were going on that weren't quite on the up-and-up, or that it was simply amazing, all that stuff she found out.

She wanted to tell him, on those nights when he watched her, that this hunger she had to find out things was no different from the need she had to shoot layups. It had nothing to do with sports: She hated basketball as a game. Everybody thought she'd be so good at it when they put her on the high school team, and she hated being on the team because the only reason they put her on the team was because she was tall. She didn't get along with anyone else on the team, couldn't stand her coach, hated being in a game when people in the stands were yelling at her to do this or that and what did they know? Playing in the game, she had too many things to worry about, and she got mad at all the nonsense about winning and losing making you better than someone else. How could you be better when it was all a matter of what happened between you and this ball that almost never did exactly what you wanted?

It was the same with journalism: What mattered was what happened between you and whatever it was you were trying to find out. Like the first few shots when she was doing layups, she would start out with expectations: The ball should go there, spin just this way, fall in like so, and definitely not snag the rim and bounce off toward the brick pile on the side of the garage. When she got an assignment, her expectations were based on what she didn't know about the subject. She would think she knew what was going on, but the more people she talked to, the more facts she piled up, the more she would investigate, the more she discovered that this truth she was seeking was not going to be anything she wanted it to be, and that she would have to just let it take her where it would. And then, somewhere in the process, she would get this charge of energy, a sense of wonder at how the truth—as much of it as she could gather—was always bigger, smaller, sillier, stranger, and sometimes so beautiful it stole your heart—than anything she could imagine.

That charge of energy would fade fast when she had to deal with faculty advisors, student editors, or angry sources insisting that they were misquoted or that she screwed up the facts. For them, it was like a game of basketball: The wonderful joy of finding something out was turned into a way of drawing attention, getting a result, making a fuss, winning a prize, or failing to win a prize. She had assumed that she could find in newspapers a place where she could just find things out, and never have to be in the game.

She didn't find it as Mr. Action. What could she find out about the anger, frustration, and hateful contempt that leaked from the readers' complaints? Somebody had screwed up? Somebody didn't do what they were supposed to? Somebody wasn't quite telling the truth? It seemed ordinary, obvious, and open-ended. She had read some of her predecessor's Mr. Action columns and saw that they were all about the same thing: A newspaper reporter with a telephone and the ability to make or break reputations could solve problems that the readers could not. The truth was that the reporter couldn't do a damned thing unless both the parties involved wanted the problem solved, and what most of them really wanted was to see themselves mentioned in the newspaper.

It seemed like her mother's gossip: Talk that filled the air so that other things were not said. Did her father want her to get that specific job at the *Press*? Did he hope it would rid her of her compulsion to find things out?

It hadn't. It had only made her more eager to find things out, not about the readers, but about him.

She sat in the car for a while, trying to will the Buick to appear. Then she went in through the kitchen door and saw an open bottle of single malt scotch standing on the butcher-block island in the center of the kitchen.

A ring of spilled liquid beside the bottle told her that her mother had been drinking. Andy went through the pantry and found her mother in the black garbardine pants, carefully rumpled nightmare-blue button-down shirt, and sport coat so dark it was almost black that she had worn into the city.

That outfit was a dark, rude shock on the white cotton couch in the wood-paneled game room that she used as an office. Andy admired how her mother could appear simultaneously in place, that is, relaxed, at peace, secure in her surroundings, and out of place, antagonistic, arrogant, utterly contemptuous. Charlotte's long and still very trim legs in very expensive, very impressive, very Manhattan art-world versions of the cheap clothes the poor artists used to buy at secondhand clothing stores clashed fiercely with the room's Johnson-era 1960's furnishings that, in truth, had made Charlotte's art world career.

During a wine party Charlotte had had a year ago for some of her buyers, Andy had overheard her mother explain she had chosen the decor for her office because "it was the last happy, purely innocent time in suburban America. The Kennedy liberals and the Eisenhower Republicans turned inward and created these precious little rec rooms, which re-created the pool rooms, social halls, and corner bars in the cities. The race riots, the hippies, the war in Vietnam were comfortably far away, and everything violent, angry, thrilling, and wrong in the world could be viewed at a safe distance, through the television."

It was a sales pitch that covered up the truth that Charlotte owed her art world career to the items in that office. The room had been the creation of the previous owner, who left much of the furnishings where they were because not even the thrift shops wanted them. Charlotte, who had just gotten a part-time job in a Bryn Mawr antique shop, had hated the room and would have hauled everything in it to a dump when she noticed in *Art & Antiques* that prices were soaring for certain kinds of 1960's pole lamps. Through the antique shop, she contacted a sixties collector in Hawaii who was notorious for buying the contents of entire rooms. The collector insisted on flying to Philadelphia to see what she had. Before the collector arrived, Charlotte went on a whirlwind trip through Salvation Army and Goodwill thrift shops, buying all kinds of junk from the period. The collector didn't buy the pole lamp, but bought just about everything else, and then gave Charlotte a list of pieces he yearned to acquire. Charlotte went back to the same thrift shops and loaded up with even better pieces. For three years this collector, and many of his friends, would make semiannual pilgrimages to the room, her house, spending wildly enough to finance both Andy's and Charlotte's college educations, until the collector had to auction his horde to pay fines and legal fees after he was convicted for fraud during the insider trading scandals of the mid 1990s.

By then Charlotte had gone to work full-time for the Kaplan Gallery in New York, which trafficked in the more lucrative originals. For Kaplan Gallery dealers to wallow in 1960s furniture and collectibles was considered declassé, and the room was, again, an anachronism, but this time, the place that was out-of-place had become Charlotte's place, and Charlotte was not beyond making little deals, on the side, when buyers saw something that they just *had* to have.

Now the room was lit from the shifting, bluish glare of the television, an old console-style "entertainment center" that had been gutted carefully to accommodate a high-definition digital screen. Charlotte studied the screen with the placid poker-face she would wear at semi-public functions when someone was giving a speech and Charlotte didn't want the world to know that she thought that this person was an absolute idiot.

Andy noticed that her mother's lower lip was quivering just above the chin that she had had tucked. Her mother's nose had been shortened and sharpened, and was like a defensive ridge between her eyes. Her hair was a short, caustic blond, cut in a slashing wave that emphasized the sweeping length of her neck.

Andy moved into the room and glanced at the game show on the screen. One of the contestants was trying to figure out which famous person had said, "History is lies that people agree with."

"Napoleon," Andy said.

The contestant thought it was Henry Ford. The game show host pointed out that Henry Ford said history was bunk, which is not quite the same thing, and the contestant was no longer in the lead.

"You were home earlier," said her mother as she moved a "smoked glass" tumbler, one of a set distributed by gas stations during the 1960s.

"Logo had people here. They wouldn't leave. I had to go somewhere."

"They didn't find what they were looking for," Charlotte sighed, taking another gulp of scotch. "They didn't know what they were looking for."

"They mentioned money missing from the bank."

"Money is always missing from that bank. They were looking for someone to blame because they can't blame the person who took it."

Charlotte put the glass on an end table where a lava lamp glowed malignantly. "I identified his body."

Andy felt her legs grow weak.

"It wasn't difficult," her mother continued, her eyes on the screen. "I was thanked. They were very appreciative. They looked at me the way I was looked at when I went to a chicken packing factory."

Andy waited. Her mother was going off and when her mother went off, you let her go wherever she had to go even if the last thing Andy wanted to hear was her mother talking about herself.

"I remember visiting one of our artists somewhere in Maryland, the Eastern Shore, I think it was. His girlfriend worked in a chicken packing factory and I didn't think, when he suggested that we all go out and collect her at the end of her shift so we could have dinner at some grotty little roadhouse, that the weekend people hadn't discovered that we'd go inside. What I remember when I went into the slaughterhouse is not the odor, but the expressions on the faces of the workers when they saw me and him. These people had nothing to look at but themselves and dead chickens, for eight hours a day. They were almost feeding on me with their eyes. And, because I was an outsider, they had expectations of how I was to behave. I was supposed to be horrified at what was going on, but I disappointed them because I was fascinated with all the machinery. Here was killing reduced to a process, something our artist had been introduced to by his girlfriend and was attempting to explore in his sculpture, in a highly stylized way, of course. Frankly, I found the real thing far more interesting than our artist's work."

Charlotte took another sip. "The process—the processing—of your father, was really quite interesting. You go into a building and there are people in robes or smocks, and each one does something different and then someone finally takes you into a room where there is something that looks like a human being, but isn't, quite. They were very nice, as correct and comforting as they could be, and when I told them I represented artists they were perplexed, of course, and I found myself talking with them about the necessity of surrounding oneself with art. They may have been listening to me just to humor me, but it did occur to me that here is a disadvantage that can be turned into an advantage."

Andy said. "Mom, you didn't try to sell them anything . . ."

"I don't sell. I provide access." She yawned. "Your father and I were really in the same occupation. He used to say, 'I don't sell nobody nothing. I get 'em together and they sell themselves.' He made it sound easy and, I suppose, sometimes it was easy."

Their eyes met briefly and Andy thought she could see into her mother's soul, at that part that was a little girl and afraid. It was the closest she had ever come to seeing her mother lose control of herself, and for a moment Andy wanted to see it happen, but Charlotte wouldn't let go and scream or cry or get mad.

Instead, she told Andy that "He did it to himself. We couldn't have stopped him. He made enemies. For years, I've wondered when I would hear that he . . . got himself dead. How would I react? What would I do? Who would be here with me?"

Andy closed her eyes. "Mom . . ."

"Sit here," her mother said, patting the couch..

Andy almost fell down beside her. She felt the warmth of her mother's leg. Her mother's hand was cold on top of hers.

"We will move through this, you and I," Charlotte said, her eyes focused on some distant point. "We will be a team. Forget about that job he got you. I have arranged a gathering tomorrow afternoon. This will lead to a series of condolence dinners with art buyers and no one will invite me without inviting you. We will be seen and heard and they will want to buy from me out of sympathy. I will sell a *ton* of objects, and I will pretend and they will pretend that this is not something we are doing for each other, that it is just business as usual, acquisition of great art.

"And while I am selling, you will be at my side and the young men will see you and you will enter society, their society, not quite in the way I wanted you to, but at least you'll be on display and if you play hard to get, they'll stay interested."

Andy shook her head and her mother put her hand on Andy's neck and rubbed it, as she had when Andy was a child and had trouble going to sleep. "That's all you should do: Maintain their interest, and take what opportunities appear. I learned how to do that when I was your age. Younger, actually. We all grew up quickly in Redmonton. We were all in such a hurry to get out and there was never a shortage of men who offered to get us out."

Charlotte let her wistful grin turn into a leer. "The best was Kellum Brickle, a marvelous, ancient old shit. He was in his fifties when he would come to the club, alone, always alone, and make a pretense of listening to the music but he would throw money on the bar, get even more drunk than he was when he arrived, and throw even more money on the bar and point to one of the working girls at the bar and have sex, or try to, in the back of his limousine. Ben, your father, would pay the girls afterward and make sure my father got his cut. Sometimes Kellum would be so drunk he would pass out on the street, and Ben would come out from behind the bar and help the chauffeur put him into the car. Ben would get more money from the tip the chauffeur gave him than whatever he made from tending bar that night."

Suddenly Charlotte turned to her. "Ever do it in a limousine? It's similar to the drive-in movie theater sex, but the seats are so much nicer . . ." She stopped when she saw Andy make a face.

Charlotte apologized and Andy was grateful that her mother had acknowledged her discomfort. But her mother wasn't apologizing for embarrassing Andy. "I forgot that your generation never knew about drive-in movies. They used to be all over Jersey. There were always a few boys in Redmonton who had cars who would take me to them. It was an adventure to get away from my father—he was so strict with me, especially when I began to enjoy the attention I would get from men. I even went once with that musician, Hooksie, they called him, the black man who played the bass in the club's house band. He was very much a gentleman because he was afraid to have sex with me because he knew my father would find out and have him killed for ruining his precious only child. He drove a noisy old MG sports car across the bridge into Camden, where he'd buy his drugs and then bring them back to the club to sell. He made sure to give my father his cut. My father got a cut of everything that happened in and around that club. And he, in turn, gave a cut to the police, the inspectors, the councilman's people. It was all terribly illegal but it was what really held the neighborhood together after the factory closed and people had to go farther and farther away to find work. The payoffs, the street money, my father used to say, was how you showed you cared. Failure to pay, or get paid, meant that you were worthless, unimportant, cut off, not worth caring about."

Andy saw, finally, the point at which her mother's gaze had been focused: The framed picture of the *Press* article about the Straight Up Club.

"Your father understood that. He was so eager to please. Rich, poor, big, small, he believed in his heart that people were more or less the same and that if he put them where they could appreciate their similarities, the world—his world—would be a better place. But he was wrong in the way that immigrants are always wrong about America. They think when we say all men are created equal, we don't mind being treated equally. But we do mind. We want our cuts, our payoffs, our tips, our kickbacks because they mean something to us more than money."

"Do you think," Andy began, "what happened to him was an accident?"

Charlotte sighed. "He had so many enemies. People hated him because he'd promised them things that didn't work out. People hated him because they thought that when things worked out, it was because Ben did something that wasn't fair. In his mind, everything he did was fair, but, in his line of work, not everyone who left the table was happy."

"Logo said that he was going to have him, and me, and some other people for lunch at Jimmy D's, but that he got killed . . ." Andy covered her eyes.

"I certainly wasn't invited," Charlotte said. "I'm sure he invited his girlfriend, Maria or Mara or whatever she's calling herself now."

Andy saw the small, younger face of her father in the article's photograph. "Why aren't you mad about that?"

"About him and Mara? She needed him and he liked feeling needed."

"What about you?"

"I stopped needing him as soon as you were born. There were plenty of people who knew me in Redmonton and would give me a job. I could have waited tables at Bep 'n' Betty's. Betty would have taken me on after Mara went off to Penn, but your father wanted to be the wage earner and have me stay at home and mind the baby, so I let him, until they threw him in the trash truck. So I had to bring in some money."

Andy didn't remember her mother working when they were living in Redmonton. "You got a job back then?"

Charlotte turned off the television set. "You know they threw him in the back of that garbage truck, even if it wasn't him that set up the sting that put Szathmary in jail. They put him in the truck because they couldn't punish the person who actually did it, so they had to blame somebody and your father was the kind of man who could have done it."

"So how did you bring in the money?"

"I made a phone call."

"Just like that? One phone call?"

"It was important for this person to show that she cared."

"Who was it?"

Charlotte stood, wobbled grandly to the center of her lair, turned around, and gave her daughter the kind of look that says, are you ready for this, because here it comes—

"Belisaria. Mrs. Brickle. I told her that you could be Kellum's daughter and that she should show she cared."

Andy was speechless.

"Belisaria kept a list of Kellum's assignations to protect her from those who claimed he was the father. Ben had Mrs. Brickle's phone number. He used it to inform Belisaria of what Kellum did, and didn't do, at the club. One night I got on the list."

Charlotte yawned again. "Don't worry about it. We never bothered to make sure one way or the other. Your father and I were also an item, though I like sex far more in a limousine than behind a bar with my father upstairs balancing the books."

Andy felt herself splitting apart. "Why didn't you find out if . . . whoever I belong to?"

"Because the money was coming in. Why push it and find out you weren't Kellum's? Then we'd have nothing but Mrs. Brickle's good-will, which doesn't go as far as it should. No, your father married me fully aware of the possibility that you were Kellum's child, and that, as long as the possibility remained a possibility, we would have a rela-tionship with an important Main Line family. Ben had proved his worth to Belisaria, long before I climbed on the list, by looking after Kellum. He once rode back in the limousine with Kellum to the Brickle estate when Kellum was ill but didn't want to go to a hospital."

Andy stared at her mother with dread. "But didn't you . . . didn't you feel really shitty asking for money?"

"I never asked Belisaria for anything when you were born. It was only when Ben was injured that I called her and she was happy to show her consideration. The relationship between our families has been fruitful ever since, though now, with this merger coming on, Logan is becoming even more annoying than he should. One reason, I'm sure, that he paid those fools to invade our house was to find other kinds of documentation, blood tests or whatever, that you might use to make a future claim upon the Brickle estate."

"But he could have done that any time. Why now?"

"Because everything the Brickles do, and have done, will be examined by the bank they're merging with, and Logan wants to know what they'll find out, first."

"But if Kellum did all those things . . ."

"He did those things and more, and money buries many things and what money won't bury, trust and affection will."

Andy stood. "I have to get a blood test tomorrow."

"Oh, put it off one more day, if you can. We'll go shopping tomorrow and we'll get you some clothes. Then, if you're not going to do your basketball exercises, you can help me hang some paintings so they'll be more visible from the salon area. . . ."

"Mom, you're not—"

Charlotte Cosicki smiled in triumph. "We must take our opportunites where we find them."

Jimmy D's is one of those places, if you walk into it, that can bring back memories, even if those memories are bittersweet. Especially if those memories are bittersweet.

The last time Ladderback had dined at Jimmy D's, he had brought a woman who had blown into his life like a summer storm that gathers overhead before anybody can notice, dumps tons of water so everybody gets thoroughly, totally, and completely soaked, and then, just when you're saying to yourself that getting soaked on such a hot, sticky day was probably the best thing that's happened to you all week, it goes.

And it was at that dinner at Jimmy D's that she let him know she had already gone. She had accomplished that rather well, Ladderback said to himself as he sipped a martini at the bar, or maybe he had fallen so heavily for her that he couldn't hate her even when she told him, in effect, that she could do better things with her life than spin wheels with an idealistic newspaper reporter who thinks he's contributing to the happiness of the world by shining up the lives of dead people until they gleam.

Ladderback glanced back at the maitre d' and saw he was seating one of the few diners the place was getting that night. Back when Ladderback first got hired at the *Press,* Jimmy D's was mobbed at dinner and lunch. You couldn't just walk in and get a table, though there were people who could, like the mayor, the head of the city's unions, the chief justice in the municipal courts, the Philadelphia Orchestra's conductor, the publishers of the *Press* and *Standard*, retired sports heroes, the head of the Philly mob, and whoever was taking bows—and getting good reviews—in the city's theaters. On some nights, you couldn't even make a reservation, things were that tied up.

The current maitre d' had done hard time in prison, started as a busboy, and worked his way up. That some of the other guys in charge of Jimmy D's dining room had strange accidents or suffered nervous breakdowns (after which they decided they'd rather be dishing out stone crabs in Florida) may have had something to do with it, but stories like that, that can make a restaurant. That, and the room's old tables, where Al Capone, Eugene Ormandy, Frank Rizzo, Mae West, Joseph Coleman, Angelo Bruno, and the Reverend Leon Sullivan had carved their initials with steak knives. It was a thing to do, if you were somebody, or if you wanted to be somebody, to leave your mark at Jimmy D's. At least, it used to be.

The place had its special drinks. The martini that Ladderback was sipping was, in truth, a Jimmy D'tini, sometimes called a Jimmy Deet, gin and vermouth made even more complicated by a shake of black pepper, which swirled around at the bottom of the glass, orbiting the olive like moons around Jupiter. The taste was strange and rude, and it, too, aroused memories that, in this case, Ladderback had always wanted to have. For a moment, he imagined himself in a smartly tailored suit in the 1920s, when Duke Ellington and Billie Holiday were making the greatest music in Harlem, and playwrights, actors, critics, and the effortlessly nasty café crowd gathered at the Algonquin Round Table in New York.

Oh, to be among those swells. As a teenager, working as a volunteer at the Philadelphia Free Library's annual used-book sale, Ladderback had found a copy of Alexander Woolcott's *While Rome Burns* and couldn't stop reading it. He went from there to the sublime sarcasm of Robert Benchley and Dorothy Parker, fully aware that, though they were bitterly cruel, threw their talent away, and died too soon, the Algonquin saints created a drunken, flashy, witty kind of cosmopolitanism that would never come around again.

He began to cut out articles from newspapers and magazines and put them in file cabinets. The articles became a collection for him, a way of reconstructing the world. He couldn't see himself doing what his parents wanted, going to medical school and lording over the secret world of dead people in a morgue.

For the Algonquin writers, the first step to that style was newspaper work, any newspaper work. Ladderback began to leave his parent's Chestnut Hill home early in the morning, with its piles of obscure, morbid medical journals, so he could go down to a drugstore on Germantown Avenue and gaze at the out-of-town newspapers on the racks, certain that somewhere in those words was the path to the Round Table. Alexander Woolcott hadn't finished Hamilton College before he got hired, and he eventually became the drama critic of the *New York Times*! Who needed college when the newspapers were hiring?

Ladderback left home, and took any job he could find that needed people who could write things. Soon he had a stack of things written—

mostly brochures and press releases for nonprofits. It was while passing by on the street outside Jimmy D's that he looked in through the glass window and saw Abe Donitz, the famously bitter editor of the *Philadelphia Press*, lingering at the bar. Ladderback walked in and told Donitz he should give him a job. Donitz, who had already had too many Jimmy Deets, asked Ladderback if he could spell "Schyulkill." Ladderbak could. Donitz asked him what his parents did for a living. Ladderback told him, and right there, Donitz told him to "See me tomorrow."

Now, so many years later, Ladderback sipped his Jimmy Deet and saw Whitey Goohan, the maitre d', talking into a phone. Ladderback put down his Jimmy Deet and motioned Goohan over.

"What you need, Mr. Ladderback?"

"I need to thank your associate for telling me about Ben coming out of St. John Cantius."

"That would be Angie. Angie knows about St. John because I come out of St. John's too. Ben and me both came out around the same time."

"You never knew your parents?"

"Never wanted to. With me, see, I have this thing with my spine called scoliosis. I have a good tailor, makes my suits look so you can't see it, but if I took of my jacket, you could see that one of my shoulders is higher than the other. So, the way I learned it, whoever had me, they took one look at me and decided they didn't want damaged goods. So I got sent to the home."

"And Ben?"

"Ben was also left at the home but he was normal, physically, but, with me, see, I never wanted to know who my real parents were, because I didn't want anybody in my life who would do a thing like they did. Ben was always making stuff up about who his folks were, having fantasies about who his folks were, and how they'd blow into the home one day with all these toys in their arms, pack him up in a limousine, and take him off to a mansion somewhere. Lots of orphan kids had fantasies like that. You can't help it, sometimes."

"Was it hard, growing up there?"

"What it was, it was easy. We had good people working there and, if you liked somebody, if you really liked somebody, you could name yourself after him. I really liked the gym teacher, Danny Goohan, an old Irish boxer with a nose like a big garlic clove. Taught me how to fight and, when nobody was looking, how to use a knife. But I would be lying to you if I said it was a paradise. We'd look outside the windows and see kids with parents and families and you wondered why they were out there and you were in this big old mansion, which used to belong to some rich family—"

"The Wadcaladers," Ladderback said. "They used it as a summer home but donated it to the Archdiocese in the nineteenth century when the city moved out to engulf it."

"Well, it was a pretty nice place, but, when you're sleeping eight kids to a room, doing everything to bells and whistles, it's not *your* place, you know what I mean? We had kids run away. Sometimes they'd come back. Sometimes you'd never see them again, and we would pretend that they found their parents and were staying with them."

"You were there for how many years?"

"At sixteen you had to leave to go into a foster home. The sarge took us both in, but I run off. Didn't stop the sarge from taking the money he got for being a foster parent for Ben and me. The sarge was like that. Anything coming to him, he wanted, even if it wasn't always coming to him. Ben stayed with the sarge, though, don't ask me why."

"Can I ask you why you weren't here when I called about Ben?"

Goohan became sad. "Hey, ain't it a shame about him dying? Brought tears to my eyes to think about it."

"Ben had a reservation here for lunch."

"Yeah, Angie took it. Party of ten, with the possibility of more."

"Any idea who some of the people in the party were?"

"I can guess, okay? Your boss, Lange? He likes to eat sweatbreads when he comes here, likes to show off he can eat something so disgusting to look at, and he called in for them today, in the morning when he came in, but then he never showed so we had to grind them up and put 'em in the soup. He didn't make a reservation or anything so he could've been in the party, or he could've been with the other parties, but that's just a guess. Like I said, Angie took it because, well, you want to know the truth?"

"Yes, Whitey," Ladderback said, "I want to know the truth."

"Ben wanted me to eat with him. He wanted me at the table. He said it was going to be kind of special, that he was having his kid, his kids with him, and would I break my own special rule and eat at my own place, and I told him I would think about it, but then, when I got the call from the cops that he got himself dead, well, it was a relief because I don't like to eat at my own place. Don't want the kitchen to poison me, you know?"

"He didn't say what was special about the luncheon?"

"He never says nothing like that. But, if he could get me to sit down with him, that was special enough."

"In what way?"

"Ben and me, back in Redmonton, we found ourselves sometimes on the opposite end of things."

"You fought?"

"Not that way. But he was with the sarge and I was with Bep Adamo and the councilman. Different kind of turf, you know?"

"What table was he going to use today?"

"It was actually a few tables. He said it was going to be for his daughter, but there were going to be at least six people. So Angie had the table Ben asked for pushed together with the other table he asked for."

"Which were those?"

"That one down there under the picture? That was a table the sarge used when he came here. There's a place him and his daughter put their names in. The other one was the table with your initials in it, Mr. Ladderback."

"Mine aren't the only ones," Ladderback said.

"Angie tells me Ben asked for the Ladderback table."

Ladderback took a sip of Deet. "Any idea why?"

"I told you, he never said nothing about what he did. With him, you had to piece things together. You had to look at the other stuff that was going on around him."

"Like Councilman Szathmary getting out of jail today?"

"Could be," Goohan said. "The councilman was an important man when he went into jail. He got me in here as a busboy. When they put him away, he got even more important, because he could make things happen from the inside in ways he couldn't on the outside. Now that he's out, though, he won't be important no more."

"How's that possible?"

"Well, I went to jail a little, you know? And in jail, you have people, and they act a certain way to each other. These same people, they have relatives, friends, enemies on the outside. What happens to people on the inside can affect people on the outside, and vice versa. When I was inside, as a juvenile offender—somebody said I'd stabbed somebody else, can you believe that?—it was all a mess. Nobody was in charge and things stayed a mess. But when the councilman got inside, some-how he got himself in charge, don't ask me how. I mean, he's not the kind of guy who is tough or mean or scary, like I tried to be when I was a kid, but, somehow, he got things working right and Ben, Ben would visit him, keep in touch, and Ben was a channel to the outside. But now, with Ben dead, all the people the councilman had around him are dead or gone or maybe not wanting to deal with him, so he's not going to be that important to anyone except maybe people in the old neigh-borhood."

"People like the Reverend?"

"I don't think there are people like the Reverend, Mr. Ladderback. He's what we call a one-of-a-kind. He was in the house band at the sarge's, but he sold the drugs and did some pimping on the side, always kicking back to the sarge. See, the way it worked, there was the sarge, and he had a piece of all the nighttime rackets, and you had Bep Adamo, backing up the councilman, and Bep had a piece of all the daytime rackets. After the sarge's place burned, and Bep put the councilman away, Hooksie took over the daytime and the nightime rackets and started buying stuff up. He owns the whole neighborhood, almost."

"What about the building where Ben was found?"

"The old Straight Up? If Hooksie don't own it, he uses it."

"But it wasn't repaired after the fire."

"So? You go by, you see all these abandoned, falling-down buildings in the city, you think it's all waste and ruin, but it isn't. The way it is in a city, stuff gets used, though what it's used for may not be legit. When I was helping Bep run the daytime rackets, and we had some stuff that we couldn't exactly get caught with, we'd park it in the old buildings."

"Drugs?"

"Don't ask me particulars. Let's just say that, if the cops found it on you, or in your bedroom, then they could get you in trouble. So you park it—that's what we called it—parking—in the old buildings that you could keep an eye on, in places where only you would think to look."

Ladderback told himself he wouldn't drink another Deet. He picked it up, took a taste, took another taste, and set it down. "So Ben was using the Straight Up to park something?"

"Him or the Reverend. Maybe both. Maybe Ben goes in there, looking for something that's his, and he finds out something that's the Reverend's. You could get yourself dead for that. No problem."

Goohan was about to leave when Ladderback said, "Lange tried to ruin Ben in print, and then he killed Ben's obituary."

Goohan said, "You read the last *Press* review of Jimmy D's?"

"The food critic gave you one star."

"Which is worse than no star. Said the soup was cold, the steak too tough. So how come Lange's got his own table here, eats here all the time whenever he's with people he wants to impress? Because Lange, see, he never pays for nothing here, but he brings in people who do, but, with what gets printed, he's got to make it seem he's not partial, so he has the food critic trash us so he can say the paper isn't kissing up because the boss gets free food. You ask me, that's why Lange did it to Ben. He owes Ben big time. But sometimes, you trash people too much, and it backfires. He might've been thinking, if I trash him, people will want to know why and they'll think it was personal. So maybe I should just shut up."

"What did Lange owe Ben?"

"Hey, I'm just a guy that shows people to their tables. But you might want to check out the last time Lange paid a parking ticket."

Ladderback put money on the bar. "I guess I still owe you."

"Don't sweat it, Mr. Ladderback," Goohan said. "You're a paying customer. You don't want to know how much I make back on the drinks."

bats

Before Andy could wake up and feel terrible, she heard sounds in the house. Her mother, who swore that she was not and never had been a "morning person," was up and buzzing about, doing things, talking on her portable phone, making lists of things that just had to get done. A small army of cleaners were moving through the house, operating noisy machines. Soon a truck from a catering company would block the driveway.

Long ago, when Andy had been in a cute mood, she had written across the bottom of the mirror in her room, "Face it, things could be worse."

Early that morning, while Andy had been sleeping, her mother had come into her room and stuck a Post-it on her mirror that said, "Gathering at 1 P.M. We have to buy clothes. Be ready at 10."

It was 9:50. In the last twenty-four hours, Andy had acquired a job that she hated, lost the man who called himself her father, and found out that he may not have been her father.

She had a headache. Her mouth was dry. The face she saw in the mirror was not a face she could recognize or wanted to encounter in a dark alley. She wanted to put on a T-shirt, shorts, and shoes and get really sweaty and smelly shooting layups for a few hours.

She picked up her phone and called Ladderback, who answered on the first ring. She asked him, "How do I get a blood test to determine who my parents are?"

He let a second go before he asked, "Why are you asking me?"

"I'm hung over and I figured that you would know."

"I do know," he said.

Andy waited. "So tell me."

"Why is it that you want one?"

"I told you. I want to find out who my parents are."

He let another second go. "Why is it that you are even questioning this?"

"Because I am, okay?"

"Did your father tell you that my parents were medical examiners?"

"I'm just asking you because you act like you know everything."

Ladderback said, "Do you know what medical examiners do?"

"Autopsies."

"Not always, but many times, yes. They also conduct tests. The results of these tests can be used as evidence in legal proceedings."

"So where do I get my blood tested?"

She heard Ladderback pause. "The test you mention will provide a measurement and a degree of similarity between sources, but it will not determine the truth. Even if the blood types are rare enough to determine a match, and this match is confirmed by genetic comparison, it will not change the fact that the man who raised you, and provided for you and loved you was the most important man in your life, and he should be honored for that."

"It sure as hell will, as far as I'm concerned."

"Your father was an orphan. Did he ever talk about that with you?"

"He never talked about anything with me," Andy said, as she heard a rhythmic banging coming from the hallway outside her room.

Ladderback said, "I am certain that he expressed himself in other ways. I received a telephone call from him the day before you arrived for work. He said, 'Make sure you look out for my girl.'"

Her mother rapped on her door and said, "*Andrea*, we must shop."

On the phone, Ladderback asked her, "Would you like an assignment? You don't have to come to work today. But if you have the opportunity, you may cover a luncheon meeting at twelve noon at the Wrightsford Inn concerning an award ceremony for the New Leaf Foundation."

The Wrightsford Inn was a colonial-era tavern that had been expanded into a restaurant and a banquet hall. It was in Rosemont, about three miles from Andy's house, on Montgomery Road down from the Bryn Mawr train station.

Andy said, "The *Press* is a city paper. If I'm from the *Press*, they're going to want to know why the *Press* cares about what happens in the suburbs."

"That we are sending a reporter is reason enough. While you're there, observe as much as you can about the persons attending as well as what the officials are saying—"

"I took journalism courses, okay? I know how to cover a meeting. That is, if I can get away."

"Whatever you can do will be helpful," Ladderback said.

Her mother rapped on the door again.

"To Lange?" Andy snapped and hung up. Then her mother opened the door. Andy turned and saw, behind her mother, the primly dressed, diminutive form of Belisaria "Bats" Brickle, chairperson of the Hampton Trust, and owner and principal stockholder of the Hampton Bank.

"Andrea!" her mother exclaimed. "You are not dressed!"

Mrs. Brickle was called "Bats" by her intimates because she was legally blind—blind as a bat—though her eyes retained enough functionality for her to amass one of the largest and most peculiar collections of art on the Main Line. Standing in the doorway, she peered at Andy as if Andy was a prized racehorse. "Oh, Cos," Bats said, "she is a fine girl. A true beauty, holding firm under the strain. Kellum would have been proud to see her this way. Truly proud."

"You think so, Bats?" Charlotte said, giving Andy a tiny wink.

Andy noticed Mrs. Brickle was leaning on a cane. Andy had never seen her before with a cane. Mrs. Brickle leaned on others, sometimes on Logo, but, since she fired most of her servants, she seemed to spend too much time leaning on Andy's mother, Charlotte. You knew you were in good with Mrs. Brickle when she told you to give a tip to someone. Mrs. Brickle never gave you any money to use for the tip because Mrs. Brickle never carried money. If she said she wanted something, and it cost money, you were expected to pay for it and *never* ask her to give your money back. Like most old-money Main Liners, Mrs. Brickle had a horror of being asked for anything, especially money. You were supposed to put her in a semipublic setting in which she could be suddenly, demonstratively generous: calling out a $1 million donation for the Orchestra, $2 million for the Art Museum, or $3 million for a neoconservative Washington, D.C., think tank that sponsored research that proved that rich people were far more interesting and important than poor people and, therefore, shouldn't pay any taxes.

"You appear strong, child," Mrs. Brickle said. "We must continue to be so, if we are ever to hold onto what is rightfully yours."

Andy couldn't figure out what it was that was rightfully hers. She noticed Mrs. Brickle wobbling slightly on her cane, favoring her right leg over her left. "Are you okay?" Andy asked her. "Did you hurt yourself, or something?"

"Or something," Mrs. Brickle said. The gaze from her milky eyes settled on Andy in a way that made Andy shiver. Then, as if she could sense that she had unnerved Andy, Mrs. Brickle turned and walked into the hallway, banging the tip of the cane on the hardwood floor as if the floor, and the privilege of banging on it, was rightfully hers.

[BBRICKLE-WAIT-OBIT]
By XXXXXXXX

Noted philanthropist Belisaria Logan Brickle, of St. Anne's, Montgomery County, died at XXXX of XXXX. She was XX years old.

Named for Belisarius, a fourth-century A.D. military leader who served the Roman Emperor Justinian, (*do we need all this?*), Mrs. Brickle was the only child of Lucian and Claudia Wadcalader, direct descendants of Augustus Logan Wadcalader (*another Roman? Is this a thing with these people?*), a founder of the city's venerated Hampton Bank. (*Aren't they having problems? How'd the Hampton get started anyway? Didn't somebody write a book about the disgusting origins of modern millionaires?*)

Belisaria Wadcalader attended St. Anne's Academy, an elite private school founded by her uncle, Augustus Wadcalader. She married philanthropist Kellum Brickle (*when?*) (*where's he from?*) at the Brickle cottage in Bermuda. Upon the death of Lucian Wadcalader (*date? Why are there no dates?*) Kellum Brickle became chairman of both the Hampton Trust and the Hampton Foundation. When Kellum suffered a stroke in XXX (*Oh, please, please, PLEASE can I see one date in here?*), Mrs. Brickle (*I heard somewhere she had a nickname, Spats or Cats or something like that*) became chairperson of both institutions (*did she give money to anyone famous?*) and used the Hampton Foundation to back conservative political issues, religious charities, and arts groups (*such as?*)

She is survived by her son, Logan (*what? No Caesar salad?*) Marius Brickle (*Marius is Roman. But is that all it is???*).

Services will be held at XXXX.

[END FILE]

Leaning back in his chair in the newsroom, Ladderback lingered over the obit, wondering how any of the reasonably well known people in the WAIT file (for God's Waiting Room) would react if they saw that their obituaries had not only been written in advance, but had also been cluttered with inserts added by unnamed editors under the guise of updates.

Like many of the people in the *Press*'s newsroom that morning,

Ladderback was wasting time. Each reporter he saw murmuring on the phone, fretting over computer solitaire, clicking through Internet web pages, reading periodicals, press releases, trade publications, and the tent-like pages of the *Morning Standard*, might have a different reason for wasting time—and Ladderback's was certainly a good one—but the result was the same: Things just weren't getting done.

Ladderback's reason did not have to do with the fuzziness he felt from the evening's three (or four?) Jimmy Deets, and the memories—good, bad, and indifferent—that they had aroused, though he hoped that the next time temptation, in the form of unremarkable but over-priced martinis, with or without pepper, crossed his path, he would step lightly away.

No, Ladderback's urge to waste time—he told himself—came from an undefined notion, a feeling, a hunch: He needed to see something, hear something, learn something before he could turn to the list of death notices and determine which decedents he would research and report.

It wasn't as simple or compulsive as drinking coffee or checking in with Lange, who was not in his office. He had a feeling that, whatever he should be doing right now, work wasn't it.

He marveled at how technological innovations had made not work-ing so easy. With a few keystrokes, he could read portions of thou-sands of publications, access the databanks of the *Press* and the *Standard*, drifting lazily over nodes of information, like a bee search-ing for the right blossom to invade.

Among the blossoms he'd reconnoitered had been the *Standard*'s web page, containing the newspaper's painfully scrupulous calendar of suburban events. His eyes lit on the New Leaf Foundation. What was this? He did a web search: There were several New Leaves, but, yes, here was one in Montgomery county, a charitable group that gave new starts to individuals who had suffered reversals of fortune.

He glanced at the list of directors and found his eyes lighting on Lange's name, as well as the *Standard*'s suburban bureau chief, Robb Schweitzer, and Beatrice Adams.

He had heard of another Adams. Or something like Adams. He had to sit still for a few minutes for his brain to deliver the connection, but it delivered and, when he pulled the file, he found her: Betty Adamo, of Bep 'n' Betty's Luncheonette in Redmonton, mistakenly referred to by Lange as The Cookie Jar. In the same file was another *Press* article Ladderback had clipped: SZATHMARY TO FEDS: EAT YOUR WORDS, a speech Szathmary delivered in front of the luncheonette in which he denounced a statement made by the Philadelphia FBI's agent-in-charge that alleged that many mom-and-pop businesses in the city's poorer neighborhoods survived only by laundering money or acting as fronts for the mob. "These slanderers should come to Bep 'n' Betty's," Szathmary had said. "They should meet these good, decent, hardworking people. Then they should either eat the scrapple, or eat their words."

Ladderback looked again at the New Leaf Foundation's board of directors and found himself lingering on another name: James R. Fenestra.

He went to the series of articles Howard Lange had written about the fall of Double-Dip Szathmary. Fenestra was the FBI agent who had posed as a parking-lot developer, come to Bep 'n' Betty's for lunch, eaten scrapple, and taped Szathmary soliciting a bribe.

Ladderback did a web search and saw that Fenestra led a private security company based in Malvern.

He went back to the *Standard*'s web pages. The group was having a meeting today. Andy lived somewhere out in Montgomery county. He would call her and possibly offer her something to do that would take her mind off her grief.

So he did, and was disconcerted at how the girl could toss him off so easily. He looked at Mr. Action's empty chair and thought of Ben Cosicki, a person he had only known as a voice on the telephone.

He did a global search through the *Press* databank, typing in "Redmonton" and then, on a hunch, "Hampton Bank" and "Redmonton." That was when the Brickle obit emerged. He found a tiny business item about the closing of Hampton's Redmonton branch. The item mentioned that the branch was one of the bank's first branches, that it had been used as a second office by Kellum Brickle, and that when it opened, it was actually outside Philadelphia's city limits, in the town located on a small red-clay promontory called Red Mound Town that was eventually incorporated into Philadelphia, though it was one of the last towns to be absorbed.

There was another article about the branch. This one, by Howard Lange, without a byline, was about Reverend Hooks buying the branch to be the new sanctuary for his First Church of God Harmonious. Hooks was quoted as saying that the purchase had been "harmonious" because "there was a time a black man couldn't walk into this building, and now a black man with the power of God has bought this building." Hooks said he had been shocked to find a roomful of books and ledgers in the building that "went back all the way to time immemorial." Hooks said he had tried to get the Hampton Bank to remove the records, but that the Hampton did not want to spend the money. He suspected that he would "probably just get rid of the stuff, if the church needs the room."

There was a final article that mentioned the bank branch. This last one, by Lange, was about Hooks purchasing the old locomotive factory and moving his church into it. "We just got too big," the Reverend was quoted. The Reverend mentioned he was grateful to Mrs. Brickle, head of the Hampton Foundation, "for giving us a grant toward the acquisition, but the bulk of the funds came from the usual sources: contributions, harmonious acts of God, and street money."

The owner of the oldest bank in the country helps a reformed drug dealer buy a factory for his church? Ladderback had a hunch that Mrs. Brickle's donation was anything but harmonious.

"If the Lord shorts a girl on her bust," Mrs. Brickle said, "he makes up for it with her legs and *those,* my dear Cos, are *legs.*"

Andy would have yelled something if she hadn't felt so tired. She closed her eyes because she didn't want to see her mother and Mrs. Brickle regarding her like a horse trader, wondering if the prize stallion might have to be taken out and shot.

Mrs. Brickle peered through her impossibly thick glasses and said, "A girl must be proud of what she's got because she never gets enough. This girl has got blood, Cos. Did you tell her about her blood, Cos?"

From a small, worn carpeted platform surrounded on one side by three mirrors that created a triptych of Andy in a ridiculous sleeveless black cocktail dress with swirling, frilly, Art Nouveau silver strands sewn into it, Andy saw her mother squirm.

"Thank *God* Kellum can't see her in this," Mrs. Brickle added. "He'd jump on her, he would." She glanced at Charlotte. "He saw women in financial terms. He said short woman, such as I, were common stock. Tall women were preferred. Did he tell you that, Cos?"

"Mom," Andy pleaded, "I don't even know how to sit down in this."

Mrs. Brickle knitted her hands. "You shall practice," she said.

"No way," Andy said. The dress stretched so tightly over Andy's legs that the only thing preventing it from riding up was pure disgust for the dress, for the tiny, stupid clothing shop, for the embalmed-but-still-twitching biddies waiting on her, and Bats in her "country" clothes: a camel-hair suit jacket over a blood-red, ankle-length pleated skirt, cordovan penny loafers, yellow-and-green argyle socks, and a pale blue button-down blouse.

She saw her mother narrow her eyes skeptically. "This is for a *funeral.*"

"Child, you're being admired." Mrs. Brickle said. "In my day, what you're wearing would have been sold to us as an undergarment. You're going to raise the dead, or get a rise out of 'em."

Andy began to boil. She remembered how Logo would tell her that he took after his mother because his mother "always gets her way because she's never *not* gotten her way. All her life, she's had more than enough money to live anywhere she wants, to buy anything she wants, and to do anything she wants. The only people she lets get near her are people who want some of her money, so nobody tells her when she's rude, nobody tells her when she goes over the line, nobody tells her when her jokes aren't funny. My father tried to get back at her by blowing the bank's money and screwing around, but, when it came to something she wanted from him, or anyone, she got it."

All through the morning, Andy could see Mrs. Brickle "getting it" from her mother: dropping loud and obvious insults, put-downs, and sharp little digs at Andy and Charlotte and even at her father, "that wonderful man whose wonders we are better off not knowing."

Mrs. Brickle turned her milky eyes on Andy's mother. "We must be sure to invite a gaggle of young bucks, if only to make Logan jealous. We'll seat them according to their inheritance, the closer to your Andrea. One must use endowments, to get endowments."

"That's enough," Andy said. "You will *not* insult me. I don't take that crap from anyone."

The short, spindly saleswoman in a coal-gray turtleneck knit consciously walked away.

"Child," Mrs. Brickle said quickly, "you may speak your mind only if you mind what you speak."

"She knows how to speak properly," her mother added in the same voice she used when Andy was a child.

"In that case, *please*, Mrs. Brickle," Andy said, "shut up."

Charlotte, in a sober, so-gray-it's-black mid-calf dress, with black mesh over her hair, rose like water spouting upward from a fire hydrant that's been knocked over by a truck.

She took a step toward Andy, her face set, her eyes glaring maximum intimidation. She said, "You will apologize to Mrs. Brickle this instant, or I will have you severely disciplined."

"Though I'd adore watching you go at it, Cos, the time for spanking has passed," Mrs. Brickle said. "You have an angry young girl on your hands. Fate has taken Ben too soon. Any girl would be infuriated at God's progress. The child must bleed her pipes so the heat can flow."

Charlotte Cosicki gave Andy a see-what-I-have-to-put-up-with look. Though Charlotte was quite capable of bleeding her own pipes, emotional detonation and improvisation was discouraged at the Stitch in Nine, a Bryn Mawr clothing boutique in what had been an old carriage house whose main house, broad lawns, and tree-lined walkways had been eaten up a century or so ago when Lancaster Avenue was widened from two lanes to four and a strip of shops catering to Bryn Mawr college girls sprouted from the Main Line train station. Stodgy and frumpy (with the exception of a shameless my-daughter-is-a-sexpot-and-you-can't-have-her rack of dresses under a hand-lettered sign that said COCKTAIL HOUR), the Stitch had that precious Main Line atmosphere that so many chain stores and copycat boutiques lacked: Its building was old in a plain, almost-but-not-quite shabby way that implied thrift, value, and a studied refutation of fashion. There were only two parking spaces in front, so that anyone driving by who would happen to see you picking out clothing through the window would look at your car and just *know* if you could afford to shop there, or if you were just pretending. Within a short walk were two "continental" café-type lunch spots where the endorphin rush derived from spending money could be celebrated with the consumption of food (it was considered bad form to carry your purchases out of the Stitch: You picked out what you wanted, got measured for alterations, put it on your charge account, and the goods were delivered that afternoon and you had two days to try them on and have the deliveryman take them back before the bill was mailed).

Even if the clothing at the Stitch was made in the same sweatshops in Mexico and China as the knock-off merchandise that clogged the chain stores, the old carriage house, the cute hand-lettered signs and the price tags that were so tiny that to look for them was considered bad form, the Stitch *said* Main Line. Anything else was, at best, an echo.

Through the window, Andy saw a car swoop by and instinctively felt the leering look of the driver (male, old, fat, almost like that guy who had burst into her house the previous day). She said, "I will not be seen in this," as the dress rolled up her thighs.

"You'll be seen no matter what you're in, child," Mrs. Brickle said merrily. "This will serve."

Charlotte Cosicki turned to the saleswoman. "We'll take the black dress with matching handbag and the pumps with half-height heels."

"Ben would have *hated* her in this," Mrs. Brickle went on.

"Then maybe I shouldn't wear it?" Andy said.

"That is every reason you should. I'm sure that by now your mother has told you of certain ambiguities in your background."

"Certain ambiguities?" Andy said, remembering her stint as an editor of student newspapers. "That's an oxymoron. An ambiguity cannot be certain. There's no such a thing."

Charlotte said, "Maybe we should save this for the car."

"From this moment onward," Mrs. Brickle went on, "your associations with me and my line will replace any previous associations you may have had, or thought you may have had. It will become known that your ties to the Brickle family may be more than merely cordial."

Andy put her hands on her hips, which, she thought, looked entirely too wide in the dress. "I'm going to get a blood test and prove this thing."

Charlotte winced.

"You will *not,* child," Mrs. Brickle said. "I do not need my opinion confirmed."

Then, in a flash, Andy figured it out. "Logo broke into my house looking for a birth certificate, didn't he?"

Mrs. Brickle curled her lip. "You should ask him."

"Not my birth certificate. His."

Mrs. Brickle's face twitched, as if water had been flicked on it. Then she grinned, and glanced at Charlotte. "Tell me, child, why would you dispute Logan's provenance?"

"I'm not disputing it," Andy said. "I'm asking why he got those jerks to break into my house."

"I wouldn't call it a break-in," Charlotte said. "The Brickles have never needed an invitation to visit us."

"They ransacked the house," Andy said. "Logo said there was a merger coming up and that the buyers didn't want anything bad coming out about the bank. It would be bad if there was even a question about who, or where the son of the bank's owner came from."

Mrs. Brickle stood. "Now is not the time to speak of this. Logo is aware that, for the next several months, he is on trial, so to speak. I am giving him a choice. He may either behave correctly and assume the character of a person who will lead the bank, or we shall find others of the right blood to do so."

Now it was Andy's turn to feel as if she'd been flicked—make that doused—with water. "Logan's blood is . . . wrong?"

"Not wrong." Mrs. Brickle sighed. "Weak, reckless, embarrassing, tasteless. Kellum could be that way, but he could also be quite the opposite."

"Like how?"

"Like you, child. Exactly like you."

Charlotte came between them and made a show of inspecting her watch. "We really must meet the caterer soon."

Andy said, "I want something for me." Andy pointed toward an ash-gray summer wool jacket with matching pants hanging from a rack labeled EXECUTIVE WEAR.

"How . . . dull," Charlotte frowned. "That looks like something your father would wear."

"I want it," Andy said.

"Let her have what she wants," Mrs. Brickle said. "For now."

While Charlotte and Mrs. Brickle muttered together, Andy got the suit, put it over the T-shirt she had worn when she came into the store. It fit beautifully. She picked out an off-white silk blouse and saw that, yes, this outfit would be the kind of thing her father would like. She examined the shoe selection and didn't like anything. She tried on the blouse, pants, jacket, and finally, her cross-trainer sneakers and shoulder bag and it all worked. Yes, she decided. This would do.

She strode up to her mother and turned to Mrs. Brickle. "What do you think, Bats?"

Mrs. Brickle beamed. "Oh, she's radiant. Buy it for her, Charl. Make her happy."

Andrea put her shorts and T-shirt on the small desk that substituted as a sales counter. She told the saleswoman she would wear the outfit. The saleswoman used a tweezer and cuticle scissors to remove price tags and said, "Anything else?"

"A notepad and an interesting pen," Andy said.

The saleswoman said, "We don't sell those."

"Farnham's Stationers is right up the road," Mrs. Brickle said. "Kellum had his pens made there."

"They closed ten years ago," the saleswoman said.

"I saw a drugstore up the road," Andy said. "They sell pads and pens."

"Whatever for?" Mrs. Brickle demanded.

"You are not doing something for that newspaper?" Charlotte said.

"I just might," Andy said.

"Procure for yourself some breath mints," Mrs. Brickle said. "The last newspaperman I encountered had appalling halitosis. Needless to say, I do not grant interviews."

"I'll see you back at the house," Andy kissed her mother on the cheek, adding in a tone she guessed was close enough to her father's to chill both women to the bone, "the very next thing!"

7 a second chance

It was nothing to blow off her mother and Mrs. Brickle: The Wrightsford Inn was about a quarter mile down Montgomery Avenue, an easy stroll in cross-training sneakers. The suit fit her loosely and the fabric let in the breeze kicked up by the vans and sport utility vehicles that roared by. On the way she popped into a discount pharmacy where she bought a cheap little pad and a wild, Day-Glo-colored pen and, just for Mrs. Brickle, a tiny aerosol breath freshener. As she came up on the inn, she saw a line of cars going into the parking lot, and that's where she saw him, the guy she met on the train, arguing with the valet parking attendant about who was going to park his MG.

It was a cute, crimson, two-seater roadster and he was in a soft, beautifully cut sport jacket that had the ruddy, almost luminous color of beach sand at dawn. Andy didn't know cars, but she knew that two kinds of guys drive two-seater roadsters, the kind that want to be seen driving them (like Logo, who was always wrecking his Porsches and then letting them get stolen because he refused to be seen in a car that wasn't shiny, new, and perfect), and the kind that merely loves the cars to death and will search automotive graveyards and haul back a load of parts with a rusting carcass and then spend hours, like a grease-streaked Dr. Frankenstein, slowly, gently, delicately nursing it back to life.

The MG this guy was driving was far from perfect. She could see a few gray blotches of primer paint on the side panels, the license plate hung askew, and the tires didn't match. But the engine thrummed like a happy, eager beast and, with the guy's voice slowly beginning to rise in anger as his strong-looking hand fondled the gearshift knob, Andy was embarrassed to discover that the combination of a well-dressed, impeccably groomed man in a rough-and-ready sports car was sexy in a manner that she thought would never, ever appeal to her.

Then she saw the plastic laminated, standard-issue press pass on the lower right corner of his windshield.

He was a journalist! A reporter, like her. She prayed he wasn't with the *Standard* because that would mean they were competitors and she really wanted to have him at her side, working with her on this idiotic assignment that most likely would never see print in the *Press*.

Andy strode up to the valet parking attendant, yet another beefy college kid from Villanova (most of the front-of-the-house labor on the Main Line was traditionally Villanova kids, and maybe, sometimes kids from St. Joe's—if you were going to Haverford or Bryn Mawr you were supposed to be too smart for manual labor and if you went to Swarthmore you were incapable of it), folded her arms, set her jaw so she would not only tower over this kid but probably scare the crap out of him and said, "You making a problem?"

The kid's bloodshot eyes took a long time to climb to her chin, and when he did, Andy could almost hear him thinking *here's a babe who looks like she owns the place and she's going to tell me what to do so why-oh-why didn't I get a job lifeguarding down the shore where babes like this would be in bathing suits and I could put that white goopy sunblock on my nose and blow my whistle and tell her not to swim where I can't see her.*

The kid said, "He won't give me his keys to park his car."

"This man is a member of the media," Andy said, using her best impersonation of her mother in a mood. "He's come here to get a story. He has a deadline to meet. He can't go waiting a half an hour for you to get his car. He needs it where he can get to it, fast."

The kid shrugged and pointed to a space by the inn's front door. Andy said to the guy, "I'll show you," and opened the passenger's door. The guy pretended not to notice as he gunned the engine, slipped into the space, gunned the engine one more time, and turned the key.

He turned and gave her a look that said he liked what he was looking at and he didn't mind her knowing it. "So, you own this place?"

Andy gave him a similar look back, and shook her head.

"Didn't think so." He pulled the keys out of the ignition and extended a hand. "I'm Drew Shaw, *Liberty Bell* magazine."

Liberty Bell was the glossy lifestyle magazine that specialized in suburban scandals, passionately intense restaurant reviews, and toppers—yearly features about the city's "top" doctors, divorce lawyers, private schools, kitchen designers, cosmetic surgeons, Jersey shore towns, Pocono mountain retreats, sex therapists.

Andy took his hand, felt the callouses in his grip, imagined him on his back under the car fixing something, and imagined herself crawling under the car next to him. "Andy Cosicki, *Philadelphia Press*."

He didn't quite let go. "What's the *Press* doing sending somebody out here?"

"What's *Liberty Bell* doing sending you out here?"

He smiled and Andy felt herself begin to melt. "You don't give up anything, do you?"

"You first," she said.

He looked at the broad front of the inn, an enormous dining room that obscured what had been a small, roadside tavern built at the interesection of Montgomery and Wrightsford roads, and then back at Andy, and Andy could hear *his* thoughts, too: *If I tell this girl the truth will she still want to have sex with me?*

Andy smiled.

Drew smiled back. "The publisher hates a guy who is on the board of the New Leaf Foundation. His house is next to the publisher's and they're suing each other over the location of an outdoor grill, which the publisher says blows smoke into his window. When I saw you on the train I was going out to look at his house. He's supposed to have all these television cameras out front and I didn't want him to scope the car."

"So you let the cameras scope you?" Andy said.

"I'm just a guy walking on the street."

"Nobody walks in the suburbs," Andy said.

He noticed her sneakers. "Except you."

Andy crossed her legs. "I'm somebody."

He let himself study her. "You sure are." He reached across her, opened the glove box, and pulled out a pad, a tiny portable tape recorder and a red, white, and blue pen on which was printed *Advertising in Liberty Bell Magazine Gets Results!*

She wanted his arm to brush—just accidently—her leg and he just might have, but he settled slowly back into the chair. "So," he began, "the deal with charities is . . ." he paused and looked her in the eyes. "I don't know if I should be telling you this."

In every other situation when she was with a guy her age who was interested in her, Andy felt like she had to come up with lines, or she had to keep score, or she had to find a way to get him under control. With this guy, she wanted the situation to go completely out of control. "Keep talking," she said.

He opened his pad. "The deal with charities is what they call in the nonprofit business the 'blow-through,' how much of what's contributed actually blows through to the people who need it, or is turned into the task or service that the charity provides, as opposed to how much pays for salaries, office supplies, meals, perks, advertising. From what I've been able to come up with, New Leaf has about fifteen percent blow-through, maybe even less, on finding hard-luck cases and giving them a new start."

"So they're just taking deductions, paying themselves salaries, and spending the rest?"

"Mostly, though you see that with a lot of nonprofits. What's weird about this one is that a lot of the people they're giving second chances to are law enforcement personnel who have screwed up big time: Justice Department investigators who slept with informants, federal auditors who took bribes, drug enforcement agents with habits, military personnel who have been dishonorably discharged, cops who went dirty, the kind of guys who have no problems doing anything illegal. They get hired by this private security company that puts them on a salary, gives them jobs doing gray-area stuff, you know, the between-the-cracks jobs that would probably get them all arrested if anybody found out about it. But nobody does, because there are enough law enforcement types out there that want to work for this company, so they cut the company slack like you wouldn't believe."

For a moment, Andy forgot that she wanted Shaw to shut up so she could kiss him. "Like, what kind of slack?"

"Now we're in a gray area ourselves. So we examine what is known as hearsay evidence: rumors, innuendo, lies, and damned lies. Such as, these guys break into an office and steal the hard drives on all the computers, the cops arrive late to the scene, and can't find any clues. They torch a building, and the investigators can't determine if it's arson."

"What if the investigator doesn't back down?"

"I'm telling you, this is gray-area stuff. They can do bribes, and if bribes don't work, people can get transferred, or put on hazardous duty, or maybe even get accidently thrown down the stairs."

Andy thought of her father doing some of this for Logo and . . . who else? Her father had always respected cops, always waved to them when he was out driving. "The toughest job there is," he'd tell her.

"Can they make a murder look like an accident?"

Shaw shrugged. "It's the cops that say if it's an accident or not. The coroner can come up with a stack of contrary evidence and a murderer's DNA can be found mixed with the blood of his victim, which can only get there one possible way, but it all boils down to what the prosecutor is willing to prosecute and the people are willing to believe."

"Who told you this?"

"I found out about it because this guy told my publisher and my publisher told me and, even if he's suing the guy, my publisher likes him. I mean, they're both so *suburban*, you know? They hate taxes, government, unions, entitlements, the city, and just about everything in it, except for maybe three restaurants and the orchestra. They keep up their homes. You should see this guy's lawn. Not a weed in it. Has his kids in private school, vacations at the Jersey shore, the whole deal."

Andy watched him stretch his right arm across the backseat until his fingers came down a few inches from the back of her neck. With his left hand, he closed his pad. "I'm supposed to go slow on this guy, just show up and let him know I'm sniffing around because the publisher will throw out the suit and call me off if he takes out a big enough ad in the magazine."

Andy caught the scent of his aftershave. "If he's got those kinds of people working for him, he probably knows you're sniffing around," she said.

"Well, yes." He looked her in the eyes again. "And you're here to . . ."

"Find stuff out," Andy said.

"Just like that?"

"No. Like this." Andy knew she was being crazy, she knew she was losing it, she knew she was sitting in a car that had no roof so that every-body could see, and she was wondering with part of her brain if, maybe, way back when her mother was her age, her mother may have felt this way, because it really felt good to put her hand on the back of his head, move forward, and touch her lips gently enough for the spark to jump.

He nodded and put his hand on the back of her neck and nudged her closer until their lips touched again.

She pulled back and he pulled back and said, "You can definitely find things out that way." Then he glanced at his watch and got out of the car. "You want to go in?"

"Do we have to?"

"We could . . . walk around."

Why was she agreeing? She felt as if she was burning up and it wasn't that hot out. She followed him through the parking lot, back around the building, where a refrigerated delicatessen truck was parked with its back facing the kitchen.

When they came upon the truck Shaw's eyes didn't quite lock with hers. But he put her hand on his waist and she wanted him to keep it there.

"Would you look at this . . . truck," Andy said.

"It is a truck, isn't it?"

"You're sure of that?"

He looked around. "We could find out if it is, in fact, a truck." He opened the doors and a delicious blast of freezing air redolent of pick-ling spices wafted over them. He glanced at her, as if he was asking permission, and then climbed in. She followed him.

It was dark and cold and wonderful when he found her and let her tangle herself in his arms. His lips were wet and cool on hers and she felt his jacket come off and his hands on her, holding her, eagerly but not greedily, as if this was a naughty joke and at any minute they would start laughing.

She found her hands on his butt, feeling it through the fabric of his pants. He stopped and waited for her to make the next move. A brief slice of light came in from the door, almost closed shut. She closed her eyes because it was more fun to feel him against her arms and legs, moving and enjoying her. She marveled at how deferential he was, as if he was a servant and he was hers to order around, torment, or tickle. She moved her hands up under his arms and he came closer, warmer, harder.

Her hands were on his pants again. "Would you look at these . . . pants."

He began, "I can't see a damned thing . . ." but she covered his mouth with his as she found his belt and opened it and the catch beneath and heard the merry buzz of the zipper descending.

"What if somebody comes in here?" he said. Andy reached behind him and pushed the door closed until it locked with a snap.

He said, "How are we going to get out of here?"

She had her hands on him and he felt himself wilt, just a little. "We can figure that out later."

"But I did a story, once," he said, "on these illegal aliens who were kept locked in a truck for three days."

"Whatever did they do?" Andy said, pulling off her blouse and thrilling as the cold air raised goosebumps on her skin that his warm hands smoothed flat. Her bra came off and she felt herself tingling in the chill.

"There's a way to get out if the outside isn't padlocked," Drew said. "At least, I think there is."

"Wonder where it is?" Andy said, pulling off his shirt and pushing him back against the wall of the truck, bumping into some cardboard boxes. She felt his hands go into her pants, through her panties and grab her butt. He lifted her off her feet and pushed her back. She yelped when she felt her naked back hit the corrugated metal.

He asked suddenly, "Are you okay?"

"I'm feeling," she licked his ear, "certain ambiguities."

"Oh, there's nothing ambiguous about this."

She peeled off her pants and panties and said, "Wait a minute." She groped for her shoulder bag, dug deep into a special change purse she kept in it, and came out with a condom.

She said, "Put this on."

She heard a rustling of cellophane. He said, "Actually, you might want to try one of mine. I did a consumer story on condoms once, and . . ."

"You tried them all?"

"I did get a lot of free samples."

"But you didn't try them?"

"You know how you do a magazine consumer story. You call three experts and you wing it."

"Who were your experts—no, don't tell me. I don't want to know."

"They were all medical. Urologist, dermatologist, gynecologist."

"And you call that responsible journalism?"

"It was part of a Valentine's Day round-up for the February issue called 'Wicked Pleasures.' We got some great ads from the sex toy stores."

"They send you free samples, too?"

"The edible underwear tasted really bad."

"Are you going to put this on or do I have to put it on for you?"

"Too many decisions," he said and put his leg between hers.

She pulled herself away and said, "Now I suppose I'm going to have to put this on myself."

"It might work better if you put it on me."

"I might work better if you shut up."

He did. She did.

"Uhh, Andy, they force you to read *For Whom the Bell Tolls* in college?"

"I had a course where they showed the movie. I almost cut off my hair so I could be Ingrid Bergman."

"Okay. So, then, just now, did the *truck* move?"

Andy thought it did, wonderfully.

It was a huge, sit-down luncheon for four hundred men and women in business clothes in a dark, wood-paneled room covered with pictures of men, horses, and dogs in hunting regalia interrupted every fifty or so feet with big black doors with glowing red exit signs over them. Half the people were clustered around the bar, an elaborately carved, black walnut Victorian monstrosity that was part of the original inn.

A perky woman with a name tag that said MEDIA CONTACT explained that the New Leaf Foundation meets every month at the Wrightsford Inn. She gave to a somewhat mussed (but no worse for wear) Andy and Drew green folders that had been embossed with the shape of leaves. The folders contained printed information that neither of them read. Drew got himself a vodka gimlet and meandered around the room, acting as if he were lost and did anyone know what was going on?

Andy had her pad and pen out. She went up to anyone in her path and immediately asked rapid, pointed questions about "the blow-through factor" and did anyone know what some of the New Leaf's employees did to earn their dishonorable discharge?

Lunch was being served but Andy was still on the prowl when she thought she saw someone who looked like Piper, with bandages on his face, standing with his back to the wall. At the front of the room, on the left side of the dais, James Fenestra was speaking into a cell phone.

Andy had been grilling a frightened woman who said, "You'll have to excuse me but I don't actually *read* newspapers," when the speeches began. Andy listened to some of them, paused to wink at Drew, and then she heard Fenestra behind her. "Miss Cosicki, a word, please."

She turned and looked down on a bulky, smiling man whose eyes were not smiling. "When I'm finished."

He put his hand on her arm and gently applied a painful pressure. "You're finished now."

Two gray-suited goons appeared on either side of him. "You've been telling people you're a journalist, correct?"

"I'm with the *Press*," Andy said.

"We have the press with us already," Fenestra said, the fumes of some fishy hors d'oeuvre on his breath. He tilted his head toward the dais. "Over there, is Mr. Schweitzer, the bureau chief of the *Standard*, and in the chair next to him, if he hasn't drunken himself into a stupor, is Mr. Lange, Lange of the *Philadelphia Press*. What press did you said you were with?"

"The *Philadelphia Press*," Andy said, her nose wrinkling at Fenestra's breath.

"We were not expecting anyone else from the *Press*." He turned to one of the goons and said, "Bring Mr. Lange here, why don't you? And call Mr. Piper, too." He moved closer to Andy. "Mr. Piper will want to escort you out."

"I'm not going anywhere," Andy said, tightening her grip on her pen. "This meeting is open to the public. We have every right to cover it."

Fenestra bared his perfect teeth. "You have no rights."

Behind her, Andy heard Lange say, "We NEVER send anybody to the suburbs." He staggered into her and looked up.

"Ms. Cosicki says she's one of yours, Mr. Lange," Fenestra said.

"I, uhhh," Lange's face began to crumple in panic. "I don't know if . . . oh, wait a minute. This is Mr. Action. He—I mean, she, does our consumer complaint column and, umm." He squinted at her. "The only person who complained about this place was, I think . . ."

Andy was about to tell him that Ladderback sent her when who should appear at her side but Prince Charming.

"Drew Shaw, *Liberty Bell*," he said, emitting vodka fumes as he shoved Lange aside and stepped between Andy and Fenestra. "Great party you have here, Jim-bo." He turned to Andy. "This is Jim-bo. He used to bust crooks but now he gives second chances to all kinds of nice, decent, convicted sex offenders, rapists, and child molesters. Even perverts have to eat, right Jim-bo?"

It happened too fast. Fenestra smacked Drew across the face, pushing him backward into Andy, who knocked Lange down and stepped on Lange's ankle. Lange screamed, causing a server to drop an hors d'oeuvre tray as Drew shot up and drove his fist into Fenestra's stomach before one of the goons got behind Drew and pinned his arms back. Fenestra took something sharp and shiny out of his suit jacket and was about to whip it across Shaw's face when Andy dropped her pad and grabbed the fallen hors d'oeuvre tray and flung it at Fenestra, who didn't quite block his face fast enough before the plate connected with the skin somewhere under his right eye.

Andy reached for the tray and was about to smash Fenestra with it again when she felt a clamp come down on her left wrist and another clamp come down around the forefinger of her left hand. She felt herself yanked up into the bandaged, leering face of Mr. Piper. She struggled but he pulled the finger back until the joint almost broke.

"You like to fight me, girl?" he sputtered at her. "I'll break it right off, I swear I will."

A group of goons had descended on Shaw. "Take him outside," Fenestra yelled, a dark red slash of blood on his cheek.

Andy tried again to get her hand away from Piper, but he cranked the finger back until she shrieked and stepped on Lange again, who screamed even louder.

Andy remembered her right hand was still holding that brightly colored Day-Glo pen she bought in the discount pharmacy.

She stabbed forward and felt it poke and almost break on the surface of his suit jacket. Piper wiggled around and cranked her finger. She didn't shriek this time—the pain was too intense for that. Her knees buckled and she kicked him with her shoes and he groaned as the soft rubber soles hit his shins. She saw him relax his grip just for a second, so he could grab her finger even more firmly. He was going to break it and he opened his mouth to tell her and she shoved the pen into his open mouth, hit the upper gum line, skidded off the gum, and ripped through the outside of his cheek.

He fell backward but still held onto her wrist, so he pulled her down on top of him and Andy, whose knees had already been bent from the pain he had inflicted on her knuckle, felt her knees bend further until they landed on a point somewhere below his belt. Piper would have yelled but he had a Day-Glo pen sticking out of his mouth, so the best he could do was a wet gabble as he let go of her wrist.

Andy wobbled to her feet, saw a crowd of people stepping back from her, their expressions going from shock to horror. She backed off and again stepped on Lange, who managed a coherent cry for help. Andy moved away from him, found herself against the wall, took a breath, and saw that she wasn't far from a door that said EMERGENCY EXIT ONLY. ALARM WILL SOUND.

She opened the door. The alarm didn't sound. She found herself in a bright, almost blistering heat, a kitchen fan blowing the aroma of hardening baked chicken in her face, a garbage Dumpster buzzing with flies on her right, and something like a path of cracked asphalt that led behind the inn, into the parking lot, where three goons were stomping Shaw beside his car. Fenestra was holding a handkerchief to his face and using what looked like a small pistol to smash the lights and rake the paint on Shaw's car.

Maybe Fenestra sensed he was being watched. He saw Andy staring at him and pulled one of the goons off Shaw and pointed toward her.

Andy took off down Montgomery Avenue toward the Bryn Mawr train station and the goon followed, his face flush with confidence, absolutely certain that he would slice through the hundred feet that lay between them. But he was wearing leather shoes and they slapped loudly on the concrete while Andy's sneakers flew over the rough surface, past some trees planted as a screen and then up a weed-choked embankment toward a fence that blocked access to the railroad tracks of the Main Line that gave the region its name.

"Stop!" the goon yelled after her. "I got a gun."

When you like shooting layups and you grow up in the city, you learn that some of the best basketball courts have fences around them and that the gates in these fences are locked to keep out people who want to shoot layups. So you learn to stick the toes of your sneakers between the links in the fence and apply just enough tension to shoot right up to the top. Then, with fences with barbed wire on the top, you stop long enough to put your hands between the sharp, twisted ends and then bring your feet up, move your hands wider apart until you can bring your legs up through your arms, and—

"Geddown from there or I'll shoot ya," the goon said.

Andy looked down and he was below her, his hands gripping a shiny, small-caliber pistol, perhaps similar to the one Fenestra had used on Shaw's car. She looked away from the hand at strands of dyed hair that had been combed over his balding scalp, and saw, from the odd way the hair was shaped, that it had been either glued to his head or attached in some way, not to make him look younger but to make him look ordinary, but, seen from above, it made him seem false and weak. He appeared to be in his forties, with wrinkles around his mouth extending into his pock-marked cheeks. Whatever hard lines his face may have had from military or law-enforcement training had softened into a puffy, flabby padding.

"I don't want to kill ya," he said, his mouth open, revealing a set of gleaming, surgically enhanced teeth.

Andy imagined herself slipping over the barbed wire, hanging onto the fence on the opposite side, dropping down onto the gravel roadbed, and then skipping over the railroad tracks to the fence on the opposite side, or maybe running toward the train station and then . . . where? Was that distant, lonesome honking sound a locomotive bearing down? Was it the SEPTA R5 Paoli Local or the Amtrak more-or-less Express bound for Harrisburg?

She recalled chase scenes from *Bullitt, North by Northwest, From Russia with Love, The French Connection*, and even *Run Lola Run*, that she had seen as part of a social anthropology class called "Suspense in Context: Danger and Redemption as Personal Narrative." There were, she remembered, two kinds of chase narratives: the prosocial, in which the pursuit brings out positive characteristics in the hero who applies these characteristics to either escape capture or outwit the anti-heroic escapee, and thereby reaffirms social order; and the antisocial, in which the chase deliberately invades dangerous, hidden, or forbidden zones, bringing a brash, sometimes farcical but ultimately liberating sense of disorder to what would typically be rigidly maintained areas of taboo and privilege. The antisocial chase climaxes with the pursuer or the pursued thwarted after obeying a rule, deciding to save a bystander from harm, or otherwise intentionally sacrificing an individual goal so that order may be restored, thus forming an ironic, contradictory or ambiguous statement on the enduring value of existing social institutions.

"Train's coming," the goon said. He took one hand off the pistol grip and extended it toward her. "Come on down now. Papa's got a little treat for ya."

Andy had been debating whether this would be an anti- or prosocial situation when that line about "Papa's got a treat" bothered her. It did more than bother her. It made her really, really angry at the big, secretive, seemingly omnipotent adult world that, despite everything that had happened in her life up to this point, insisted on patronizing her, denying her the respect, consideration, and dignity that any human being was due, because she was young, tall, female, and, now, fatherless.

She got very angry at this goon, the kind of anger that is red, hot, and dangerously sure of itself. As she turned her feet around until her toes pointed away from the fence, she said, "what sort of treat?"

The goon said, "The kind of treat you've been missing—"

Of course, Andy wasn't missing anything that this goon could supply. But, by taking up space under her, he provided a target for her anger and something that she needed—a landing platform for the big, wide soles of her sneakers, that came down straight on the goon's shoulders as she jumped off the top of the fence and drove him crashing back into the ground.

Was that a snap of a broken collarbone she had heard, or had that asshole actually fired his pistol? She landed in a crouch, sprung up, and brought both feet down on the hand holding the gun. Was that a groan of pain she had heard? She shifted her weight to her left foot, which kept the hand holding the gun pinned, and brought her right foot up and down on his elbow. When that only got a "you bitch," she stomped on his stomach for a louder groan, then pounced on the hand holding the gun, pulled the gun away and aimed it at the guy's face.

He swore again at her as he reached into his jacket pocket and came out with a cell phone when Andy brought her foot down on that hand and the phone. Both broke, or seemed to. He groaned, brought his legs up, and would have grabbed at her if he hadn't discovered that his collarbone really was broken and that trying to do anything with his right arm now hurt more than anything Andy could do to him.

Well, almost anything. Andy kicked the cell phone away and was about to kick him somewhere when she saw she still had the gun in her hand. She pointed the gun at him, flipped the safety off, and held it steady as he said, "Now, don't you . . . oh, God, ma'am, please don't—"

She could hear the clanging bell of an approaching train—from the snarling sound of it, the SEPTA R5, the same train she had met Shaw on, though this one was bound for the city.

She caught the stench of the man losing his bowels. She saw a stain appear at the crotch of the goon's pants and her anger left her. As threatening as he had been to her, he was now quite obviously less than what he was.

She stood back as the ground beneath began to tremble from the approaching train. The guy writhed around. He was crying and she wondered if there might be in nature a species of animal that protects itself by becoming too pathetic for its predator to harm.

"You could use a second chance," she said. "Take it or leave it." She tossed the gun over the fence, tore past the goon, shot across Wrightsford Avenue just as a gray Lincoln was pulling up with more goons inside, raced the fifty yards to the train station, got on the train, and saw, through a window, another Lincoln pull up at the station, a pair of goons come out, stop, look around, argue with each other—*no way she could've got this far*—as the train slowly, slowly, slowly pulled out.

job security

It took Ladderback longer than he anticipated to find the letter among the unopened mail on Mr. Action's desk. He put it beside Mr. Action's telephone.

Then he took out a pad and wrote down two telephone numbers. He went to his file cabinet and removed the thick folder marked PARKING AUTHORITY. He compared the list he had written to telephone numbers written in the file.

They were identical. It had been several months since he had written an obituary of a former parking-authority meter maid, but he could recall the numbers instantly, and accurately.

He wasn't ready for early retirement. Not yet.

Then he heard the baying jackass of a yawn in the newsroom that told him Bardo Nackels, the night city editor, hadn't left yet, even though he should have left hours ago. Nackels had his legs up by the copy desk, propped up on either side of his computer terminal. His khaki pants drooped down to show off the black pointed toes and hand-tooled tedium of western boots that would have been his trade-mark had anyone in the newsroom bothered to look at his feet.

Nackels was also one of the rare journalistic types who was born with ink in his blood. He lived for deadlines, never took vacations, never called in sick, never took a personal day since he had been hired as a copy boy while going to night school at Temple, and was notorious for staying way past his shift. The night after he was mugged on the way to get his car in the garage two blocks from the *Press*'s building, he showed up for work, his face swollen and bruised, his beer gut pushing out a gray sweatshirt on which was printed, "YOU SHOULD'VE SEEN THE OTHER GUY."

As a thorough newspaper slave who was born, raised, educated, married, divorced, and victimized in Philadelphia, Nackels maintained that he was an expert on all things local, especially inside stories, scams, conspiracies, and under-the-counter deals. He was fifteen years younger than Ladderback, but the job had weighed heavily on him over the years, as if so much venality and vibrant sleaziness (and not the gooey Reuben sandwiches and gallons of coffee that he guzzled while editing copy) had battered him so much that his skin had thickened on him, forming an armor capable of absorbing any shock or revelation.

From his desk opposite the water cooler and the photocopying machine, Ladderback steeled himself for Nackels's departure ritual. He watched as Nackels placed each boot on the floor, shoved himself off his chair until he was standing, yawned that painfully loud jackass bray, and then moved with his heavy, foot-dropping trudge to the photocopying machine near Ladderback's desk, where he made copies of the night city list, an index of stories that had been edited and approved for inclusion in the *Press*'s afternoon edition. While the copy machine was humming, clicking, and too frequently jamming itself with incompletely copied paper, Nackels would put his face into the limp dribble of the water cooler, lean back, gargle, then bring his face down like an executioner's blade about to sever a head, and spit his very soul into the drain.

He looked at Ladderback. "Shep," Nackels said. "Since when do you have an assistant?"

Ladderbacked turned around. "Lange hired her."

"Because of the Lunchman," Nackels said. "If I was editor, I'd never let anybody like the Lunchman tell me who I was going to hire."

"She went to Penn," Ladderback said. "She did good work there."

"Yeah, and I went to Temple and I did good work there. But nobody got hired in our day for doing good work. They still don't. When I was coming in, newspapers were all about power, which is all about who you know and who knows you. Donitz hired me because my uncle was a police captain and Donitz thought, through me, he'd have access to the cops. Was he ever wrong. I never, ever in my life discussed anything we did here with my uncle."

"But if Donitz wanted to speak with your uncle informally," Ladderback said, "he could certainly get him on the phone."

"Same reason he hired Lange—his father was a partner in the mayor's law firm. But you, we could never figure out why you got on. Why'd he hire you?"

"I could spell Schuylkill."

"And what else?"

"My parents were medical examiners."

"See? What'd I tell you: Donitz wanted the paper as connected as it could get. Lange's no different. Now that Lange's got you an assistant, you know he's going to get rid of you."

"Not yet," Ladderback said, turning back to his keyboard.

Nackels ambled over and sat down heavily in Mr. Action's chair. He looked at the pile of unanswered mail. "She called in on her cell phone, said we had to run a story about some tussle at a banquet hall out on the Main Line. Something about a private criminal army and guys in gray suits trying to kill her. She said that Lange was there, but he was drunk. You know what I told her?"

"That if Lange was drunk, it meant he wasn't paying for the liquor," Ladderback said, "which meant that any story that reflects negatively on a person or organization who is paying for Lange's liquor must first be cleared by Lange himself."

"I didn't put it exactly that way," Nackles said.

"You told her that suburban stories weren't within the interest of the newspaper's readers, unless they involved personalities known to the readers or a death."

Nackles chewed his lip. "I've never been a good liar."

"If you told her either of those things, you would have told the truth."

"What I told her is that I had no knowledge she was out there and that until I found out why she was out there, we were taking nothing from her. She said she was on assignment from you."

"She was," Ladderback said.

"So how come Lange called in a half hour ago from some hospital emergency room and told me to fire her?"

Ladderback said nothing.

"Shep," Nickles began, "you've been here the longest of anybody and I shouldn't be the one to tell you editors make assignments, not staff writers."

"She is my assistant. I can assign my assistant to do specific tasks relating to my work."

"How is her going out to eat rubber chicken at some charity bash relating to your work?"

Ladderback said, "Background."

Nickles grinned. "Last time I used that word, I was trying to bull-shit a source into telling me something he didn't want to tell me, but I sure as hell wanted to know."

"The boundaries between the city and the suburbs no longer exist," Ladderback said. "What happens in one place affects the other."

"You know what I think? I think you sent her out there so she could watch Lange work the room. You wanted her to get something on him, maybe see him getting schmoozed by an advertiser or groping some babe's behind, so you could use that to keep your job."

That was not Ladderback's reason but Ladderback saw that Nackels was certain that it was. The only thing Nackles wanted from Ladderback was an admission that he was right.

Ladderback had seen this in many editors over the years, especially those who believed they knew the city, if not the entire world, even if all they had experienced of it was the flow of words that they chopped, tweaked, puffed, or squeezed to fit the spaces between the ads, pictures, and cartoons. You could not contradict these editors, you could not show them that the facts showed otherwise, you could not remind them it was possible to be 100 percent certain about something and be 100 percent wrong at the same time, because these editors went by their gut feelings and their guts, which were mostly big by the time they reached any level of power, could not be wrong.

About the best you can do is distract them. "I wonder how the paper might be different if Abe Donitz made you editor instead of Lange," Ladderback said.

Nackels rubbed his broken nose. "I think, if I were running it, I'd've put it out of business because, to me, the truth has always been ugly. I came up thinking, if two reporters for the *Washington Post* can dig up enough dirt to bring down the president of the United States, what could I do? But now, with the Internet and radio and TV and so many other places people can turn to for news in any size, shape, or flavor they want, you can't afford to print too much ugly, or you lose readers who don't want ugly. And you can't be too subversive, because the sources you depend on will just cut you off and give what you need to the competition. The premiums on liability insurance have gone through the roof and if someone decides to sue, the cost of defending a libel suit is so high that, even if you win, you lose. And then you got the publisher breathing down your neck—cut costs, do it cheaper, early retirement, find another way to save money so I'll look good to the shareholders and the stock price will stay high."

He spun around on the chair and settled his gaze on Ladderback. "What I don't understand is why you're still here, Shep. I mean, you got hired, for whatever reason, and you found that whatever you thought the newspaper business was on the outside, on the inside it's the same pile of greasy, stinking horseshit that you step in anywhere, but it's worse because we're supposed to be selling the truth, but we're not. We're selling ourselves, over and over again."

"We sell what we know," Ladderback said.

"And what we know can be piss poor, more often than not," Nackels replied. "So why have you stayed?"

Ladderback thought about it for a long time. "I owe things to people," he said finally.

Nackels's sagging face sagged further when he heard that. "So you're no better than Lange," he said as he pulled himself out of his chair and headed toward the exit.

"No better," Ladderback said quietly to himself. "But not worse."

Ladderback had almost finished his second obituary when Andy rushed into the newsroom in a rumpled gray suit. She was out of breath when she dropped into Mr. Action's chair and said to him, "I have . . . I have to tell you. You're not going to believe this."

Ladderback was typing and told Andy to open her mail.

"I almost got killed and you want me to open my mail?"

"The envelope beside your telephone. Open it and call the person who wrote it."

"Oh, like, I'm Mr. Action? What I found out is going to blow Mr. Action away."

He said, "It's important that you do it now."

She fired up her terminal and said, "Whatever it is, it can wait."

Ladderback turned to her and quietly said, "Right now."

She blinked. "Okay." The letter had been hand-addressed to Mr. Action. She noticed it was two months old. She opened the envelope and read a story about some restaurant hiring a waitress and firing the woman's daughter—a student at Villanova—in the middle of the week, not paying her the three days she had earned in salary. There was a phone number at the bottom.

Andy looked at Ladderback and made a show of dialing the phone. To her surprise, a woman answered it, the same woman who had written the letter, and she was so grateful that Andy called because the bitch who runs the Ristferin shouldn't get away with holding back on what she owes her daughter.

Andy got out a notepad and said, "Run the problem by me again."

Seems her daughter got a job working a banquet at the Ristferin.

"Could you spell Ristferin, please?"

Andy heard Ladderback whisper behind her: "Mrs. Schweitzer is from Florida. She has an accent."

On the phone, the woman spelled "W-R-I-G-H-T-S-F-O-R-D. That's the name of the place."

Andy looked at what she had just written on her pad. "You're talking about the Wrightsford Inn?"

"The Ristferin."

"I . . . was just there, today, an hour ago," Andy said. She looked at Ladderback, who pretended not to see her.

"I wrote that letter two months ago but then the column stopped and, well, I know Ennis Aadderack because he did an obituary for the friend of a friend and even though we're really much more a *Morning*

Standard kind of demographic, I still read the *Press* because the *Standard* is so boring and they don't have a Mr. Action column and, what's going to happen if you're a young girl going to Villanova and you get a job, not because she needed the money, mind you, but every girl should have a job, don't you think? And when they fire you because you find out the chef is living hot with the owner, and the owner's laundering money for the drug dealers and the bitch doesn't pay my daughter what she's owed. It's really pretty terrible, don't you think? So I called Ennis a few weeks back but he said that Mr. Action had been suspended and he doubted if they would ever send Mr. Action out to Montgomery county but that if they did he would let me know. You said you were out there?"

Andy was about to add that she was on a different assignment and that she was almost killed and that some suburban slimeball had a private army with some fat former FBI agent in charge who stomped this guy Andy was thinking about falling in love with, when she said, "Yes. I was at the inn."

"So you saw what kind of operation they run, the people they cater to—people like us, you know, who are well off, but also groups and things, and a girl can make herself some money, though, my husband Robb, you know Robb Schweitzer, he's the Montgomery County bureau chief of the *Standard*, well, he said he just could not be-*lieve* a place like that would fire a girl and not pay her and that it must be our daughter's fault and he would *not* investigate or put any of his reporters on it, because, as far as *he's* concerned they don't do those kinds of things in the suburbs and that's what she gets for not telling them who she is and whose daughter she is."

Mrs. Schweitzer took a breath. "Personally, I think it's wonderful that you care enough about these things to take them personally. By the way, did you happen to see my husband with . . . anyone else? He has an assistant editor, a terribly ambitious little snoop who thinks she's so fine because she's got an Emmy from Lombya."

"What was that?"

"Lombya Jool a Sherlism."

"Columbia School of Journalism?" Andy said. "Penn undergrads are even better, if you ask me."

"There are mornings I try to get him on the phone and they say he's in meetings. I drive by and his car isn't in the lot, and what do you think that can mean? There are only so many things you can force your staff to lie about and I don't know if they've been seeing too much of each other, but if they are, I think a wife's got a right to know about it, don't you think?"

Andy thought back to the morning she had waited fruitlessly for the editor to come out of his meeting. "That's not the kind of thing we check on here, Mrs. Schweitzer."

"Well, I feel better, knowing you were there. I'm going to let him know that the *Press* had someone out there and see if his ears get red the way they do when he's covering something up. His ears weren't red when you saw him, were they?"

Andy said they weren't and let the woman wind down. When the conversation ended, she said to Ladderback, "Was that why you assigned me to go out there?"

"No," Ladderback replied, looking at his computer screen. "But you will say that was why you were sent."

"To check up on some waitress who got stiffed for a few days' work?"

"You will refer to her by name and mention what her father does for a living."

"Why don't you tell me the real reason you sent me out there?"

Ladderback said, "Write these down." He recited three telephone numbers. "Call them. Identify yourself as Mr. Action and say that you are pursuing information on parking summons adjudication."

"What's that supposed to mean?"

"Many of Mr. Action's complaints are about parking matters. Some of your complainers are even suggesting that it is possible to fix tickets. Is there a list of people who have had tickets fixed? What should you tell your readers?"

She glared at him. "Aren't you interested in what happened to me out there?"

"Yes," Ladderback said. "But first do this."

"Why?"

"Job security."

She didn't know what that meant but she dialed the first number, and got a recording that told her to call a different number which happened to be the second number, which was a phone tree for departments within the parking authority she didn't understand. She dialed the third number and got "Adjudication, Ganeesh Ryan."

Andy asked, "What's a Ganeesh?"

"An Indian god with the head of an elephant. You can call me Ryan. My parents were hippie flakes."

Andy did exactly as Ladderback told her and heard Ryan laugh. "You're not shitting me are you? This is the *Press* and you're Mr. Action?"

"You have Caller I.D.?"

"I do, but, you doing a ticket fixing story is like, a joke. One of the biggest scofflaws we have—you know, a scofflaw is someone who doesn't pay his fines—is your editor, Howard Lange. He's got this blue Jaguar and he just won't feed a meter and the tickets and the fines rack up until the word comes down and we mark them uncollectible. Don't ask me what he does to get them fixed, but, well, are you really doing the story or are you just finding out how to screw him?"

"I beg your pardon?"

"You'll have to do better than that. I work in Adjudication: All day, people are coming in, saying the meter was broken or the enforcement officer got the wrong car. I get my pardon begged all the time. You work in the city, I wouldn't be surprised if I haven't seen you come in begging."

"You have not," Andy said.

"I bet you I have. What's your last name? I got it all on the computer here. It's all public record, collectibles and uncollectibles. Give me your last name."

"Cosicki."

"You related to Benny Lunch?"

"My father," Andy said.

"You're not on the computer."

"How do you know?"

"Benny Lunch was a real, true character, who will be missed," Ryan said. "We get a lot of people asking for favors from us, but him, it was a pleasure. There are maybe three dozen people—you're not quoting me are you? In the city there are maybe fifty people—call it a club—who don't get ticketed because, well, *because*, and he's one of them. You, too, as a courtesy to him, though you probably didn't notice. Your guy, Lange, always wanted to be in the club, because his opposite number at the *Standard* is in the club and Lange probably would've gotten himself in, sooner or later, if he just maybe fed a few meters every once in a while and pretended he could be a regular guy. But, you know, some people think they're better than everybody else and get really mad when other people don't exactly agree with them, and that's why he's always going to be out and people like your father are always going to be in. Your father used to send us over big boxes of soup and sandwiches from Jimmy D's. Last time he sent over a lunchbox was just a few days ago . . ." she heard him tap into the computer. "Under uncollectible, we have $696 in fines for a blue Jaguar, registered to Howard Hogarth Lange, license plate number—you don't need a license plate number, do you?"

Andy started to cry.

Ryan went on, "I guess if you're calling from the *Press*, that could have something to do with you getting in there?"

She hung up on him, looked around for something to cry into, ripped some pages out of her pad—

A clean, pressed handkerchief appeared in front of her. The hand holding it was soft, plump, dusted with light hairs and liver spots. "I'm sorry," Ladderback said.

She covered her eyes, forced the tears back. "You don't know," she said.

"You wanted to get a job at a newspaper because you are competent and because you want to accomplish important things," Ladderback said.

"I wanted to find stuff out," Andy said, wiping her eyes.

"And so you have," Ladderback said.

"So now I found out about a foundation that's a front for a private army—"

"It is not a front. The foundation does exactly what it says."

"What I want to know is, what does any of this have to do with my father?" Andy said.

"It may have everything to do with your father," Ladderback replied. "Or it may not."

She closed her eyes. She could shoot layups for the next two hours. Or she could eat.

"I could go home and eat," she said. "My mother whipped up a catered affair at my house. She's hoping that people will pity her and want to buy art." She expected Ladderback to share her indignation. "Is that crass or what?"

"Your mother is being brave," Ladderback said.

"Oh come on, you don't know her. If she can make a buck selling something, she will."

Ladderback folded his hands. "One of the most common strategies for dealing with grief is to make yourself busy, preferably doing some-

174

thing that you can do well, that offers immediate gratification or satisfaction."

"I don't see that as brave."

"You would rather have her be miserable? In my experience, there is far too much time for that and, as miserable as we have every right to be, we cannot remain that way for long. Each must find grief, and leave it, in whatever way possible. Parties, shopping sprees, vacations, aggressive behavior, lovemaking—"

Andy blushed.

Ladderback turned back to his terminal.

getting back on the horse

Lange's call came half an hour later. "What were you doing spying for Schweitzer's wife?"

She motioned for Ladderback to listen in. Ladderback just pointed at her, as if to say, *you can handle it.*

Andy picked up the letter and said, "Mrs. Schweitzer wrote Mr. Action regarding a labor dispute at the Wrightsford Inn."

"Yeah, her and her daughter. She's called me on that, too. Thinks we should do a really big story about the owner sleeping with the chef and laundering mob money. I don't know if you had any direct effect, but that fling he's having with the Columbia babe is about to become old news. I'd normally be inclined to give you a raise for that kind of thing, but not when I end up at home with a sprained ankle, doped up on painkillers and a pair of crutches. Are you normally this clumsy or was it for my benefit?"

"You really want me to answer that?"

"What I really want you to do is get the fuck out of my newsroom and never come back. I told you, if you ever crossed me, I'd run over you with a truck."

Andy imagined herself staring down at him. "I didn't cross you."

"What kind of shitty act were you pulling, asking about blow-backs and return percentages?"

"It wasn't an act," Andy said.

"You were just curious."

"Shouldn't you be?"

"The foundation does good work. I'm proud to be on the board. They get free ad space in the Situations Wanted section."

"You and Fenestra must have great barbecues together."

"As a matter of fact, we have. Fenestra and I go way back. He helped me out when I needed sources inside the FBI. We owe a lot to each other."

"You came when he called."

"Andrea, I don't like what I'm hearing from you. You're being extremely unprofessional. I don't think I'll sue you for assault, but I think I really am going to fire you."

"You won't," Andy said.

"This is your second day on the job and I haven't seen a word from you yet."

"You will. My lead for Mr. Action is about parking tickets."

His tone changed. "What about them?"

"About how some people don't pay their tickets and rack up these big fines and then the fines disappear, but they don't really disappear. They are just marked as uncollectible, but they keep a record of the amounts on the computer in the Parking Authority's Adjudication Department. I'm thinking of making a list of the people who have had the most uncollectibles and starting off with that."

"I don't know about that," Lange said. "Parking ticket stories only interest readers with cars and a lot of our readers don't own cars."

"Enough of them do."

"I think we can do a better lead, the kind of lead that only someone with your special talent can pull off. Or you can quit. Do you want to quit? Why not quit?"

"Because there are things I need to find out."

"Then find out about . . . a lot of our readers live near people who have dogs and these people with the dogs let them bark and crap all over the place. People complain about that. There's some city law about owners having to clean up after dogs, fines up to three hundred dollars," Lange went on. "Find out if anybody's ever been arrested and charged for failing to scoop the poop, and lead with that. There's got to be at least one in there. Get a shovel and dig."

"And if I don't find anything?"

"Make one up," Lange said. "Nobody'll know the difference unless you win a Pulitzer."

Andy slammed down the phone. Then she turned to Ladderback. Should she thank him for saving her job, even if it was a job she wasn't sure she wanted? Or should she get mad at him for sending her to a place where these goons in suits tried to kill her?

Ladderback's finger's raced over the keyboard. He seemed eager to finish his third and last obituary of the day when he suddenly stopped writing and said, "Do you want another assignment?"

"Not if it's going to be like the last one you gave me."

He listened to her explain to him what had happened. (She didn't tell him about what went on with Shaw in the refrigerator truck, but who would?) She added that she had seen Fenestra coming out of a bar one morning while she was with her father. "My father said something about a man of God not liking him much. Then he and his goons came and broke into my house."

"They were looking for something," Ladderback said. "Did they find what they were looking for?"

"I hope not," Andy said. "I, sort of, got rid of them."

Ladderback went to his file cabinet. "For your next assignment . . ."

"Lange wants me to find out about dog-poop fines."

Ladderback closed one file drawer, went to another. "Then you must do so."

"He's trying to get me to quit."

"Possibly. He might also be helping you."

"How is finding out about dog poop going to help me?"

"When was the last time someone lied to you?"

"It happens every day."

Ladderback ignored her sarcasm. "When a source lies to you, or attempts to prevent you from gaining information that the source is aware of, you can usually hear a change in the tone of voice or detect some other sign of increased tension. Sources typically overcompensate when they try to lead you astray, and these overcompensations offer insights into the source's personality. You may not get exactly what you want, but what you get may prove to be more important."

"We're talking about dog poop," Andy said. She put her hand on her phone. "How do I find out what hospital a person's been taken to, if he's been beaten up?"

"You call them," Ladderback said. He turned away from her and began to work on the last obituary of the day.

So Andy began to call. She was on the phone with the fourth hospital admissions department when the newsroom receptionist called out, "Anybody work here named Cosicki?"

She waved, put the hospital on hold, and her heart jumped when she heard his voice, slurred and somewhat sluggish, "You got a car?"

"Sure I do. But, how are you? Are you all right?"

"You should never ask me how I am because I am the kind of person, when people ask me how I am, I tell them. Exactly. I have three cracked ribs. A fat lip. These disgusting yellow bruises around my eyes and mouth that will turn all kinds of fancy colors. I've been told I have had a minor concussion. And the forefinger of my left hand is broken, don't ask me how."

She broke the connection on the other line and asked him again if he was all right.

"I am not all right. I am not even half right. I'm calling to ask you for two favors. The first is, do you have a car so you can drive me home from this hospital and help me up the stairs to my apartment?"

He told her where he was and she saw that that was the second hospital she had called and the hospital had no Drew Shaws registered.

"They say you don't exist."

"I exist. My real name is Vidor Isidore Warshofsky. My family came over during the Glasnost immigrations. V. I. Warshawski and King Vidor were already taken, okay? Now, you have a car?"

"It's at home. I'd have to take a train to get to it."

"I can wait. Or you could get one from the motor pool. Don't they have cars reporters can take if they need to go someplace?"

"What's the second favor?"

"I want to see you naked."

"Drew, anyone could be listening on this phone."

"Should I speak louder? Naked. I want to see you. It has to do with the healing process. I did a story once on alternate therapies and there's this thing, it's actually in the Bible, where King David was so old they didn't know if he was alive or not so they put this young naked girl next to him and, surprise, surprise!"

She asked him for a number that she could use to call him back. She hung up and stared for a few minutes at a pile of mail.

"How do I get a car?" she asked Ladderback. "I need to go someplace and my car isn't here."

"You want to see him?" Ladderback said.

She blushed.

"You must have an assignment," Ladderback said. "They'll let you sign a vehicle out, but it will come back to Lange. He has to approve it."

"I was going to do a list, for Mr. Action, of people who had the most unpaid parking tickets, and Lange didn't think that was a good idea. He wanted me to write about people complaining about dog poop."

"Write this down," Ladderback said. He recited a telephone number. "This will put you into the city's Department of Streets. Tell them you are making a list of places in the city where dog droppings have been most evident."

"There is no way that the city would pay someone to keep track of that."

Ladderback returned to his work. Andy dialed. Not only was there a person who had the list, but the information was used to secure state and federal sanitation improvement grants and the *Standard* was preparing a five-part, what's-wrong-with-Philadelphia series on street sanitation. Was it a coincidence that she called or was the *Press* trying to beat the *Standard* to the punch?

Andy got a list of the top three of fifteen sites—one was near a public park bordering her old neighborhood.

"Would that be Mut Haven?" Ladderback said, going to his file cabinet.

She told him to stop listening in on her conversations. She called up the newspaper's motor pool and yes, there was a car but because she was a new employee and still on probation, Lange would have to sign it out for her.

"If I get this in by deadline we're going to beat the *Standard*," Andy said.

In that case, she was told, she could have the car immediately.

She picked up her shoulder bag and left Ladderback holding the file. He opened it, and looked at the yellow clipping of an article by Howard Lange about the dedication of a public park for dog walkers on what had been the exercise grounds of the St. John Cantius Home for Boys and Girls. The article ran with a photo that showed Councilman Szathmary and other dignitaries and some former members of the home. There, on Szathmary's side, was a fellow who could have been Ben Cosicki, but the caption identified him as "B. Brickle."

Ladderback hoped Andy would make it back before the deadline.

Everything really was going to work out okay, Drew Shaw explained as Andy almost carried him up the stairs to his third floor apartment in the Bellavista neighborhood.

"I'm getting paid sick leave and the publisher says he'll try to lease me a car while my MG is getting fixed. Uhh, go easy there."

"And the article you were writing about Fenestra?"

"On the back burner."

"All because Fenestra is taking out an ad," Andy grumbled.

"You should see the size of it. My publisher is dropping his suit and . . ." he paused as he stood in front of the apartment's door and brought out his keys with his one good hand, "I get to see you naked."

He tried to kiss her but she didn't want to be kissed, so he banged his bruised lips against her chin. "If I wasn't on painkillers, that would have really hurt."

She turned the key in his apartment door and smelled dust and engine oil. "The light switch is a little hard to find," he said.

She found it and saw a small sitting room with piles of books—biographies of Edward R. Murrow, Lincoln Steffens, Joseph Pulitzer, H. L. Mencken, Lafcadio Hearn—and boxed MG automobile parts in the corners spilling out onto the floor. She pushed away a laundry basket filled with clean but unfolded sheets and pillowcases that had been left in the center of the sitting area. She looked into his dark bedroom and saw that the bed hadn't been made.

"I didn't think I was going to have my finger broken when I went out," he said, painfully easing himself onto a threadbare convertible couch. "How good are you at making beds?"

"Good enough," she said. She carried the laundry basket into his bedroom and saw that it was surrounded by closets that bulged with more clothes: suits, sport jackets, an entire wall of polo and golf shirts. A huge mirror hung on the back of the bedroom door. Above the mirror was a banner: "You're brilliant, good-looking and bound to be rich. Get over it."

The sheets had been washed so much they were almost translucent. Andy put the bed together, came out and saw him looking glum. When he noticed her, he tried to raise his head, winced, and brightened.

There was no other chair in the sitting room so she sat on a stack of automobile parts. "So," she said. "Who's your lawyer?"

He shook his head, and winced.

Andy said, "You don't have one?"

"I have uncles in firms that deal only with Russian Mafia."

"Use them."

"No need."

He tried to shrug. "It's amazing what you can't do with broken ribs."

"The publisher is suing, then?"

"I told you, the publisher got what he wanted and he'll make sure I get what I want." He noticed she was scowling. "I hope it's not me you're mad at. I mean, if anybody has a right to get mad, it's me."

"So what you were doing in there, it was all a set up?"

"It wasn't a set up. But what I told you, about the publisher using me to get Fenestra to go along to get along . . ."

Andy stared at him for a while. "You want to know what happened to me after they took you outside?"

"I know what happened to you," he said. "I wasn't there, but, I can figure it out. They were concentrating on me, so you could get away, go back to the city, write up what happened and get told that the Press either isn't running it, or it's running it so small nobody's going to notice. Am I right?"

"They're not going to run the story," Andy said.

"Because it's the suburbs and . . ."

She let him talk. She could stop him and tell him what had happened beside the railroad tracks, but he seemed like he had to talk, he had to put the experience into words to make sense out of it, and even if he was leaving things out, or his reasoning was wrong, or if he was patronizing her without realizing he was doing so, she let him keep talking because to be strong, right now, she had to shut up, even if she wanted to scream at him that there was absolutely no excuse for letting himself be used like this, and that journalists whose biographies he had acquired and possibly even read would have been enraged to hear of what he had been put through, and how easily he had backed down.

But as he spoke Andy found herself doing something that she didn't think she would have done with anyone—it had to do with what Ladderback had told her about how people change their tone when they lie, or when they want to cover something up. And it also had to do with what her mother had told her, about how people talk about some things to keep other things quiet.

She saw that this banged-up, beautiful man who had made beautiful love to her was trying to hide the fact he was terrified. She had seen rape victims react in a similar, glib, I-know-what's-going-on, the powers-that-be-are-going-to-make-everything-right when she wrote about a rape crisis center near the Penn Campus. It didn't matter how horribly the women had been treated by their assailants—they all tried, at one point or another after the incident had occurred, to talk it out, rationalize away the after-images that haunted them, the strange hallucinations they experienced when they saw in shadows the face or hands of their assailant, the hideous memories triggered by odors, colors, half-remembered images of car seats, stairwells, odd places in their lives that they would normally not even notice, that had since been turned into symbols of helpless terror.

Andy had interviewed the director of the center, as well as one of the aides, each of whom had been a victim of assaults, as well as two women who had recently been treated at the center. And she had learned that, no matter how much post-trauma counseling is offered, no matter how long therapeutic strategies are employed, no matter how much the rapist is punished, or how relatively normal a person's life may be after the attack, there is no "getting over it," as the director told her. "It's not like getting back on the horse after you've been thrown. It's like knowing that, at any time, what you think is safe and secure, can turn into a nightmare. The only way you can begin to get past it, even in a small way, it to understand that the only person you can trust and rely on, no matter how much you think you failed or that it's your fault, is yourself."

How would it have been, Andy asked herself, if she had not fought back and knocked that goon down? What might have happened if she hadn't landed on him, if he had overpowered her and harmed her in some way? Would she be where he was now, trying to find a reason to believe that just doing nothing would put Humpty Dumpty together again?

"Uh, Drew," she interrupted him. "You shouldn't be alone tonight. Do you have family you can call?"

"Too much family. When this gets out I'll be surrounded by sisters, day and night. Sisters I don't need. You, I need."

"Drew . . ."

"Okay, I don't exactly need you. I can manage. I can sit here, in pain, while my sisters jam black bread and overcooked cabbage down my throat. But, I did this story once on the medicinal use of sexual arousal for healing purposes. The doctor had a Grenadan M.D. with this huge, multimedia porn collection but the funding he got from these Hollywood moguls for his research you wouldn't believe. He said sex has a very positive effect on the healing mechanism."

"So does fighting back," Andy said.

He looked away and she wanted to hold him, then. She came up to him, gently kissed his swollen lip. "Of all the people I'd want to be with tonight, you're . . . up there, okay? But I have to do something first."

"The bathroom's right over there."

"It's work related."

"It can wait."

"It can wait. But I can't. I have to find out if I'm right about something."

"You can use my computer and do a search on the Internet."

"I have to find out . . ." should she tell him? She looked at the darkening bruises around his eyes and saw that, right now, he wanted her to be with him, to hold him, to tell him that things would be all right.

But things wouldn't be all right until she found if, after her father was almost killed in that trash truck, he, too, learned to trust himself, and only himself, and that, just possibly, the reason that he got himself dead, was that you can trust yourself and still end up horribly, terribly wrong.

10 last word

Though she had loaded up the meter, Andy found several parking tickets stuck under the windshield wiper of the *Press*'s dented Ford Taurus. Was it because the *Press*'s banner logo was printed on both sides of the car? Was there, perhaps, a meter maid (or man) who didn't like the *Press*'s editorial policy?

Then Andy noticed from the plate numbers on the tickets that all the tickets had been made out to other cars, and that they had been placed under her car's windshield wiper. She looked down the narrow street of three-story row houses and saw the Parking Authority tow truck hooking up another car that had been decorated by a blizzard of parking tickets.

She then scanned the windows of the row houses. Was this some neighborhood asshole's cute way of getting rid of cars on the street? Jam a bunch of old tickets on the car at right about the time the tow truck passes through? If the tow truck operator doesn't check license plates, he'll assume that whoever parked the car is a hardened offender and tow the vehicle.

She thought of her father's yellow Buick. The police report said it had been locked. So what happened to the car? Was it still sitting out in front of the club where he died?

Andy pulled the stack of tickets off the window, threw them in the backseat with the dessicated, half-eaten container of cheese fries that the previous driver had left. She started the car and moved out onto Kirkman Street, took a right turn at Fifth, and headed north through the edge of Society Hill toward Redmonton.

At a red light she opened her shoulder bag and checked her notepad. One of the dog "infestation" sites—Mut Haven—was in Yorkvale, a neighborhood on the edge of Redmonton that she would have to pass through in order to reach Sackawinick Street, where her father's car might be.

Like Redmonton, Yorkvale was a grid of row houses that had sheltered factory workers during the nineteenth century. While Redmonton had decayed after the closing of the locomotive factory, Yorkvale had gentrified. Corner bars and grocery stores turned into cafés and gourmet take-outs as what had been cheap housing for immigrant laborers was bought and renovated during the 1970s and "gentrified" into tidy, primly renovated yuppie habitats, with stained-glass window inserts, bright red doors, polished brass door-knockers, carefully tended floral displays in sidewalk barrels and planter boxes, and streets lined with high-end import sedans.

Redmonton was less than a mile farther from Center City, but the wave of gentrification had stopped at the grassy park lined by benches and flower boxes, surrounded by a waist-high stone wall, where, at the open gateway leading to the park, a small bronze statue of a bull terrier gazed southward toward the distant towers of Center City.

She left the car in a space on the Redmonton side of the park, where she could see the broad dome of the old Hampton Bank branch next to the dark cupola surmounting the blotched, tin roof of the locomotive factory.

She entered the park through a smaller gateway beside a cluster of 1960's "modern" row houses—sharp angles, edges, corners, and *fenestrations* (was that the right word?) of glass block windows, skylights, and open vestibules barred by wrought-iron gates. On the corner of the cluster was a blue historic marker that identified this as the former site of the St. John Cantius Home for Boys and Girls.

What had it been like when her father lived there? She tried to imagine a dark, gloomy Victorian structure, but it just didn't fit in the bright afternoon sun. She looked into the park and saw an old man sitting on one of the benches watching a middle-aged woman in a Philadelphia-lawyer tweed jacket and khaki skirt talking on a cell phone as she walked what appeared to be a dust mop with feet.

Andy got out her pad and pen and approached the woman. Before Andy could even identify herself, the woman shook her head at Andy, slapped the cell phone shut, yanked her dog away, and headed purposefully out of the park.

"Wait," Andy shouted, "this is about dogs."

The woman stopped, gave Andy a once-over.

"I'm doing something on dogs and this park and people complaining."

"Complaining about the media?"

"About people not cleaning up after their dogs."

The woman stared suspiciously at Andy, then she pointed to the old man on the bench. "You should ask him. He came here yesterday morning and he can't get enough of the place."

"But, ma'am—"

The woman's dog started barking at Andy. "You'll excuse us," the woman said. "We don't *talk* to the media." She pulled her dust-mop-with-feet away and marched quickly, her ankles wobbling on high heels, back to one of the modern row houses.

That left the old man, who sat on a bench on the Yorkvale side of the park, facing Redmonton.

Andy approached him, identified herself, and said, "Look, I'm not here for any big reason, I just want to ask people about the dogs in the park, okay?"

Andy felt the man scrutinizing her and so she decided to scrutinize him. His skin was blotched and thin, his cheeks marred by shaving cuts. He had dark, horn-rim sunglasses over his eyes, a faded driver's cap with a dark stain on the rim. Though it was hot enough to make Andy wish for shade, the man wore a rumpled yellow, windbreaker zipped up to his neck. His dark blue pants, which were clearly two sizes too big, had that shine of frequently washed polyester. On his feet were a pair of brown-and-white-striped suede sneakers.

"Can I ask you some things?" Andy said.

He took a long, slow breath that puffed up the windbreaker. "Of course, young lady," he said with a voice that, though thin, seemed to project through her. "Can I call you young lady? Some ladies who are also young can be touchy about that."

Andy let him.

"Forgive me if I assume that it isn't the dogs you're interested in, but the way this park affects those who live near it. That's the real story, I think, and it's never really been covered because people think this is just a place for people to walk dogs. But it's much more than that. Much more. This park is a monument to a very difficult struggle that residents of Yorkvale and Redmonton fought with a suburban developer who thought a city was like some blank canvas, and he could do what he wanted without showing consideration to the people who lived there. He bought the old orphanage that used to stand up the hill there, promised that he would remodel it as residential condos, and then tore it down when the city didn't give him the tax breaks he was after. That orphanage was very important to the residents here. It was something we all used to point to when we wanted to feel as if we gave a darn about the unwanted children in the world, even if, the truth was, not a lot of the residents here cared a whit about the children themselves. They just wanted something they could point to, and when the developer tore the place down and wanted to turn this field here, where the orphan kids used to play, into a parking lot, we all got together and hit him with everything we had. He hit back, too. Got all kinds of consultants and paid flunkies on his side, but we got him because the only loyalty he had on his side was what he could buy, and you can only buy so much. We had a lot of spirit."

He gazed proudly at the open area. "This park is a monument to that spirit. Never doubt for a minute the value of human spirit. That's a lesson I've learned, and forgotten, and learned again."

Something about the man's voice brought Andy back to a moment when, as a youngster, she crawled up the stairs outside of Bep 'n' Betty's and heard a voice that sounded just like that.

"Our point-man on this fight," he went on, "was a fellow come back from the Vietnam War without an idea in his head what he'd do with himself, not much more than a pot washer in a restaurant. Our point-man had no family to speak of. He had no experience with local politics, trusted some of the wrong people, but ended up getting himself elected to the City Council because he was Hungarian and nobody around here had ever elected a Hungarian to City Council. It wasn't exactly a David and Goliath situation, but, sometimes, spirit is all you really need. The way the deal was cut, the developer had the land the orphanage stood on, but re-zoned for row houses, and we got this rezoned as a wildlife sanctuary."

"*This* is a wildlife sanctuary?"

"For funding purposes, yes. The city gets federal money to maintain it, though aside from cutting the lawn occasionally, the city stays clear. Those flowers you see are all put there by the people who live here. Not everybody likes this, of course. There's a cussedness in human nature that'll oppose any darn thing, especially now, with all the lawyers and professional types moving in, chasing out the working people who used to live here."

"And the dog statue?"

"That's a story, too. When we dedicated it, the media came out, and one of the former orphanage kids we rounded up told the reporter, a rather foolish individual, that he was the bastard son of some rich man, and the reporter was too stupid to see that the kid was pulling his leg and got into some trouble when he printed it. For a while after that, we got no coverage from anybody. Taught me a lesson about the media: Never make fools of them. They always have the last word. Am I correct, young lady?"

Andy had been listening to to him all this time and hadn't even opened her pad. "Okay. You live around here, right?"

"That depends on what you mean by 'here.' My home was, still is, in Yorkvale. Had my office in Redmonton. I used to walk through here every day on my commute."

"So you saw a lot of people walking dogs?"

"Every day, rain or shine."

She wrote that down. "Did you hear people complaining about people not cleaning up after them?"

"I heard people complaining, about that and other things. It was my job to listen to people. Part of it."

"Did you ever see anyone try to do anything about it?"

He crossed his legs. "I'm afraid I don't understand you. By see, do you mean, with my eyes? Because when I used my eyes, I tried only to see the good things, though, I assure you, there was enough opposition, more than enough, if I wanted to see it."

Andy had written *see only good things* and *more than enough opposition*. "There's a city law that says people who don't clean up after their dogs can get fined three hundred dollars. Its the same as littering. Did you ever see anyone call the cops or get arrested for not cleaning up after their dogs?"

He thought about that. "Let me make sure I understand you. You said that a law exists and that the law provides a penalty, in the form of a fine, and did I ever see anyone call the cops or get arrested. Are you asking me if I've ever been arrested? Are you really asking me that?"

Andy counted to ten. She had once interviewed a group of old, retired, University of Pennsylvania employees living in a group home near the Penn campus, and some of them acted a little crazy when she asked questions about how things had changed over the years and this guy was certainly acting a little crazy.

She heard the angry sound of a car screeching to a halt at the stop sign on the street outside the park.

"They drive too fast, those professionals with their ridiculous cars," the man said. "They run stop signs. Their alarms go off all the time. I've always hated cars. I've never learned how to drive and I've never owned a car in my life and I get done in by a federal agent pimping a parking lot!"

Before she could say anything, it was as if his anger had opened an escape valve and all the steam had blown off. He sighed and said, "Forgive me. It's been a while since I've talked to the media."

"That was also part of your job?"

"It was not part of the job but I was expected to do it, and to refuse to do it was to confess that I had done something underhanded or had something to hide, though I never, ever, in my entire life as an elected official, had anything to hide."

Andy stared at the words she had written down. "You were the point-man."

"And you were much smaller when your father introduced me to you, Ms. Cosicki. It would be pleasant to see you now, but the circumstances are not. I have no willingness to talk to the media and I am no longer under any obligation to do so. And don't tell me about how I can finally tell my story—that's how the *Standard* tried to get me to talk to them and I refused them and I sincerely hope that your paper did not dream up this dog business as a pretext and sent you to interview—what did you rascals call me?—"Double Dip" Szathmary, because they were afraid to send anyone else."

He got up and walked awkwardly past the dog statue and out of the park.

Andy went after him. "Nobody sent me," she said. "I picked this place. It was convenient. It was close. I wanted to see what happened to my father's car. It was my idea to come here."

"So fate sent you," he said sourly as he braced himself with his hand on the park's wall, as if the effort of moving quickly had tired him. "Your father drove me home from the jail yesterday morning in that car. I assume it's still parked in front of your grandfather's nightclub, unless the Reverend's boys have decided to strip it for scrap."

He started moving slowly on the sidewalk outside the park, one hand on the wall to steady himself. "I haven't gone beyond this park since I got out, Ms. Cosicki. Your father wanted me to come to lunch with him, but I refused. My good memories are here, I told him. He was persistent, I'll admit. He kept trying."

"Was this yesterday?"

"When else? He said it was just going to be a lunch, he said, but I knew him better. He wanted me to sit down and make peace. But I'm not at war with anyone. If there are people who don't like me, well, I'm sorry but I no longer have anything left to give. I told him that. He said, 'What about that spirit?' I told him that now that I have become an old man, I want to be only an old man."

Another car raced by, or was it the same car? Andy saw the receding taillights of a Lincoln.

Szathmary stopped again, put his hand on his middle. "I'm sorry, Ms. Cosicki. If I had been with your father . . . If I had gone with him instead of staying in this park, if I had been with him when he went looking for whatever he wanted, they would have killed me, most likely, but not him. He could keep secrets. I could never keep them. I never wanted to hide anything."

"Who were these people?" Andy said.

He shook his head. "He never said. He didn't have to. It's not the people, it's the cussedness of human beings that I can no longer tolerate. In the prison I found I could rise above it, because we were all united in our pathetic hatred for the things that put us there. So it didn't make a difference, to me, and somehow, my people sensed that. Know what they called me in jail? The judge. They thought that I could settle things, make things right, and they trusted me because I never hid anything. I was honest. Why couldn't they let me be that way here?"

"You solicited a bribe," Andy said.

Szathmary raised himself up. "I did not. The tapes were altered to suggest that. What I said was that anyone coming into the city or a neighborhood making any kind of change must show consideration."

"And put out street money?" Andy said. "That's not a bribe?"

"As far as I'm concerned, street money is an act of grace," Szathmary said. "It is a contribution to a community's welfare. It is a way to show that you care. It is a way of acknowledging spirit. People in this city have their dignity. They are not stupid, they won't sell their vote for a ten dollar bill. But they'll be loyal to the death for a person they believe respects them, cares for them, looks out for them."

"All for a ten dollar bill?"

"No!" Szathmary shouted. "Didn't your father tell you anything? It's not about what you get, it's about what you owe."

"Then why, when you were on trial, didn't you try to fight back? Why did you let them cut you to shreds?"

He came to the corner and he almost collapsed. Andy moved in to help him but he waved her away. "I did what I thought was right."

She stepped out toward him but he waved her off. "This interview is over, Ms. Cosicki."

"Councilman, you look like you could use some help."

He smiled. "Funny, how your father said the same thing. Just about every day I saw him when he would visit me in jail, and he said it yesterday, he did. And I told him the same that I told anyone who supported me. I said to him, 'Thank you, but I owe you so much already.' "

He continued across the street. Andy watched him for a minute, then turned and was halfway back to the park when she heard the screech of the car's brakes and a hideous thump. Szathmary's body flew up over the car's front end and fell on the windshield like a flimsy marionette. A panicky teenager in the driver's seat put his hand over his mouth, looked like he was going to be sick, and sped off.

Andy would later tell the police that she didn't see a license plate, but she was sure it wasn't a gray Lincoln.

11 our andrea

"That," Bardo Nackels said to Andy when he put down the phone, "was the publisher."

Nackels put his cowboy boots back up on the copy desk, rubbed his nose, and turned to Andy, who sat beside him in the painfully hard wooden chair editors had reporters sit in when editors were editing the reporter's work. "He said Howard Lange is an absolute genius for hiring you; hear that, How?"

"Loud and clear," Lange's voice quaked through the speakerphone. "If you check the files, you'll find that I gave Szathmary his first interview, right at that very park. It must've stuck in my mind when I gave our Andrea the assignment."

Andy folded her arms. She was tired, more tired than she'd ever imagined she could be. She wished she could close her eyes and be home in bed when she opened them.

Lange said, "I'd come in and do a column on it, but I'm here and you're there and let's just see how it plays. You want to do a page one refer?"

Andy's heart jumped. A refer was a reference, a notice on page one that a big story—her story—was inside.

"Considering that Szathmary turned down everybody that tried to get to him when he got out of jail yesterday," Nackels continued, speaking loud enough so Lange could hear him through the speakerphone, "I think a refer is cool. Just answer me one thing, How. Why didn't we send somebody down to interview him?"

"Because I was thinking of doing a column on him myself," Lange said. "You know, I got all those awards for the series that put him away. I'd had something set up for lunch, but it didn't work out."

"He didn't like sweetbreads?" Nackels said.

"I think it's pretty damned impressive what I turned in," Lange snapped.

Andy wanted to jump into the speakerphone and pull herself through the miles of telephone wires and come out at Lange's home and ask him if it was her father who had set up that lunch, but she was just too tired.

It had been hard enough to see Szathmary die because she had never seen anyone die and maybe that was why she couldn't really let go and let the grief about her father's death finally claim her. She had felt it coming on but couldn't give in to it immediately because she had to run out into the street and prevent the cars from running over the councilman's still warm but so completely and thoroughly dead body. Then she had to drag him away, which she thought would have been easy but was almost unbearably difficult because he was so heavy, far too heavy for someone who seemed so thin and frail. She looked pleadingly at the windows of the row houses. Had anyone been watching? Could some just rush out here and take over so Andy could sit down and cry?

No one came out. Maybe they weren't home, or maybe they didn't want to get involved. Andy grabbed Szathmary by his arm but felt the skin stretching around a broken bone. She dropped the arm and put her hands under his underarms and his battered head began to drag on the asphalt. Then she smelled urine and saw that his sphincters had let go.

There was just no easy way to do it. Not only was he heavy but the cars along the street had parked so close together that she had to drag him down three car-lengths before she found an opening wide enough. She would have called an ambulance but while she was dragging him she set off a proximity alarm in one of the cars and she had to wait until it cycled off before she got out her cell phone and dialed 911.

She sat down next to him, watching the blood stream out of his mouth as she called in to the newsroom what she remembered of his conversation with her, leaving out the parts about her father.

People came out when the first police car arrived. Three police cars pulled up, blocking traffic around the park, only to let some of the traffic flow through because the ambulance had to get in and the ambulance was stuck in the traffic.

The police were surprisingly nice, asking her again and again who she was, where she lived, if she had any I.D., why she was here, where her car was parked, where she had been standing when she saw the car hit Szathmary, what the car *might have* looked like, if she could tell what kind of license plate the car might have had, what the driver might have looked like, if the councilman rushed into the street, if the car rushed into the councilman. Finally someone arrived, a Lieutenant Everson, and said, "You look like you might have been through a lot today," and, after taking her telephone number, gave her his card and said, "You've been very decent. We'll call you if we need you. You think of anything you want me to know, you call me. If not, you might want to get some rest. Though," he paused, his eye probing her, "I don't think you're going to sleep much. If you need to see somebody to talk it over with, I can give you some names."

It took a long time to get the *Press* car past the police car blocking the road because cars and trucks from the other media had blocked the street, too. She recognized a TV reporter in front of one of the satellite-dish trucks looking at her contemptuously, curious about what a reporter for the *Press* did that was so special that the cops let the *Press* in, but kept everyone else out.

Andy drove the *Press* car through the warren of row houses that opened onto a street that was a few blocks from the house she had lived in when she was a baby. The apartment was in the top half of a row house on Pardue Street, one among so many others forming a wall of dull, tired, rust-colored brick. A few houses had sprouted bay windows, cut-glass transoms, carved wood doors, flags, window boxes, and carefully restored ornaments that mark a structure that has been officially gentrified.

But most were boarded up, slashed by the bright paint of graffiti, the cellar windows broken open. Even on the worst streets, there was movement: a lone kid swaggering toward town, an old couple waiting for a bus, a guy crouching on the sidewalk fussing with the front tire of his car.

Every house on the street was made of the same brick, but go in any direction and, though you couldn't see how the tiny details on the houses changed, you would eventually come to a corner and feel so unfamiliar that you could have gone into a different city.

She drove to Sackawinick, the wide street ending at the domed Hampton Bank branch building, its front door blackened from a failed arson attempt. Her grandfather's old nightclub was so much smaller than she remembered from when her father would push her by in her stroller.

Along the street, the sodium vapor lamps were beginning to flicker to life and under their weird, orange-pink glow, it was easy to spot the ruined entrance to the bar where her grandfather had burned to death and now, her father had been found. A recently tied strip of yellow police crime-scene tape hung listlessly from a vacant, rotting door frame.

Her father's car was gone.

She turned off the engine and stared at the building under the twilight sky. Like many buildings that had suffered under suspicious circumstances, it had never been rebuilt, becoming one more wound in the body of the city that never healed. Above the narrow, boarded-up front window the remnants of a sign hung, its words indistinguishable but its faded orange and green colors miraculously surviving the neglect, fire, and weather that had doomed the rest of the structure, and most of the other houses in the row.

The weathered, painted sign, whose lights had long been ripped away, proclaimed that this was the Straight Up Club. On the brick facade were other signs—graffiti tags in wild, violent slashes of spray paint.

She became furious without knowing why. What was it about this life that took things from people without reason? Her grandfather should not have died in the fire. Her father *should not* have died, either. Her father *should not* have even been here, with or without Szathmary.

Why had her father gone in there in the first place? He certainly hadn't gone inside when he was with her. It had come up every once in a while in conversation with her parents. Her mother would occasionally say things about how much fun it was to work where they had such great music, and that her grandfather would have loved her, had he lived to see her.

And her father would get really quiet.

As she stared at the place, she wanted to believe in ghosts, so she could imagine herself in her grandfather's presence and have her grandfather reveal, like the ghost of Hamlet's father, the secrets that would turn so many of the people around her into villains and fools.

Though a faint breeze ruffled the crime-scene tape, the ruined facade of the old nightclub remained mute.

Movement around another facade, about fifty yards past the well-lit billboard for the First Church of God Harmonious; she saw, or rather smelled, the odors of roasting garlic and simmering tomatoes coming out of what had been Bep 'n' Betty's Luncheonette. Judging from the apparently homeless people who were lingering in front of it, this was the soup kitchen where her father's girlfriend worked.

She had never met the woman and her father had pretended she didn't exist. This was one of his secrets that he could not keep well. He said nothing, of course, but the smell of the cooking odors on his clothes, and the swagger that came into his movements when he came home from seeing her, indicated that whatever this woman did for him, it changed him slightly, as if he were just a little bit drunk, or, maybe, a little bit happy.

Andy drove by the soup kitchen, continued down to Broad Street, and then to Market Street and the *Press* building. She left the car with the others in the motor pool behind the loading dock where bundles of freshly printed newspapers—the *Press*'s final, evening edition was still going out—were loaded into the delivery trucks. She took the elevator up to the newsroom and was ashamed to admit to herself that she was incredibly proud of the fact that the first time her byline appeared in the newspaper, it would be over the last fateful interview of an important political figure, and not some stupid Mr. Action about dog manure.

Ladderback was working when she arrived. He glanced at her but said nothing. Nackels told her to wait while he edited three other stories. She put her head down on the pile of mail and then Nackels called her over to the hard chair and said, "Incredible work. Lange's on speakerphone. Sit tight and—"

That was when the publisher called. "Not only do we have the story," Nackels had replied, "but we had a staffer get an interview from him before it happened."

She watched Nackels run his fingers over the keyboard. He pulled up a facsimile of tomorrow's front page. It had a color picture of a Phillies baseball player, Aaron Miltcheck, stumbling while running, with large block type, SPILLED MILT. Nackels moved the cursor to the upper right-hand corner, opened a box, and typed: "I HATE CARS!" CONVICTED CITY POL SZATHMARY'S LAST WORDS BEFORE HIT-AND-RUN DEATH, PAGE SEVEN.

Andy said, "What he actually said was, 'I've always hated cars.' He was talking about inconsiderate drivers and car alarms."

Nackels hit a key that tried, and failed, to squeeze the text into the box. "Too many words," Nackels said. He wrote CONVICTED CAR-HATER SZATHMARY'S LAST WORDS.

He read it aloud to Lange.

"I don't think you can get convicted for hating cars," Lange said on the speakerphone. "How about, SZATHMARY: HATE CARS AND DIE."

"If only he didn't have such a long name," Nackels said. "You think anybody will remember him? When did he go to jail, twenty years ago?"

"SZATH'S LAST HATE?" Lange offered.

"We need more description," Nackles chewed his lip, "or they'll think he's on the Phillies' coaching staff."

A moment of silence passed when Lange said, "I got it. HATE AND DIE: JAILED POL'S LAST WORDS."

Andy wanted to say that Szathmary was out of jail, but she didn't have the energy.

Nackels typed it in. "It fits."

"Of course it fits," Lange said. "I'm done. Is our Andrea there?"

"I'm here," Andy said.

"Szathmary ate up a full page so we took it out of your column. Save the dogshit stuff for tomorrow, and lead with a different place, okay big girl?"

Andy said nothing.

"Call me if anything else comes up."

Nackles pulled up page seven. Andy saw two photos of Szathmary, one of them showing a grim prison mug-shot, the other of him smiling with a group of people in front of the dog statue. Szathmary was standing next to a person who looked like—

"You don't like the headline?" Nackels said. "Tough."

The headline read HIT-AND-RUN CLAIMS EX-CON COUNCILMAN. Below it was a byline: By Howard H. Lange, Editor-in-Chief.

"Lange sent this in a little while after the police report came in," Nackels said. "It's pretty tight. We didn't know you were with him, so we had to drop one of the pictures to make room for what you called in."

He pointed to three paragraphs at the bottom of the story. Andy read, "Moments before a hit-and-run driver would take his life, Szathmary bared his fangs at passing vehicles. 'I hate cars!' he snarled, insisting that he was a victim of a Federal agent pimping a parking lot."

Nackles changed it to *"I've always hated cars."* "Great quote," Nackels said.

"He didn't snarl," Andy said. "It was a nice day and the guy who killed him was driving too fast and making noise with his brakes."

"He might have snarled," Nackles said.

Andy read further.

Szathmary claimed to have "seen only good things" and that he encountered "more than enough opposition" as an elected official. He insisted that he was framed and that tapes made of him soliciting bribes were "altered," and that he was considering spending his way back into politics because "people in this city are not stupid," they're "loyal to the death" to candidates who "show consideration," which, for the Double-Dipper, was always known as street money.

"It's all about what you owe," Szathmary intoned as he stepped into the path of a speeding car.

"But that's not what he meant when he said those things," Andy said.

Nackles called up the quotes that Andy had dictated over her cell phone. "You called them in," Nackles said. "I sent a copy out to Lange. He put them in the text and sent it back. You got your notes, you tell me what's right."

Andy opened her notepad and saw that, yes, the quotes were there but the sense of what had been said was not. "He didn't say anything about running for office again. The feeling I got was that he wanted nothing more to do with politics."

"That's a feeling," Nackles said. "Politicians are charismatic people. They can make you feel anything they want you to feel to get what they want."

"But he didn't want anything," Andy said. She was about to tell him that Szathmary had turned down the lunch with her father, but she stopped herself.

"A convicted extortionist gets out of jail and all he wants to do is wiggle his toes in the breeze," Nackels said. "Sure, but what about the next day? Or the day after that? These politicians, they can't quit. Once they get a taste of power, they're like junkies. They just have to get another fix."

"But he really wasn't that way. He didn't intone anything. He wasn't ominous. He was harmless."

"He might have been," Nackels said.

At the very bottom of the column, she saw a line: *Press staff writers contributed to this report.*

"Who's the other writer?" Andy asked.

"Shep came up with that quote about him being at the orphanage."

He pointed and Andy read. "Before he enlisted in the army to serve in Vietnam, Szathmary was a counselor at the St. John Cantius Home for Boys and Girls, where he had previously been a resident. 'He always felt he had to be an example to us,' recalled Patrick Goohan, a former resident of the home. 'He wanted to be somebody we could look up to.' "

"Must've been pretty tall," Nackels said.

She had left her shoulder bag on Mr. Action's chair. As she returned to get it, Ladderback said, "Check your messages."

She was too tired to do anything more than glare at him and say, "No."

"A journalist always returns telephone calls," Ladderback muttered as he stood over his desk, cutting out articles from the *Press.*

"I'm quitting." She slumped in her chair. A light on her phone indicated she had voicemail messages.

Ladderback used the scissors like a barber, clipping quickly but delicately. He lifted a clipping, admired its clean, freshly-sheared edges, and gently put it in a file folder. "The job," he said, "comes with benefits."

"Free copies of the *Press*."

"And the *Standard* and *Liberty Bell*, if we ask for it," Ladderback agreed. "Then there is the benefit that accrues when your name is connected with everything you do."

"But I want my name on what I write."

"It can be to your advantage when others take the credit, especially when you are not pleased with the result."

She closed her eyes.

"Another is that research always yields valuable information that, for one reason or another, fails to make it into print."

She nodded at that.

"You were going to meet your father for lunch," Ladderback went on. "Lange was among those invited. He may not have known that you were also invited, but he did know that your father had died before you left to meet him yesterday."

He opened his file and showed Andy the clipping of Szathmary at the dedication of the dog park.

"Your father's relationship with Lange began here. This was among Lange's first assignments as a staff reporter. Your father told him that he was 'Ben Brickle.' The original article contained a quote from Ben Brickle."

His pale, stubby finger pointed at a line in the text. " 'Anything that's unwanted can come here, just like us kids did, when it was part of the Home.' Why would your father call himself Ben Brickle?"

He opened another file with an obituary page in an edition dated two days after Lange's piece. "You'll note, at the bottom, a box entitled 'Correction'. It says that one of the people quoted and pictured in the article was not identified correctly. He should have been identified as Ben Cosicki. Notice the spelling."

He showed Andy a third file. "Here is the clipping about the reunion of residents at the Cantius Home. At the reunion, it mentioned that they were starting a scholarship for orphans and that they were naming at after a tailor who made the children's clothes. This tailor was so popular that, according to Patrick Goohan, 'We all wanted to be his kid.' The scholarship is called the Kozceky Fund."

"Goohan's the one you got that quote from about Szathmary."

"Goohan was also invited to this luncheon," Ladderback said. "He said that your father mentioned that the luncheon would be for Ben's kids and some others. Did your father mention to you anyone else he wanted to bring?"

"Kids?" Andy said, emphasizing the plural.

"Getting these people together must have taken time. It is likely that your father could have been transporting some of the people, or meeting them, at the nightclub when he died. The police report mentioned that his automobile was found locked. You said your father never locked his car. Someone he was with, who witnessed his death and may not have known that he didn't lock his car, could have locked it and taken some other form of transportation away from the nightclub. Did you or your mother claim his car?"

"It was supposed to be where he left it," Andy said, "but I didn't see it when I drove through."

"You were looking for it?"

"I just had to go there, okay?"

"Before or after your interview with Szathmary?" When she did not reply, Ladderback said, "After. Szathmary said something to you to make you want to go there."

She took a long breath. "He said a lot of things. He said, back when the park was dedicated, he brought with him some kids who had been at the Home with him. He told me he was always open with the media and that he had nothing to hide. He said that my father had picked him up at the jail and wanted him to go to the lunch with him 'to make peace' and that he refused because he didn't want to."

"So your father, who was known for staging lunches in which mutual antagonists settle their differences, could have been doing something similar, with you as an observer, possibly even a participant. Szathmary certainly has no love for Lange, whose articles in the *Press* portrayed him in a negative light."

"He said kids?"

"I believe so. That was what the source said."

"And that was?"

"Whitey Goohan. He's the maitre d' and part owner of Jimmy D's."

"Kids," Andy repeated. "The only other person he would call a kid is Logo, Logan Brickle."

"Of the banking family?"

"My father used to get him out of trouble. We sort of grew up together. When my parents and his mother got together, Logo and I were supposed to go off and play somewhere else."

"Your parents were friendly with the Brickles," Ladderback said, as if that was the oddest thing in the world.

"My father knew Kellum because Kellum would come to my grandfather's nightclub and my father would sort of, take care of him."

"Keep him out of trouble?"

"I guess that's what you could call it."

"So we have the following luncheon guests," Ladderback said. "Douglas Szathmary, former councilman, former counselor at the Home—"

"He said, before he ran for councilman, he worked in a restaurant."

Ladderback went to his files. "That would be Bep 'n' Betty's. Anthony Adamo owned the restaurant with his wife. He also managed slum apartment dwellings in Redmonton and in other neighborhoods, the kind of places where rent is paid in cash." He opened a file that contained several clippings from the *Press* and *Standard*, as well as *Liberty Bell* magazine. "His office was allegedly used to launder funds for the South Philadelphia crime families. He backed Szathmary and managed his office, as you know."

"Why would Szathmary have had anything to do with him?" Andy said. "Szathmary wanted people to look up to him, but with somebody like *him* with him . . ."

"We never found an answer to that," Ladderback said. "Our editorial writers specialize in asking such questions because, sometimes, posing a question that can't be answered obscures a truth that we already know but don't want to face."

"That Szathmary made a deal with the devil?"

"Politics is the science of making deals, with every kind of individual or group, at every level of society. When Szathmary returned from Vietnam, the orphanage that had employed him was closed and sold to a developer who would soon demolish it. The children with whom he had lived at the orphanage had all been placed in foster homes. Adamo gave him a job, the kind of job where Szathmary would be aware of Adamo's criminal activities. When Szathmary decided to fight to preserve the orphanage's exercise grounds, Adamo could have helped in that fight."

"Szathmary told me that they hit the developer—those were his words, they 'hit' him—with everything they had."

"Perhaps Adamo's criminal relationships were part of that hit."

"Szathmary said that they won because of spirit, and that, sometimes, spirit could be enough."

Ladderback nodded. "A spirit that, as he would see it, cut across divisions, boundaries, notions of good and bad, and unified a community around a single issue. This would not exclude criminal activity."

"But I don't see Szathmary letting himself get trashed at his trial and go to jail just because his boss, who had betrayed him, had helped him out a long time ago."

Ladderback went to his file cabinet. "Every neighborhood in the city has criminal elements operating within it, and though the nature of the crimes vary considerably, you can get a sense of a neighborhood's relative peace, or lack of it, by the number of calls made for police assistance. The *Standard* does a yearly ranking of the city's safest neighborhoods, based on calls to the police as well as types of crimes. It groups the statistics by neighborhood, as if it is a neighborhood's fault that crimes take place within it. Here are the statistics for the Redmonton and Yorkvale neighborhoods. Notice that during the years that Szathmary was on the city council, the number of crimes reported to the police in these neighborhoods were at their lowest. While there are many theories as to why the number and varieties of crime in neighborhoods change, and also about why people do and do not report crimes, it is clear that, while Szathmary was in office, Redmonton and Yorkvale were as relatively safe and peaceful as the more affluent neighborhoods like Chestnut Hill. Adamo was supposed to have managed some of the criminal elements operating in Redmonton."

"Another deal with the devil?" Andy said.

"Not just the devil." He removed a clipping from his file cabinet, this one from the *Press*. "This is how the *Press* does what is essentially the same story. Instead of listing statistics about crimes in a spreadsheet, the *Press* generates a map of the city and uses it to blame crime on the police."

He showed her a map of the city with numerous areas shaded or cross-hatched. Above the map was a headline WHERE THE COPS ARE. "This specific map was also compiled during Szathmary's political career."

Andy looked at the map and saw a huge, dark blotch covering Redmonton and Yorkvale representing the highest number of police patrols in the city.

"You don't get that number of police patrols," Ladderback added, "by merely calling the police commissioner on the phone and asking for them. You align yourself with political forces affecting the police, involve yourselves in fund-raisers benefiting police charities, and you block or inhibit legislation aimed at police budget reduction or changes in manpower."

She could sense he was going to say something else, so she said it for him. "And you look the other way when a retired police sergeant has a nightclub where people from the suburbs can have their fun and go home."

"Possibly, yes. Your grandfather was in the vice squad. He was certainly aware of illegal activities within the city."

"He was more than aware of them."

Ladderback showed her another clipping from the *Press*: SEPTA SAYS, MORE BUCKS, MORE BUSSES. "The *Press* doesn't portray public transportation in quite the same way the *Standard* does. The *Standard* looks at public transportation as a diseased organ within a dying city that, if it were run correctly, would cut down on automobile congestion along commuter roads, but because it is run incorrectly, has become a kind of righteous punishment for suburbanites who can't drive to work. The *Press* sees public transportation as directly symbolic of the city's lifeblood: People take busses, trains, and trolleys in order to move about the city, and most of those who use public transportation within the city, including the majority of SEPTA's employees, read the *Press*. So the *Press* looks at SEPTA as a cultural entity, an element of urban life that is distinctive and vital.

"This article, also dated during Szathmary's political reign, shows how funds from a fare increase were to be spent. Notice two new bus routes going through Redmonton and Yorkvale."

"Another deal?" Andy said.

"You don't get a new bus route by asking the driver to go down your favorite street. It is a political favor that can only be obtained at high levels."

"So why, if he was doing such a great job, didn't he say that when he was on trial? Why didn't he fight back?"

"You asked him that," Ladderback said, "and what was his reply?"

"He said he was doing what he thought was right. Just before that, he got mad at me, like I wasn't understanding something."

"And that was?"

"He said, didn't my father tell me anything—it wasn't about what you got, but about what you owe."

"We have our answer then," Ladderback said.

"To why he didn't fight back?"

"To why Szathmary refused to accompany your father to his peace-making luncheon, and, possibly, to the identity of the person responsible for your father's death."

He folded his hands. "Do you want another assignment?"

"Aren't you going to tell me who killed him?"

He repeated, "Do you want another assignment?"

She said, "I'm tired. I'm hungry. I . . ." she sighed. "I want to go home."

"Check your messages," he said.

She glared at him, stabbed the phone, and listened to Mrs. Schweitzer give her suggestions for other stories she could write that her husband just wasn't paying attention to, and Ganeesh Ryan, from the Parking Authority, calling about a "yellow Buick. If I'm not in the office when you get back, you can call my cell phone." He left the number. Andy dialed it.

"We towed the car because someone stuck a wad of tickets under the windshield and the driver didn't bother to check if it was, you know, on the list," Ryan told her. "You'll find it in the impoundment lot on Delaware Avenue. I can't waive the towing charges because your father isn't on the list anymore."

"It's okay."

"If you can get $79.50 in cash, a valid driver's license, and mention my name, it's yours."

"I'll do that," Andy said. "And, thanks, by the way."

"One more thing. You're doing that Mr. Action thing?"

"I am but . . . who told you?"

"There's a guy, some preacher, who has a church and has started these nighttime services with all this music and, well, I live in York-vale, and the church is all the way in Redmonton, but it's pretty loud, you know?"

"You want the preacher to turn his music down?"

"Just a little. I can hear it even when I have the air conditioner on."

"I can't promise anything."

"If you print it up, just use my initials. He's a big guy in Redmonton. For somebody in the Parking Authority to complain wouldn't be quite right, you know?"

"He's on your list?"

"He's on them all."

12 car talk

After Andy left, Ladderback took the elevator down and asked the doorman at the *Press* Building to call him a cab. He went through the revolving door and toward the cab with his eyes almost shut. He could see shadows and changing patterns of light and make out, in the hazy space between his eyelashes, the driver, a thick, overweight Hispanic man who tapped his hands restlessly on the steering wheel. Ladderback opened the door, slid in, and closed it gently. Ladderback kept his eyelids down, but gripped the door handle so tightly that his knuckles glowed white under his skin.

He was used to cab drivers assuming that he was blind, or that he was so tired that he was about to fall asleep. He was, after all, at the age when people expect a plump man with thick glasses and soft, sagging features to lack the strength to keep his guard up. Some drivers, when seeing Ladderback's eyelids droop, would turn down their radios and then begin to deviate from the most efficient route. Ladderback would correct them, carefully but firmly, having memorized the route by studying the fingerprint-smeared Philadelphia street map on a wall over the *Press*'s metro desk.

Ladderback gave the driver an address.

The driver said, "This time of night, why you want to go to Redmonton?"

What could he tell him that would make sense? "It isn't far," Ladderback said. Though his partially shut eyes, he saw the driver observing him in the rearview mirror.

The ride was short, not more than three miles, with the driver running stop signs and peering warily into the shadows beyond the streetlights' glare, as if the muggers, killers, and drug addicts that were supposed to haunt the ruined sections of the city were about to come forward and identify themselves.

"This is it, man," the driver said, stopping suddenly.

Every moment in the cab was agony as Ladderback tried not to think of the vast open spaces just outside the cab, and the danger and uncertainty those spaces could bring. He forced himself to concentrate on the greasy handle of the door. It's just a lever. Move it one way, the door opens. There. Push outward. Raise up a foot. Put the foot down on the asphalt and hear the crunch of broken glass. Turn. Put the other foot down. Stand. Step back—

He didn't have time to close the door. The cab pulled away from him and Ladderback, his eyes still closed, stepped carefully backward, reasoning that he was somewhere near the sidewalk. He approached what he guessed was the old Straight Up Club.

With his eyes closed, he heard distant sounds of the city, the muted chatter of television sets playing behind open windows, the slamming of a car door, the thud of music blasting from a passing car.

He was trembling as he forced himself to remain standing. He felt the panic rising in him. He became short of breath. He could not bring himself to go into the building. He couldn't open his eyes.

Again, he told himself that agoraphobia was a *condition*, a set of *symptoms* and that, even if he had adverse reactions to the current drugs on the market, he could tell himself that there was nothing to be afraid of, that he was merely in a place that didn't have a roof and that he could easily get to a place that had a roof, so just calm down, try to control the breathing, slow it down until he could think clearly and just . . . open . . . your . . . eyes.

He did not know he had wandered into the street when he heard the sudden roar of the bus, a shriek of horns, and his eyes flew open as he fell, hitting hard on his left side, lying still, frightened, as he smelled the odor of the diesel engine, felt the heat of the motor waft toward him, heard the horn sound again and again, and then the hands of the driver, cursing about drunks, pulling him over, fingers going to his face, voice rough and weary, "You sober, or what?"

"I'm okay," Ladderback said.

"I don't think so."

"Just give me a few minutes," Ladderback panted, again forcing his breathing to become regular. "Thank you for your kindness."

"Only thing for you to thank me for is not running you over. The people out and about now are going to the Reverend's. Don't tell me you're one of his."

"I could speak with him," Ladderback said. He felt his panic subside, so he stood, opened one eye, and was so overwhelmed with vertigo that he fell down again.

"You're not going to do much walking, are you, old man?"

"I can crawl," Ladderback said. "How is the traffic?"

"It's traffic, what it is." The driver lifted Ladderback to his feet, and said, "I'm putting you in the bus and I'm putting you off the bus at the Sisters of Zion."

"I don't need a hospital."

"I'm not leaving you here." The driver walked him past the idling bus, and then stopped and rang a bell beside on a thick, steel door wide enough to admit a truck. "You *sure* it's the Reverend you're wanting to see?"

Ladderback smelled an oily, burnt aroma. Could this be the former Hampton Bank branch, where the arson attempt had been reported? He heard locks slide away and a door open.

The bus driver said, "This guy says he wants to see the Reverend."

"The Reverend don't see white people without an appointment, unless they belong."

"Tell him . . ." Ladderback tried to remember what he'd read about the Reverend in his clippings. "Tell him I want to talk to him. I talked to him a long time ago, on the phone."

"We don't obey the commands of white oppressors."

"I was hoping to get information about a person who died."

Ladderback heard a sharp, resonant, commanding voice. "Why do you come to a House of Harmony to speak of death?"

Ladderback opened his eyes just enough to see, in the baleful glow of street lamps, a reedy, narrow-eyed figure standing before him distinguished by a large hearing aid filling one ear. He had a face that had once been handsome, but had sharpened with age into a gaunt, angry mask. He was Hooks, surrounded by huge, beefy bodyguards.

Ladderback said, "I write obituaries for the *Philadelphia Press*. I spoke to Mr. Hooks many years ago, about Sergeant Francis McMann."

"And what did you do with what I told you?" Hooks said. "Did you tell the world that he was murdered, and that they burned down his club and made him out to be a saint, to cover it up?"

"I did what I thought was right," Ladderback said.

"If you call printing lies, and cheating murderers of God's judgment, the *right thing*, then you are in need of education."

"Educate me, then," Ladderback said weakly. He *had* to go inside.

"What are you really after, old man?"

Ladderback hesitated.

An older voice cut through. "He's here for the same reason anybody else is, Reverend. He needs to be healed."

It was a shriveled, pale-skinned fellow in glasses and a Teamsters baseball cap who had been trying to stretch his neck over the bodyguards to get a better view. He came forward and Ladderback risked another glance and saw thick glasses, a drooping nose, and a face long and lined by trouble. "We've never met, Mr. Ladderback. I'm Hank Norwood. I used to drive a *Press* delivery truck."

"Now Brother Norwood drives for me," Hooks said. "He has shaken off his burden and accepted a life in harmony with God."

Ladderback felt Norwood's hands on his arm. "Mr. Ladderback's okay, Reverend," Norwood said.

The temperature changed and Ladderback heard his steps echoing. He opened his eyes and saw that he was in a magnificent domed atrium, a marble-encrusted copy of the Roman Pantheon illuminated by naked lightbulbs hanging down from darkened chandeliers.

He looked closer: It wasn't marble but rotting, peeling, wood paneling painted to look like marble.

"We will go to the sacristy," the Reverend commanded. "And there we will give him what he truly wants."

The Reverend stopped and turned and Ladderback saw above the metallic green bow tie a face only slightly darker than his own. Hooks had thin lips, a broken nose bent to the right, and eyes framed by a pair of red horn-rimmed trifocal spectacles. Riding above that was a thick mat of rust-colored hair, holding so tightly to the skin that it suggested an unnatural attachment.

"You can't be healed unless you get down on your knees and beg for forgiveness," the Reverend said. He turned and the men closed in on Ladderback.

"I don't think forgiveness will help," Ladderback said.

"Nothing will help unless you're in harmony with God. So, you going to worship with us, now? You going to get on your knees in front of the Living Lord?"

"If you'll give me a few minutes of your time," Ladderback said.

"He wants to make deals!" the Reverend chuckled. "Everyone wants a few minutes of my time. What they really want is for me to do for them what they can't do for themselves."

He spun around, moving past a line of at least forty people who were leaning against a rotting wall of inlaid paneling. He entered a broad set of doors into what could have been the bank's boardroom, where more people sat on mismatched chairs, and then into a small, ruined but ornately trimmed office that must have once belonged to a senior bank executive, if not the president.

"Because you are an older man," the Reverend said, patronizing him, "I will let you sit. But you will have to watch and listen. Then you will have your turn."

Ladderback thanked him and sat on a hardwood chair that could have been from the same factory that made the torture seat near Abe Donitz's desk. He saw that a woman was there, sitting on a threadbare, flower-print couch that faced a dented steel secretary desk.

"I could give you a list of deserving folks that no white newspaper ever wrote up," Hooks continued. "But you don't have room for the deserving. You got too many disrespecting scum to write up, to show the black man and the black woman and the black children that learn the white European's language that black people are criminals or basketball stars but nothing in between."

"I believe you were written up once, in the *Press*, Reverend," Ladderback said.

"More than once, but that's a ghost life." He sat behind the desk and told the woman facing him to talk to him about her son.

The son had been paroled last week but hadn't come home. Could the Reverend say a prayer? The Reverend asked her if she was saying prayers and she said that she was, but she wanted the Reverend to pray also because she thought he was closer to God.

"I am no closer than you are," the Reverend said. "As close as you can be to anyone, God is always closer. But I will pray for him because everyone is worth praying for."

She thanked him and, on the way out, put some money in a sack held by the bodyguard closest to the door. A man came in, complaining that the police weren't chasing away the riff-raff around his bodega. The Reverend said, "We will talk to the police," and asked the man about his family. The talk shifted to sports and the man asked if, the next time the famous basketball star had some free time, he would be happy to have him visit the shop and maybe have his picture taken.

The Reverend said he would talk to the basketball star.

Again, money went into the sack, though, from the lack of sound, Ladderback guessed these were dollar bills.

Then came a flabby-faced house painter and a hatchet-faced woman who had hired him to paint her living room. The man wouldn't finish the job unless the woman gave him money to buy more paint. The woman complained that she had given the painter more than enough, but that he had drunk it up.

The Reverend secured a confession from the man—he had been drinking, but he also stated that the sum he had agreed on to paint the woman's living room was far too low, even if the woman had very little money. The Reverend nodded to the man with the sack, who dolled out what the Reverend believed was a proper amount.

"You will make sure that whatever you buy with this goes up on the wall," the Reverend said.

The supplicants continued, appealing to the Reverend for favors, hand-outs and, once, for revenge. "You should send your boys to get those drug dealers off the corner!" An old man yelled at him.

The Reverend waited until the man quieted down and said, "The person you call a drug dealer is a businessman. He pays for the privilege of being in business. It is not an easy business. He has enemies. He has competitors. He has to worry about people who would cheat him, rob him, or kill him. Why should he worry about you? He is not harming you. If he was harming anyone on your block, he would not be there."

The man said, "It's the folks he deals with. They're acting-up kinds of folks. They're calling me words."

"We will speak to them about their actions and their words," the Reverend concluded and money dropped into the sack.

A balding man entered with a dark five o'clock shadow across his face, in a freshly pressed, tan suit. He had a red carnation in one lapel, and a blue campaign button in his other lapel with his face on it, and the words WARSHOFSKY and JUDGE.

He extended a hand and the Reverend said, "You're running for a municipal judgeship."

He looked around the room and began with heavily accented English, "You got it, Reverend. Now, my family, we came from Russia, so we know what's like to be excluded—"

"No one excludes me!" the Reverend barked. "You want money or votes?"

"Any support you and your people would give . . ."

"You're in a firm?"

"Sure I am. We do a lot of work for the, well, I suppose you'd call them the Russian mob."

"Leave your card," the Reverend said. "Within the next two weeks I will send people to your firm who will indentify themselves as indigent. They will be represented by your firm on a pro bono basis by your most competent attorneys."

"Reverend, I'm not allowed to exactly *promise* any of this . . ."

"You are not promising anything. I'm telling you what will happen. I don't have to tell you what will happen if what I want does not occur." The Reverend looked away and Warshofsky looked around the room again, saying, "I'll be a good judge, by the way. I'll put the bad guys away. I'll give you safe streets."

The Reverend made a cutting motion under his chin. Warshofsky stopped and said, "Well, see you later." He passed by the man with the sack and reached in his pocket but the Reverend shook his head and the sack was not offered. Warshofsky handed over his card instead and said, "Bye, bye, now!"

Ladderback watched the Reverend's face grow heavy as the requests, entreaties, pleas, and cries for justice or divine intervention continued. As much as the Reverend maintained a dignified distance, the needfulness of the people wore him down.

When the last person left, the Reverend looked at Ladderback.

Ladderback waited for just enough silence to slip by before he said, "I want to ask you about Ben Cosicki. He died in the building next door."

Hooks stared at Ladderback until the silence was almost unendurable. "You want to know why he died. He died because I did not want him to live. Who was he with? He was not with me, though he wanted me to accompany him. Did he speak with me before he died? Everyone speaks to me, but only God speaks with me. Your questions have been answered."

Ladderback didn't move.

"You want me to say I killed him?" the Reverend went on. He leaned back in his throne chair and gazed at a piece of dingy, corroding paneling on a wall that, perhaps a century ago would have held a portrait of the bank's founder.

"I'll take the credit or the blame for anything bad that happens to a white man around here, because that's what you do, isn't it? You decide what happens and why and you point the finger at the man you want to blame. We got black folks perishing every day around here, and nobody's asking about them. A white man dies and suddenly we got visitors popping in." He grinned at his bodyguards. One of them said, "Amen."

He laughed and the bodyguards laughed with him, except for Norwood, who seemed embarrassed. "Reverend, I told you, Mr. Ladderback's okay. When they had the driver's strike at the *Press* after I backed my truck into that editor's car, one of the drivers had a mother who died and Mr. Ladderback gave a very nice write-up to her in such a way that management didn't know she was the mother of a striker, but, for us, it was like a message, that, as bad as it was to have to walk off a job, we were all on the same level when it comes to people living and dying."

Norwood gripped his hat nervously. "I don't know how that sounds to you, Reverend, but to me, it's a lot like what you preach."

The Reverend eyed Norwood as if Norwood was a bug that ran into the room from nowhere and that the Reverend didn't know if it would mess up his shoes to step on him. He said to Norwood, "Leave."

Norwood said, "I think I'll finish up in the motor pool. Nice to see you, Mr. Ladderback. After worship, I drive home some of the folks. You need a lift, stick around."

The Reverend watched him go. "I remember our conversation," the Reverend said. "I believe you called me because you wanted an African-American quotation in an obituary about an Irish cop."

Ladderback said, "You once performed at the Straight Up Club."

"It was no performance," the Reverend replied. "It was my first touch with God. We was playing the kind of tunes that inspired drunkenness and fornication, but the music came straight from the Lord."

"I was once given a list of telephone numbers relating to illegal activities at the Straight Up Club. Your telephone number was one of them."

The Reverend narrowed his eyes. "What you trying to put before me?"

"Ben Cosicki was a bartender at that club. After I wrote Francis

McMann's obituary, Cosicki called me and said that the sarge presided over many illicit activities and that if I ever wanted a real story, I should start with the phone numbers."

"You didn't call me," the Reverend said warily. He folded his hands and regarded Ladderback.

Ladderback said nothing. He had interviewed enough people to know that he and the Reverend had reached a point in which the Reverend was either going to welcome the interview as a chance to tell a story seldom told, set things straight, and bask warmly in the glow that attention from the media, even from an obituary writer, can bring.

Or he would end it and have his bodyguards throw Ladderback out.

Moments like this are fragile and sometimes require a gentle nudge. If the interviewer flatters the subject, or confesses personal admiration or sympathy, the sentiment must seem sincere. A shared interest, perhaps, or curiosity over an article of clothing, a picture of loved ones, a hobby in which the subject indulges, an odd possession—

The Reverend turned away from Ladderback and said, "Go from my sight, old man."

The bodyguards moved when Ladderback said, "That's a painting, isn't it?"

The Reverend smiled wryly and, as a pair of guards pulled Ladderback to his feet, the Reverend motioned Ladderback toward the dingy panel and said, "Tell me why you think it's a painting."

The guards released Ladderback and he moved slowly toward the panel that, Ladderback could see, was, in fact, a rectangular section of what could be decaying fabric or possibly even leather that was mostly flat, unreflective black, with smears of brown and very dark red.

"The placement," Ladderback said. He put his hand on the paneling beside it. "The wood here is faded slightly. A framed painting hung here some time ago, that could be viewed from where you're sitting. But there is also the work itself."

"Yes," the Reverend said. "Tell me about the work itself."

"I don't know anything about it."

"Don't be too sure, old man."

"It's dark, in the manner of Mark Rothko's major canvases, though it doesn't have Rothko's use of color to create space or set off areas within the painting. Here the colors suggest a chaotic formlessness, a . . ." Ladderback paused.

"Say it," the Reverend commanded.

"A mess from which things may cohere, but may not."

"You're calling this a mess?" the Reverend said.

"I'm saying that it depicts disorder," Ladderback said.

"You didn't say if you think it's beautiful."

"I don't think it's beautiful," Ladderback said. "The more I look at it, the more I don't think it's a painting. The colors here aren't from paint. There doesn't seem to be much that's intentional about it, except for these creases through the middle." He pointed toward a few cracked and flaking grooves running across the center. "This reminds me of a book jacket, or binding, actually. A covering that would go over a large book, perhaps."

"Perhaps," the Reverend repeated. He reached up and pulled it off the wall. "One of my parishoners put this in the sack. Said some of his kids found it while running through the sarge's place, that it looked old and had writing on it. Now, I'd never seen this in the sarge's place. For me it, was just a gig and a place to keep a stash."

He turned it over and Ladderback saw, carved into what was cured leather, *Record of Account and Trade. Hampton Colony Bank and Public Exchange.*

"So what looks like nothing on this side—what'd you call it—a mess that may cohere—is, when you turn it over, the cover of a book. So I asked these kids, was there a book, and they said it was rolled up with lots of papers and I said show me the papers and they showed me stuff that had been put in a part of the wall, that had been part of the vault of the very first bank that stood right here, that the fire opened up. Later, I found out that before they turned it into a nightclub, the sarge's place had been a warehouse for storing stuff that was recorded in these papers, most of them, which fell apart when I touched them but not before I got enough of them out, and saw what they had written on them, and saw my life, my history, every minute I had lived and doubted and refused to see the hand of God leading me through life."

He opened a desk drawer, took out a folder, removed one of a stack of brown, stained sheafs. "Look at this. All in rows and columns. You want beauty? Here's your beauty. Some man—and it would have to be a man because way back in colonial times, they didn't have women working in banks, did they? Look how careful the writing is. Look at how beautifully ordered it is. What do you see here in these rows and columns? So many barrels of this, so many casks of that and, what's over here? Do those look like names to you? With prices next to them? In pounds and shillings. Tell me what you think you're looking at. Tell me what's cohering."

"Slaves," Ladderback said.

"My grandpa worked at that locomotive factory and he told me, he told me that a black man couldn't walk in this building, even if it was to get his own money that he worked for. And he told me that it didn't bother him, because he would not want to go into this building to get his money because *his* grandfather told him that this building, and this bank, was built from money made from buying and selling all kinds of stuff, and most of it was slaves."

"But the Quakers banned slavery in Philadelphia," Ladderback said. "Philadelphia was a free city."

"But Redmonton was not part of Philadelphia until very late," the Reverend said, his voice growing louder with excitement. "So who cared if a refined colonial gentleman who had brought in a boatload of slaves, happened to unload it just a little further up the Delaware and march his cargo up the Sackawinick Creek to the Red Mountain, where, my grandfather told me, there was a tree with wrist- and leg-irons hammered into it for displaying the merchandise, and a branding iron cooking so the refined colonial gentlemen could put a mark upon their purchases after they worked out their transaction right here, on this spot, which is now owned, full, clear, and legal, by a man whose forefathers may be in this book, or another, or another."

"Have you told anyone—" Ladderback began.

"That I have evidence that the oldest bank in the country aided and abetted the slave trade? The B-Man knew. When I wanted money to buy the locomotive factory, the B-Man let it be known to the Hampton people, and, lo, did they provide so generously the funds for the purchase, on the agreement that I donate these very important artifacts to the bank's archives, which, I believe, is in an oil furnace, or some such destructive device. I only gave him a few pages and I never saw much of him, and then, who should appear on my doorstep yesterday but the B-Man himself, asking me if I would like to come with him to lunch and meet some people and settle some things. And I told him I have my connections, I have my lines of communication, I know the Hampton Bank is going to get itself bought out but that they can't afford a major scandal, and that I won't give it to them, unless they've shaken off the burden of selling tens of thousands, maybe a hundreds of thousands of African souls. And there's only one way of shaking off that burden that I can think of."

"You wanted more money?"

"I want a piece of the bank. Big one. Something I can't swallow in one bite. I want a seat on the board of directors. I want stock and options to buy more. And I'm going to get it, because they owe me, and what they don't owe me, they owe my people, and what they don't owe my people, they owe to God."

"What did Ben say when you told him this?"

"He said he would handle it. Then, yesterday morning, he called me from his car, telling me he wanted me to settle my differences with some people. I told him I don't settle differences. I fight back. He asked me to get into his car. I told him I have my own limo. I don't get into anybody's car for no reason.

"Then I went about my business, the business of finding harmony in this place that people have turned their back on, and who should arrive, but the cops. Mr. Co-sick-ee has died. And then, Mr. Fenestra, thinking I won't recognize the FBI scum that tried to bust me back before I found God, Mr. Fenestra comes around with all his body-guards around him, asking me, 'Any documents you can provide?' You think I'm surprised, after he's up and gone, somebody throws a fire-bomb at this building?"

"An arson report came in to the newspaper," Ladderback said.

"The outside of this building is stone and the front door is iron. You'd have to drive a truck through it before you could start anything worth worrying about."

Hooks carefully rehung the binding, put his papers away. Then he went to an armoire in a corner and removed a shimmering green eccle-siastical robe.

"Time for you to start praying, white man," he said.

Andy got the cash and took a cab to the impound lot. It was a rectan-gular, fenced-in tongue of asphalt sticking into the Delaware River behind the monumentally huge trash-smashing pier where the garbage trucks lined up at all hours of the day and night, their engines grum-bling and groaning as the drivers soaked up overtime while waiting to dump their collected horde into the stinking noisy, clanking contrap-tion that would sort it and crush it into bundles that would go onto barges that would go down to Delaware to places nobody wanted to think about, and come back empty.

She could spot her father's yellow Buick among the rows of vehi-cles, old and new, slumbering under the baleful floodlights. It wasn't the only yellow car in the place, but it was the only yellow Buick, a truly hideous shade of curdled lemon that had faded into a hue Andy's mother called "burnt dust."

Among the most significant questions a child of the suburbs asks a parent, even one as taciturn and unrevealing as Ben Cosicki, is, "Why'd you get this car?" Suburban vehicles are mobile, perishable statements of wealth, sex, power, social class, aspiration, and, occasionally, transportation. Children, even if they were born in a city, raised in a row-house apartment, and then transplanted into the suburbs as the rise of their parents' affluence seemed natural and inevitable, sense this, even if they can't articulate it. They're smart enough to see, from their car seats and seat-belt harnesses, that a car is both fact and fancy, necessity and luxury, a thing to get other things, a thing to make other people pay attention, or look away.

Children think that buying a car is like buying groceries: You go to this big place where they have too many brightly colored things that are almost but not quite alike, you pretend that you can tell the difference from one to the other, you pick one and then load up on all this other junk that you don't really need but you might-as-well get, and then pay for it on the way out. Because parents never want to have their children witness teasing, coddling, and humiliation from car salesmen (especially that stone-faced guy they keep in the back who is so cruel and efficient as he fills out the loan application), the new car arrives like a new baby: The parents park the kids with a trusted adult, depart with an air of expectation, and return with this new, strange, oddly aromatic shiny beast.

Andy remembered coming down the stairs of the row house to see her father's first car, a banged up, former yellow cab whose signage had been ineptly covered over with bee-sting-yellow spray paint that failed to match the car's faded buff. When she asked him why he got the thing, her father actually answered her: "With that color, people can see me coming."

Later, she learned that her father only bought American-made sedans so as not to offend the union executives he worked with, and that he made a point of buying them used, with a few dings in the side panels and maybe some rust around the wheel wells, so nobody would think he was so rich he could afford a new car. There was only one accessory he insisted that each of his yellow cars have: a decent tape player. Because he never locked his cars, the tape player was always getting stolen.

He would listen to music on those long and tedious errands, some of it from the radio, most of it on tapes he'd make in his office. Sometimes he'd bring along a tape from the collection he'd made when he was bartending at her grandfather's nightclub.

Andy could never figure out why anyone would want to listen to music. For her, it was just a bunch of sounds that went up and down, repeated, throbbed, and, if she waited long enough, stopped. Riding in a car with the music playing, was cruel, but usual, punishment. Her father would do things that a lot of people do when they listen to music: bang his hands or his fingers on the steering wheel, sing or hum or say some of the lyrics or go "dah-do dah-do dah-do," *badly*. It seemed so dumb, especially when he'd turn to her and say, "This really don't sound like nothing to you?"

She would shake her head. Later, she learned that President Ulysses S. Grant may have also had amusa, an aversion to, or an inability to hear, music. Grant never went to concerts, hated marching bands, and never danced, and when she told her father that, he said, "But he won a war somewhere. You win a war, they put you on a dollar bill, and everything that's wrong with you is suddenly right. I got that dyslexic thing. I see words, and they're nothing much. I can't think of no war I want to win, nothing I want my picture on. I got no folks I can blame for screwing me up. What I got to do, I got to make it right every day. I got to tell myself that it's okay to have no folks who want to know me, to have this thing that means I can't read and write like normal people. Or else I don't try—I just sit there, you know? Like I'm in traffic and it's jammed up. Nothing happened to nobody that just sat there."

She would want to tell him that Gautama Siddhartha, the prince who founded Buddhism, just sat under a tree until he figured out everything he had to figure out and he has statues all over the world.

Now, as she groped under the left rear wheel well for the tiny magnetic container that was stuck just inside the well, where her father kept an extra set of car keys, she remembered his words, and asked herself if it was his need to be making things right every day that doomed him. How many times had she tried to tell herself that there was nothing wrong with being smart, capable, talented, tall, and not resembling the half-dozen actresses and fashion models whose faces and figures made men think of beauty, only to find out that there was, indeed, something wrong, in that those who were *not* what she was seemed to be getting the jobs, having the fun, and getting the respect and attention.

She wished that there were a basketball court handy, and a ball that she could throw around. She was in the right shoes and to hell with these clothes she was wearing. Give her a ball and a basket and she'd just go . . .

She hesitated before putting the key into the door lock. The car should not have been locked. Whoever locked it did not know her father never locked the car. If she could pretend she was a psychic, she could touch the car and "see" the person who had been with her father, who had seen him die, who had locked the car out of habit.

She looked in. From what she could see, the seats were empty. She saw no debris in the foot wells. The ashtrays were closed and apparently empty. Her father sometimes carried papers with him to his luncheon meetings, but he tended to keep the car clean. He would look at the piles of newspapers, wilted food wrappers, and fading hand-outs left over from Penn cluttering every horizontal surface of her car and tell her to clean it out "because people see what's in a car and they think they know you. You don't want nobody to know you, do you?"

I want to know you, she said to his memory. *I want to know who killed you.*

She put the key in the lock, gave it a twist, and the nub over the door popped up. She opened the door and smelled the dry, musty aroma of a car interior that was old enough not to smell new, but not so old as to smell rotten.

She sat in a seat that was too high and too far forward, draped with that beaded mat her father used on the driver's seat for his bad back. It felt really uncomfortable, like something clawing at her through her clothes, but, instead of getting out, she let herself sink slowly into it, as if she were settling into a cold pool of water on a hot day.

She closed the door and felt the stifling, close air of the car's interior bearing in on her. She reached for the window crank that she had in her car, and then remembered that Buicks had power windows and to make them work you had to put the key in the ignition. She put it in and gave it a twist and the engine groaned, strained, shuddered, and roused itself.

A blast of hot air hit her in her face. She saw that her father had had the air conditioning on. Unless it was raining, he always drove with the windows cracked, if not wide open, even in the winter time (with the heater blasting) and he *never* had the air-conditioning on, even if that would make him a sweating mess when he arrived at his appointments. "People perspire when it's hot out," he would say to her when she would plead for him to put the air-conditioning on. "It's natural."

So he had been with someone who had persuaded him to turn the air-conditioning on. Andy made a quick list in her mind of people she knew who insisted on automobile air-conditioning: her mother, Mrs. Brickle, Logo . . .

Just about everyone except her. Why did he *not* turn the air-conditioning on for his daughter? Why did she have to suffer? Would he turn the air-conditioning on for his clients? Sure he would. What about his girlfriend, the singer who worked in the soup kitchen?

She suddenly felt a pang in her stomach. She put the car in gear, backed it out, narrowly avoiding the armored grill of a sport utility vehicle, paused at the stop sign near the exit to the lot, and then, just as the blowing out of the dashboard vents was cooling, she turned the air-conditioning off and rolled down the window.

The Buick had an unwieldy shape and mushy power steering that was far too eager to turn her hesitant twitches and flashes of indecision into direct commands to be followed to the death. The power brakes stopped the car so rapidly that she felt as if the back end would rise up and flip over.

When she found a break in the traffic, the car glided gently onto Delaware Avenue as if it was reading her mind. She wished she'd pulled away the beaded mat—she wasn't getting used to it. The car went faster and faster before she noticed she was going 65 miles per hour and tapped the brake *gently* to slow it down.

Something was missing. She glanced at the tape player and saw that a tape was in it and playing but the volume was down. He *never* turned the volume down on his tapes unless he was having a conversation, and her father didn't have conversations as much as he'd listen to another person prattle on and on and then he'd say a few clipped, terse, badly constructed sentences that would hang in the air like a weird odor that would take too long to dissipate and . . .

So, he had been talking to whoever had been in the car.

She reached for the volume knob, hesitated, and asked herself if she was ready for this. She took a breath and turned it up.

She heard a woman singing. She had heard this woman before. She was one of her father's favorite singers, his girlfriend, who called her-self Mara Rimes on his tapes but was really Maria Adamo, Bep 'n'

Betty's daughter who threw her career away to work in that soup kitchen.

The words Mara sang were distinct, though she liked to slur them and vary the speed at which she spoke. The music subsided and people applauded and the woman thanked the crowd and said some insane things about the next song and Andy winced as another song began.

While Mara sang, Andy could hear a few indistinct conversations—evidently her father had kept the tape recorder's microphone near the bar so the music was tainted with stray words and sentences about sex and smack and tea.

The tape continued that way for a few songs as Andy made her way to the Schyulkill Expressway and joined the traffic heading west. She was negotiating the tricky left-hand exit onto Route 1, City Line Avenue South and almost didn't hear Mara say on the tape how honored she was that people from the record companies were in the audience tonight, and that they were welcome to stay after the show and give her recording contracts to autograph. She was going to sing a song for Charl, her best girlfriend, who was sick upstairs, but first, a big hand for the man who was her biggest fan. "Why don't you come on up and say a few words to the people, Mr. Gold Bricks?"

Andy merged with the red taillights crowding onto City Line Avenue as the applause crested and a drunk with a flat, almost-but-not-quite New England accent that you hear among the cloistered rich spoke. Mr. Gold Bricks—no, it was Kellum Brickle—said hello and that he was happy to be here, always happy when Mara was singing, and hoped Charl would get well soon.

Mara started with another song and there was a rustling sound, followed by the thunk and smash of breaking glass, and a voice, low and enraged, "YOU DID WHAT TO HER?"

"You know exactly what I did, Sarge," Brickle said. "Don't push it, Sarge. You know I didn't do anything anybody else could've done."

Another thunk. "What the *hell* do you mean by that?"

Then her father's voice, younger, higher, and thinner, popped up. "Hey now, I gotta tell you grown-ups to cool it down?"

"Tell him, Ben," Brickle said. "Tell this . . . this son-of-a-bitch that handcuffs his pregnant daughter to a radiator and beat her senseless, tell him . . . I'm calling an ambulance right now."

She heard a loud smack and more glass breaking. "Hey, now," her father said, "I gotta get a mop. You come up off the floor, now, Mr. Brickle."

"I'll kick him again, I will," the sarge said. "I'll beat the shit out of him, too. I'll fucking kill him. But first, he's going to pay to fix her. He's going to pay double. Triple."

"What kind of monster are you?" Brickle said. "Is money all you want?"

"I want you to be there with the baby-killer," the sarge said. "I want you to watch the blood flow."

"There's people here, Sarge," Ben said carefully. "This is Mara's night. Let's just everybody have a good time."

"Frannie!" A sad, drunken voice said. "Keep it down."

"Am I bleeding?" Brickle said. "B-Man, am I bleeding?"

"You'll be okay, Mr. Brickle," her father said. "You come sit over here."

"You should've seen what he did to her," Brickle said. "It's criminal."

"The FUCK you say," her grandfather bellowed.

"The fuck I do say," Brickle said with a sneer. "You've got a lawsuit on your hands, you asshole."

Andy heard a panic enter Mara's voice as her father said, "Back down, Sarge!"

A different voice, dour and drunk, "What'er you ancients doing spoiling the mood?"

"None a your business, Abe," the sarge growled.

"You know better 'an to tell me that, Sarge," the drunk said. "I run a newspaper. Everything's my business, Sarge."

"Mr. Brickle and I are going downstairs to discuss this privately," the sarge growled.

"Wait a minute, Sarge. I think you should let me . . ." His voice faded out and all Andy heard was singing for several minutes.

"Sounds like I better get to the next number," Mara replied. "One of my favorites, about what's going to happen if my dreams and your dreams and everybody's dreams don't quite come true the way we want it. I'm sending this one out to you, Mr. Gold Bricks, and everybody else that's a little bit afraid of how their life's going to work itself out."

It was "Please Don't Talk about Me When I'm Gone," and she laughed when it began and rushed the words, so it was like a plea, as if she was begging everyone to keep things quiet.

At a red light on City Line Avenue, Andy stopped the tape, rewound it to the beginning, heard a resonant voice welcome Miss Mara Rimes to the stage, the sound of drinks being mixed, and then her father's voice, more recognizable now, just under the music: "I said, Charlotte hasn't come down all night. The sarge was up with her in her room upstairs and it didn't sound so good."

"I'll go up and bring her down," Brickle said. "She's says my money always looks better when I smile."

"That may be," Andy's father said, "but you're in no condition to climb stairs. "Maybe Abe, here. You want to go upstairs, Mr. Donuts, let the sarge's daughter out?"

Abe Donitz said, "I'll take another bourbon and water, B-Man."

"Coming up, Mr. Donuts."

"How many times I have to tell you it's Donitz. Like the German admiral. You know there was a German admiral named Donitz, B-Man?"

"There's a whole mess of stuff I don't know, Mr. Do-nits."

"And a mess of stuff he does," Brickle said. "I like your idea for that turn-around charity you talked about. The councilman said it just might fly. How does New Leaf Foundation sound?"

"It was just an idea," her father said uneasily. "You know, how it shouldn't make a difference where you come from, or who your folks are, or what's wrong or right with you, that you really can make yourself into what you want to be. If I ever had a kid, that's what I'd want my kid to know."

Andy turned right off City Line and was driving through the gently curving streets of Merion Station when she heard a series of rapid, confused movements, and her father saying, "We have to clean this up."

Abe Donitz said, "You're going to call this kid I just hired. He's from a family of medical examiners. He'll tell you what to do."

"What if he doesn't?" her father asked.

"You don't think that way," Donitz boomed. "When I was a reporter, every interview I ever did, I went in fully confident that whoever I was talking to was going to say exactly what I needed to make him sound exactly the way I wanted."

"Christ, I think I'm having a stroke," Brickle said, "My arm's numb. I didn't mean to hit him. I told him not to push me. You heard me. I said don't come any closer and, you saw. It was self-defense. Jesus, Ben, I'm the head of a bank. Okay, so I married into it, but the head of a bank can't be caught in this kind of thing. Ben, get me out of here. I don't care what it costs."

"You don't fix this with money," her father said as he dialed a rotary phone. "Yeah, is this Mr. Ladderback? This is Ben Cosicki, the B-Man from the Straight Up Club, how you doing? We had an incident here and . . . it's like, well, somebody got himself dead, somebody who sort of had it coming—I'm not saying he deserved it but, maybe it's okay, now that it happened, and the people involved, well, they're good people and your boss is here and he said you'd know what to do."

Andy slowed the car in front of her house as she hoped the tape would run out before she heard her father say, "Thanks. I owe you one." There was the sound of the phone being hung up, and then her father said one word, "Fire."

Andy turned the car around and headed back toward the city.

13 please don't talk about me when i'm gone

They went across the street in a procession, the Reverend in his green robe, flanked by bodyguards in darker robes that Ladderback remembered as being almost the color of the ledger cover that the Reverend had hanging in his sacristy.

Ladderback had shut his eyes tightly, tried to ignore the delicious aromas from the soup kitchen and the cool touch of night air on his skin. He began to sweat. He held onto Hank Norwood's arm, and stayed among the last people in the procession.

Ladderback opened his eyes when he felt the air change and heard the low chant of the Reverend and his guards begin to echo. A low shed of what had been a parts-storage room in the locomotive factory opened into the tremendous cavern of the assembly area lit from above by baleful industrial lights. Large slabs of plywood had been fitted across the grooved tracks in the concrete. Propped up against the large doors that, a century ago, would have opened proudly when a new locomotive was ready to go out into the world, were two dark stacks of loudspeakers pounding out a low, pulsing bass vamp.

The Reverend and his bodyguards went up a series of stairs to a makeshift altar on a flatbed trailer, where five musicians in green robes were pounding out the bass vamp. Norwood led Ladderback down an aisle between rows of mismatched chairs and benches, some of them made from ripped-down remains of shelving. Those seats were mostly full with an extraordinarily mixed group; some, judging from their dress, were poor, but many of them obviously not.

Norwood led Ladderback past the eagerly seated congregation to a row in the back. "If you're like me, you'll want to get the effect of the music," Norwood said. "You'll also not want to find yourself surrounded by too many of the faithful. It can get weird, the way they hang onto what he says."

Ladderback said nothing as he assumed his seat.

Norwood sensed his discomfort. "He's a good man, Mr. Ladderback. He's angry and crazy because the city makes you that way. You can be angry and crazy and still be a good man."

Ladderback folded his arms. "If you say so."

"I say so because I know so. I never used to have anything to do with him. I had my garage down the street and he was just another parasite you see in places that start to go downhill. When he got busted, we hoped we'd be rid of him and when they let him off, none of us wanted anything to do with him. We all figured he was crazy for starting this church. We couldn't take his religious ideas seriously but there were some, mostly from out of the neighborhood, that did, and some of them, they moved in here. To be close. The others would drive in on the weekends. We heard stories about him preaching hate and those of us that were still here, we kept our distance.

"But, you look around, and sometimes what looks like a bad thing at the beginning can look a little different. You start thinking about how much you have to pay for living in a place and not getting your house broken into, for walking down a street and not getting mugged at night. When the newspaper drivers went on strike, I got to the point

244

where I needed money to pay my bills. Ben Cosicki visited us on the picket line and he told the Reverend I needed some cash money. He told me the Reverend needed some work done on his car, so I did the work to get the money and one of his people just handed me this sack of cash and said, 'Take what you need.'

"That's when I decided to stick with the Reverend, Mr. Ladderback. I have to admit, I don't like half of what he says, and I hear things about people crossing him and disappearing. But you can go to him for help and not feel ashamed to get the help he gives. And you can look up to the man. Being able to look up to somebody always counts for something in this town."

"But at what cost?" Ladderback thought as the Reverend picked up a battered upright bass and began to play.

Andy got no answer when she called Ladderback's newsroom number on her portable phone. So she drove back to the street where her grandfather had had his nightclub and put her father's car right back where it had been.

She turned off the car and again regarded the dark ruin set off with its bright yellow string of crime-scene tape.

She smelled garlic and tomato sauce coming from the soup kitchen, and felt a low, throbbing pulse that almost shook the car. She looked down and across the street at the First Church of God Harmonious. It was loud enough for her to feel the vibrations coming up through the Buick. Ganeesh Ryan said he could hear those vibrations where he lived and that was at least a half a mile south.

So she would ask the guy, this Reverend, why it was so important to play music so loud on a weekday night in a residential neighbhorhood. She would ask him and maybe he would tell her it's religious and she'd print both sides of the story and nothing would happen.

She went across the street to the big, iron doors of the old locomotive factory. She looked for a button she could press, or a door knocker, or something that would signal that she wanted to get in. She banged on the door with her fists until they hurt, but the door didn't open.

Then Andy caught another whiff of the soup kitchen. She went across Eighteenth Street to the door that once had glass in it, but had been covered by curling sections of plywood on which had been painted the words, FOOD IF YOU NEED IT.

She needed it but she hesitated. Her father's girlfriend was supposed to work in this place. Andy was curious but . . .

She pushed open the door and saw, past the people holding trays moving toward what had been the lunch counter, a short, harried woman with tired eyes, gray hair, and a paper cap on her head. She was putting a two-inch pan of sliced meatloaf into a steamer tray and almost dropped it when Andy said, "I'm Andy, Ben's girl."

The woman gave Andy a sour look and said, "Ben who?"

"You're his girlfriend, right?"

"As a matter of fact, no." She made a face and went back through a kitchen door that was almost falling off its hinges. Andy stepped behind the counter (it seemed so much smaller and narrower than when her father had hoisted her onto the stools and commanded that a huge dish of ice cream be put before her) and followed her into the kitchen, where the woman slipped beside some male helpers and peered into a grimy gas oven, glanced at a large gray pot, and went to a gray metal table near the pot sink. A sack of onions lay beside the table. The woman picked up a ten-inch chopping blade, grabbed an onion, sliced off the top and bottom, and began to peel away the skin.

Andy said, "You going to ignore me?"

"You any good with a knife?" she said, her eyes tearing as she began to slice the onion.

"As a matter of fact, no," Andy said, picking up a smaller paring knife. "I never learned to cook."

"So I heard," the woman said. "What I want you to do, is take the point of the knife, see, and carve out the top of the onion, like this, and then slice the bottom. Then you put a piece of skin against the knife and peel it away from you."

"This is starting to get to my eyes," Andy said.

"Try not to cut yourself," the woman said, wiping her face with a rag. "And don't touch your eyes with your fingers. It'll just make it worse."

Andy began, "What I want to ask you . . ."

The woman hoisted up the sack of onions and spilled it onto the edge of block. "This, first."

Andy wiped her eyes on her sleeve. "Can it wait? Can I get any food around here?"

The woman put the knife down, got a chipped plate from the dishwasher rack, went to a slab of meatloaf that had just come out of the oven, lopped off a chunk, popped it on the plate, ladled on red gravy from the pot on the stove, and put the plate in front of Andy.

Andy found a fork from another rack near the dishwasher. "You won't need a knife," the woman told her.

"Thanks, Mara, is it?"

"Maria," the woman said.

Andy took a bite and the rich, salty, sweet, tomato-mushroom-onion-and-garlic explosion shoved her straight into heaven. "What's in this?" she said.

"Loving kindness," Maria said, "and whatever else we had lying around." She took up the knife, wiped her eyes again with the rag, and continued to chop the onions.

Andy took another bite and tried to see what had drawn her father to this woman. She was of medium height, where Andy's mother was tall. Her mother's face was sharp and strikingly attractive; Maria would have passed unnoticed. Her mother's complexion flawless, her nose, chin, and throat carved and tightened to surgical perfection; the skin around Maria's eyes and mouth was lined, her face was spotted with a few moles. Her mother's body was toned from sessions spent in a health club; Maria looked like she liked the food she cooked, and wasn't ashamed to eat it.

Andy took a third bite and tried to do as she had been instructed with the paring knife. She blinked away the tears.

"He said you learned quick," Maria said. "He said you'd probably hate the job he got for you."

Andy put down the knife. "He talked to you about me?"

"All the time," Maria said, as if only the onions were bringing tears to her face.

The music was unlike anything Ladderback had ever heard.

At first, Ladderback told himself he had merely forgotten how beautiful music is when it is performed spontaneously before an audience. There is the theatrical aspect: Fingers pluck, hands flutter over keyboards, mouths open, an arm moves a trombone's slide back and forth as a man's face swells with a breath, and then forces that breath into a tarnished brass tube.

Then Ladderback recognized some melodies in what appeared to be a freeform service, but as soon as he identified a fragment from a familiar composition, it changed into something else. He thought he caught the bass vamp from John Coltrane's "A Love Supreme." Another time he smiled at what resembled a quote from Bach's "Jesu" that melted into the haunting modal wanderings of the Hebrew prayers.

But because there were no breaks in the music, no moments or directions to pause, stand, or sit, Ladderback found himself quickly enveloped by sensation. He could not pause, he could not consider, he could not judge, evaluate, or reflect on the inexpressible loveliness of the sounds. And, because there were no prayer books to read, no catechisms to recite, no rituals of eating or drinking, the music became an inescapable, overwhelming presence that washed over him that rapidly worked its way into his brain until the music was all he could think of, until he could not distinguish where the music ended and the collection of chemicals, synapses, fluids, and phobias called Neville Shepherd Ladderback began.

Some people stood and sang, others swayed in their seats, eyes shut tight as the low notes of the organ and the Reverend's groaning bass reverberated through their bodies. Words, chords, and voices came together and separated without plan, a seamless improvisation as the organ and the bass played off each other and the congregation, bringing to life a blend of sound that was, at times, heartbreakingly beautiful to behold.

For a moment it seemed that any sound he wished to make, no matter how calculated or incidental, would be accepted into the great rush of sensation. It was almost like hearing a miracle, a musical flow that sought to unite the fragmentary, the disparate, the shattered, and the incomplete into one perfect act of creation. It suggested that if people could come together and make such wonderful sounds, and these sounds could fit and blend or fall away and still evoke a sense of wonder, then other equally wonderful things were still possible in the world.

Was it silly to think that in this grim, forbidding, abandoned industrial ruin, he could hear a city of brotherly love?

Then the Reverend put his bass down, picked up a microphone, and delivered a sermon that was vicious with antagonism, hideous with cant, and murderous with rage.

They finished the onions and Maria got herself a piece of meatloaf and a glass of iced tea. Andy followed her out to one of the booths in the dining area.

"Some things I want to know," Andy began.

Maria tasted the meatloaf like a mechanic listening to the sound of an engine. "He said you had no social graces."

"What's that supposed to mean?"

"He actually liked that. He said you wouldn't take crap from people. He took crap from people every day. But, you, he said, you'd be the kind to throw it right back, and get in all kinds of trouble after that."

Andy's anger flared. What was this woman doing telling her things like that? "So," Andy began, "how long have you been screwing my father?"

"If I told you we didn't, would you believe me?" Maria shook her head.

"My mother said you were his girlfriend."

"I'm a girl and I was his friend," Maria said, wiping her eyes. "But we didn't sleep together. Your father and I had similar tastes, in that we were attracted to powerful people. He was overwhelmed by Charlotte, in much the same way I was taken with powerful men."

"Like Kellum Brickle?"

Maria shook her head. "I used to tell Ben that he should sit you down and just tell you everything, answer every question you could come up with, and stop being so protective of you."

"He wasn't protective of me! He never said anything."

"He did but maybe you didn't know how to listen, or you may not have noticed, but, because he was an orphan, he believed that who your parents were and whatever they did with each other before you were born really didn't matter."

"But those things do matter. They matter to me."

"I'll admit, they did to me, for a while," Maria said. "I wanted to be a singer because my parents hated your grandfather's nightclub and when Ben sneaked me in at nights, I thought it was the most wonderful, glamorous thing to be up there on a stage in front of people. I wanted to be exactly what my parents didn't like."

"You were going to get a recording contract that night of the fire."

Maria regarded her. "Ben must have played that tape for you. You've heard it?"

Andy nodded.

"Scariest thing, isn't it? Some of my best work was on that tape, and Jeff's—the Reverend, the man who owns this place, was in fabulous form that night. And on the same tape, you hear how powerful and terrible a man your grandfather was. He was aware of everything that went on in that place. He wanted Charlotte to get pregnant by Mr. Gold Bricks. He thought he could squeeze money out of Kellum Brickle the same way he squeezed money out of the whores, johns, and perverts when he was on the vice squad. He just might have gotten something out of him, if he hadn't hurt your mother and threatened to abort her baby."

Andy said. "That's why they killed him."

"They didn't kill him."

"He didn't just die. Who killed him?"

"Ben wouldn't tell me, but he let me know that he would tell me if I asked him. I never did. I had wanted so much to be a singer and something about the fire, and the reasons for the fire . . . I just couldn't go back to that, or anything connected with it."

She took a bite. "Your father wasn't a fool: He knew how corrupt your grandfather was. But he was fascinated by him—and by Charlotte, who could get more attention by just walking into a room than I would if I sang all my songs naked—the same way I was attracted to . . . the men I was attracted to."

"Jeff Hooks?"

"Of course." Her tone suggested to Andy that she wanted to say more.

"Who else?" Andy asked.

Maria smiled wistfully. "I wish that your father had told you more about what it meant to him to be an orphan. He told me that he would look out of the windows of the Home and see people older than he was and think, so many of these people could be my parents. They could have made love, for whatever reason, and had him, so you want to love everyone who is older than you and who looks a little bit like you, because, hey, this could be the person that gave you life. But this also could be the person who did not want you, who could not or would not give you the love you wanted more than anything else. So you want to hate them for the pain they caused you, and for the pain they caused every child that they spurned. This was how he felt when he was your age and it took raising you for him to understand the other side of the problem, that parents, who seem so powerful and important when you're young, are never as powerful and important as they want to be.

"That was why, about two years after the fire at your grandfather's club, when I became pregnant, your father urged me to have and raise my baby. My parents wanted me to abort it, especially when they found out who the father was."

"Hooks?"

"Hooks was very cool with his music and his drugs, but I was never attracted to him then, and I think too much that what he's become now is . . . ugly. At times I think he has no right to be where he is, but I don't see anyone any better wanting to take his place. He's a lot like the councilman: He's made some big mistakes, made some deals with criminals. He can also be unforgiving with people who get on his bad side, but, on the whole, things are working out. The cops come here when we call them. The buses run on time. I have this kitchen. I take self-defense courses in our job-training school. We also have a child-care center, homeless shelter, substance-abuse outreach center, a used clothing and furniture exchange, and, because the cabs don't come here, we have a small transportation service that takes our people where they need to go. We want to start a charter school and try to get some business to come back into the neighborhood."

"That'll take some money," Andy said.

"We have money. I do the church's accounting and we're doing okay. What we need is businesses from the outside willing to come in and be part of what we're doing here. Ben was working on that for us. He was trying to get the Hampton to buy and renovate the Straight Up Club as a bank branch."

"I can't see Mrs. Brickle wanting to do that," Andy said. "The bank isn't doing too well. There's talk of a merger."

"Ben said he was working on her son."

"Logo is hopeless," Andy said.

"Ben had a lot of confidence in him. Ben had confidence in me, when I wanted to be a singer. As much as Ben and I are attracted to powerful people, we have a weakness for hopeless cases."

"But you never . . . got together?"

"I told you, we didn't sleep together because we had too much in common." Maria looked up at the shelves, now laden with boxes of donated canned goods, that used to have the cookie jars on them. "There was only really one powerful individual here that I was drawn to."

"The councilman?"

"He was so admirable and righteous where everyone else seemed corrupt. My mother used to give me orders of food to take upstairs. He was working late in his office one night, and alone, and I was looking for someone to tell me I wasn't going to spend the rest of my life waiting tables in my parent's restaurant, and he did that."

"That's why your mother hated him," Andy said.

"When my father wouldn't lift a finger against him, she went to the FBI. Doug had had other affairs, but he was always very discreet. There was no question in my mind that there was something special between us, that he wanted a baby as much as I did. The reason, I think, that he let them convict him was that he felt he had done something wrong and that the indictment and the conviction was his penance. But he had only done what was right. I needed him at that time in my life, and he needed me."

"But what happened to the baby?"

She said, "Ben said he knew of a couple that wanted one, and that they would pay for me to have it and give it to them, if I agreed to a closed adoption. They would have paid me but I didn't want any money."

"Was it a boy or a girl?"

"A boy. I'm told he didn't look like me."

"But you knew the couple?"

Maria was quiet for a while. "Ben kept the secret, handled the details, but he told me that, at any time, he would tell me. He was going to tell me tomorrow. That was the reason he was setting up that luncheon."

"And you didn't go?"

"Because I didn't want it known. You can get comfortable about not knowing something. It can change the way you think. I was trying to make a living singing and waitressing, but I'd look out at the kids on the street, and I found myself thinking, the same way Ben used to think when he was in the Home, that so many of these kids could have been mine. And then I saw this article in the *Press* about kids who were found starving in a row house right around the block from here, and how the the Reverend had promised to set up a mission to feed people, so I got on the bus and came down here and . . ."

Andy did the math. Maria's child *could* be Logo Brickle. "But you've never wanted to know who he is and if he's okay?"

"I've wanted to know every day since the day I had him," Maria said, tears in her eyes. "But some things are worth more when you don't know."

"Tell me, why was my father in the club when he died?"

"Ben told me that if something ever happened to him and I wanted to know who my son was, I could go in there and find out."

"That's it?"

"He told me I wouldn't have to look too hard."

*   *   *

Andy put her hands on the yellow crime-scene tape in front of the vacant door of the Straight Up Club and pulled it apart. Then she stepped over the shattered marble threshold.

She didn't have a flashlight and, for a moment, she wanted to go back to her father's car to see if he had one. As she recoiled at the stench of filth and garbage, she saw that the glare from the streetlights seeped through places where boards had fallen off the windows. The place was creepy and disgusting and it could fall in on her at any minute, but she had to be here. Something had called her here, and she would not leave before she found out what it was.

She took another step, and halted before a sea of trash, broken furniture, and rotten piles of clothing ending in a fringe of charred boards. She let her eyes adjust to the darkness, gradually seeing an open pit where the bar must have been. She clambered over some of the trash and looked into the pit. She could barely make out more garbage down there, in what had once been the basement.

She looked up and saw that the fire had climbed straight up from the basement, burned a large opening in the first floor, and burned a smaller one in the ceiling over her head. If he had, in fact, fallen through that hole, he would have gone straight down onto whatever lay below.

She could see no chalk outline where her father's body had lain. The debris in the basement provided no surface flat enough for a line.

She looked up again and saw that, though fire, water damage, and years of neglect had obliterated much of the ground floor, most of the ceiling was intact. The second floor had survived. As far as she could see, there was no way to the second floor from inside. The bricks in the walls of the first floor had been exposed in places, but they were all in their courses, rigid and apparently strong.

She went out and glanced down an alley on the club's side. She went into the alley and found, about ten feet in, an open threshold with a rusted sign suspended over it. The sign said, LADIES' ENTRANCE.

Inside, a series of sagging wooden steps led up. The floor up there was probably weak, especially around the area where her father had fallen. No. Not fallen. Her father was a careful man. He had lived part of his life in this place. If he had a reason to come back, he wouldn't have just rushed in.

What would that reason be?

Andy put a tentative foot on the first stair, and then raced up to the top. The door on the top had fallen off its hinges long ago. You'd think anybody who would put anything important in a dump like this would fix the door and put a lock on it.

But then she remembered that her father never locked anything, not even his car. *"If you want to let the whole world know you got something worth stealing, you lock it up."*

She went through the door, and found herself in a huge, smelly room that covered the entire top of the club. The glass that had been in the windows had dropped out long ago, letting in small animals and birds. Shoved up against one wall was a battered chair and decaying sofa that appeared to have been ripped up by animals. There was a desk covered with bird droppings. Shoved against one wall, an open door at the far end led to what might have been a bedroom.

In the back of the room, against the charred brick wall farthest from the street, the floor ended in a gaping hole. The fire must have climbed up the far wall and started burning away the floor before it was put out.

The gap in the floor was about four feet by six feet, certainly big enough for a man to fall through.

But not accidently.

She stepped to the edge of that hole and felt around the edges. They were solid enough to support her. Her father couldn't have been standing here and then slipped down.

She backed carefully away and let her eyes grow accustomed to the faint glare coming in through the windows. Had something been hidden here that he had wanted to bring to the luncheon? Or did he want to show something to whoever he had brought with him?

And where would you put it? It would have to be easy to get to, but not so obvious that someone blundering in would find it, and not so accessible that the animals would get to it.

She bumped into a desk a few feet from the hole. It was filthy with bird droppings and grime. She groped under it but didn't find anything.

Then she saw, almost invisible in the gloom, the outlines of a kitchen sink. Beside that was an oven, a stack of cabinets whose doors had been torn off, and an ancient refrigerator with a rusted dinette chair in front of it.

She approached the refrigerator and put her hand on the door. She tried to move the door but the hinges were so corroded that it would not move.

Whatever was going to be hidden in this room had to be put where scavengers hunting for scrap metal wouldn't find it. It would have to be easy enough to reach because her father wasn't a tall man, but not so accessible that anyone would see it.

The fixtures and most of the pipes had been torn off the sink. The oven door was rusted shut and didn't appear to have been opened in years. She gave it a good yank but it wouldn't budge.

She stood up, glanced again around the room but didn't see anything. It had to be here, she told herself.

Outside she heard the grinding gears of a bus, or was it a truck? A breeze found its way into the apartment and the stench from the sofa almost overwhelmed her. Her father wouldn't put anything of value near that. She found herself thinking about something that was in the obituary Ladderback had written about her father.

It was a quote from the mayor's aide. "Whatever he took from the cookie jar, he shared."

257

She turned around and there it was, a twin of the one that they had at home: A pink and blue Bep 'n' Betty's Luncheonette cookie jar was sitting on top of the refrigerator.

She was tall enough to put her hands on it. Her father would have had to use a step stool, or a chair, to get to it, or maybe he would have whoever he was with reach for it.

The jar was cold and grimy, but not quite as grimy as the rest of the junk around her. It had been put here *after* the fire. She brought it close to a window and opened the lid. She didn't see anything. She didn't quite want to put her hand in—who knows what could be inside there. So she turned it over and a packet of papers wrapped in plastic fell out.

Where did it go? It was right there, in front of her, somewhere around her feet. She moved her feet. She started to search the darker areas of the floor when she heard a voice outside that almost made her want to scream. The voice, somewhat thick but still recognizeable, said, "I thought they towed this car."

"The car *was* towed, Mr. Piper," James Fenestra replied. "And now it's back. Call one of our own wreckers this time."

"What do you think got it back here?" Piper continued.

"My source at the Parking Authority said it was the Cosicki girl, the same girl who broke Mr. Tuhoy's collarbone, hit you with a brick, and popped that hole in your mouth. You're fortunate that I provide dental and reconstructive surgery benefits, Mr. Piper, or you might not have been able to work in public. People remember a man with a scar or any kind of disfigurement."

"Yeah, well, she'll have more than a scar if I find her. I really don't like that bitch," Piper said.

"Watch your language. You never know who might be listening."

Andy heard what sounded like the back of a truck opening. Piper said, "If I stick her in her butt, I won't have to look at that face. But it is fun to look at 'em when you hurt 'em, you know what I mean, boss?"

"Concentrate on the task before you, Mr. Piper. I do believe you've spilled the gelignite on yourself."

"What do we need this stuff, if we're just going to crash a fuel truck into the place?"

"We need a hot, long-burning conflagration to destroy everything and anything. Fuel oil is a slow and relatively sluggish combustible. Gelignite soaks in and stays lit until it burns itself out. Put the two together at the few remote-controlled incendiaries that we planted previously, and you'll get the job done."

Andy moved closer to the front window and saw through a crack in the window boards a large fuel oil delivery truck idling beside her father's car. Piper, a fat bandage on his right cheek, and Fenestra were in their gray suits, wearing gloves and carrying large drums of liquid from a rack behind the truck and spilling them on the street, and in through the front door of the club.

Fenestra gave Piper a two-gallon plastic container. "I want you to go upstairs and scatter this around. Leave the container and don't, I repeat, don't, get this on you. It's a highly toxic industrial solvent that will show up when the arson inspectors arrive. They'll find that this is a toxic site, which will require Mr. Hooks to demolish it completely and have it brought up to code, or cede it to the city. Very expensive, but necessary. Since we don't know where the documents are, we have to make sure that anything that could contain the documents is destroyed and carted away."

"What kind of documents are these, boss?"

"Don't ask, don't tell, Mr. Piper. Let's review the escape procedure. We walk, don't run. Run and you draw attention to yourself. You can also trip and fall and hurt yourself. Not a good move. And stay on the sidewalk. The street is filled with potholes. I cannot tell you how many times I've twisted my damned ankles on these potholes. Avoid potholes."

"Yes, sir."

"We escape in opposite directions. I go to the Lincoln up the street. You go to the Lincoln on Seventeenth Street. Understood?"

"Yes, sir. But, well, what I don't understand is why do we have to take this place out? This sure is a dumb place to put something, for what we charge for a takeout operation like this."

Fenestra said, "Some people think it's real smart in these parts to hide things where anyone can get them, but nobody knows where to look. I should have told you this is a pro bono job, Mr. Piper. I owe this to Mr. Hooks. My career in law enforcement would have been different if he had been convicted of his crimes. Alas, the Lord works in devious ways."

"Think we should pray before we torch the place?"

"I always do, Mr. Piper. I always do."

Andy heard him coming up the stairs. She held onto the cookie jar and took a position behind the open refrigerator door. She heard Piper's pause on the stairs. "Anybody up there?" he called.

Andy didn't breathe.

He came again, bounded into the room, opened the door, and shined a flashlight in until he saw the opening in the floor. He stepped to the edge, put the flashlight under his arm, opened the jug, and was just about to spill it down the hole in the floor when he froze.

The tired floorboards under Andy's feet had made a tiny squeak as she rose.

And that was enough to make Piper spin around. The flashlight found her eyes, blinding her so that maybe her aim was off, just a little bit, when she launched the cookie jar at him, seeing this as just one in a series of layups, with the basket and hoop just a little lower than usual.

Unfortuntely the jar didn't quite go exactly as she wanted it to go and instead hit him below the face, on his chest, where it bounced off harmlessly.

But it fell straight down and shattered on the floorboards with an explosive crash that made Piper jump back, just a little bit, and come down in what he thought was a fighting crouch, and probably would have been a fighting crouch, if one foot wasn't on rotting, burned-out, weather-damaged floorboards, and the other was on nothing at all.

Andy was out of the room and going down the stairs before she heard the crash and the scream. She ran out the ladies' entrance and was almost at the street when a blast of light hit her eyes and another blast, so deep that if she had had any more food in her stomach than a few bites of meatloaf it would have blown right back up. The blast caught right in her gut, followed by another quick blast right under her breastbone. She fell backward on the brick, heard but did not quite feel her head bounce, and didn't know how long she had been staring at the way the dark sides of the alley framed the patch of open, red-tinged night sky overhead as she heard Fenestra say, from inside the club, "Okay, Mr. Piper, I can see you. I'm going to put a board across, like so, and this piece of molding, like so. Just hold on a little longer and . . . that's it. Ease yourself down. That's it. Quick thinking, grabbing onto the edge like that. That's why I hired you, Mr. Piper. Plenty of former jailhouse screws can think on their feet, but off their feet, that's another matter."

Andy wondered why she couldn't get up and run away and then she saw one of those big drums of gelignite pinning a plank across her middle. If she moved in any direction, the drum would fall on her, and judging from the smell the drum appeared to be open.

That, and the back of her head was beginning to hurt really, really bad.

She found that she still had her shoulder bag on her arm and she groped in it, looking for something she could use as a weapon when the bottom of a shoe appeared over her face dropping bits of grit into her eyes.

"What say I stomp her now, boss?"

"Please remove your foot, Mr. Piper." Fenestra crouched down beside her. "You put me in a difficult situation, Ms. Cosicki. You know who I am and you may know why I'm here and both of those are no-win situations for you, strategically."

His rotten, sulphuric breath made her want to gag, until she remembered purchasing the aerosol breath spray, the one item that her mother said Andy absolutely *had* to have if she was going to meet people.

"But I have a great deal of respect for your father, who, you may be surprised to know, invited me to have lunch with him yesterday."

"You refused?"

"I declined. We don't eat lunch in my business, Ms. Cosicki. It dulls the mind. Now, my respect for your father makes me want to search for some way of resolving this without making you a tragic victim of circumstances, if you know what I mean."

"I know what you mean," Andy said as she wrapped her hand around it. It was still in its blister-pack card. How was she going to open that one-handed without nails? She'd cut her fingernails close because you can't do layups and have long fingernails because the ball will bounce back and tear the nail off.

She ran her thumb around the back and found a perforated groove in the cardboard. She dug in her thumb, felt the cardboard gouge her cuticle, and winced.

"Something troubling you, Ms. Cosicki?"

"Uh, no."

Piper said, "Just let me have her, boss. I think I owe her something on the order of what you owe this Hooks guy."

He frowned. "You have a point, Mr. Piper." He stood and banged his fist against the drum of gelignite. A clammy, cold, syrupy liquid descended on her pants and soaked through to her skin. "Mr. Piper, I recall from your marijuana ingestion incident with Mr. Brickle yesterday that you carry a cigarette lighter. Please produce that cigarette lighter."

Andy had the aerosol out of the card but the spray nozzle was sealed in tamper-proof plastic. She poked it with her thumb and the nozzle fell off and disappeared into her shoulderbag.

Piper came out with the lighter.

"Mr. Piper, light your lighter."

Piper found his gloves cumbersome. He took them off and then brought out the lighter.

Andy began to panic. "Aren't you worried about anyone seeing you?" she said.

"Ms. Cosicki, this is a city. Everyone watches. No one does a thing."

"I can scream."

"You won't be heard over the music. And if you should get as far as the church, you'll find the doors locked. Mr. Hooks locks his church while he's preaching. I think you have no alternative, Ms. Cosicki."

"Ms. Cosicki, the substance on your clothing is a close relative of napalm. It is designed to stick to a variety of surfaces including those containing water. If it's lit and you throw water on it, it will stay lit and burn you so badly that, should you survive, you will never have normal use of your legs. Now, can we come to some kind of agreement here, or do I let Mr. Piper light his lighter?"

"Uh, sure," Andy said as she touched the plastic tube sticking out of the aerosol and felt it squirt a tiny jet into her fingers.

"Now, if we let you up, you're going to get in your car and drive off, saying nothing about this to anyone. If you do, I'll find you and you'll regret it, severely. Do we have an agreement?"

"Sure," Andy said.

"If you do anything else, or if you make us think you're doing anything else, Mr. Piper will drop his lighter and you will most likely die horribly. Do we agree?"

"I'm not going to die," Andy said, her hand tight on the breath spray.

"Mr. Piper, put your right foot on these planks while I lift the gelignite off Ms. Cosicki. If she tries to move, drop your lighter on her."

He rolled the drum off her, carried it into the ladies' entrance and dumped it inside.

"Boss," Piper called. "You said I could have her."

Fenestra emerged and gazed down at Andy. "Mr. Piper, you will notice that Ms. Cosicki's arm is in her shoulder bag. As you step off these boards, put your foot right here, where her wrist would be. I want you to pin the wrist. Don't break the bone. Just prevent her from moving."

"You want me to keep my lighter on?"

"Yes, Mr. Piper. And I want you to put your other foot here, pinning Ms. Cosicki's shoulder." Fenestra removed a small switchblade from his pocket as he kicked the boards away. "Now, Ms. Cosicki, I'm going to cut away your shoulder bag. I will put it on the hood of your car."

Andy enclosed her fist around the breath spray and hoped it would not be seen. It wasn't.

Ladderback felt blindsided, wincing from words that seemed to hurt as much as blows.

How could the Reverend do this? How could anyone follow such tonal bliss with such atonal ugliness?

"Oppressors sicken me to the death," he boomed, "because they will never be anything but what they are: Oppressors who abandon commitment, who deny community, who betray trust in order to keep us from our destiny. When people betray that trust, when they exploit you, when they pollute their space with their evil, they must be cast down. They must be named. They must be labeled. They must be accused, resisted, defiled, and annihilated. They must be removed from creation!"

Removed from creation? By whom, Ladderback wanted to know, and on whose authority?

"When institutions in this city," the Reverend thundered, "are found to have profited on slavery and degradation—that so thoroughly disgusts me that I must fight it with all my anger, all my hate, all the rage in my heart."

What was there to fight? Every life that Ladderback had summarized in obituaries might have contained embarrassments, venalities, events that, for one generation, might be just and true, but for another were crimes of the lowest sort. The Reverend certainly had damaging information, in the form of records indicating the Hampton Bank's participation in the slave trade. But, instead of tendering those records to historians, who could use them to gain a better understanding of a turbulent era, the Reverend was using those records to justify the kind of antagonism that prevents any kind of understanding or healing of old wounds from occurring.

"Now you may ask if telling the oppressor that he is disgusting in your sight is going to make him go away. No way, he's gonna stay. You tell him what he is and he's going to oppress us even more. He'll start by telling you you've got to have an abortion because the world is no place for your child, while the oppressor has a whole pack of brats growing up to be just like him."

Cries of "Amen" rose around him.

"Then he'll fire you for being uppity," the Reverend continued, "for not being grateful. By giving us the paycheck, the boss is buying our silence with every corrupting, sinful, disgusting thing he wants us to do, whether or not it's in the letter of the law, whether or not the union's going to file a grievance, whether or not this working for a living is poisoning our soul, raping us of our dignity, depriving us of the joy and hope of raising our families. What can we do to these oppressors, these devils, these blights upon our lives? I say unto you, I have the answer, I have the answer:

"We fight back!"

Andy began to breathe again when she reached her father's car. Piper doused his lighter as she grabbed the shredded shoulder bag and discovered that her car keys were not inside.

She turned around and saw Fenestra's knife too close to her face. "I have your keys, Ms. Cosicki. I kept them because I wasn't sure if you should go just yet."

She leaned back, away from the knife.

"Every good general must let his troops enjoy the pleasures of conquest," Fenestra said. "I left the FBI for that very reason. The work builds up tensions that must be released and you, Ms. Cosicki, have provided us with far too many tensions for me to merely let you go."

"My mother is a friend of Mrs. Brickle," Andy said. "I'll tell her what you're doing."

"Mrs. Brickle sees what she wants to see. As for what she hears, you won't say a thing, Ms. Cosicki, because I'm about to crush your spirit. Yes. I think that's exactly what must be done with you."

He pushed her back toward the alley. "Mr. Piper has been very loyal to me, the only one of my staffers who is not afraid of Mr. Hooks's criminal organization. He also has expressed an urge to sack the city, as it were."

Piper said, "Boss, you are the greatest. Can I break her finger, too?"

"Mr. Piper, you have my permission to have your way with, but not kill, Ms. Cosicki. You will do it in the alley here, just far enough from the chemical spills." He looked at his watch. "I will stand guard and witness the proceedings so that you may feel free to indulge yourself. You will take no more than five minutes."

"Boss, I don't know if I can do it that fast."

"You raped those prison inmates. That's how you lost your job at the jail, am I correct?"

"But I could take my time there and . . . those were guys."

"Six minutes, then."

Andy was so shocked she could not move. "You don't want to do this."

Fenestra smiled. "To tell you the truth, we do." He put the knife under her nose, and locked his arm over and around her neck. "Feel free to resist. We like a struggle."

She was still aching from the blows to her stomach. He stepped behind her and shoved her toward Piper, who wrapped one arm around her, enclosing her arms and chest, and threw her against the wall.

14 all fall down

"No way you're going to bean me with those bricks now," Piper said as he fumbled with his belt.

Andy forced herself to stay in control. She still had the aerosol spray in her left hand, though she felt herself bleeding on her face after Piper had shoved her into the wall. "You said you had respect for my father," she said. "Just let me go."

"We will," Fenestra said, checking his wristwatch, "in five and a half minutes."

Piper fell against her. She felt his weight shift and a droplet of his sweat fell onto her neck, which made her shrink just enough so that the fist he was trying to send into her face slid by. The band on his wristwatch grabbed and pulled some of the hair from her head but she had the satisfaction of hearing him howl when his knuckles smashed against the wall.

"One point for Ms. Cosicki. Mr. Piper? Your serve."

She twisted under him as he pulled back. His knuckles were just beginning to spout blood. Piper shook his hand like a dust mop, wincing, and then opened and closed his fingers. Andy chose that moment to try to put her leg out and twist away. He stopped her by putting the palm of his uninjured hand flat on her neck and leaning forward. She flinched as he touched her—his hand had a nauseating odor of sweat and toxic chemicals. She decided she didn't care if Fenestra had a knife. She twisted again and brought her left fist up and boxed him as hard as she could on his ear.

That didn't hurt him at all. He smiled at her and with her right hand she grabbed a chunk of stucco that had fallen off the wall and smashed that against his other ear. Piper tried to dodge the blow by twisting his head away, opening a hideously deep gash that started somewhere inside his ear and ended near his chin.

Then he really smiled. Andy didn't ask why he was smiling as his blood sprayed on her. He tightened his legs around her, pinning her legs, and sputtered something about being baptized in the blood of the lamb as he positioned his left fist up about two feet above her nose. He was about to bring it down when Fenestra said, "Mr. Piper. Let's cut to the chase."

He pinned her with his legs and Andy tried to think of the rape counseling story she had done and what you're supposed to do when you're in this situation and her mind just blanked out.

You're not supposed to get scared, she told herself. Movie heroines don't get scared unless they're being fed to a monster, and that's just so the hero can rescue them, or vice versa in the role-reversal films of the mid 1980s onward. Cultural heroines were *never* supposed to give in to fear. They were supposed to stay cool, have a plan, look for an edge.

He put a hand on her throat. With the hand that wasn't on her throat, he pulled one of her free arms across her chest, folded her other arm on it, then bent her shoulder and pushed until she yelped and had to turn over or he would break her collarbone.

She wanted to cry as she felt him push her face down. The dirt in the alley stuck to her skin. She felt him pulling down her pants.

"Piper, please, don't you do this to me."

"Shut yourself up, bitch."

"GET OFF ME!" She yelled as she felt the open air on her buttocks, and his fingers touching her. He responded by shoving her face deeper into the dirt. Then he moved his stinking right hand through her hair, down and over her mouth, covering her mouth and then suddenly yanking her head back until she thought her neck would break.

He put his face next to hers. "Feel that? That could've been it for you. I could've pulled your head back and given it a little twist, and that would be it. When I'm done, I'm going to break each and every one of your fingers. It's going to be fun seeing you drive that car. Or maybe we'll call you a cab?"

"Mr. Piper," Fenestra said. "You have established your dominant position. Get it over with."

Andy tried to scream again but his hand was over her mouth. About the best she did was open her jaw to keep breathing. His blood-slicked fingers moved past her lips until one was so far inside her that it was pushing her tongue flat against her jaw.

She hated the smell of his hand, the taste of his fingers violating her. She gagged and it made her bite down, hard, with a deep, primal fury that cut skin, cut bone, and made a squishy crunching sound as her teeth cut right through the first two fingers on his hand until they broke away like warm lumps in her mouth, the blood rushing in, viscous and vile.

Why did it take so long for the synapses in his hand to travel up to his arm to his brain and tell him that parts of him had been *removed?*

His blood filled her mouth. She turned her head as his hand loosened and she spat out two glistening crimson lumps.

He made no sound as she felt his weight shift on her. Suddenly it was easy to squirm out, under, and away from him. She scraped her naked legs against the stucco but she almost welcomed the sensation as she pulled her pants back up, stood with her back to the wall, and faced him.

He was in a half crouch, his right hand curled into his lap, twin spurts of red ejaculating onto his pants. He brought the hand to his face, saw what was missing, then he looked at her.

Andy asked herself later if it was the shock of what had just happened to him, or the way she appeared—towering over him, her eyes afire, her mouth smeared red with his ichor, that made him jump back as if she was his worst nightmare come true.

He fell down on his butt and put his right hand down to steady himself, jamming his two stumps into the dirt.

Fenestra raised his pistol and Piper chose that moment to scream "MY HAND! WHUD YOU DO TO MY HAND?!"

She grabbed the bloody lumps, sprang off the wall, and threw them at Fenestra, who tried to knock them away with the hand holding the knife. One of them hit him in the face and he flinched. Andy jabbed her fist toward him. He moved his head back but Andy managed to get close enough to him to knock his eyeglasses off. As Fenestra reached to pull them back on, Andy pressed the plastic button on the breath spray and a thin jet of minty, highly concentrated liquid streaked out and sprayed across his eyes.

Fenestra made a sound like an automobile transmission seizing up. Andy ran past him, grabbed her shredded shoulder bag as she ducked past her father's car, crossed Sackawinick, and almost slammed into the locomotive factory's shuttered doors.

She turned back and saw Fenestra clambering out onto the street, one hand over his eyes, the other groping for the steps leading up to the cab on the fuel oil truck.

Andy ran into the soup kitchen, found Maria and said, "They're going to blow up the building across the street."

Maria's eyes widened as she saw the dirt and blood on Andy's face. "What's happened to you?"

"You have to get somebody out here. These guys . . ." Andy began to hyperventilate.

"What guys?"

Andy pointed toward the street and took off. Maria followed. By the time they were on the street, they heard the fuel truck roaring as it backed away from the nightclub. They saw Piper wobble out into the street, gripping his hand, moaning, "*Somebody, somebody lookit my hand, what she do to my hand?!*"

"Is that the guy who did this to you?" Maria said to Andy. Andy was about to say something when the the fuel truck shifted gears, and bore down on Piper, who froze like an animal in the truck's headlights until the truck's grill hit him and seemed to suck him under the wheels. The truck's left front tire rose slightly as it crushed Piper into the street.

They heard an angry crump as the truck plowed into the yellow Buick, squashing it like a candy wrapper and pushing it into and through the old nightclub, ripping out a corner wall, continuing until it pushed itself halfway into the side of the Hampton Bank building. Then the truck's driver-side door swung open. Fenestra hopped out and started walking calmly up the sidewalk.

"STOP RIGHT THERE!" Andy screamed and took off after him.

Fenestra, who was not wearing his eyeglasses, turned and looked around wildly. He pulled out his gun but could not be sure exactly where Andy was. Andy grabbed her shoulder bag with both hands, hauled back, and slammed it into his face.

It wasn't much of a blow, but it was enough to make Fenestra lose his cool. He stepped back, slipped down the curb, and found himself in the street. Andy smacked him again and he ran.

He was big, overweight, half blind, and wearing the clothing and shoes that nobody should run in. And he was running on a Philadelphia street that, even with the Reverend's vast political power, was still a mess of cracked asphalt and potholes. He stumbled and went down. He tried to stand and his right ankle collapsed like wet cardboard.

She stood over him and watched him writhe in pain. "I believe my ankle is sufficiently injured so that I cannot stand. I think it's time to renegotiate our position, Ms. Cosicki."

"Then you tell me something."

"Anything you want."

"Did you kill my father?"

"What if I tell you I could have prevented it, by going along with him?"

"But you didn't go with him."

"I didn't go with him because, to be honest, I didn't trust him. When I saw Ben negotiating in a purely business fashion, he was very casual, quiet and reserved. But when he called me yesterday morning, he was animated, nervous, in a way that indicated to me that he had some personal stake in this meeting. I've learned to be careful when people get personally involved. They tend to . . . lose perspective."

Maria came up to Andy, followed by some of the people in the kitchen.

"He the one that tried to hurt you?" Maria said.

"Be careful," Andy said. "He's got a gun and a knife."

Maria reached under her apron and pulled out a sharpened broad-bladed, ten-inch chopping knife. "Mine's bigger."

"You'll excuse me," Fenestra said, "I have to make a call."

Andy saw the cell phone in Fenestra's right hand. Before she could ask why he had a cell phone in his hand, she saw his thumb find the autodialer and press it.

"We must fight back by naming names!" the Reverend shouted. "We must point to the oppressor and tell him that he is not in harmony, and that those who do not know harmony, who have not heard the sweet vibrations of heavenly power, who have not merged themselves with the rhythms of life and love and honor and pride, will shortly wither and die, and stay dead."

That wouldn't stop Lange from firing anyone, Ladderback thought.

"This is exactly what the oppressor does not want to hear. But what is naming the oppressor going to do against guns and knives, drugs and abortions, a burning cross and a hanging rope?"

The organ swelled with dissonant chords, as if it, too, was indignant at the injustices the Reverend described.

"I will tell you, brothers and sisters. By calling out the oppressor, we recognize our God-given right to feel. And what we feel, brothers and sisters, is always real. And in feeling what is real, we give expression to our individuality. We become aware, and grateful, that we are not that which oppresses us. Once we recognize what has made us sick, it cannot make us sick again if we refuse to make it part of us. It is a part of a demon's hell that is crumbling on its own foundations, that will fall and topple around us and, like Daniel in the lion's den, leave us safe and unscathed."

Perhaps it was because the music had been so beautiful that the revulsion gripped Ladderback. Suddenly the old factory had grown large and limitless and he was alone and vulnerable. He shut his eyes to this, told himself that the Reverend was wrong, that emotional responses were not an indication of reality, that unresolved fear can be a manifestation of inner turmoil.

When he opened his eyes he saw that the people assembled around him appeared to be enthralled. As the Reverend pounded out his dangerously misleading message, Ladderback heard cries of "Amen" and nods of agreement that evolved into a catechism, a back-and-forth question-and-answer session in which what the Reverend asked, and what the assembled replied, was not as significant as the rhythm of the exchange. The oppressors he vilified previously, the incidents from public life that he had distorted in his sermon, the crude antagonists that were so thinly defined that they were more myth than factual, were rhetorical devices to bring speaker and audience to a relationship where one stimulated, celebrated, and reinforced the fears and hopes of the other.

Which was not all that different from the relationship a newspaper had with its community of readers, Ladderback reflected. At the core of both relationships was a sense of trust that would not tolerate contradiction, competition, or distraction. Suddenly a loud crash reverberated up from the floor, followed by one of the bodyguards rushing in, shouting that the "Walls are tumbling down!"

The blast had thrown Andy and the woman forward. Both fell near Fenestra, with Maria closer to him. He grabbed her and put the knife to her throat. "Now you're going to be calm," Fenestra said, "and you and Ms. Cosicki are going get me up and moving toward that Lincoln parked there."

Andy saw Maria's knife on the asphalt.

"Ms. Cosicki, if you do anything other than what I say, I'll kill this woman here."

"I doubt that," Maria said. She clamped both hands on Fenestra's, pushed the knife just far enough from her throat to be out of danger, rolled away, grabbed a finger holding the blade, and yanked the finger back.

Andy heard the pop of the knuckle breaking apart, and another one of Fenestra's deep groans, as the woman rolled off him and stomped hard on Fenestra's left hand, the one that had been holding the cell phone. He groaned a third time as she pulled away his knife. "He got a gun?" she asked Andy.

"Somewhere."

"He won't be able to use it," she said as the Reverend's bodyguards ran up and surrounded them, parting to admit him.

The Reverend looked at the flames licking up over the dome of the bank building, and then back at Fenestra. "You," he said. "You did this?"

"I've been injured and I will pay for assistance," Fenestra said.

"I know who you are and what you are," the Reverend said. He picked up the chopping knife. "I had a vision that you would return to me, to my hands."

Maria stepped forward. "Jeff, don't!"

He paused, saw the knife in her hands. "He used this?"

"He tried to," Maria said. "Jeff, please—"

"DON'T doubt me!" he shouted at her, the bodyguards and parishoners around him. "We must fight the oppressor!" He took the knife. Andy felt the crowd around her tense.

The Reverend poked the knife into Fenestra's neck, cut to one ear, and then back to the other. Fenestra made a wet, gagging sound as people in the crowd looked away.

Andy watched the Reverend hold the knife in the air in triumph. He expect the crowd's adulation, and found himself getting a different response, a shocked revulsion. The Reverend understood instantly that he had crossed a line that they hadn't wanted him to cross. It was one thing to talk about fighting, it was another thing to murder an injured man on a public street.

"The oppressor dies so we will live!" the Reverend shouted, but the crowd wasn't buying it. "They used fire to destroy us, but they won't destroy us. The flames will consume them, but not us!"

As a wail of sirens began to fill the air, he told his bodyguards to throw Fenestra's and Piper's bodies into the flames, but he saw that even his guards weren't listening to him with the same fervor as before. He turned to Maria, who couldn't face him, and Andy imagined that the Reverend was feeling what Napoleon must have felt, and Hitler and Caesar and Alexander, when those leaders understood, finally, that the source of their power was in providing to their followers an unending series of enemies whom those followers could fight and win, and that as long as they were united against a common threat, those followers would not see the flaws, doubts, and darkness in their lives that had made a demogogue's simplistic exhortations so vividly compelling.

"We must save the future!" he cried, his voice thin against the sirens and the heat of the fire. "In there," he pointed toward the bank building, "is our future!"

He began to walk purposely toward the burning bank building. Maria tried to run but was stopped by the heat. She called after him. "Jeff!"

He turned around, aware that everyone was watching him. He seemed to grow an inch, feeding on the power so much attention can bring.

"No one, no thing, no power can harm a man of harmony!" he shouted. "No one can keep from us the God-given truth!"

He walked and then ran, past the hulk of the burning truck, toward the inferno of the bank building. The old doors had been blown off their frames. He paused on the threshold, looked back at his flock, turned, and ran in.

Time stopped on the street, and then started again. They heard an awful wrenching sound and saw a gust of flames shoot from the open doors. The dome slipped from its moorings, slid forward, and fell all the way down.

15 fits and starts

The police and fire trucks closed off Sackawinick and Eighteenth Streets. Andy watched them aim great, rushing cascades of water into the blaze, as she sat on a wobbling, partially corroded dinette chair before one of the two windows in the small sitting room above the soup kitchen.

What had been Councilman Szathmary's office had been converted back into a two-bedroom apartment containing glued, braced, patched-up, and otherwise mismatched furniture. The door to what had been Szathmary's personal office contained Maria's bed, shelves of books, sound equipment, a television set, and a collection of recordings. The second bedroom was an office, with file cabinets, a computer, and equipment.

Maria let Andy clean herself up in the bathroom. When Andy emerged, she saw a worn pair of black denim pants, a cracked leather belt, and a faded, brown-and-white batik print blouse on Maria's bed.

"I found those out in the clothing exchange," Maria said. "They should be your size, or close to it."

Andy had never worn used clothing and, though the garments were clean, the fact that someone else had inhabited them unnerved her, until she touched the pants. The cotton had been washed so many times that it was soft and pliant in ways that pre-washed clothing could never be. The blouse was made of synthetic fabric, but it, too, felt smooth and comforting as she pulled it over her shoulders.

Andy sat in the front of the apartment watching the firemen as Maria went into the bathroom. She came out in a shapeless blue smock of a dress. She did not appear to have been grieving. She sat down on another dinette chair before the other window.

"Nothing's blowing this way," Andy said. "The fire seems to be staying put."

Maria took a seat by the second window, and folded her arms.

"The Reverend was important to you," Andy said.

"He was important to many people. We'll do his funeral. And the councilman's. I'm going to have a small service for Ben, even if Charlotte does something on her own."

Andy saw Maria trying to be strong in front of her, almost in the same way that Andy had tried to be strong in front of Ladderback hours after she'd learned her father had died.

"Is there someone you could be with tonight?" Andy asked.

"There are plenty of people downstairs who need to eat."

"I mean loved ones," Andy said.

Maria shook her head. "I don't have any."

"Your mother?"

"We really don't speak to each other. She thinks this place, and the people in it, ruined my life. Sometimes I agree with her, but I don't tell her that."

"Did you ever want to settle up with her?"

"You sound like Ben. Sure I did. But if it's going to happen, it's going to be on my terms. It's enough that she launders the money from the numbers-runners and the drug dealers."

Andy blinked. "Do you know I work for the *Press*?"

"Ben told me he was getting you in."

"What you just told me, about the money laundering . . ."

"Won't go past this room. Howard Lange is on our board of directors."

Ladderback regarded Bardo Nackels's famously broken nose as Nackels wrote in a box on the front page, "FIGHT BACK" DRUG DEALER-TURNED-PREACHER SAYS BEFORE FIERY DEATH. EXCLUSIVE INTERVIEW, PAGE 6.

Nackels pressed a button on the keyboard. "Doesn't fit."

FIGHTING PRIEST STRICKEN IN FATAL BLAZE. HIS LAST WORDS AND MORE, PAGE 6.

"He never boxed professionally," Ladderback said. "He wasn't Catholic and most deaths due to fire are caused by asphyxiation—smoke inhalation."

"I know, I know," Nackels said. "I was just seeing if it would work. This fire, it was arson?"

"The investigators have not determined the cause, though they believe it could have to do with a fuel truck whose driver lost control and collided with a building where toxic chemicals were illegally stored on the site. Two bodies have been tentatively identified as the driver and a passenger."

"How was it that you were there, by the way?"

"Background," Ladderback said.

"That Reverend was up to his ass in a lot of criminal shit, politics, racism. I mean, the guy was disgusting. You can't tell me you went there just to listen to some music. You were trying to get something on the preacher dude, right? You know Agnew wanted some kick-ass stuff. Why is it, after all these years, you're starting to kick ass?"

Ladderback said, "Please," and put his hands on the keyboard. He typed, PREACHER DIES IN FIRE, page 6.

"That's not enough words. We don't say what kind of hate-

281

mongering crook he was. I want that in there, but, somehow, I don't think that's going to fit."

"He was killed attempting a rescue in one of the buildings," Ladderback said.

"I'm getting tired of this," Nackles said. "We have a pile-up on I-95—overturned tractor trailer, the driver and one motorist critical; snatch-and-grab at an ATM on South Street—sixty dollars taken; two-alarm fire in a restaurant on Cheltenham Avenue; one firefighter hospitalized for smoke inhalation; underwear burglar strikes again in Yeadon—nothing taken but bras and panties, and the house that was robbed only had one person living in it and he was a guy; shots fired in Mantua—no injuries; and a three car smack-up on Broad and Old York Road. On top of that, a car bomb went off in Jerusalem in front of an Israeli day-care center. There are other things happening, you know that, Shep? So if this doesn't fit. . . ."

Nackles changed the type-size, altered the size of the box, and typed a new headline without the reference to page 6: INFERNO OF DEATH. "FIGHT BACK!" DYING PREACHER CRIES.

It fit.

The driver with the Harmonious transportation service offered to take Andy back to her house in Merion but she directed him back to the Olde City neighborhood.

She buzzed Drew Shaw's apartment. When she told him she wanted to see him, he said, "I don't know if I should let you. I don't want to feel too lucky."

"You won't," Andy said.

He was standing by the door in boxer shorts when she came in. She put her arms around him, felt the tape across his chest where his ribs had been broken. The injuries made it awkward to hold him, so she let him hold her. She let him kiss her with his swollen lips. She didn't look at the dark bruises on his face.

He offered to get her something from the kitchen. She told him that the only thing she wanted was to be somewhere safe. He began to tell her that she came to the wrong place, that two apartments on the first floor had been broken into last month, when she said, "You know what I mean."

They ended up on his bed, not touching but close enough to touch each other. He turned off the reading light. She asked him if he would mind if she cried for a while.

He said he wouldn't mind and, somehow, she didn't need to cry anymore. She moved closer and wanted to feel his skin against hers. She kicked off her clothes, pulled up the sheet, and curled into him.

He tried to put his arm around her but the movement hurt him too much. "Uh, Andy, what I said earlier, about having sex, I don't think I'll be able to . . ."

She wanted him to shut up and he sensed that because he didn't say anything for a long time. His breathing became low and steady and it didn't occur to her that he may have fallen asleep when she said, "Drew, I've never been to a funeral."

"They're not fun, but there's a lot of changes going on in the business," he said. "I did a story once on the New Funeral Directors and—"

She sat up and he stopped talking. She wondered if he was thinking what she was thinking, about how it is possible to be with some people for your entire life and not know who they were, and not get a straight answer when you asked them a question.

"Drew," she said, "if I had to go to a funeral, would you come with me if I asked you to?"

She expected him to make a crack, ask her if going to funeral was her idea of a date, or tell her about a story he wrote about it, but he just said one word, and he said it in just the right way.

He said, "Yes."

It became very easy to sleep after that.

16 you do it his way

As he did every workday morning, Ladderback locked his apartment door and took the elevator down to the subbasement. He passed what had been the building's laundry room, went down a corridor that used to have the barber and sundry shop, and through a heavy metal door that opened onto a wide, grim pedestrian concourse that shuddered and trembled with the sound of passing subway trains.

The concourse linked the Hi-Speed line, which ran below Locust Street eastward to the Benjamin Franklin Bridge and New Jersey, with a second, wider concourse that served the Broad Street subway, which, in turn, intersected with the Market East underground shopping mall. It was possible to walk from Ladderback's Locust Street apartment building, all the way to the *Press* Building at Eleventh and Market Streets, without once seeing sunlight.

He was negotiating the tunnels leading into the Market East mall when he sensed that something was off. He moved eastward into a maze of cracked yellow tile walls, grimy floors, insect-spattered lights, and the inevitable odd corners reeking of urine, to see that the flood of pedestrians heading east had ebbed. Over the shattering roar of the subway trains, he heard a deep throbbing of machinery ahead, just beyond a line of yellow police barricades. At the center of the tunnel, under the white-hot glare of portable floodlights, stood a group of workmen in dark navy, sweat-stained T-shirts emblazoned with the faded white flame logo of the Philadelphia Gas Works. They talked, scratched their guts, drank from Styrofoam coffee cups, and pointed occasionally at the yawning crevice in the last stretch of tunnel leading toward Market Street.

One of the workers, a short, wide woman in a hardhat, noticed him and nodded toward a battered white sign with big, blue, block letters that said SIDEWALK CLOSED—FOLLOW ARROWS TO DETOUR.

Ladderback did not see a sidewalk or any arrows. The crevice was small enough for him to walk around.

The woman said, "Outside, to the street."

Ladderback felt the drone of the machinery coming from the crevice vibrating through him. He didn't move.

"C'mon, outside, outside," she called out to others who had gathered behind Ladderback. She made a corkscrew motion with her finger, advising them to turn around and seek the stairway leading up and out.

A woman behind Ladderback asked what the problem was. "Somebody said they smell gas. What can you do about it?"

Ladderback said, "How long—"

"As long as it takes. And then a day for the concrete to set. C'mon, turn around, you gotta go outside."

A man asked where the arrows were.

"We couldn't find any on the truck," the woman in the helmet said, crushing her coffee cup. "Either they forgot to load 'em on the truck or they ran out at the depot. Cost-cutting measure, no doubt. You want to see some arrows, next time, pay your gas bill."

"I don't use gas," the man said sourly.

"So you can't come through anyway, okay? It's a nice day outside. Stairs are just around the bend." She turned to a fellow worker. "You sure you got no arrows? Must be some arrows around here someplace."

Ladderback closed his eyes, took a breath, opened them, and then merged with the flow of disgruntled commuters heading toward the stairs. In all the years he had used the tunnels, whatever construction had to take place had always been where the passages could be kept open.

He paused at the metal railing leading up. It gleamed from the light above. People nudged him, bumped him. He heard some say "'Scuse me." Others cursed.

A transit policeman would appear soon, Ladderback knew. The cop would want to know if there was a problem, which meant that he really didn't want to know if there was a problem, he just wanted Ladderback to move.

Ladderback wanted to move also. This would be the perfect time, he told himself, to climb the stairs, feel the sunlight on his face, and discover he was cured, that his agoraphobia was retreating now.

It was silly, he told himself, to fear the outdoors. It was something in his brain, an imbalance of chemicals that could probably be cured with a pill.

But to go to the psychiatrist he'd have to go outside, or take a cab to his office, and he'd have to talk about it and Ladderback didn't like talking about himself. Let other people tell him the story of their lives. His story was no one else's business.

He put his hand on the greasy railing and a foot on the lowest stair. He felt his eyelids descending and he forced them to stay open. He brought another foot up. He let his hand slide up.

He began to panic shortly after he smelled the mix of bus fumes, pizza, and burnt dust wafting down from the street. He told himself he didn't have to feel this way, that there was nothing threatening about where he was going, and that, with so many buildings around, he would have something resembling walls on one side of him.

He felt it first in his back, a tightening of his muscles as if he were about to be hit. His breath grew shorter and his mouth dried up. His head became loose on his neck. He became dizzy and nauseous. He put a hand over his mouth. He wanted to make himself small enough to fit into someplace in which he could hide.

He froze halfway up the stairs and people began to curse at him again. He lifted another foot up and put it down.

Then he remembered that he was close enough to the access corridor leading into the subbasement of an office building. This corridor had a door that led into the basement kitchen of Jimmy D's. He used this corridor when he went to see Whitey Goohan.

He went back downstairs, found that corridor, and paused beside the door to the restaurant, then continued into the office building and into another concourse that wrapped around and back to Market East.

The detour made Ladderback arrive later than usual in the newsroom. He found Andy at Mr. Action's desk, writing furiously.

He hung his jacket on a hanger at the coatrack and wandered over to the copy desk, where Bardo Nackels, a growth of stubble on his cheeks indicating that he hadn't gone home yet, was working on the front-page headlines of tomorrow's newspaper.

It was another sports cover, about a basketball player, but, in a small box in the upper right-hand corner, Ladderback saw GOT A GRIPE? CALL MR. ACTION. Page 23.

He went to another side of the U-shaped copy desk, where the deputy editors were using the word processor's page layout features to trim news stories and size photographs so they would fit the spaces between advertisements. He found an editor working on page 23.

The headline on Mr. Action's column was CHURCH NOT A VOLUME BUSINESS. The lead paragraph was about a Yorkvale resident identified as G. R. complaining about the loudness of the music coming from the First Church of God Harmonious.

Dear G. R., Mr. Action replied. *The evening services have been louder than necessary, agreed Church Director Maria Adamo, and, as part of a plan to attract new business to the Redmonton neighborhood, the sound will be much more moderate from now on. Ms. Adamo explained that the church's founder, the late Reverend Jeffery Hooks, set the church's P.A. system at high levels because he was hard of hearing.*

After this was WORST SPOTS FOR DOGGIE DROPS, an explanation of the Sanitation Department's new anti-organic-litter initiative, and a toll-free number to call to get a brochure about litter enforcement and a schedule of fines.

That was followed by a request from "Waitress, name withheld": What to do if you're fired because the owner did something "under the counter."

Dear Waitress: Blowing the whistle on an employer can be an emotionally difficult thing to do, but it can sometimes be the only way to fight for what you feel is right. If you feel you were harassed, discriminated against, cheated, or unfairly taken advantage of, or you think that what you saw represents a serious violation of state or federal laws, fight back by calling any of the following toll-free whistle-blower hotlines: numbers . . .

The last item was from "Name withheld, art lover," who had discovered an old painting in an attic. How can she find out if the painting is valuable?

Dear Art Lover: Cos Cosicki, an executive with New York's Kaplan Gallery, says you are the best judge of how valuable a painting is. "If you like it, keep it," Mrs. Cosicki told Mr. Action. "But if you want to sell it, here are a few simple steps to follow."

Ladderback went to his desk, signed on to his terminal.

"Aren't you going to congratulate me about the column?" Andy said. "My name isn't on it, but, I think it looks pretty good."

"It does look good," Ladderback said.

"I threw in my mother because, well, she was calling me on my cell phone this morning, wanting to know where I'd been, so I told her I was working, and I sort of . . ."

"Made something up," Ladderback said.

"My mother gets questions like that all the time. The information is valid."

When Ladderback turned to his terminal, Andy said, "There are two things I want to ask you."

Ladderback checked his e-mail.

"You said, yesterday, that you knew who had killed my father. How about telling me?"

"You were discussing the comments Councilman Szathmary made about himself and his relationship with your father," Ladderback began. "The councilman said, 'It wasn't about what you got, but about what you owe.' I said that this provided us with an answer as to why the councilman did not accompany your father to this luncheon he had arranged, and that this can be used to identify the person responsible for your father's death. I did not say I knew who killed him."

"So you don't really know?"

"What I know is that your father had a relationship with every person he invited to this luncheon, and that these people had a great deal of animosity for each other, but that they shared a common bond in knowing your father. Your father wanted to use the luncheon to settle these animosities for reasons that were far more than professional."

"He wanted to prove something to himself."

"And to you and, presumably, everyone who would attend. But no one wanted to attend."

"He was turned down by everyone except me and . . ." Andy got it, in a flash, "whoever he was with when he died. He had picked someone up. That person was in his car. That person was probably in the place with him when he died."

"But everyone you talked to," Ladderback said, "denied being with him."

"How did you know that?"

"I talked to one of them. Whitey Goohan, maitre d' at Jimmy D's. He suggested that he did not want to be in the same room with his adversaries, but the real reason was that he was aware that your father wanted to prove something to himself and he didn't want to be part of that. So, how many people could he have invited?" Ladderback said.

Andy made a mental list: herself, Howard Lange, Councilman Szathmary, the Reverend, Maria Adamo, Betty Adamo, Fenestra. "I have seven, and with your guy, eight, and if what he said about wanting it to be for his kids is true, then we can add Logo to it. That makes nine. With him, that's ten. One of those people could have killed him, right?"

"Not necessarily," Ladderback said. "There could be others. He told Whitey that it would be a party of ten, with the possibility of others."

"So what are we going to do?" Andy said.

"Are you asking me for help?"

"What does it sound like I'm asking you for?"

"Call up Jimmy D's. Get Whitey on the phone. Make the same reservation for lunch tomorrow. Say you found out something very important about how your father died. Then call and invite every one of your suspects and tell them the same thing, that you found out something important about how your father died."

"But I haven't found out anything important," Andy said. "What am I going to say when they show up?"

"You have found many things that are important," Ladderback said. "But you won't have to say a thing."

"I don't get you," Andy said. "I'm just going to go there and say nothing, like my father used to when he was Benny Lunch?"

"Yes," Ladderback said. "That's exactly what you're going to do. Because the person who was responsible for your father's death will be the only one among these people who will be afraid of what you might know. The others will stay away for the same reasons that they stayed away originally: They have nothing to gain from your father settling their differences. But this person who is afraid will show up, on time, because he or she has everything to lose if you act on what you know."

Andy thought about it. "I want you there with me."

"I can't be there with you. The person will see me and leave. Only if you're sitting at that table, alone, will the person responsible come forward."

"But you're supposed to look out for me," Andy said. "My father asked you."

"That isn't the only thing your father has asked me."

Andy frowned and picked up her phone. Ladderback examined the death notices. About a third of the way down the page, he saw, *Fenestra, James R., former FBI Agent.*

He picked up his phone, dialed the funeral director, and got the funeral director's voicemail. Ladderback identified himself, and said, "I'm gathering background for an obituary we may publish about Mr. Fenestra. If you provide me with sources—"

He heard Andy slam down her phone.

"—that could shed light on his life and character, I would appreciate it." He put down his phone *gently* and saw Andy, in a beautiful earth-toned batik printed blouse, glaring at him.

"How about asking me?" Andy said.

Ladderback almost didn't recognize her. The tension, the wariness, the angry, haunted expression she had worn, had softened, mellowed, ever so slightly.

But she was glaring at him, nonetheless. "You're not really going to do him, are you?"

"Very little of what I research sees print," Ladderback said.

"So you're doing it for—?"

"Background," Ladderback said.

"You want to know how he died?"

"The how and the why are never as important as the fact of death itself." Ladderback examined the death notice.

"Especially since the fire can cover up a murder, right?"

He took his hands off his keyboard. He put his hands back on the keyboard.

Andy said, "The night Kellum Brickle killed my grandfather, your boss, Abe Donitz, told my father to call you because your parents were medical examiners and you would know what to do. You told him to burn the club down."

Ladderback deleted some junk e-mails. "Our job is to report important, factual information in a direct, accurate, and unbiased fashion."

"That's what they teach in journalism school," Andy said.

He took his hands off his keyboard. "We like to pretend that we are observers, that we only report the facts, and that what we report and the manner in which we report it has nothing to do with who and what we imagine ourselves to be. We pretend those things, and we are wrong."

He took a breath. "By the ethics of this profession, I should have refused to say anything more and reported the fact of his call to the police."

"But you didn't because your editor was there," Andy said.

Ladderback shook his head. "Your father was sincerely afraid that this world in which he had found comfort, prestige, and no small degree of love, had just come crashing down around him and he was appealing to me for help. I gave him that help."

"You told him to burn the place down—"

"I told him to open any windows or vents leading into the basement area. I told him to get a cigarette butt out of an ashtray, one that wasn't crushed out. Then, to break open some bottles near your grandfather, something with a high alcohol content. I told him to put the cigarette butt in the alcohol, as if your grandfather threw it away without thinking. Then I told him to light the alcohol, as close as he could to where the butt was, with a cigarette lighter, if he could. If he used a match, I told him to make sure that he took the entire match with him. I told him to tell the police that your grandfather had gone down to the basement and by the time he was missed, he smelled smoke. I told him to get everyone out of there before he called the fire department."

"You covered up a murder," Andy said, "and look what happened."

"Yes," Ladderback said, his eyes on her, "I do believe I am looking at what happened."

17 andy lunch

On the morning that Mr. Action made her triumphant return to the pages of the *Philadelphia Press*, Charlotte Cosicki had pinned a note to Andy's door, informing her that she had to catch an early train for New York.

Andy put on shorts, a T-shirt, and basketball shoes and did layups for two hours, missing more shots than normal, because she was wondering if Betty Adamo—or Beatrice Adams—was going to call her back and ask for a lift into town. Betty had never learned to drive, so Andy could have imagined her going up the ruined stairs of the Straight Up Club and giving Andy's father a push.

Or maybe the person who had killed him was dead. Szathmary could have been lying to her when he said that he had refused to go any further than his "wildlife sanctuary." Fenestra, who supposedly was skillful at making murders seem accidental, could have zoomed away from the nightclub in one of his gray Lincolns. Or maybe the Reverend had let his temper get the better of him and given her father a shove.

She told them to call Jimmy D's if they weren't going to make it. She was pretty sure that Howard Lange wasn't a suspect, though he looked at her oddly when she had invited him to the lunch yesterday. She had left a message on Maria Adamo's answering machine. Maria had claimed to have not wanted to know who her child was. Could she have killed him to keep its identity secret?

Thinking about Logo had made her call him the previous evening. She said she was lonely, and that she wanted to see him, and he could tell that she was lying, that she really wasn't lonely but that she still wanted to see him. When he had asked her why, she didn't tell him that she wanted to see how closely he resembled Maria Adamo or Councilman Szathmary. The more she thought about it, the more he didn't resemble anyone but himself.

He stayed on the phone with her and actually apologized for raiding her house. Then he asked her how she was dealing with the loss of her father.

She said she was doing more than dealing with it, and that she was going to meet her father's killer for a lunch at Jimmy D's.

Why Jimmy D's? Logo wanted to know.

"I want to settle our differences," Andy said.

Betty Adamo never called back. Andy got Drew on the phone but he was delirious from painkillers.

She told herself she could bag it, call in sick, come up with an excuse, and be like Maria Adamo, so proud of what she didn't know that she let it change her life.

Or she could find something out.

Maybe that was why, in the end, Andy put on that leggy, knock-'em-dead suit that her mother had bought her in New York, drove in, parked her car on the street near the *Press* Building, went up to the newsroom, and Ladderback was there, waiting for her, with his coat on.

"Follow me," he said. He took the elevator down to the *Press* Building's subbasement, past the security guard who said, "Morning, or is it afternoon?" through the glass doors into the underground shopping, subway train, and commuter rail concourse below Market Street. The T-shirt shops and fast-food arcades were open now, and the place was flooded with pedestrians moving between the more than one hundred different bus and train lines converging on this five-block trench under Market Street.

Ladderback didn't walk as much as he lurched just a few more inches forward then back, a bulky lump in a khaki raincoat that never saw rain. Pedestrians zoomed past them, everyone was either in a hurry or dawdling in a lazy stupor. Ladderback moved so slow, like royalty going to the toilet. Why was he moving so slow? You don't move slow anywhere. You don't give people time to look at you, size you up, figure out whether or not you're worth pouncing on. You move, fast forward, unless you're Ben Cosicki, who would drive Andy nuts by the amount of time he would spend in his car, parked just past a street corner somewhere in the city with the windows down, just watching the entrance to a union hall or a restaurant or an office building or sometimes somebody's house, as if he were a spy or a detective, without any word for his daughter, who had come along because he had offered to take her into the city and drop her off at the campus, or maybe she was having another of those odd mornings when she had an incredible curiosity about what exactly her father did to put food on the table.

She was so taken with the memory that she almost didn't notice that Ladderback had stopped his lurching shamble and had his left hand on a dark column between the shops.

He moved his finger on the embossed words IN MEMORY, then dropped them lower, on the list of names.

"People died building this," Ladderback said. He turned left and went over the brutal aluminum-and-glass-block bridge spanning the Market Frankford subway trench. Instead of climbing up to the street, he proceeded further west and entered the dark wood and thick hunter-green-carpeted subbasement of an office building that had been turned into a convention hotel. He led her past a dry cleaner and sundry shop into another, more forbidding corridor of bleary yellow brick and scuffed concrete, passing a few storefronts that had been boarded up and bricked in, their doors painted the same sickly yellow that coated the brick.

Then Andy caught a scent of something that just didn't belong. When she'd been in the pedestrian tunnels below Market and Broad Streets previously, the overwhelming odors had been the searing fumes of ozone and filth from the subways, and the sour stench of human urine. So why was it, down who-knows-how-many-feet below the street, she was inhaling the sharp scent of onions and garlic sizzling in hot olive oil, the automatic, aromatic signal of Philadelphia cuisine?

Ladderback put his hands on an unmarked set of steel double doors that she would have missed even though they weren't painted. He nudged them open and they entered a swirling, frantic kitchen of steamy garlic fumes, bright lights, people shouting in Spanish, Italian, and just a little bit of English as blue flames leaped from a six-burner stove below racks of rounded aluminum pots, pans, trays, utensils, and devices pointed, edged, and bent to purposes Andy could not imagine.

Heads in paper toques turned and Ladderback was *noticed*. The kitchen crew in white spattered coats and dingy gray houndstooth pants spied him and moved past their simmering saucepans, piles of beef, and chopped vegetables to approach him, surround him, give him a heroes' welcome in their many languages, and then peel off toward their stations, spoons waving, demanding that he taste the sauce, bite into a meatball, smell clouds of salty chicken brine wafting from the big pot on the stove.

Finally, someone—a small man with an Asian face and dark eyes that told her nothing—noticed *her* and was impolite enough to ask if she was "with him?" Before Andy could qualify that statement he drew close, without any food in his hands, and said in an absolutely perfect South Philly kaplink-kaplonk accent that she was "lucky to be with him" because Ladderback was "some important man. Did some nice write-ups of people used to work here."

Andy said, "I'm not with him. I'm just here, you know?"

"Anything you say."

"Mister Ladderback," boomed Chef Gee, a round-faced, ash-haired, droopy-nosed man wearing the gaudiest pair of gold-rimmed spectacles Andy had ever seen, was sticking a basil leaf on a mound of angel-hair pasta on a plate, when he saw Andy, put the plate down, and said "Oh my God, what a beauty."

Andy wished she had an internal switch that would stop her from blushing when people said that. She was vertical, she took up space, she had attitude—but she was never beautiful and hated the compliment game guys played when they said what *they* thought was nice so that she would now owe them something. What was she supposed to say? *Sorry, but I know what I am and I don't share your delusions?* It was another annoying situation men liked to put women in, especially older men like Chef Gee (whose face, she noticed, sagged slightly on one side, indicating that he might have had a stroke) and she didn't want to give anyone the satisfaction of a response.

So why, in spite of so much unimpeachably correct self-knowledge, did she have to blush? And why did it have to be here, with all these scurrying male Ladderback fans (okay, there was one woman maybe half her mother's age chopping parsley)? And why did Chef Gee have to approach her, pick up her hand and bow and say, "Giovanni Domanecci the Third," and do this utterly embarrassing old-fashioned hand-kiss act?

He gave Ladderback a look that would best be translated: *The fiery ones are always best in bed.* Then he went to a bank of three dumb-waiters against a far wall, where food on plates went rising into the dining room above, returning as soiled dishes to be pushed through steaming clouds toward the dishwasher. He lifted a telephone with a flourish, dialed number two, and said, "Two for dinner, coming up, the best table."

He collected Ladderback's arm, brought him to Andy, put Andy's hand in Ladderback's and walked them to a narrow stairway leading up. Andy saw that the steps had been worn so smooth that they seemed to sag in the middle. "This is how we used to do it," Domanecci explained, "everything up and down. Then nobody ever got fat working our dining room. Up and down, thousands of times a day. Stay healthy. Work it off."

Ladderback gripped the stairs as if he were anticipating a challenge. "Didn't the customers come down here, too, in Prohibition, when there was a raid?"

Domanecci's face clouded. "Nobody ever raided this place, as long as it was in the family. Not when my grandfather, not when my father owned it. Too many bigshots ate here. Mahoffs. What they want with a raid? We serve a certain kind of customer who don't want the world knowing what he's doing, where he's eating, and who with. This certain kind of customer, come in through the kitchen and up the stairs, he leave through the kitchen. Always an honor."

He put his mouth close to Andy's ear. "Al Capone, before he got arrested and they put him in jail, he come here, through the kitchen. My grandfather said he was batty, you know? In the head. Now. You go. You go up and you get the best table and you relax."

He winked at her and Andy was about to tell him what he could do with his wink when Ladderback clamped his hand on her wrist and up she went, her eyes on the back of his coat, his steps moving so slowly she wanted to push him.

The stairs opened up behind the podium where the man she had seen when she had been at the bar waiting for her father bent and twisted to see what tables were open.

She crossed Whitey Goohan off her list.

"Angie," Ladderback said, "Ms. Cosicki has a reservation for the dining room."

Angie took a pencil out of his ear and went down the list and said, "We had the table but some people called in to say they weren't going to make it."

"Counting Whitey Goohan, it was a party of six," Andy said. "Two Adamos, a Brickle, and Howard Lange and me."

"I'm at the bar," Ladderback said.

Angie said, "I got cancellations from Brickle, Adams, Adamo, Lange and, you know, the boss, he's got stuff to do today. I think it's down to Mr. Ladderback and the lady."

"Put Ms. Cosicki at a table," Ladderback said. "I will be at the bar."

"You bring a lady to Jimmy D's," Angie said, "and you're not going sit with her?"

"She's meeting someone."

"Then you should both be at the bar."

"I will be at the bar. Ms. Cosicki will be more visible at a table."

"If you don't mind my saying, she's as visible as she's going to get," Angie said. He checked his list of tables. "And it looks like, yes it is, the Ladderback table is opening up right now."

"You have your own table here?" Andy asked him.

"Make sure you sit facing the entrance," Ladderback said. "You must see the person before that person sees you."

"But they all canceled," Andy said.

Ladderback turned toward the bar. Angie led her to a dark table for four whose top was scarred with the initials of people she didn't know. "My father use to come here," Andy said. "Is this where he sat?"

"Your father was Ben Cosicki? How come he was so short and . . . well, Benny Lunch, he sat all over the room. Different tables all the time. But this was a table he'd ask for occasionally." He gave her a menu, signaled a waiter, who put down a plate of roasted red peppers, a loaf of warm Italian bread, a dish of roasted garlic in oil, and a chilled highball glass of Ukrainian pepper vodka.

"I didn't ask for this," Andy said.

The waiter shrugged and pointed to Ladderback, who acted as if he hadn't seen a thing.

Then she was suddenly alone, a woman by herself at a table for four, surrounded by people jabbering, eating, waving credit cards, having a good time, leaning forward in that ridiculous getting-down-to-business pose that means something has to happen so the tab can go on an expense account.

Andy sat there, opened the menu, and wondered if her father felt this way before one of his lunches, and then she said, no, he would never do it this way. He would never just sit in a place and let people see him alone. Her father always liked to be in the background, in the shadows.

Just then, a shadow passed over the open menu. Andy looked up.

"So nobody showed," Logo said.

"You did."

"I'm just here, you know?"

"So sit down."

"Just for a minute or two," he looked around, as if he expected to see someone who would fly over and snatch him away from the table.

Andy pointed to a chair. He sat. He folded his hands. He looked at the bread.

Andy tore off a chunk and handed it to him. Logo stared at the chunk of bread and said, "It really was an accident."

"Your father was driving me and my mother into the city because the Reverend was threatening us again and my mother was all set to throw more money at him when your father said that money wouldn't work anymore, and that it was time to sit down and settle it. So he came out for us and got me and my mother into the car. She didn't want to go but he told her that she should do this for me. Good old-fashioned guilt. Then he said, whatever we decided to do with the merger, the Reverend was going to keep at us until we met with him.

"It got very strange, with my mother in the car, and him playing that tape of what went on at this nightclub that my father used to go to. She made him turn the air-conditioning on high so she couldn't hear it. It got even stranger when we made the side trip to the prison. This man your father kept calling the councilman was there, just getting out. He took one look at me and my mother and it was like getting in the car was the last thing he wanted to do.

"Your father didn't say much as he drove us through the city. He called up a lot of people on his cell phone, but I couldn't hear what he was saying. He stopped the car at this place that the councilman used to live at, and told the councilman he was setting something up for his kids, but the councilman wouldn't have anything to do with it. The guy bolted out of that car like it was radioactive. Your father began to get a little edgy—normally he's so cool, you never know what he's thinking. But this time, he started to get worried.

"So we drove off and your father made some more calls. We ended up on this street in these slums in front of that old nightclub. Your father said he had to show us something that, he said, was hidden here. As soon as she heard that, my mother got real eager to go in there."

"Did he say what he was going to show you?"

"He just had us go with him into that alley, and then down these stairs into the basement. It was a dirty, smelly mess, but my mother seemed real interested when he showed her where this fire that had started twenty years ago had burned away the wall that separated the nightclub from the old vault in the bank building. Parts of it had broken open, and there seemed to be a mess of rotting books and papers stuffed into it. My mother started sticking her hands into the mess and pulling things out and tearing them up, but she really couldn't get to all of it and insisted that your father take us out of there.

"He said he had to show me some things. You can imagine how strange it was—he never talked to me like this, and I could see it was really important to him that I listen. The first thing he showed me was a place in the basement where he said he used to sleep when this was his foster home. He said the sarge locked him and this other orphan kid named Whitey Goohan in the basement at night so they wouldn't run off, and then the sarge and Charlotte would go upstairs to the second floor, where they had an apartment. Your father said, sleeping down there, he never wanted to run off, like Whitey did. He said, 'For me, life was about moving up to the second floor, and living someplace, anyplace where there would be no locks.'"

Andy remembered how happy her father had been in his office on the second floor of their home, and how he would never use a lock, for anything, or any reason.

"So he said he had to show me something else, so he led me and my mother up the stairs to the second floor. As we were going up the stairs, he told my mother that this place belongs to the Reverend, and that he has plans for it and the bank branch that just might make the neighborhood a better place, and that she shouldn't be afraid to meet with him.

"She got mad, going on about how people with weak blood are always trying to squeeze money out of her, and your father said, 'This guy is different. You can't buy him off. What he wants is to feel included, accepted, respected. The problem isn't the records. The problem is he's angry, he's got power in the city and he's got money, too, and if you don't deal with him, he can use that power and money to hurt you, maybe even buy up enough shares to put him in a position to screw up the merger.'

"My mother said that the Reverend was a mentally defective criminal with inferior blood and Mr. Fenestra knew how to handle him. Your father told her Fenestra would only give the Reverend an enemy to fight. 'You don't want to be an enemy to him. You want to open the door, sit down with him, let him feel that you think he's important. It's kind of like handing out street money. You give it out as a way of letting people feel that they're important to you.'

"My mother was yelling about how he was definitely not important to her, when we got to the top of the stairs and into the kitchen area. Your father was dragging a chair over to the refrigerator when my mother threw a fit. She said her family moved out of the city before she was born so they could get away from places like this and people like the Reverend and that the reason she hated my father was that he kept coming back here, for what, she didn't know. Your father said to her, 'You know exactly why Kellum came here.' And that shut her up. Believe me, I never saw her shut up like that before. It was like she'd been hit with something, because she just backed off.

"Then your father put his arm around me and said that the reason I was spending so much time getting into trouble was that I was waiting for my life to begin, and that, for him, his life didn't really begin until he was here, in this place, on that night when he'd made the tape he played for me in the car. The sarge was dead and it looked like he was going to lose everything. He said, 'Then I picked up the phone, got to the right person, found out what to do, and got the job done. At that moment, I figured out that power isn't about winning or losing, it's about getting people to settle their differences and share what they already have.'

"He put the chair in front of the refrigerator and said, 'So what I'm doing now, is sharing with you what I have.'

"Then my mother either tripped or stepped on something she couldn't see, but she fell and your father was there, right there, trying to help her, but she was kicking him away and yelling to me to call Fenestra when your father almost got her up but she shoved him away, toward that opening in the floor, and he went straight down and made this painful noise when he hit. My mother demanded I help her up, which I did, and I got her down the stairs and told her to wait while I

305

checked on your father. She told me we were leaving him, and that he was fired and that we would never see him or you or your mother again. I let her go on while I went back to the basement and found him on his back with his neck bent and the back of his head broken open . . ."

"You left him there."

He couldn't face her. "I never saw anybody dead before. I just couldn't deal with it. My mother was screaming and I just wanted to get out. I used the cell phone to call Fenestra. He said, don't worry, don't touch anything, don't let anyone see us on the street. I told him my mother had hurt her leg and he said he'd have a cane in the car. He sent one of those gray Lincolns to pick us up, and there was this cane that my mother began to bang on the floor of the car. Fenestra arranged it so the cops would come when we were gone. We were just leaving when my mother—you know how she sees things sometimes—said I should lock your father's car because the city was full of thieves and she didn't want anyone to steal anything."

"So you locked the car?"

"I couldn't touch it. One of Fenestra's people, Piper, locked it. My mother thought he was so nice and polite that she told me to give him a tip."

Ladderback waited for more than an hour at the bar but Andy and the slovenly fellow kept talking. He could have slept in his oversized black shirt. He was unshaven and possibly unbathed.

They seemed to know each other very well. They seemed to care for each other but there was none of the casual affection that indicated intimacy.

First the fellow had said things that made Andy's hands tense, her body hunch over. Ladderback saw her use the napkin to dab her eyes. The fellow tried to put his arm around her but she would not let him.

Then it was Andy's turn to say things to the fellow that made him fold his arms tightly, cover his eyes with his hand, and shrink into the chair. She tried to give him a napkin but he refused to take it.

There was some urgent conversation going back and forth, some expressions of anguish, and then a feeling of relief. They slouched in their chairs. Andy put her hand on his and they ordered food.

Ladderback instructed Angie to put the lunch on Ladderback's credit card. Then he went back downstairs to the kitchen and returned to the newsroom. He found it difficult to get into his work because he could not stop wondering if, having reached a level of understanding about her father's death, Andy would forsake whatever career she might have, and, perhaps, do something better with her life.

Ladderback stared at the file cabinets behind his desk. How many times had he been certain that there were better things to do than reduce human beings to a three-to-five-paragraph formula?

He was into his second obit when his phone rang.

"It's Andy," she said. "I didn't ask you to pay for my tab. You don't pay for my tab anymore, ever again, is that clear?"

"If you wish," Ladderback said. "Did you learn what you wanted?"

"Of course not! I mean, I found out what happened, but, it wasn't right! He shouldn't have died that way."

Ladderback waited. Then he said, "You remember what I said about the how and the why of death not changing the fact of death."

"But it changes something for me. When I think of him, and I think of his life, it's amazing how things got so screwed up. My parents, when they were my age, really didn't know what they were doing."

"But they thought they did," Ladderback said. He changed his tone. "Would you like another assignment?"

"I don't know. Logo—the guy I was talking to back at Jimmy D's— is going on this trip to sort things out for himself about what he wants to do with his life. He's rich, he can do that. I'd rather do the same thing but, not really traveling. How about we go after Bats Brickle? How about we nail her to the wall?"

"I believe you have an ethical conflict regarding that," Ladderback said.

"So what? Ethics never stopped you."

"We each have our reasons for persevering."

"You're a hundred percent right about that. I guess I should quit."

"I would like you to you stay."

"Give me a reason."

"Because you're good," Ladderback said.

"I know I'm good. But that doesn't mean anything to anyone in that newsroom."

"It means something to me," Ladderback said, hoping that she wouldn't hear the urgency in his voice: "I learn things from you."

"I thought it was supposed to be the other way around."

"If you've taught me one thing, Ms. Cosicki—"

"It's Andy or you'll never see me again."

"—it's that we can accomplish great things when we're on our own."

He waited.

"You might see me again," Andy said. "You just might."